HYPERION'S BIER

Book 4 of The Scarecrow Trials

Tamara Brigham

For those who stand strong

against the darkness…

And those who struggle to do so.

Our wills and fates do so contrary run
That our devices still are overthrown;
Our thoughts are ours, their ends none of our own.
Hamlet Act 3, Scene 2

❧Chapter 1❧

The Talkers rushed the unsteady platform. Scarecrow sensed them out of his periphery though his gaze moved from the blood on his black-gloved fingers to the bugger lieutenant standing over him and the prone man he cradled. Lieutenant Young saw the Talkers' movement too, the nearest threat amongst a sea of frightened salt protestors screaming, lurching, writhing in every direction as the roar of the Five Falls swallowed the fading echo of the second popper shot that followed hard upon the first. She kicked with one foot, catching the lead Talker across the sternum as he crested the platform, reaching for the slack hand of the man in Scarecrow's arms.

Lieutenant Young nodded once at the vigi as the Talker was flung back into his companions.

That threat was only the first.

Scarecrow nodded too and, with one hand, freed the unused injectors from the strap at his hip, grateful now that Tamner had insisted he take them. Buggers nearest the stage struggled to beat back the protestors who pressed to fill the void left by the fallen Talker now trying to rise without being trampled. Brako agitators likewise pushed in, eager for the prizes on the platform that many sought, eager for clashes with the bugorra that might gain them a few extra ticks from the one who paid them.

That one, Scarecrow determined with a glance across the heads around him, was no longer visible.

He offered the injectors. Lieutenant Young accepted them after a moment's hesitation without considering that she was working with a man she had, before today, believed to be the enemy.

Maybe tomorrow she would think of him the same again.

Today, she had no better choice than to accept their alliance.

In the intersection lit only by the blue-green glow of perimeter alglamps, the sporadic Igraci sandwich boards littered and trampled amongst the rioters, and the sizzling glow of the torches some of the buggers carried, the priorities of the lieutenant and Scarecrow were, for once, the same.

The crowd had to be controlled.

Haythem Kemway had to be taken to safety.

Scarecrow slithered backward, body low to shield the fallen man he dragged with him, seeking an opening in the thinner crowd at the rear of the platform. An alley two doors away looked to be his best chance of escape. As he dropped to the metal grate walkway and prepared to hoist Kemway over his uninjured shoulder, the platform shuddered as the crowd pushed against it.

There was no thought to the reaction. Sensors in his hood, in his eyepieces, and years of reflexive training and experience spun him around to hurl the modified throwing star-blade pulled from his chest strap into the face of the masked brako on the other side of the stage.

Lieutenant Young crumpled, a victim of the shattering strike of the brako's nightstick against her knee.

Scarecrow did not believe the blade in the brako's mask was enough to kill him.

As Young used the alglamp post to struggle to her feet, he also did not believe that a shattered kneecap would prevent the lieutenant from doing her duty any more than the chaos around them would keep him from doing his.

Lieutenant Young whistled her buggers to her side.

Scarecrow adjusted Kemway's weight across his shoulder, ignoring the ringing in his ears from the earlier popper shot, the ache in his ribs and shoulders from the injuries Vanderwall had inflicted, and barreled through the thin rear-edge crowd, unheeded, it seemed, by those embroiled in a battle with fear and outrage.

Clutching his shoulder, unaware of the struggle on the platform blocked from his view by the throng, Skelter used the greasy coattails of the nearest fellow to hoist himself to his feet. The bellowing man, one fist pumping the air as another man lashed out at some hapless individual nearby, turned his beak-masked head to leer at the offending redhead and thrust a swinging fist in Skelter's direction.

The enhanced eye patch Tox had provided offered Skelter enough warning of the blow to enable him to weave to the side out of the fist's trajectory. There was no time to pull the blade from his walking stick to strike back, and in the push and pull of the throng, Skelter dismissed the impulse to fight.

This was not the time or the place.

Molly had done this. He was damn sure of it. That one popper shot aimed at Skelter…or had it been two…had been enough to stir the already agitated crowd into a frothing frenzy. Before Molly found him again, before he was trampled by this directionless swarm, Skelter thought it wisest to disengage.

Tox's shop and Vapors were closer than home. Her kesfek vindi typically contained a bit of everything; she would undoubtedly have whatever was needed to patch his bleeding shoulder.

She would also not fuss over him the way he expected Otta to.

He had to get to Tox…if he could squirm his way out of this bloody crowd.

With the popper knocked out of his hand and kicked away by those scurrying in panic around him, Molly lost sight of his target. The broad, water-slicked shoulders of a brako brute knocked against him, twisting Molly's torso one way on legs that did not move, creating a wrenching shot of pain that forced his feet to follow his body's trajectory. Facing backward now, away from Skelter, away from the platform, away from those rushing towards it, and instead into the current of those attempting to flee the scene as arriving buggers rattled the nearest stairs, Molly relented to the tide. The mass carried him, thinning as some turned off at first one staircase and then another, into side paths and alleys until he could peel off from them.

He ducked into the doorless entry of a vacant squat and scurried deep into its shadows where he did not expect anyone to see him. Knees pulled to his chest, making himself as small as possible, he fumbled in his pocket for the last of the loose Hebbies lodged there. Two fell from his shaking fingers and skittered across the floor to slip and wedge into a dirty crevice dank with thick, green slime. But the last made it into his mouth and was swallowed despite the dry fear that coated his throat.

It was only one. Until he felt safe enough to move, to retrieve the others, one had to be enough.

Too many brako.

The Talkers were swallowed into the crowd, less determined to reach the platform now that Founder Kemway was no longer there. Ilya noted the figures in Talker robes struggling to sift to the side of the platform as if to follow wherever Scarecrow had gone, but in the thrust of panicking protestors, those Talkers too disappeared. Given his affinity for the shadows, she doubted the Talkers would find him.

She doubted she would find him either if he did not want her to, but he would, she trusted, keep the Founder safe.

The first injector was emptied into the shoulder of a screeching woman flailing in the grip of the two buggers attempting to divert her Heb-induced fury away from the platform. The jostle of bodies against the barely sturdy stage shook Ilya too, resulting in the loss of the empty injector, but she still clung to the second, the fracture in her wrist making her grip unsteady. When one of her officers, seeing her injured and otherwise unarmed, thrust a baton into her vacant hand, she dropped that injector in favor of a weapon that felt more comfortable and useful.

The arrival of reinforcements elicited a smug smile but she had no illusion that the handful of buggers arriving from every side of the intersection would be enough to subdue the crowd. Unable to leave her position without collapsing on a knee that would not support her, she whistled and pointed. The descending buggers obeyed the command and launched into the thickest knot of discontent in the hopes of untangling it.

The Igraci were among the first to disengage. The loss of their sandwich board glows made the intersection darker.

The neon of vindi lights failed to reignite.

A tall figure, bald and broader than most, flung someone aside in his effort to reach the crowd's edge. That individual screamed and landed with a wet hemp sack thud somewhere in the crowd.

Ilya wiped the dripping blood out of her eye, whistled again and pointed there, but there were no buggers to stop the retreating figure or aid the fallen.

The dispassionate brute whom she assumed to be brako though he wore no mask, had reached a down-angled stairwell and was gone.

The huge fellow charging through the crowd like a fish through an uphill current afforded Switz a path to follow, a way out of a horde that would crush a small man if he remained lost in it too long. Not the sort to seek physical altercations if he could avoid them, he would be too easily trampled…

…or else the infiltrating bugorra would get him first.

He dropped the injector as he squeezed between pressing bodies, intent on keeping his leader in his sights. He had struck his target, he was sure. Kemway would be incapacitated, asleep for hours, but Switz had little hope that it would be long enough for him to reach the man undoubtedly now in bugorra custody. The best Switz could hope for was that sleep would be enough to erase any memories the Founder had of him, of their time together, that it would allow Switz time to go to ground ahead of an inevitable manhunt for Kemway's abductors, his imprisoners.

The brute reached the stairs and started down.

Someone pushed past Switz and followed. The man on the stairs looked back to meet the pursuer's gaze and growled. Unheeding the warning, the unidentifiable figure in a rain slicker that covered from head to ankle took two more steps.

The brute caught his arm and yanked, throwing the form to the base of the stairs where it did not move again. He met Switz's gaze long enough to issue a threat of the same before he continued alone.

Switz did not move.

No one else followed.

Déjà vu. If he investigated the body at the base of the stairs, he would be hunted all over again.

Switz took the nearest available option.

He wiggled into an alley between recycle boxes and compost bins, between pallets awaiting reclamation and a pair of strung-out Heb users oblivious to his passing.

It did not matter where the path took him. It only mattered that it took him away from here.

Ginna did not speak his name when she saw him. She did not call out. If her sister heard her, an unlikely thing over the shouts and screams and the stomping and squealing of boots on metal, it would distract Ilya from the responsibility of restoring order.

It was obvious to her, when she spotted the familiar solitary figure struggling through the thinner crowd, avoiding grabbing hands and the occasional thrown punch, that he needed help. Whatever else this incident was, whatever had happened in the intersection before Ginna's arrival, Founder Kemway needed to be taken to safety. Scarecrow might succeed without her, as he always did, but this time he was not going to do so easily on his own.

She caught his arm. He lurched around as if to strike the shadows, but he recognized the young woman in time to avoid injuring her.

"There's a lift..." she murmured as another whistle from the square split the air.

"Not gonna work." While the filts and electronics in his mask and body armor continued to function, the barely adequate external trickle of power he sensed moving through Hebenon's support systems would not permit the lifts to operate until more power could be rerouted to them or the system was restored. Stored battery power might permit brief operations, but he chose to leave that for key personnel, for buggers and fire suppression crews, to use if they needed it.

The possibility of being trapped in a lift, vulnerable, until the city systems were restored was too great.

Realizing he was right as soon as she made her offer, Ginna nodded and beckoned him to follow. "Know a place."

He did not question her as she maneuvered toward a descending stairwell and a walkway that led between rows of planting sheds. At the base of the stairs, Ginna let fly a birdcall whistle that would bring the nearest Spinks. The Spinks knew Hebenon's veins nearly as well as Scarecrow. Perhaps better. With Ginna's guidance, he trusted they could get Kemway out of the cold long enough to assess the man's condition and perhaps seek help.

If anyone could help, the lost children of Hebenon would do so.

The birdcall untangled the mass of young bodies who had thrown themselves over Enoch and Ulynda with the first crack of popper fire. Ulynda, screaming, "Poppa!" now that she could no longer see the father she had just regained, attempted to dash away. Enoch caught her in his short arms and held her back from folly as he barked to the Spinks, "Go!"

Whatever the whistle meant, whether a battle cry, a summoning call to retreat, or a plea for assistance from other Spinks, Enoch expected they would be safer away from him and the girl thrust into his care than they would be if they stayed.

The Spinks were already scattering.

The swirl of rioters, whipped by fear and uncertainty, and, for some, by the opportunity to create further chaos by picking fights with the accumulating brako and bugorra, was working its way towards the stairs of the rise where Enoch and Ulynda stood.

Soon, they would be caught in it.

"Got to go. Not safe…"

"Poppa needs…"

"Buggers got him; they'll take care of him. We won't be safe if we don't…"

The attempted rational argument was cut off by the fist that fell against the side of his head as the rattling beneath his feet, previously attributed to the rioters, announced the arrival of three brako in beaked horror-masks from the shadows at Enoch's back. He was knocked to the ground, but not without taking a swipe at the long-coated figure nearest him. The blow failed to connect with anything solid except the grating onto which he collapsed.

The last thing his senses registered was Ulynda being snatched off her feet, still screaming "Poppa!" to a city that failed to heed her pleas.

❧Chapter 2❧

"**C**azzing inconvenient," Feena Wulfe muttered, more to herself than to the trio of men with her, men dressed in tailored, high fashion suits rather than the long coats and stolen Crow masks of the majority of her subordinates. Despite her recent encouragement to phase away from those masks, to leave them to the splinter faction that allied themselves with Mam Kemway, many continued to cling to the anonymity and intimidation factor the beaked masks provided.

With a glance at the unlit vindi signs she passed, she sighed. Masks would not protect anyone much longer. The people of Hebanthe Falls, whether brako or not, would need more than masks and breathers to survive if they were forced to subsist on minimal power for more than a few days. The sandwich sign of a passing Igraci once more announced that the end of their city was at hand, a sentiment the near-darkness of vindi lights and vacancy of street vendors mimicked.

Those with her had been able to pry open the doors of the lift she had been in, affording her an escape from an indeterminate period of uncomfortable incarceration. The trio shielded her from the shoving, noisy horde escaping the raucous rabble somewhere ahead and the snapping crack of popper fire that was too far away to be a threat.

Bugorra trying to break up another protest, Feena assumed. There had been several of those since the closing of the mines as people sought relief from salt shortages and a host of other perceived injustices that may or may not have been valid.

She had heard snippets of a guest speaker's words over the cheering crowd before the chaos erupted, but not enough of it to identify the subject matter or the speaker. She only cared about such protests for the inconveniences they caused, or the opportunities.

The loss of city power was more troublesome.

Twice, she and her guards detoured from the lift to descend to reach the Den.

Twice they had been forced to turn back, to seek another path.

The third time, as a cluster of beaked shadows barged past with a squirming bundle protected between them, its head and shoulders covered in a hemp sack to muffle protesting screams, Feena was determined not to turn away.

A child. Likely one of those streeter Spinks she had heard about, children who had become increasingly irritating like stones in her shoes. She paused against the rail to allow them to pass, curious what the child had done to warrant abduction, but it was not the child, nor even the masked brako who may or may not have been her own, that forced her to hesitate longer than her guards preferred.

Rather, it was the prone figure lying awkwardly twisted and abandoned on the walkway in front of them, near another incapacitated lift, around whom those fleeing the riot swarmed.

He could have been anyone.

He could have been no one.

But Feena knew his face.

"Bring him."

The man nearest her grunted, a questioning sound expressing uncertainty about the wisdom of the order without verbally questioning his boss's request.

"You heard me," Feena huffed as another gaggle rushed by with a bugger in pursuit, shouting for the runners to stop.

The bugger ignored the dwarf. He paid Feena and her companions no heed either except to push one of the men aside. The third lunged at the bugger but Feena restrained him with a hand on his arm. Her irritation with the inconsiderate treatment by a man doing his job was not worth addressing.

The other two guards lifted the dwarf between them.

"Don't hurt him."

He might already be dead. If he was breathing, she intended to make certain he continued to do so in the hopes he would respond to her charity with an appropriate measure of gratitude.

If he was not breathing, Founder help the bastards who had killed the one she considered to be Hebenon's best hope for peace.

❧*☙

Spinks tumbled out of the shadows, small forms like spiders pushing against the crowd, throwing shards of glass, pieces of broken hemp crates and furniture, or rotting food to deter their pursuers before skittering as if afraid of the light when the adults they assaulted took offense. If a blow landed, if one of their number was pushed to the walkway where they were in danger of being trampled, other Spinks swarmed to protect their own and make their opponents suffer enough that they would reconsider attacking children in the future.

Scarecrow did not see it happen, only heard each cry of pain, of outrage, each grunt of exertion and whoop of glee that punctuated the scrambling rattle of feet on the grate and the skidding thumps whenever someone fell. The Spinks could take care of themselves better, perhaps, than the majority of adults in the city.

They had to.

His focus remained on the man whose feet dragged behind as he and Ginna maneuvered him up one set of stairs, down another, through cluttered alleys and empty structures on a route that took them away from the riotous intersection and gradually left most of the Spinks, and anyone who thought to follow, behind. He did not question their direction, nor the haphazard nature of the lean-to structure built to shield the broken-off door of an abandoned vindi on a street that looked to have been unused since the Coup.

Perhaps it was the absence of vindi lights that made the street look empty, but the building they entered, cold and damp and lined with empty counters, had stood unused for at least that long. The takeaway containers and empty bottles, wadded mounds of discolored blankets, and a meager assortment of dirty sacks and pouches deflated by age-stained emptiness that Ginna kicked aside, suggested what this place was now.

A streeter squat or a Spinks hideaway.

Neither mattered. The space was empty now. As long as no one followed them here, as long as no one confronted them for invading this place, they were safe.

From the light, cautious noises in the shadows outside, the Spinks taking lookout roosts to stand protectively against any enemies, Scarecrow believed this place was as secure as it could be.

"Here."

Giving the Founder's full weight to Scarecrow, Ginna pulled aside a moldy curtain, its weight suggestive of the value it once had, to reveal a metal door on the back wall of the room. Very little air moved through the vents on either side of it. No sounds came from within. It took both hands for her to turn the hatch wheel in the center of the door but the hinges did not creak or groan when she pulled the heavy door open.

It was used often enough to be in well-cared-for condition.

Again, slinging her arm around the Founder's torso and pulling his limp arm over her shoulder, Ginna helped Scarecrow maneuver him through the round, low-ceilinged door and down onto an old, but still usable, spring cot surrounded by a collection of food, liquor bottles, and other goods organized and stored in stolen recycle crates.

Though curious to know what this place was, this was not the time for questions as Scarecrow eased his burden down and pulled a battery torch from his belt. Its glaring beam was the only light in the room.

"He's breathing," he murmured as he handed the light to Ginna. That breathing was ragged and the amount of blood staining the Founder's wet, dingy shirt did not bode well for survival without a doctor. The disheveled man occasionally muttered delirious words beneath those struggling breaths but the advanced audio modules in his hood did not enable Scarecrow to make sense of what the Founder was saying. "Stay with him while I…"

"I don't know how…I shouldn't…you're hurt…" Ginna pointed at the wet smears staining the front of Scarecrow's leather coat.

"Not mine," he shrugged. "I'll send help…but we can't leave him alone. Not safe to move him out there yet. Need you here with him…I'm needed out there."

Despite her frustrated sigh, Ginna grimly nodded and slid a crate into place beside the cot, agreeing to his words without saying so. She wanted to do her part out there too, help her sister, help the Spinks. Help make Hebenon a safer place. But Scarecrow's skills made him better suited to it than hers ever would. He would reach help before she could. Her duty, assumed by the offer she had made to get them to this secure shelter, was to ensure the Founder's safety.

Scarecrow clasped her shoulder, a reassuring gesture despite the intimidating visage of his mask, his suit, and the digitized tone of his voice. "Do what you can. I'll be back soon as I can."

This time, her nod was more resolute, but he did not see the gesture as he slid back through the circular doorway and pushed the door most of the way closed.

The slight movement of air hissing through the grated shaft into the room meant she and the Founder would not suffocate, and the handle on the door's interior meant that she would not be trapped if he closed it, but he did not want her to feel like a prisoner. He only wanted both to be safe. Despite the Spinks outside, he needed to do more to protect them than covering the door with the curtain.

Punching the buttons on his wrist ICD, he muttered, "Doctor, need you down here. Follow this signal. You'll know what to do."

There was no signal from the other end of the connection. No response. Whatever had robbed Hebenon of power had robbed it of its communication capabilities. The ICD was useless for that, but it would continue to emit the programmed distress beacon he coded into it to the doctor's line for as long as it could.

He broke it free of his wrist guard and secured it into the crevice of the slightly open door.

If, when, Tamner got the message, he would come. If that had not happened by the time Scarecrow returned, he would find a way to bring Kemway to Tamner.

He did not believe either scenario would come soon enough to benefit the Founder.

The moldy curtain, brittle beneath his gloved fingers, was drawn into place to hide the door, and then he glanced over his shoulder at the Spink silhouetted in the entrance from the lean-to.

"Go Up. Get a message to Doctor Tamner. Bring him here…and only him. Don't speak to anyone about this…tell the others in the riot to stand down. Don't need to be there. Best they get out. Understood?"

"Yeah," said the girl, swiping her dirty blonde braid off her shoulder before dashing away.

Scarecrow looked back at the curtain. Maybe he should stay. Protect them both.

But Vanderwall was out there, even if Scarecrow had lost sight of him in the crowd. There was an attempted assassin to find. And he had to make certain Enoch and Ulynda were safe.

He had to trust that Ginna would do everything she could and that the Spinks standing watch outside would keep those inside safe.

He had to trust them all to do the right thing.

❧*❧

"Stay here."

Otta cinched her drab brown coat at the waist, new to her but not new, weightier, thicker, and warmer than anything she had worn inside the prison where she had been born, and threw a stern glower at the collection of children who had come out of the Core with her. They were not afraid of this unexpected darkness, were accustomed to periods of power loss within their subterranean world, and were not afraid to be left unattended. Even the shuddering of the city walls was a familiar, quaking hazard.

The woman's shift in demeanor, however, the concern in her voice she tried unsuccessfully to hide, etched their faces with a mirrored concern that prompted her to take action. If she remained with them, they would fail to trust her inactivity as her worry for Skelter bled into them. She would be surrounded by little monsters of fear she did not know how to help.

She could help them by doing something. They understood being asked to stay put while the adults addressed the dangers. They would obey her. In the Core, children who did not obey often died. The faces watching her understood that. She hoped taking action would be enough to ease their fears…and hers.

There was little she could do here, but she could find and help Skelter. He was smart, wily, and resourceful; he knew people, knew this city, better than she did. But he was no fighter. In her opinion, he had done enough. Fought enough. It was her turn to help and protect him. She nodded at the children and stepped outside.

On the walkway, a glance left and right revealed no hint of the direction Skelter had taken. Business, he had said, but with whom and where he was going, he had not revealed. The world was as dark outside as in, lit on this path only by the sporadic alglamps at the corners of buildings or in front of a few occupied dwellings. Something significant had happened. Something bad. Something she could not fix. Something she hoped had nothing to do with Skelter.

He was the only one she could help…except, perhaps, her father.

Pushing her black hair out of her face, the dyed color nearly displaced by the passage of time and new growth, Otta listened to the distant sounds of raised voices, shouts, and cries that told of too-familiar discontent. Knowing Skelter's propensity for involvement in such matters, that skirmish seemed a good place to start.

"Stay here," she repeated before closing the door.

❧*❧

The men who stared wide-eyed and nervous at the Echo screen, Oliver Grainger, Rafe Tamner, the man called Lash, and a handful of techs assigned to address the damaged external solar array, shielded their eyes against the flash and crackle that burst across the feed, wiping the view of the shell from sight. They did not see one man fall, did not see the sparks that spewed into the face of the other. By the time the flare subsided and their eyes adjusted to the returning normalcy of the now barely lit room and the dimmer-than-before screen, all they could see was one man stomping out a small spitting fire where the new interface had been installed, and the lead tech laying slack at the end of the line designed to prevent all shell crews from falling to their deaths.

It was impossible to tell the man's condition on the screen. The other, in his efforts to put out the fire, shielded his face with one hand. Red seeped between his fingers, and around the edges of his hand, charred facial flesh could be seen.

"Get them in here," Grainger shouted as he spun, aiming his fist at the thin, stringy-haired man nearest him.

Lash ducked out of the way, but was unable to avoid the eruptive, "You did this!" that followed.

Tamner pushed between them, pulling Lash back, as Grainger barked, "Arrest him!" to the pair of buggers standing at the office door.

"Captain," the doctor began, hoping to redirect the man's fury.

"And them too!" the captain continued, gesturing at the screen, ignoring the doctor except to step around him to try to grab Lash's bare arm.

His fist came up empty.

"They didn't…" Tamner started again.

"I won't have sabotage! It's his equipment…his instruction…"

"Modules can fail," said one of the techs, "We don't know…"

"Could have been a primary board failure," Lash growled defensively, as taken aback by the unexpected chain of events as everyone else. He had not been on the outside, on the shell, to inspect the unit. He had been given ICD images to work with and had only the word of the inspecting solar techs to go by. Now that both the module he had built with parts supplied by Tox and Zara, and the main inverter board set into the city's shell were both irretrievably damaged, it would take more time than before to replace one more board to restore solar power to Hebanthe Falls.

"We need the footage…need to see what was missed," Lash continued, escaping Grainger's hand but not the gloved grips of the buggers who caught him by both biceps and began to drag him from the room despite Tamner's efforts to intervene.

"You've done enough! I'll have your balls for this as well as your tongue…"

Grainger's threat was cut short by the chirp of the emergency Echo channel, a surprising sound now that the screen had faded to black with the dimming of the lights. Expecting the message to spawn a barrage of complaints about the abrupt city-wide power cut and yet hoping that the sound heralded Jaron trying to reach him, the captain slammed the side of his hand into the comm buttons and barked, "What?" as the pneumatic door struggled open and then failed to close after Lash was dragged out through it.

Tamner did not move.

"Captain…we have a situation…"

The voice on the other end of the connection was unrecognizable, cracked with static pops and sounding faint as if echoing from the far end of a tunnel. There was the background chaos of shouts and screams, sounds that made both Grainger and Tamner frown.

"Founder Kemway was…" Crackle. "…to the rioters…" Pop. Sizzle. "Scarecrow…" Hiss. Snap. "…shots…"

Screeching erupted close to the speaker and made Grainger and those with him wince.

Silence.

Tamner could hear it. Feel it. See it. The tension across the captain's shoulders at the mention of the missing Founder and

Scarecrow in the same attempted message. If anyone could protect Kemway, Tamner believed it was Scarecrow, but he did not expect Grainger to agree to that assessment. He was about to speak when the captain's fist cracked down on the desk again, and the dark-skinned man glared at one of the few people still present.

To the tech, a young woman with few visible years of experience, Grainger barked, "I want that location. I want to see what…"

"Hub's down, Captain," the tech mumbled anxiously, her mien conveying the intimidation she felt in the shade of Grainger's outrage. "But I'll…"

He cut her off with another growl and a wave of his hand as he tried to reestablish a communication connection on his ICD with the individual who had tried to reach him. "You'll do more than try."

When his effort failed to produce the desired result as the tech hastened to the Hub in the hopes of getting communications back up at the source, Grainger tried to contact the other person he expected to have answers…or who would be able to get them.

Lieutenant Ilya also failed to respond.

There was no proof that his efforts were connecting, that anyone could hear him.

Tamner cleared his throat. Learning what was happening in the Levs where the message had seemingly originated, where the Founder may have been located, where he might, at last, be in bugger custody, was important. But in the dim room, with an obvious audible whine in the filt systems that brought with it a noticeable increase in temperature and the slow stagnation of the room's air, other equally pressing matters needed to be addressed.

"Might I recommend we shut down non-life systems until we can assess the damage…see if we can repair…" he began.

Without lifting his head, Grainger hissed. "I can't just…"

"You can. You have to. I'll convene the Nau, get a ruling…a plan…but if we don't shut down every non-essential system, there won't be enough power to run anything. The batteries will fail. We risk blowing the hydros' capacity…cazzing the whole system."

They stared at one another, one irritated that such necessities had to be pointed out to him in his distraction, the other stern-faced and focused on practicalities that he was more used to managing though he was only a doctor, a scientist, by practice. This was not Grainger's fault. He was no Founder. No city manager. He was a law enforcement officer thrust into a position of leadership he had never needed to shoulder before. Tamner, despite his career, had been exposed to the mechanics of ruling through a lifetime of interaction with the Founder, the defunct Doctet, and the Nau.

Establishing order, Grainger could do.

Maneuvering through politics and thinking through the myriad of citywide issues that came with it, he would gladly leave for Tamner.

"Do it…and take care of those two." His sweeping gesture indicated the injured techs on the city's shell they could no longer see. "Get someone up there to assess the damage and inventory our equipment while I…"

Tamner nodded and finished, "…find Founder Kemway."

Grainger scowled but nodded, too. Right now, that felt to him to be a more pressing matter than anything else. If Kemway was found, if he lived, the deposed Founder, mad or not, could ruin everything.

❧*❧

He had been in the thick of the crowd earlier, a faceless savior to some, a shadow-demon to others. With the crowd's focus intent on protesting the salt shortage and other ills they believed Hebenon's leaders were facilitating, and then on the missing Founder's unexpected rise and chaotic, verbal plea, Scarecrow was able to pass through the gathering without hindrance.

The man he sought, however, as he pulled brako off civilians and civilians off buggers, trying to assist in peacekeeping as he hunted, was no longer here.

If he were Vanderwall, he would have used the riot to escape notice, now that his identity had been unmasked. Few would have recognized him as brako without the mask he often wore, unless he failed to remove the identifying yellow band from his arm. But his Crow coat would be enough to signify his brako allegiance. In a sea of combat between his minions, the bugorra, and the people of Hebenon, that was something Vanderwall did not need. Retreat had been the wise, judicious choice.

Scarecrow had lost him, but not for long.

He had seen the man's face.

Soon, he would know who he was, where to find him.

When the riot settled, when the Founder was secure and the city was as calm as the power outage permitted, the hunt for Vanderwall would begin again.

Now he had to think only of the Founder.

❧*☙

Clinging to the power pole with her injured arm, ignoring the searing throb in a knee that barely balanced her weight, Ilya whistled and shouted and pointed commands from the now lopsided platform, directing the bugorra into the tightest clusters of discontent she could identify from her vantage point. When hands tried to dislodge her, sometimes brako, sometimes disgruntled civilians looking to lash out at the powers that controlled their lives or seeking only to take advantage of the tumult as an excuse for mischief, she struck out with the baton she had been given, cracking wrists and hands and skulls with enough force to bruise or fracture bones but rarely with enough force to drive would-be assailants away.

Only the presence of two officers who had positioned themselves near her could keep the worst of the monsters at bay. When the first of the two was dragged into the crowd by a screeching woman under attack by multiple assailants, and the second was knocked off her feet by Igraci Players grappling with a group of Talkers, Ilya found herself unprotected and at the mercy of whatever foe would reach her next.

That foe was greeted by a curdling blood-cry of a broad-shouldered woman who shot out of Ilya's peripheral vision and launched into the fight with a fury the lieutenant had rarely seen. At first, she expected her protector to be Scarecrow, but the fringes of purple in the unfamiliar woman's hair and the sweat sheen on her dark skin proved her to be as human, as normal, as Ilya. The stranger struck the Talker who tried to clamber onto the stage between his legs with a fist. The Talker rolled off the stage with an agonized bellow. The woman then scooped up the nearby bullhorn the Founder had dropped that had been out of Ilya's reach before and thrust it into the lieutenant's hand without a word.

Ilya nodded, tucked the baton under her arm, and took the bullhorn. If the power systems in the city were compromised, she could not count on backup from the captain or anyone else. Ilya had to manage this situation on her own. The crowd was thin, the buggers slowly gaining the upper hand, but it was not happening fast enough.

She brought the bullhorn to her mouth. The woman at the base of the platform clocked an outraged fellow who tried, along with his comrade, to help the downed Talker to his feet. All three stumbled with the force of the blow and fell back. Ilya had barely shouted, "Stop!" through the bullhorn when something flew from the far side of the stage, knocked the horn from her hand, and in her instinctive, reflexive effort to dodge the impact, was forced to twist sideways and release the pole.

She crashed to the platform with a yelp of excruciating pain when another thrown object struck her already damaged knee.

❧*❧

"Tell him…he's done…enough…"

Ginna turned the battery light on and leaned closer to the man on the sagging mattress. "Tell who?" she whispered, ignoring the unsettling visage the shadows molded out of the man's face.

He did not continue. The eyes that had snapped open with the flickering of the light, staring at first with dilated fear, fluttered and grew gradually unfocused as if he could no longer see her face or the light that illuminated it.

The filt system's hiss was but a murmur but it was louder, she mused, than the life breath that escaped in lessening rattling wheezes, until the man's chest rose and fell one last time, expelling its remaining contents before ceasing to rise again with the closing of his eyes as if to sleep. The hand held in hers, which had clenched so desperately at the utterance of those words, grew slack.

Ginna squeezed tighter as if doing so would anchor his breath to his body, as if it would bring strength and life back into the man whose family had been the backbone of Hebanthe Falls since its inception.

The last Founder.

There was no one else.

If she could have captured and clung to his dying words and breath to give it back to the decaying city, she would have done so.

With his hand still in hers, the last kindness she could offer, Ginna sat in Hebenon's darkness alone.

❧Chapter 3❧

There was no point in screaming at Nanny, accusing her of causing the devouring dark and the dwindling purr of the life systems that made the roar of the Five Falls more pronounced. That fact had not tempered Neoma's outbursts, however. Though she vaguely regretted her eruption in the engulfing silent solitude that remained after the other woman fumbled from the living room towards the kitchen panel where battery systems and fuses were housed, her regret was not enough to prompt Neoma to push aside her temper to summon Nanny back or apologize.

She was no stranger to solitude. She often preferred it unless she was the center of attention. Such silence, such darkness as this, however, was new, and after peeping through the window to expose the unlit paths of the city, she realized how alone she truly was.

Not even Ulynda was here to distract her.

No one but Nanny and her own tempestuous thoughts.

Nanny eventually returned with the glow of a candle in one hand and an unlit battery torch in the other. The meager flame cast withering flashes against the wall when she set it on the table nearest the liquor cabinet and then Nanny lit the torch and hurried out of the room.

Neoma did not ask what she intended to do.

Reaching the table for a drink she hoped would steady her nerves, Neoma listened to Nanny's footsteps. There would be no cooking. If there was running water, there would not be enough to clean dishes or make lukewarm algtea. There were no Echo voices to announce the source of distress and nothing in the room but the wine to distract her. She swallowed the contents of the first glass, wishing for a better vintage or something stronger before pouring another.

Footsteps outside brought a curt knock and the muffled sounds of a struggle at the door. Warily, the wine carafe in her hand in case she needed a weapon, Neoma peered through the window at the side of the door again. She recognized the three there as brako, but not the bundle that struggled in their midst. Behind the Crow masks, they could be her supporters, or they could be Feena's, but seeing them there was comfort enough to prompt her to open the door in the hopes that their company would provide security if not a distraction.

If they were Feena's men, they would not have the gall to kill her, knowing who she was. They would not dare.

The door was barely cracked open when the thrashing bundle kicked and flung it back with a shriek of outrage. The man carrying it was forced to drop his hold so that the small figure stumbled and fell across the threshold.

"Looking for this?" that man grunted as another yanked the hood from the girl's head. The child began to crab away, but under the gaze of the woman looming over her, she froze and fell silent, her fury at being manhandled and carried across the city like a cat in a sack now metamorphosed into the terror of realizing she was home with the woman she had tried to escape.

There was a moment of unsuspecting shock before Neoma's voice returned and she cried, "Ulynda!" as she bent towards her daughter. Without a sound, Ulynda skittered away from the reaching hands so that they came short of touching her.

"Found her at the salt riots," the third spoke, "with the dwarf."

Whether pretending not to be affronted by her daughter's avoidance or relieved and satisfied to change the subject to avoid the intimacy of welcome she was unaccustomed to expressing, Neoma straightened and snarled at the speaker, so focused on him now that it was as if she had forgotten Ulynda was there. "You found him? You didn't bring him to me?"

"…listening to the Founder…" the man continued as her questions trampled over his words.

His last word cut short the rant as Ulynda cried, "They shot him!"

"Wasn't us," the first man rushed to assure the woman as building outrage at one interruption after another, without anyone answering her questions, darkened Neoma's narrow face. Her fury lent a death's head air to her pale visage, a look that drove Ulynda further away and past her and made the three brako square their shoulders. "Someone in the crowd…"

"He's dead!" Ulynda cried as she started to rise. "Enoch too!"

"Not dead," said the second brako. "Buggers trying to…"

"Might have been Talkers," said the third.

"Or the Players," the first added.

"Everyone's dead!" Ulynda wailed between the frightened sobs that pushed to the surface despite her desire to remain invisible.

"Enough!"

Though uncertain who the demand was directed at, the brako fell silent as Ulynda choked on her tears and continued to inch backward toward her bedroom. Neoma did not recognize her daughter's clothes, only that they made her look like a streeter. She did not appear to be harmed, only filthy and ungroomed, but the way she had been dragged home and dropped into the room were reasons enough for the child to be dirty and hysterical.

Seeing a father believed dead was another, although Neoma was skeptical that any of them had seen the things they claimed.

Haythem was gone. He was never coming back.

Yet for the first time since the Coup, Neoma felt hope.

"Send Vanderwall to me," she demanded, the carafe finally set down on the windowsill next to the door so she could wipe her hand down the front of her blouse to smooth it. "And bring me that dwarf."

At the mention of the one who had tried to save and protect her from the brako…men she now realized were in her mother's thrall…Ulynda forgot her fear of her mother. "Leave him alone!" she cried in a vain attempt to race out the door past the brako. She did not understand why her mother was more interested in her protective friend than her father, but this was not the first time she failed to fathom Neoma's motivations.

She had to warn Enoch if he was still alive. She had to find Scarecrow. They would take her to her father.

The barricade of brako prevented her from escaping and allowed her mother to grab her shoulder and yank her off her feet. The violence of the thrust threw Ulynda against the nearest cushioned chair. She slid to the floor with a wide-eyed, dazed expression.

"Get out of those disgusting clothes! And you," Neoma snarled again at the men in the doorway, "Why are you still here? I want Vanderwall!"

"Leave him alone," Ulynda again dared to challenge as she wiggled to her feet.

Neoma took a step towards her.

Ulynda fled to her room, slamming and locking the door behind her. The brako were left on the walkway with the door slamming shut.

Alone again now, Neoma let out a single long, hissing breath. Ulynda could not be right. She could not mean any of the things she had said. She was a foolish, traumatized child.

The brako merely wanted to rile her.

Vanderwall was the only person likely to give the tale to her straight, if there was any tale to tell.

If there was some reward forthcoming for the return of the Founder's only living child, the three who stalked into the darkness knew they would not see it.

❧*❧

Blayd wiped his gloved hands on the front of his mist-damp jacket, surveyed the walkway, structures, and alleys nearby to verify he was alone and unobserved, and then closed the door of the vacant warehouse behind him. Other people emerged from the nearest businesses, shift workers left without duties who raised their eyes upward or looked towards the falls, seeking the source of the sudden loss of power. The glow of neon signs was supplanted by near darkness. The steam that had belched nonstop from the nearest plants and the rattling whirr of exhaust fans that vented farm sheds into the street had ceased too, leaving only the ever-present roar of the Five Falls that continued to spill their flow over the roofs and streets of the Levs and the confused murmurs of those people he could see.

Someone glanced at him and bobbed their head, but with the coat hood pulled up, the individual's face was obscured, unrecognizable. Blayd neither nodded to acknowledge the gesture nor spoke.

No one here knew him.

No one had a reason to.

They had not seen him arrive. They had not seen what he had done or what business he had come out of. Intent on the silent darkness, none of them would notice his departure. To them, he was no more than another worker observing the unknown. As soon as the individual resumed speaking to those nearby, Blayd headed quietly away, ignoring the muscled brute who barreled past and threw open the door of a warehouse similar to the one Blayd had just left.

Tempers were short.

A loss of power was bad for business, particularly if it lasted too long. It was bad for survival, too.

For Blayd, the loss of power was an inconvenience of a different sort, but it might also be a boon.

Everything was in place. There was only one more thing to do.

It might have to wait until the power was restored. But he had waited this long. He could wait another few hours.

By then, Neoma would rue the day she had turned on him. The day she had threatened him and refused to take him back.

He no longer wanted that.

It was done now. The bridges between them were burned…and she would pay.

❧*❧

"Why'd you do it?"

Vanderwall kept his voice low as the perpetual rumbles of functioning city systems no longer masked his voice or his barely contained fury. But that anger was evident as the door clattered closed behind him, barely cutting off his voice from any of the people outside seeking answers where there were none. The limp figure bound and suspended by chains that hung over the meat rails above their heads lifted his face in the direction of the new, unfamiliar voice but he did not speak. He did nothing more than hiss out a weak groan between thirst-swollen lips and try to face his captor through the glare of the sparking flare held between them.

Different voice. Different face. Not one of those who had dragged him here, bound him, spoke to him in belittling whispered jeers and jabs before leaving him alone. That had been hours ago, or he assumed it was hours. Hours in the dark, in the cold, with only a single cup of water brought to him that he refused to drink.

He was sure the water was drugged. He was sure it was poisoned.

He was equally certain about why he had been brought here, even if he could not remember where he had been found, how he had been delivered to this place. Even if he did not recognize any of the distorted voices and faces that paraded before him.

The masks of the Crows told him enough.

"Tell me what I need to know and I'll end this."

'End this' was not a promise to let him go. Rather, it sounded preferable, he mused on the head of the fist that caught him beneath the ribs and left him gasping for breath, to unending torture.

No one knew he was here. No one was coming for him.

He doubted, when the man with the flare caught a fist of damp curls and pulled his head up so that they could stare into each other's faces, that anyone was looking.

Vanderwall scowled, noting the dullness of the captive's eyes and the tiny electrical pops emitted by the remnants of the damaged speecher units at the man's throat and temples. Deciding to test the obvious hypothesis, he growled, "Where's Scarecrow?"

There was life in those eyes, a hint of defiance matched by a furious burst of activity from the speecher that might have produced words if it was still capable. It was not that the captive refused to answer questions. Rather, he could not, at least not questions that demanded anything more than a yes or no answer.

The interrogator smirked.

"Did you kill Vanderwall?"

The captive's defiance morphed into something perceived as panic that spread noticeable shivers through his body. The chains around his wrists rattled. Toes dragging against the floor sought purchase as if to retreat from the accusation.

Before he could answer, however, with either a nod or a shake of his head, someone pounded on the warehouse door in a sequence that made Vanderwall snarl and scowl. His companion opened the door far enough to hear, "Mam's looking for you, sir. We found the girl."

The metal door closed with a bang.

"Don't touch him till I'm back," the big man grunted at his underling. "I'll have the hands of anyone who does." He yanked the captive's head up again by the fist of hair he still clenched and hissed, close enough that their noses nearly touched. "Think carefully about what you say to me next. One chance. You won't get another."

Jaron's head dropped so that his chin bumped his chest, and he closed his eyes against the darkness that returned after the door opened and closed again.

He did not need to answer.

The brako already knew the truth.

He was as good as dead.

❧Chapter 4❧

Senior Kal crouched in the space beneath his desk, trying to ignore his shuddering, listening to the fading screams of surprise, shock, and fear in the Hall. The onslaught had begun with breaking windows, banging on the exterior walls, and the squeal of pry bars against any opening that might allow intruders into a building that had, until recently, been perpetually open to any in search of the wisdom and indulgences the Voices of Faith meted out in exchange for ticks or return favors. Since the abduction of Founder Kemway, a crime that burdened the Senior and the Voices with unproven guilt, the need to lock the doors of Primary Hall had been the only way those living within were able to feel a sliver of unmolested peace.

Sleep had been his intention, but he doubted, as the ruckus continued, rattling his teeth with every crash against the nearest wall, that the night would be a peaceful one. He could not make out the shouted words, muffled as they were by hands pressed tight to his ears and the intrusive assault on the walls of his office. He could not tell who was winning the invasive confrontation. When someone pushed open his office door, his breath caught behind the choking fear of impending slaughter. Using the hemplastic kick barrier at the front of the desk to hide behind, he pulled into a tighter ball and squeezed his eyes closed as if the inability to see what was coming would shield him from its inevitability.

As dark as the room was, without even an alglamp to lend a soft glow to the ambiance or a neon glow from the nearby hostel to stretch red fingers through the window, there was little to see and no way for anyone to see him. If not for the shouts and clatter of clashing Talkers and civilians, the office, as insulated as it was, would be dark and silent. Despite his morbid curiosity, his overwhelming terror spared him the presence of mind to ponder other important matters.

"Senior? Are you safe? Are you here?"

A slivery shaft of light swept the room, drawing a yellow line on the dull white surfaces in a seeking arc from one side to the other. Relics and digital frames with images of Kal and other Talkers and dignitaries at various Voices of Faith functions had fallen from shelves or dangled askew on the walls. The room's single window was cracked but remained in place. On the desk, the Echo screen tilted on its stand, dark without energy to power it. With the fractured window clinging to its frame and no other way of escaping the office without facing the unidentified assailants, there was nowhere else for the Senior to be except within his private sleeping chamber.

It was unknown if the speaker had already looked there.

There were few places in his office to hide.

Kal recognized the voice of his secretary, Bene, a middle-aged fellow a few years younger, with salt and pepper hair and deep creases around his mouth that made him appear older. The familiarity of his voice was not reassuring, for how could Kal know if the man who had served him for more than twenty years was a participant in the Hall assault? He forced his eyes open and lowered his hands from his head to hear clearly, but his arms and legs refused to uncoil from the terror shield they created around his body.

"Senior? Are you here?"

The note of concern in Bene's beseeching plea sounded earnest enough to prompt Kal to creep from under the desk, his movement aching and shaky as he used the lip of the desk to pull to his feet. His eyes made a darting scan of the room, noting that the banging on his wall and window had ceased, and he swallowed hard before forcing words out of his too-tight throat.

"Are they gone? Is it over?"

Despite the effort to sound and appear calm, his limbs continued to tremble, so he had to sit to avoid falling. Once seated, the quaver in his voice was quenched by the dregs from the wine glass left when the attack had started.

Kal was amazed the glass had not tipped when the shaking began.

"We got 'em…at least two of 'em…the others are gone, I think."

"Brako?" He searched the periphery of the lantern's illumination, noting the inconvenient damage but seeing nothing of import harmed. Only the broken window might be a problem once the outside air and moisture began to find a way through the cracks.

Brako were the assailants he expected, men sent by Neoma in response to their growing enmity and distrust. Brako…or else bugorra.

Such a shame. The Kemways and the Voices of Faith had been allies since the founding of the city. They should still be so now as life in Hebanthe Falls spluttered and collapsed around them.

"Don't know about all of them. I didn't get a look. Most fled when Samsen and Charles were…"

Bene's voice faltered and he fiddled with the light's settings to make the beam brighter.

Kal scowled. "What?"

Bene shrugged but it was several moments before he morosely muttered, "Caught by a moli. Got the fire out but they didn't make it. There's others pretty cut up by the glass…sent for a medic but they should be fine. You oughta come see the damage…"

Kal bobbed his head but reached for the wine bottle again without speaking. It was one of the bottles Feena had brought him, with just enough remaining to refill his glass. Rather than savor the rare, expensive gift, he leaned on the alcohol's medicinal properties to give strength to his weak legs. He wiped his mouth across the back of his hand, not bothering to tug his handkerchief from his pocket, pulled his coat from the back of his chair, and then stood again to don it with a gesture to Bene to lead the way.

The Hall was silent except for the murmurs of Talkers trying to right the wrongs done to their sanctuary. There was evidence of damage from the shaking, ritual items and images that had fallen, the speaking podium having toppled from the platform where it stood, emptying its stored contents across the floor. Every colored hempglass window had been shattered, the glass imploded inward at the mercy of building hemp bricks, bottles, and bits of stone hurled through them. The Hall entrance doors were pried open and broken from their hinges. The nearest benches, the hemp-planked floor, and the faded blue-patterned carpet that ran the length of the aisle to the podium were burned and frayed for several feet around where the moli had shattered towards the front of the Hall. Kal could see the impact point, see where two of his most stalwart Talkers had given their lives for their Faith. Talkers and civilians were scattered in frightened huddles about the sanctuary while others, less bloody and more focused, tended to the injuries of those who had taken the brunt of the assault.

Some threw critical glances at their Senior as if he were to blame, but no one spoke to him or voiced their thoughts. No one approached as he picked his way over the splotches of what he believed to be burnt flesh and blood to peer outside into the square.

Kal swallowed the bile in his throat and kept his eyes forward.

Two individuals were bound at the side of the room, non-descript men in non-descript apparel, unmasked if they were brako, bearing no distinguishing attire or mark of affiliation that might identify them.

A passion crime of opportunity, perhaps, Kal frowned as he passed through the empty portal onto the Hall steps into a world darker than he had ever seen it.

No neon glowed. A few battery-operated emergency lights offered struggling flickers to the feeble efforts of the dozen or so alglamps atop their poles or on the corners of buildings, but it was not enough to counteract the darkness. The park fountain had ceased gurgling and the people gathered there, shoppers, diners, and recreationists, stared up through the twisting layers of Lev walkways as if expecting to find an answer.

Not one of them had come to the aid of the Talkers in the Hall.

He could see no evidence of it and imagined that fear had kept them away. Perhaps some or all of them had been participants.

His frown deepened.

"Senior." Bene gestured behind them.

The walls on both sides of the door were slathered with new graffiti, slurs, and crude symbols in still-wet yellow, white, and red. Hijo de puta. Malakes. Schweinhund. Afatottari. Rise up or fall, a common Igraci slogan born on many sandwich boards. The increasingly familiar stylized inverted haz symbol which served as a plea and rally cry of support for Scarecrow. The painted scrawls continued around all sides of the Hall, up as high as a person could reach, variations on messages of hate and discontent once reserved for, and primarily directed at, Founder Kemway and his family.

But no more.

Pejorative degradation in neon in the minutes after the city had grown dark and the attack had begun. Too much of it to support the conjecture that this had been a spur-of-the-moment opportunity crime.

This had been orchestrated.

"Clean this up…inventory the damage…the losses," Kal snapped, cinching his belt as his glower returned to the park crowd, some of whom watched him with what Kal believed to be more than curiosity.

"Where are you…?" started Bene, eyeing the onlookers too as the Senior descended the Hall steps alone.

"Gonna find out who did this." He could question the captives but he did not believe either would tell him what he wanted to know. He suspected they did not have the answers he sought.

There were likely only three who could provide what he wanted.

He intended to hammer each of them until he had the truth.

❧*❧

Gritting her teeth, she ignored the clatter of thrown objects and the shouts of fury that continued in an ongoing barrage from Ulynda's locked room, an uncharacteristic tantrum that Neoma attributed to her father, to the dwarf, to the brutes who had brought her home like a hostage. Knowing only a single way to address such tantrums, she was kept from doing so by the one-fisted single-pounding thump at her door that announced Vanderwall's delinquent arrival. She opened it, muttering beneath her breath, deeming her business with him to be more pressing than dealing with the unruly child, and let the bald man inside. She hoped her disapproving scowl was interpreted as displeasure with his delayed arrival and the dripping mess left on her floor rather than being rooted in Ulynda's offensive outburst.

"Haythem's been seen," she began, her tone a more clipped, high-pitched questioning squeak than she intended.

Refusing to remove either his gloves or the brimmed hat he wore, refusing to enter further into a room in which he expected not to be invited to stay, Vanderwall shrugged and grunted, "I know." He kept his head low, shielding his bruised chin. The SCAMs were down, the prodcasts too, but he was not surprised that Mam had already heard that her husband had been seen. That sort of news was undoubtedly spreading like fire. "Saw him."

Casting him a narrow-eyed glare, marginally aware of the abrupt silence in Ulynda's room, she hissed, "You know and didn't...?"

He shrugged unapologetically. "There were complications."

"No complications are an excuse for keeping..."

"Buggers...and Scarecrow...things to do..."

"Didn't think you're afraid of..."

"Not afraid." Frowning, eyes creased with a hint of offense he tried to swallow, he grunted, "You weren't there." The accusation of cowardice made his broad face flush but he was not willing to admit that Scarecrow had seen his face and might be able to expose him to the bugorra. Doing so would raise additional ire and questions about his suitability for the position he had obtained. He preferred to deal with that problem without Mam's interference.

He also chose not to mention the popper fire or the possibility that those shots had been aimed at her husband.

That they might have struck their mark.

As soon as the prods were up, she would learn those details from someone other than him.

"You'll find him and bring him to me."

"Yes." It was easier to agree than to argue. He had enough resources that someone out on the street ought to be able to find the Founder…even though they had failed to do so before.

"And I want you to find the dwarf Enoch and…"

Another roar of outrage and the pounding of impotent fists on the locked bedroom door began anew. Neoma flinched and grimaced, angry shadows digging creases of intolerance at the corners of her eyes and mouth as she added, "Find him and get rid of him."

"Kill him?"

Neoma was grateful in that renewed flurry of destructive force that Ulynda could not hear the man's question.

"I don't care how. I just need him gone."

Before he further corrupts my daughter.

Without questioning the dwarf's significance to the Mam, Vanderwall grunted, "Consider it done."

He was aware of a connection between Scarecrow and the dwarf. He had seen them together, a connection he might be able to use to pluck the vigi thorn from his foot and bury them both in the turbulent river. The more lures he had to draw Scarecrow out, the more likely it was that he could catch that particular spiny fish.

Neoma grunted too and stalked across the room to the liquor cabinet where the burning candle threatened to go out, leaving Vanderwall at the door. He watched her, expecting to be dismissed, expecting her to say something else, but instead, she poured a glass of something pungent he could smell across the room and drank it with her back to him.

"Anything else?"

No title. No polite address. Only the question.

Ulynda screamed and kicked the door.

"Get out!" Neoma snapped, the glass thrown in fury at the girl's door, its contents splashing Vanderwall as it flew past.

He narrowed his eyes, pursed his lips, and left.

Neoma stormed into her bedroom and slammed the door.

❧*❧

The room smelled of stagnant perfume, a floral scent that tickled his memory but one he could not identify as he struggled toward consciousness. He heard nothing, no hum or buzz or hiss, no voices or footsteps. He tasted only the flat, metallic remnants of blood on the swollen tongue stuck to the roof of his mouth. When he turned his head, it was with a creaking ache and pop that brought with it the remembrance of the blow that preceded this waking. That turning brought a sound, the audible nervous clicking whose source was assessed to be a woman's nails on the polished end table near his head. He cracked open his eyes.

Feena Wulfe.

Her scowl forced his eyes open the rest of the way, prompting him to stretch and slowly sit up, a movement that drew her focus from whatever musings accompanied her vacant-eyed stare out the window at her shoulder.

"Good. You're awake." She smiled, gently caught his shoulder to prevent him from rising, and then pushed a cup of wine within his reach. "Drink this. It'll help." It smelled expensive, but in those initial waking moments, the tang of alcohol made his stomach turn.

"Doubt that." Her tone grated against his groggy nerves, a reminder of something forgotten, something hidden. Brushing away her efforts to keep him down, he wormed his way into a fully seated position and glanced in the direction she had been staring.

Something stronger than wine might have done the trick, but the throbbing in his skull, connected to the sharp pain at the base of his neck and across his shoulders, decried even that remedy. He did not trust whatever she was offering, whatever she might have added to the contents of that cup.

"Where am I?"

"Found you trampled by the mob." Feena's peculiar tone hung between concern and ambivalence that made the back of his neck prickle. "If only they'd known who you…"

Enoch shook his head so that his shaggy curls flopped across his forehead, and he pushed them back with one hand as the other pushed the offered wine away. He did not recognize the cerulean blue shirt of expensive, shimmery fabric that he wore, nor the brand-new pair of sturdy trousers, both of which he was tempted to return in favor of his familiar, threadbare clothes. That would have left him momentarily naked, however, and though he wondered who had undressed and then dressed him again, who had washed his hair and tended to his injuries, he chose not to speak of clothes or medical care as if he had not noticed either. "If they knew who I am, they'd have come after me, too."

"Too?" Unoffended by the rejection of one gift and the ignoring of the others, she lifted the glass to her pink-rouged lips and sipped its contents as if to prove that it was not poisoned.

Instead of watching her, Enoch perused the room, the lavender and pink coloration reminiscent enough of the Den that he gauged it to be the business office of that bar. The pink hemp-leather sofa he sat on was the only item of unbusinesslike luxury in the room. An alglantern on the desk, customized to fill the room with a faint pink ambiance instead of the usual blue or green, provided enough light to see by but there was little he was interested in seeing.

His original clothes were nowhere in sight. Only the boots on his feet, clean though they were now, were his own.

Trying to remember what had prompted his words, the vivid images of the rioters, Founder Kemway on the speaker's platform, and the subsequent popper fire were disjointed enough that he could not be sure of the sequence of events. What he did remember was the crow-faced brako snatching Ulynda and her plea for rescue before the blow incapacitated him.

His gaze stopped at the open door and the silent fellow standing beside it that Enoch had not noticed before, his hands clasped in front of him, his gaze straight ahead as though also staring through the window into the dark or perhaps not staring at anything. Wondering why the fellow was there, if he was andi or human, if Feena was afraid of him or hoped to discourage him from leaving, Enoch slid to the floor using his hand on the sofa arm until his equilibrium was steady. He did not feel dizzy or weak, despite the ache at the back of his skull, but he did feel reluctant to stay here any longer.

"I have to go."

"You just got here."

"Didn't get anywhere…and it's been long enough." He had been brought here against his will, long enough ago to regain consciousness. Despite any gratitude he might owe the elegant woman for saving his life and for the tailored attire he now wore, he knew what she wanted. Her intent for him was evident in her opening words.

Before he could remove his hand from the sofa, she covered it with hers.

He pulled away.

"People need me."

Feena's voice lowered into a warm, insistent, determined purr. "Yes, they do," she agreed. "I'm glad you see that now. I won't stop you from leaving…just remember…"

Enoch met her gaze for the first time, anticipating the words that would come next, reminders of a debt he had not agreed to by waking up here. Instead of speaking to them, the woman smiled evasively, stood to draw a new leather coat from where it hung on the back of a nearby chair, and handed it to him saying, "Darwin will see you out. After that, I'm sure you can find your way."

He hesitated to accept another gift, but going out into the city without a coat's protection from the damp and cold was inviting sickness. He suspected that refusing this offer would carry a similar risk, though she had made no threats. Without a word, he accepted the coat, pulled it on with a grunt that might have expressed gratitude or annoyance, and after adjusting it at the waist and collar, he wobbled through the door following the man who waited there.

He might not intend to grant her the repayment she hoped for, but he did not want to stubbornly die either.

At least not until he made certain Ulynda was safe.

Not until he knew what had happened to Kemway on that intersection platform.

Not until he found…his brother.

❧Hyperion's Bier❧

❧Chapter 5❧

The attempts to provide emergency lighting could only assuage Vapors' guests for so long. When the second power drop came and the battery units of personal Echos around the room began to run dry, when the limits of Maemi's offering of free alcohol and appetizers that did not need cooking was reached, the wary, weary patrons began to brave the dark streets in the hopes of reaching home before tragedy befell them. Colyx escorted many of them, alone, in pairs, or in small groups, in the direction they intended to go as far as the first set of stairs or intersection they reached, alert to the potential presence and interference of the brako or any other threat.

A single Igraci, white hood pulled low to shield their face from the wet and possible recognition, stood at the closest intersection with a neon-tubed signboard that announced the end of Hebenon.

Colyx paused to stare at the figure and the sign for many moments after escorting the last of Vapors' guests away and then limped back into the nearly empty bar with a ponderous expression.

"Lasting too long," muttered Nigel as he tied the filmy mauve robe around his naked waist. He was the only male andi in Zara's entourage, a trio who provided daily entertainment to Vapors' patrons. Sitting on the edge of the dance stage with his lean legs swinging nervously, he only stilled when Hiana, the phosphorescent makeup on her dark skin glistening in the dim light, covered his hand on his knee with hers. The third andi, seated on his other side, the pale, silver-haired Ebenee, nodded in silent agreement but did not lift her clenched hands from her lap. They should take the opportunity to rest, to recharge for another day's shift, but there was a sense of security here with Maemi, Colyx, and Jonner gathered at the bar so that none had convinced themselves to depart.

Even the cook was gone now.

There was an unspoken expectation that Zara would come for them if they waited long enough.

"Should go up…out…see if it's night or day," Jonner offered, swirling a finger in his lukewarm drink, watching the amber liquid circle the glass when his finger was taken away.

"Lifts won't work," Maemi reminded him, fidgeting with the bar rag beneath her hand as she watched the beaded curtains that served as Vapors' door. Usually, they swayed with the drafts created by air moving through the filt systems. Now they hung still. She wondered if she should close and lock the door now that it seemed unlikely there would be any patrons until the power was restored.

"It'll come back," she added mulishly. "You're welcome till it does…all of you." This was her vindi. Without her cooks or other swivers, she would remain behind the bar until the lights came on.

The only other option was locking the door.

It had not been locked in all the years she had owned Vapors.

Jonner sighed, bobbed his head, and drank the last of the whiskey.

Adjusting the beaded blue shawl around her bare shoulders, Ebenee sighed too. "You think so? It'll come back?"

"Always does," Maemi assured her, hoping to instill as much confidence in the others as she could in herself.

Despite the distance across the room that prevented Ebenee from seeing the swiver's eyes, she, too, knew the truth. Doubt and dread would settle more heavily with each hour of systems silence, black neon, and the absence of the normally present brown noise of prodcast blather they were all accustomed to.

"We can clean up for tomorrow's crowd," Hiana offered encouragingly, choosing to shift her focus onto a positive future instead of an uncertain present.

"Yes," Nigel said with a nod before climbing to his feet on the stage and holding his hands down to the women. There were things they could do. It was better than sitting in the dark doing nothing.

❧*☙

"What do you mean 'can't be fixed'?"

Andre Nunn's tone of offense prompted Tamner to rub his face long enough to take a frustrated breath behind his hands as he formulated a reply. It was Caminda Vaughn, however, her long blonde hair pulled into a tail that accentuated the roundness of her youthful face, who began with, "The fire didn't start itself…"

"I didn't start it either," barked Nunn, his offense growing at the presumed accusation.

"No one's saying you did," Lydon Folaw soothed, stroking his short, black beard as he often did when anxious and uncertain.

"Thought someone was working on the array…"

"Something went wrong," Tamner replied to Warren Pisso's question. "Main board failure…or the replacement unit…"

"Should've let me…" began Nunn.

"Blueprints were lost in the crash," Folaw reminded him. "There's no trace of 'em in the Archives…"

"And the fire took what parts we had left." Woster Pisso, Warren's twin brother, leaned back in his chair with a resolute expression that mirrored the concerns of everyone in the room.

"If we manufactured more, divided the store…"

Folaw cut off Fahti Dandridge, the last surviving member of the dynasty who had spearheaded hemp processing and manufacturing since the city's founding, with a dismissive hand wave. "Impossible to do that without the blueprints."

"Should've tried to recover and replace what we lost." Stace Sargins, elected to the Nau from the Levs along with the Pissos, Folaw, and Pearl Xeng, swept a hand through his short strawberry blond hair and wiped it down his flushed cheek. Without the flow of air through the filt and temp systems, the Nau chamber was growing hot and stagnant with the cluster of so many bodies in the same room. Sargins was not the only one to look as miserable as he felt.

"There've been priorities," Fahti said with a haughty huff.

"Not the right ones." Nunn crossed his arms over his chest and leaned back from the table as if doing so might afford a degree of cooler air.

"Arguing about what was is not helping now," Tamner grunted, hoping to bring the Nau back to the purpose they had convened to address. "We need to redesign tech so that new components can be made. We need to step up manufacturing. Until that's done, we're running on hydros and batteries. Systems can't maintain the load, and the batteries need to be preserved. They go, we won't have anything. If we don't cut non-essential systems and redirect…"

"The factories cannot function without…" protested Fahti.

"They've got their own panels. If the hydros go down, there won't be anyone to manufacture for. It'll be worse than the Coup," Sargins snorted, the first to argue in favor of the people living in the Levs, the first to seemingly agree with Tamner's assertion of power priorities.

Nunn wiped his nose on a cloth. "Who's to say what's essential?"

"Filts, water, air, temperature regulation…we need those things," Warren pointed out.

"We need to manage waste or we'll be neck deep in it," added Woster.

"Food…we need food," Sargins began.

"Grows can do without the lights until we get the array in place," Tamner offered. "We can trade with the parah for more." He ignored the bristling expressions on several faces as he continued, "We keep the alglamps tended to have light…distribute torches and candles and battery packs. Keep the waste and filt systems active, allow enough power for cooking at staggered intervals to spread the usage…avoid usage spikes…and establish water rations per household. Businesses are going to have to make do with what's left…or shut down until…."

"The economy…" hissed Fahti.

Pearl and Delora met each other's gazes and reluctantly nodded at Tamner. Having her point ignored, Fahti snorted and kept her pinched face otherwise neutral.

"I suggest we shut down all lifts except for priority use," offered Caminda.

"I'm sure you think you've got priority," Woster snorted.

"Not about me. Peacekeeping, repairs. The Source for distributing aid. Reinstate the passcard priority to restrict movement but reprogram…"

"You'd like that," Sargins glowered at the blond opposite him. Caminda shrugged, refusing to be baited.

"Temporary measure until the array's online, nothing permanent."

Delora splayed her hands upon the table and coughed softly, the sound drawing attention. "We're not addressing the primary issue, the real solution…"

"Which is?" Nunn, Fahti, and Delora were the longest-standing members of the Nau, having served the Doctet before the Coup and being selected to continue their leadership roles with forced political reform. The three had a begrudging respect for one another and a strained alliance intended to safeguard the power the Uppers had clung to for so many centuries. Of those at the table, those two women, and Tamner, who was not a member of the Nau, were the ones Nunn was most likely to listen to, even when he did not agree with them.

"We need to increase emigration…get people outside…reduce the drain…enforce…"

"I am not going out there," Folaw hissed with horrified tension creasing the corners of his eyes.

"We can't force anyone to…" began Nunn.

"Maybe not force, but…" Delora took a breath, held it, and released it as others waited for her to continue. "How long will it take to build designs? Make prints? Reprogram the printers? To process hemp to print new parts? How long to print them and then repair the damage and upgrade the systems? I don't think we can wait that long."

She met Tamner's gaze from the other end of the table, nodding as if he had voiced those questions, as if knowing those arguments weighed heavily on the practical scientist's mind. "The hydros haven't been upgraded in years. How long before they fail with this increased workload? How long can we hold manufacturing at partial capacity when the people are…?"

"There's already rioting," Sargins reluctantly agreed.

"We close the doors." People stared at Fahti. "If we're restricting the lifts, we can't have prossers and crossers clogging the stairs; traffic will be unmanageable. Let the prossers go out if they want. Everyone else stays where they are until the situation's in hand. Restrict the lifts as you say," she glanced at Caminda, "keep the systems working at minimum…"

"…and restore the prods," added Folaw.

"You would say that," grumbled Nunn.

"If we don't tell people what's happening, there'll be more riots. More fighting. The brako will grow bolder. People need to know."

"Like they'll believe anything we…" Fahti interrupted.

"They'll respect the Pissos," Caminda offered. "They always do. People will believe in us if they do the talking."

"Doctor Tamner is a better choice…better spokesman and negotiator," began Delora.

Fahti vehemently shook her head. "He's more valuable out there, with the parah. They know you. If we'll be forced to rely on them…interact with them…we'll need you there." Her gaze held Tamner's. "The Levs don't…"

"Then it's time those in the Levs meet him too," countered Delora stubbornly, speaking with arms-crossed defiance although the older woman had not lifted her hands from the table.

"If we're not letting anyone in or out anyhow…" Folaw snipped.

Fahti again shook her head. "If we rely on trade…hemp and food…we need a mediator."

Nunn banged the table with the flat of his hand. "We haven't decided to…"

"Please." Tamner swallowed his trepidation and stood, adjusting his jacket as he did so. He did not understand why the Nau continued to insist on his input in these meetings, how he had stumbled into the role of intermediary when their debates reached an impasse or fever pitch. In such moments as this, he felt as if he were managing a group of unruly children.

The parah were, so far, easier to negotiate with.

"Can we at least agree that the lifts need to be restricted…and passage into and out of the city managed while we develop blueprints," he glanced at Nunn, "that we coordinate manufacturing and power from the factory arrays," he looked at Fahti, "and that we direct as much existing hydropower as we can to keep the city livable? Once we get started, when we see how things hold up, we reconvene tomorrow and iron out what's next."

Though the majority around the table continued to express dissatisfaction with the day's progress through the frown lines on their faces, the nine exchanged glances and finally nodded their combined agreement. "See it's done," Nunn grumbled to Tamner, the first to likewise stand and the first to leave the room.

Tamner sighed and resisted rubbing his face and eyes again until he was alone. He should not be the one to negotiate authority. He was not the Founder. If anyone should be where he was, Tamner believed it should be Captain Grainger. For now, the captain had his own burdens to shoulder.

❧*❧

Scarecrow had not returned.

Founder Kemway was dead.

The darkness was silent except for the ongoing wheezing struggle of the barely operating filt system.

She was hungry, thirsty…and afraid of remaining here alone.

She tried her ICD, but its screen refused to activate. There was no way to reach out to her sister, who was likely still engaged with the gradually fainter echoes of the salt protest and the aftermath of the Founder's speech. She dared not send one of the Spinks to find Scarecrow, who undoubtedly had more important matters to tend to and had promised he would be back as soon as he could be.

There was Tox and Skelter and Maemi, but she did not want them to know the truth of the Founder's demise. She could not take that risk.

She could think of only one other person. After prying the dead man's hand from hers, she got up, pushed open the hatch, listened for threats, and then carefully picked her way through the room's debris. At the lean-to's entrance, she whistled a single low tone and waited.

A small girl in tattered clothes wearing a stolen Crow mask over her little head, responded to the summons, dropping from the roof of the building across the path and landing in a crouch beneath the blue-green glow of a corner alglamp on the Lev above. Her abrupt arrival, her unexpected attire, and the clang and shudder of her impact on the walkway, startled Ginna but only long enough for her to crouch defensively as well in preparation to either attack or flee.

The little girl giggled and got up with her empty hands spread before her. Ginna sighed, "Go to Vapors. Bring Colyx here."

"The big man?"

Ginna nodded.

The child nodded too and sprinted away.

Ginna watched until the girl was no longer visible, until she could no longer hear her retreating steps. The distant riot sounded quieter. Perhaps she should reach out to Ilya. But she shook her head to the argument with her inner thoughts, and then, despite her reluctance to loiter with the phantoms of the dead, she retreated into the structure and returned to the Founder's side to again clench his hand. The action felt awkward and did nothing to ease her fearful feelings of solitude, but she hoped, as she waited, that wherever he was now, the Founder appreciated her efforts not to leave him alone.

❧51☙

❧*52*❧

❧Chapter 6❧

The Den was as dark as the streets, lit by a pinkish glow from the customized alglanterns lining the bar. The perfumed scent he was accustomed to lingered stale and weak, the ventilation system's usual hiss too faint to add additional circulation and suck it from the air or infuse it with more. Kal found the silence and faded smell unnerving but after scolding himself during his entire descent through the city for not bringing his standard entourage with him, he was relieved to duck into the Den to find Feena at the bar, her nails tapping absently on the shiny surface, a pensive, thoughtful look on her face.

Perhaps she regretted the absence of the bodyguards who most often lingered in her orbit, shielding her from the worst elements of Hebanthe Falls. She was alone, without even the Den's swiver on hand, but unless she had filled the glass her other hand toyed with, Kal assumed the swiver would return. When she looked up at the footsteps entering the vindi, her relieved smile took some of the bite out of Kal's frustrated anger.

Her expression lasted long enough for him to lower the hood of his coat and swipe the mist-damp from his face and back through his disheveled, graying hair.

"Don't suppose you had a hand in this?" Despite his reluctance to accept the summoning gesture of her empty hand, he grunted and sauntered towards the bar as if to join her without the invitation. By the time he stopped beside her, the fullness of his anger had returned.

"You give me too much credit." She slid the open wine bottle towards him. There was no empty glass on the counter and he refused to reach behind the bar for one or drink directly from the bottle, and so he ignored her offer.

Opting not to sit, he propped one foot on the hemplastic foot rail that ran the length of the bar. "The Hall," he snapped. He was familiar with her neutral, offhanded tone. It was never innocent. He knew her too well to assume that, and she knew him too well to try to bluff.

It was why, when she leaned forward with an arm on the bar and asked, "What happened?" he knew she was not directly responsible for the vandalism and the death of his Talkers.

If the brako had been involved, it had not been at her bidding.

That left two other possibilities.

"Come by Primary Hall and see," he huffed. "Good men died…I won't have it."

"Bozhe moy…"

Kal's frown deepened. "What do you know about a riot?" He had heard talk on his way down, but as he was uninterested in gossip, he had not stopped to ask for details.

Offering a single-shouldered shrug, Feena continued to toy with her glass. "I don't have details." If he had passed the intersection where the riot occurred, he knew as much as she did. "I got caught in it, on the fringes. Quite the mess. The usual start I imagine, protestors, Igraci, buggers."

"Probably a few of yours in there…Neoma's too…"

"No doubt." Though she had not ordered or sanctioned such activity, and her people's involvement in such nonsense would not benefit her goals, some people did not need a reason to surrender to the lure of mayhem. Mayhem had been the nursery of the brako until she and Neoma reined the chaos in and gave that mayhem a direction and purpose.

Individuals going back to their roots did not surprise her.

"Doubt there's a connection…Hall's too far from there." Without details airing on the prods, without knowing the timing of events…the attack on the Hall, the riot, and the city-wide loss of power, connecting the three things would not be easy.

Hebenon was a big place. Things happened all the time. It did not mean they stemmed from the same root.

"The power?"

"I'd guess the quake." She had seen nothing in the riot's vicinity to account for the blackout, but sometimes the shaking, shifting earth disrupted the power until the city settled on its long, metal support arms and legs that secured it into the riverbed and the canyon walls. This would not be the first time it had happened.

Again, Kal grunted. "They knew it was coming…took advantage of the chance to damage the Hall…"

Whoever they were.

"No one in Hebenon's that organized…not even me…or you." Certainly not the buggers, the Nau, or the Igraci. Despite her efforts, certainly not the brako. The Voices of Faith and the Founder had once kept the city so.

But not anymore.

"You'll let me know if you hear anything." He pushed the wine bottle back toward her and stepped away from the bar.

"I'll ask around. If it's any of mine…you'll know…and they won't do it again." It was the most she could commit to.

"Hold you to that," he muttered, leaving demands of restitution for later as he brushed aside the beaded curtain that swayed in the doorway. He expected the next conversation on his list to be less cordial and productive, but it had to be done.

"Kal?"

He looked back, a fistful of pink beads clenched in his hand.

The words Feena intended died on her lips. The dwarf was no longer here, and she was not certain that finding him, rescuing him from an unknown fate, and the interlude afterward presented anything worthwhile the Senior needed to know. He had thus far failed to win the long-missing Kemway to their cause, in cementing a rapport with him. She did not need him to interfere in her efforts. It was likely wisest, she mused, if Kal and his Talkers stayed out of her affairs.

"Do you want an escort?"

From the twitch at the corners of her mouth and eyes, Kal knew that question had not been what she had begun to ask. Harboring enough suspicion about the brako to think that anyone she chose to send with him might assault him instead, he shook his head.

"I'll be fine."

Their gazes held for several heartbeats. She nodded. "Be careful."

Kal nodded too. "I always am."

❧*☙

Colyx did not question the summons the child brought. Someone needed his help. That was all that mattered. Ginna and the Spinks had become part of his extended family since coming out of the Core as Otta took them, and the orphaned Core children, under her wing. Family deserved to be helped. The limping man assumed the request had come through Otta and worried that some harm had come to his daughter and her unborn child with the quake and loss of power. He followed as fast as the leg braces protecting both knees permitted. The direction he was led, however, was away from the hostel. His surprise and confusion faded as they skirted the remnants of a fight in one of the intersections they passed, where buggers and medics hovered over bodies, both groaning and still, that lay amidst broken glass and debris and a platform that listed on mangled legs.

He knew the aftermath of a fight when he saw it. It was reason enough for a detour, either meant to show him the damage or because the fight had spread as far as the hostel. In the Core, where there had been no outside peacekeepers, fights had been common, a means of thinning the population when their meager supplies ran thin. Here, amongst the injured, men and women in Player white, their sandwich boards of doom messages set aside, offered water and encouragement alongside the always generous herpa.

One woman seen in Vapors in the weeks after his escape from the Core lifted her head to watch him, pulled along by the child's hand.

He did not know her, had never heard her name. Until today, he had never connected her to the Igraci. She glanced at another nearby who shoved a water bottle into her hand and did not meet his gaze again.

Colyx continued past, pondering what had happened here.

Winded, his knees throbbing with the exertion of trying to keep up with the Spink, he was thankful when the girl finally stopped at the entrance of a metal and hemplastic lean-to that shielded the door of the building before them, vacant-looking in its darkness.

"Colyx? Is it you?"

His worry for his daughter, or that he was being led into a trap, faded.

The dragging steps entering the shop were familiar after working and living with the big man and his family for several weeks. Ginna peered from behind the hatch to see his broad shadow in the pale light of the battery torch he carried and motioned for him to join her.

"Trouble?" She looked relieved to see him, which made his effort to reach her worth his time.

"I…" She shuffled aside so he could join her. It was a struggle for him to lift his braced legs through the hatch opening, and when he saw the figure on the makeshift cot in the small chamber, he paused mid-step and almost lost his balance.

He did not know the man, did not recognize him. But he knew without closer examination that the man was dead from the awkward tilt of his head and the slackness of his facial features.

"Been watching him 'til Scarecrow's…or Doctor Tamner comes," Ginna explained as she assisted him the rest of the way into the room.

"Tamner's a good man," Colyx said with a nod. So, he agreed without saying it, was Scarecrow.

He might not be alive without Scarecrow's help.

"Was alive when we got him here," Ginna swallowed, shuffled her feet, and added, "Don't want to sit alone with him 'til then. It's too quiet outside…"

"You were there…in the intersection. Whatever happened looks to be over…"

"They're not likely to come looking here…but still…"

The whistle of the Spinks outside cut her off, and she pulled Colyx awkwardly down beside her, motioning for him to be quiet as several heavy sets of boots passed the lean-to. Buggers or brako, they did not know, but Ginna did not want either of them to find her with Founder Kemway's body. The repercussions of that would be dire.

"Can you stay with me 'til they get here?"

Colyx nodded, shifting his legs into a more comfortable position upon the empty crates where he sat. "I can stay."

He had left, telling Maemi there was something he needed to do. She would assume that something involved his daughter.

Vapors was empty and likely to remain so until the power was restored.

He trusted that Otta and Skelter were safe.

No one would look for him.

Especially not here.

∾*∾

Residents and crossers bore witness to the sudden darkening of the lights of the metal nest. For Marbordo's people, this was not the first time such darkness had occurred. For those who had migrated out of Hebanthe Falls to live and work in this new world, that darkness was familiar too. Power issues and maintenance needs sometimes required darkness to accomplish. Most thought little of it.

Following a quake that had pulled every parah out of their homes to avoid the potential of being crushed in a structural collapse, the winking out of the city lights was expected.

After the fire flash on the dome, however, and the scramble to get the specks of humanity off the shell and back inside, Venn and the other crossers understood the source of the darkness better than the parah could

But none of them knew what it meant.

It was the creeping passage of time, the delay in the light's return, that was new. Young Agnys and Cori Tamner, pressed into the responsibility of pulling down dry clothing from a hemp rope strung between Venn's home and the one nearest to it, watched the unchanging spectacle, the parah girl with curiosity, the boy with concern for the father still inside.

Raised voices crossed the empty hillock void between Marbordo and the city doors. Anger. Fear. Frustration. Figures nearest the dome remained to pound and shout in protest while others trudged back to the village with their shoulders thrown back in defiance or slumped in perplexed defeat.

"Closing us out," someone pushing a cart of harvested hemp mumbled as he passed Venn on his stool, where he sorted and folded the clothing the children brought to him.

Venn dropped the half-folded tunic into the basket and lurched up, his brow knitted across his furrowed forehead. "What do you mean?"

The speaker shuffled on without replying.

Behind him, a younger man, bald and thin, with broad hands and dirty nails, shrugged when Venn grabbed him by both arms, nearly causing him to drop the bundle of pelts he carried.

"What does that mean?" Venn hissed.

The man pulled free with annoyance and adjusted his bundle with a frustrated glower. "Didn't get an explanation. Just said it's a security measure and they'll reopen when it's dealt with."

"Do you think Father…?" started Cori in a squeaking whisper.

Agnys took his hand and stepped to the side so the man with the pelts could pass, drawing her friend with her. "Before you came, the doors were always closed. He's okay."

Trying to appear more confident than he felt, he squeezed her hand and bobbed his head. "That was then…but he's there and I'm here…"

"He'll come…or he'll send for you," Venn murmured despite the terse set of his mouth and narrowed eyes. A security issue could mean many things. The earlier flash on the dome and the vented plume of interior smoke suggested mechanical issues. Closing the door might be to conserve power until the damages were repaired. Political squabbles would have arisen as bureaucrats argued about repairs, and the protests of frightened people seeking answers would need to be resolved and prevented from spilling into Marbordo. An outbreak of sickness would need to be controlled, and the death of someone of importance, caused either by the outage or some other means, natural or not, were also possible causes.

"Whatever it is," said a passing woman with three toddlers in tow, as though reading Venn's swirling thoughts, "they're worried."

Struggling to keep the scowl off his face at the inference her words carried and the possibility that Rhyd was again at the center of controversy, Venn patted Cori's head and purposely settled on his stool, and resumed sorting and folding clothes as if the matter was irrelevant. Events inside Hebenon had not mattered to him in several years. The city was no longer his home and nothing he could do would open the doors or change anything. There were those he knew and loved inside, however, trapped as they had been their entire lives, once again denied the opportunity to escape, and that concerned him.

For their sakes, for the sake of Cori's father, for Rhyd, Venn prayed to whatever power existed in the universe that the lights came back on and the doors of the city opened again.

And he prayed, as he watched the pair of children resume their task, talking in muted whispers as Agnys did her best to distract Cori from his fears, that this time, whatever was happening inside the city would be enough to prompt Rhyd to come out for good.

"Why in the Founder's name aren't you doing something?"

Kal no longer carried the passcard once required to operate the city lifts. The Coup had punctured the barriers between Uppers and Levs, facilitating access to Outside, rendering passcards obsolete by

Oliver Grainger's executive order. Today, most of the lifts were unmoving without the power to hoist them, and those that functioned did so only to allow faster passage of the bugorra and other emergency personnel from one Lev to another in their ongoing efforts to keep the peace and secure citywide welfare.

Kal had seen the swiping of passes as he had walked, but he had not thought their use would apply to him.

Forced to take the stairs to his intended destination, he cursed the dead lifts, the blackness, cursed Grainger and the bugorra and whoever had chosen to deny him the access his privilege had always provided.

Didn't they know who he was?

Grainger rubbed his temples and lifted his gaze from the dim Echo screen on his desk without raising his head to look at the annoyance barging into his office unannounced. Minimal function had restored the Echos in the Uppers to allow the Nau and the bugorra to do their jobs on the city's behalf, to permit techs to focus on restoring life systems, and to permit public service notices and news prods to those trapped in the Levs. Access to the SCAMs remained unavailable, meaning that Grainger had yet to get details from the riot site, and there had been no updates on the progress of repairs to the array.

There had been no communication with Lieutenant Young, and the Archives remained inaccessible. There was no word from Jaron.

"You'll have to be more specific," he grunted, unsure if he was relieved when the Senior did not sit across from him or further annoyed by the man's agitated pacing.

"Do you know how many flights of stairs I had to…?"

"Necessary, I'm afraid, until the power systems are repaired unless you want to run out of air, water, and heat. We have to reduce power consumption where we can."

"But the lifts?" Kal flailed his hands in frustration. "And where the posa are the bugorra? The Prime was attacked! Vandalized! People were killed and I haven't seen a single…"

Vandals were far too common, an ongoing scourge that had yet to be solved since the final years of the Founder's rule. It was a thorn that festered in deference to more pressing social ills in the hopes that a satiated population would reduce the compulsion to lash out in pain on the city's walls. The word attacked, however, piqued Grainger's interest, as it suggested that Kal's outrage might be connected to the salt riot that may or may not have brought the missing Founder back to the surface. The reality of people being killed was what caught his attention, however, even if it was a problem he could do little about without a means of communicating with his officers.

"Killed? Who? Where?"

"Voice's Prime. They threw molies…two of my Talkers died from burns, and the damage the fire caused is…"

"Did you see who? Do you know…?"

Again, Kal threw his hands in the air, an unusual action from the typically reserved and self-controlled man. "Brako? Igraci? How the cazz do I know? That's not my job! It's yours! This isn't supposed to happen. It's what the bugorra are for. We deserve protection too, no matter what you think I have done. If the Founder was here…"

"Well, he isn't, thanks to you," Grainger rebutted, lifting his head at last. Kal and the Talkers had nothing to do with deposing the Founder, but while enough evidence of his kidnapping had yet to be uncovered to prompt an arrest, Grainger clung to the belief that the Voices were ultimately behind it. How else had Talkers disguised as buggers come to be at the scene? Who else but Talkers could have gained access to secure corridors in the Uppers to swipe the Founder from under everyone's noses?

He half-believed this tale Kal told was instigated by the senior's hand to elicit public sympathy and support, and further distance the Voices from the truth of the kidnapping charge.

Hearing the doubt in the captain's voice, Kal snapped, "You think I'm lying?"

Rather than reply, Grainger gestured to the room lit only by a half dozen alglamps, his Echo's screen, the stars beyond the dome, and the dots of fires visible in Marbordo. "I've got more important things to worry about than vandalism. Spread a little thin if you haven't noticed. If you can't give me details…soon as I reach anyone down there, I'll get someone to take statements and have a look."

"You'll send someone with me now!"

Silence burned between them as they stared at one another, Kal demanding action, Grainger struggling not to utter the things that sprang to mind or snatch the Senior's lapels across the desk and throw him out of the office. He was taller, broader, younger, and though once the Voices of Faith had been a powerful force throughout Hebenon, now their influence, and Kal's with them, was waning.

Kal's fury, his demands, came without the teeth to back them up, and Grainger did not have the patience to coddle him.

"No one to send. You're welcome to wait in the anteroom, if you want, until someone…"

Kal began to retort but swallowed his words. Given the emergency measures undoubtedly in place to ease the city through the energy crisis, a wait in a dark room could last for hours. Maybe days. He could not wait that long. He would not. Kal had places to be, other people to see…including one he had put off to come here. That destination was one he would rather the captain and bugorra not be privy to.

His arms dropped to his side and his fists clenched. "See you get someone there at once. The dead aren't going to keep…and we're not leaving the damage unrepaired indefinitely."

Given the state of city resources, however, Kal was aware that indefinite might be his only option. Both knew it as he stalked out of the room with the same bluster with which he had arrived.

The Echo beeped, announcing the arrival of another report from the solar array repair team. Grainger turned his attention to it, the Talkers and Senior Kal largely forgotten.

❧ * ❦

Tamner, like those around the conference table, was alerted to the restoration of the communication systems by the simultaneous beeping, buzzing, and whirring of each ICD in the room, children, spouses, family, and friends breaking the stalemate of the Nau's second conference today with their efforts to determine the safety of those they had previously been unable to reach. The interruption was as good a reason to break away as any other, and as Nau members scurried from the table to engage in conversation in what little privacy the large oval room allowed, Tamner, too, looked to his ICD for the incoming messages stored there.

Cori, asking when he would be allowed to come inside, when his father would come to him, if his father was okay.

Grainger testing the system and asking for an update on the Nau's business.

And one message he was not expecting.

He frowned.

"I have to see to my daughter," said Fahti, bustling out of the room without fanfare and without waiting for the meeting's adjournment.

"My mother is stuck in a lift," Caminda huffed, following the older woman out.

"We reconvene later?" asked Warren, the only member who had not pushed away from the table, the only one who did not seem troubled, distracted, or distressed by messages they had received.

"Family comes first." Nunn swiped his Echo-P from the table, tucked it under his arm, and nodded at Tamner. The hour was already late, although, in the perpetual darkness, timekeeping meant little. No one had eaten or slept much since the disaster had struck.

They might as well do so now, Grainger be damned.

"In the morning," Tamner agreed, patting his pocket to ascertain possession of the passcard tucked there. He had not thought to need it. Hopefully, by morning, he would be available, though the Nau could see to their duties without him.

Hopefully, by morning, he would know what Scarecrow wanted and would be done with that business too.

Whatever it was, Tamner imagined it was not good.

He doubted Scarecrow would reach out to him otherwise.

❧*❧

The place where he had fallen, where he had last seen her, was damp with the ever-present mist of the falls, cleared of evidence by the passage of footsteps, the scouring of the buggers, and time. The intersection had been emptied of everyone except a few uniformed peacekeepers congregated at its center, poppers ready, daring passersby to challenge them as others hunted for evidence and explanations of what had transpired. Four Igraci huddled on one side beneath a dripping awning, repairing their signboards, speaking in hushed murmurs to avoid being overheard. The platform where Enoch had last seen Haythem sloped to one side, its left legs broken, and the fractured pole beside it with its stretched-tight power lines remained upright only because of the tension of those lines.

There was no sign of Ulynda and none of Haythem. Niece and brother he had not met before today, kin he did not know how he felt about and did not want to consider too deeply. The buggers were undoubtedly seeking the deposed Founder but had not likely known that the man's only remaining heir had been there too. Enoch wondered if he should tell them the girl had been taken by the brako, but then he would have to explain why she had been there, in his company, why they had been at the riot, who he was.

Enoch doubted the officers, or Captain Grainger, would be compelled to believe what he said.

There was likewise no evidence of Scarecrow at the scene, an unsurprising fact. For Enoch, finding Scarecrow would be easier than tracking Ulynda; if anyone could find the girl, it would be Hebenon's infamous vigi. Enoch only had to return to Vapors and wait. Inside Vapors, regardless of the power conditions, he would be safe from the dangers in the streets, including those he believed had followed him away from the Den at Feena Wulfe's bidding.

The brako had pursued him before. So had the Talkers. Whoever was following him, perhaps they thought to kill him or else pressure him into accepting the offer that brako and Talkers alike presented. He chose not to allow them the opportunity to influence the course of his life. Vapors it was.

At the staircase platform, an audible static pop reverberated through the stagnant mist as every Echo flickered and flashed to life, though street and vindi lights remained dark. The unexpected glare made everyone in the intersection blink, wince, and squint behind shielding hands. On the screen, captured by the SCAMs around the intersection, Haythem once again paced the now-damaged platform surrounded by the mob of salt protestors, the words of his disjointed speech overlaid by Kenneth Ximenez's impassioned plea for information regarding the shots fired into the crowd of protestors and the whereabouts of Founder Kemway. Any details about Scarecrow people could offer. On the platform, between the bugger lieutenant and the masked vigi, the Founder went down but it was unclear if he had been struck by the fired shots or had been pulled out of harm's way by the individuals beside him. Talkers rushed the stage.

It was the first time the Founder had been seen on camera since before his presumed death during the Coup. Knowing that SCAMs did not record sound, Enoch did not know how Kemway's incoherent monologue had been recorded and dubbed into the SCAM footage, but that was unimportant.

What was important, to Enoch and many others, was that this was the only time since his emergence into Hebenon that the whole of the city had been given a glimpse of Scarecrow.

Enoch groaned. Though Rhyd had chosen to be there, he was going to be pissed when he saw himself on camera.

❧*❦

❧ 66 ❦

With her daughter's impotent rage continuing to bleed from behind the bedroom door, deciding it was better not to engage the child until they were both in a more subdued frame of mind, Neoma paced and swallowed one drink after another until she forgot that the wall Echo had been on when the city's power was cut. When the screen burst to life with a flash that illuminated the room, it was jarring enough to cause her to drop the wine glass she had been refilling and spill the contents on her bare feet as she spun towards the screen. The sound was muted as it had been earlier, but the writhing evidence of the riot gleaned from the SCAMs brightened the room. She could not hear the voice-over Kenneth provided from the corner image on the screen, but she did not need a voice to know what she saw.

Haythem.

Addressing the throng.

The bottle dropped from her hand.

"Volume up!" she croaked. The Echosys obeyed. She barely acknowledged Kenneth's voice as her focus lasered in on the barely distinguishable words Haythem spewed as he paced with aberrant, disjointed, passionate haste from one side of the platform to the other.

His words mattered less than the revelation that he was alive. Free of his abductors. That he would come for her, for Ulynda. He would come, and it might not be in her favor when he did.

Neoma's hands curled. Her lips pursed. Her eyes narrowed.

The muted recording popped like a hemp cork ejected from a liquor bottle. Scarecrow was there. Haythem fell, swallowed from view by a swarm of panicked rioters and Talkers. Kenneth's deceptively desperate intonation masked neutrality or even glee that Neoma had heard from him before, but it took several moments before his words seeped deeper into her head.

Shots fired.

Potential assassin sought.

Founder missing.

Again.

Panic.

There was pounding at the door that made Neoma wheel about with eyes that wildly sought anything that could serve as a weapon.

Haythem had come for her.

Or this new attempted assassin had.

If someone had killed Haythem, or tried to, whoever they were, they would seek her and Ulynda next.

"Mam! It's Molly! Please…let me in!"

Neoma's hesitation was brief. She was alone. Nanny had skulked out for emergency nessies, for information, to escape her employer, one less person's company Neoma had to tolerate. She had been glad for it before, but now that there was a new threat, she did not want to be alone.

She barely knew the squirrelly man who had offered his prodcast skill. He sounded as frightened as she felt, out of breath as if he was pursued. He might have led Haythem or an assassin to her door. But he had not seemed like a killer to her, had seemed to be more of a survivor than a fool despite his obvious Heb addiction. Right now, Molly Netzer was the only ally she had.

She pulled open the door enough to grab his wrist and yank him into the flat. The door was slammed and locked behind him, shaking the flat with its force as he stumbled free of her suddenly-released grip.

He tumbled to the floor with a squawk.

"What do you want?" she growled, hoping her tone sounded angrier at his interruption than afraid of the abrupt shift in her reality.

"Brako everywhere…not yours but the others. Buggers too," Molly chattered, his clothes and skin wet, his cheeks flushed in the frightened pale of his face. "Soon as the lights went out…they're everywhere. What's…?" He coughed, sputtered, and wiped the back of his damp sleeve across his dripping nose. "What's goin' on?"

Eyes narrowed still, a look of disdain and distrust he recognized in those of a higher social station than he would ever attain, she hissed, "You don't know?"

He had been out there. He had to know something.

But Hebanthe Falls was a big place. There was no reason to think he had been at the epicenter of the city's latest crisis. If house Echos were broadcasting again, every external Echo likely was as well, but there were places where external screens did not work, where they had been broken or tinged. If Molly was fleeing both brako and bugorra, both groups overactive in their responses to the darkness, he might not have paid attention to the active screens he had passed on his flight.

"That," she spat, pointing at the screen.

"I…" he started, wide eyes darting to the images of light and shadow on the Echo, grainy SCAM footage replaying what Neoma had already watched. "What's…?"

Neoma ignored his question and grabbed her ankle-length coat from the hooks at the side of the door. Continuing to disregard the pounding fists on the inside of Ulynda's door, Neoma shoved her arms through the sleeves as if punching the air and thrust her feet into her boots. "Stay here. You'll be safe. Don't let anyone in…except Blayd."

Yes, she thought. She should call Blayd. Despite their differences, their falling out, she trusted him. He would come if her life was at risk.

In the interim, until he did, there was someone else she had to see.

"Momma!" Ulynda cried in ongoing rage. "Leave him alone!"

Pointing at the door that trembled with each fist and foot that hit it, Molly croaked, "I'm not a…"

"You want to stay here, you'll be anything I need you to be…or you can leave." She glared at him as she yanked open the front door. "If you're not here when I return, I'll give you to Vanderwall myself."

Vanderwall had spared Molly before, but only because Molly had proven useful to the Mam. Defying her demands might mean losing the only protection he had. Until the streets were calm, until the power came back on, this flat was the best place, the warmest, with alcohol on the counter and food in the kitchen, for him to hide. Molly understood he was safer here than anywhere else he could be.

Banging brat to tolerate or not.

❧Chapter 7❧

She did not remember how she had gotten here, this crowded, cluttered, dingy, disorganized medical room somewhere in the Levs, but the throbbing in her immobilized knee, in her wrapped forearm, and beneath the gauze bandaging above her eye reminded her why she was here. The beds around her in this communal ward, crammed together to make room for an overspill of patients, were occupied by the moaning, the groaning, the weeping of the freshly injured and afraid, likely collected from the upheaval point where she had been found. But there was no one, medical staff, buggers, or the purple-haired woman who had fought with her and protected her, to answer questions as she rubbed her eyes to clear her vision.

Ilya believed that woman had brought her here, but she had no memory of it happening.

Judging by the minimal, generator-provided light in the room and the corridor beyond the door, her officers would be occupied with the more pressing duties of keeping control of the city rather than waiting here for her to wake up.

They would be looking for Scarecrow.

Looking for Founder Kemway.

Finding whoever had fired the two shots she was sure she had heard. Unless her memory was faulty, her perception skewed by the chaos, there had been two shooters, but which one had made the striking shot would be difficult to gauge. Until the truth was known, she wanted them both.

The captain would want them both.

Using her uninjured arm to wiggle into a semi-seated position against the headboard of the medical cot, a difficult feat with her leg bound in straps and lines that held it off the bed, she reassured herself that, despite the wet stain on Scarecrow's glove, despite the blood on the Founder's sweat-soiled shirt, this had only been an attempt. There had not been a successful assassination. Surely she and Scarecrow had acted fast enough to thwart it. Saving the Founder would be a bright mark on her record, so long as she found where Scarecrow had taken him and brought him to the Uppers for care.

Permitting an assassination, regardless of her efforts to the contrary, and allowing Scarecrow to spirit him away where he could not be found, would not.

There had been no choice but to trust the vigi in the thick of the fight. Someone had to care for Kemway, protect him, remove him from the crowd, and get him to safety. Scarecrow had been the only person available to do it. Given his part in the tussle with Vanderwall minutes before, Ilya believed for the first time that the Founder's death was not Scarecrow's agenda. They wanted the same thing.

Stopping Vanderwall.

If their agendas had been at cross purposes, he would have let her die and abandoned Kemway to his fate on that platform rather than risk public exposure and death.

She assumed the power grid was still down, suffering from what must have been a failed attempt to repair the array. Why else would the lights be in emergency mode and the air filts remain functioning at a hissing fraction of their capacity?

She tried to move her leg as she tapped on her unresponsive ICD and winced at the pain that shot from her knee into her foot and hip. Even if the damage was repaired, the muscles and tendons would take days to heal. Too many days when Hebenon needed her. Her arm, while wrapped and likely repaired with plasts, would be quicker to heal, and the head injury was insignificant. She needed to reach Grainger. He needed to know what was happening in the Levs if he did not already. He needed to know that the Founder was alive.

Needed to know about yet another salt protest, the subsequent riot it had birthed, and about her near-apprehension of Vanderwall.

But there were meds in her body, meant to counteract the worst of the pain and keep her groggy enough to inhibit undue motion. Enough meds to make her drop her head against the headboard and close her eyes to halt the spinning room. Trying to count the pain away, listening to her father's voice in her head ticking off numbers, her head eventually lolled sideways into an awkward angle that she would regret when slumber eventually gave way to waking again.

⌘*⌘

The crowded soaper stuffed with underlings, some in Crow masks, some barefaced with heads uncovered or with scarves wrapped over their mouths and noses, smelled of sweat, wet leather, and the traces of hemp smoke that lingered on the skin, clothes, and breaths of many. Not all of his people were here, the brako aligned under his leadership, as they could not all fit into this space even if word of the impromptu conclave had reached every member from Lev 1 to the Ups. But there were enough men, disenfranchised, disgruntled, and disillusioned, or else bored and eager for mayhem, that he was confident his words would spread to everyone else. His wishes, as always, would be known and obeyed. As he climbed onto the desk so his already imposing mass could be seen by everyone in the room, favoring the leg where the buzzer's burn had seared his flesh, his raised fists drew their eyes to his masked visage. The shuffling, muttering collection stilled to a low rustling of feet and fabric so they could hear what the one called Vanderwall wanted to say.

None of them noticed the faint grimace the stretching of his bruised shoulder created. He should get that injury looked at…but not now. Not while people might know his face.

He rarely spoke to most of them directly. Most never crossed his path. Behind the mask, most would never see his face to know that he was an impostor, not the man who had originally carried the

Vanderwall mantle. Always the orders trickled through an established chain of command that had been in place since the congealing of the brako beneath his predecessor's fist.

Hearing him was an honor that would amplify unity. Solidarity was what was needed as Hebenon continued its spiral of misrule.

"Forget what was before. Forget Wulfe. Forget the Mam. Forget the buggers and their rules of the some. We find the Founder. We find Scarecrow. We find the dwarf Enoch who some of you know. I don't want excuses. I won't tolerate failure. We take what Hebenon offers while it is unprotected, rip out its throat, end those who get in the way. All of them. Do this and Hebenon is ours. We will begin again and build a city that no longer holds its boot on our necks."

A short speech, hardly worth the effort it took to collect those accumulated here. But the uproarious cheer of agreement that followed as he climbed down and slipped into the back room proved that it had been speech enough to unite them.

The brako had to act. They had to be free of the pair of women holding their tethers if they were going to prosper. He did not know the dwarf's importance, beyond being wanted by the Mam, by Wulfe, and by the Talkers. Once they had him, Vanderwall would figure out who he was and why he mattered. Scarecrow was important only because the vigi stood in the way of their progress…and had now seen Vanderwall's face. That was one too many who could identify him, and thus his brako had to close their fists around him before the knowledge of his identity spread and cut off the tentacles of their reach. Before Scarecrow ruined everything.

❧*❧

Rolling his aching shoulders, listening to the fading echoes of the man's words and trying to pick his location out from the host gathered in the soaper with him, Scarecrow hunched on the roof of the nearest building, wondering how long he dared to wait for his quarry to come to him. It was not the first time his hunt for Vanderwall had brought him to the soaper, but it was the first time he had found the man in the place he expected him to be. It was tempting to swing in, to confront him now, to end the game they had been playing for too long. But he was weary, not at his peak. There were too many in the soaper and no way he could fight them all. They would overpower him before he got his hands on Vanderwall. And with the ICDs down, he could not call the bugorra as backup to arrest and overpower enough of those inside to thin the herd, to make his pursuit of Vanderwall easier.

Besides, he thought with a mental sigh, when it became obvious that enough of those gathered inside were lingering instead of obeying the boss's order to hit the streets, he had a promise to keep. Kemway had to be his priority.

Now that he had proof that the soaper was one of Vanderwall's haunts, he knew he would be back. The brako boss would not escape him indefinitely.

❧*❧

"Did you see it? Is it true, Neoma? Is Haythem alive?"

The eager, panting note of excitement in Leslie Isaac's reedy voice made Neoma's jaw clench, creating an ache in her teeth that permeated into her head and resulted in a pounding she should have anticipated. Despite the passage of years, the thin, rakish woman with boyish brown hair and pinched features, oddly reminiscent of Neoma's blond-rimmed face, had never given up on the hope of marrying Haythem, not even when marriage and children of her own had intruded on the dream. Despite the irritation of those people Neoma had known before, men and women of the Uppers who had survived the Coup and Factory Plague, Leslie was one of the few Neoma thought she might have a small chance of swaying to her cause.

There were no such allies for her in the Levs, except perhaps a handful of brako she could count on only for what she could offer in return. In the Uppers, the members of the Nau were too busy with the fallout of persistent supply shortages and the loss of power to listen.

The few she had reached out to thus far, Zeb and Rabia Faure and Ogden Castle, had offered support in platitudes and surface words only, promises of backing when the right time came, but offering nothing Neoma could use now.

That right time was the present, she argued without the show of desperation that bubbled beneath her station, her rank, her dignity.

That right time, the three countered, would come when Hebenon's struggles were behind them and life was at peace again. Why add more fuel to the seething fire trying to ignite Hebenon's belly by forcing such political matters into the fore?

Life had not been at peace since that damn parah girl had fallen into the Levs. The bugorra captain ran the city in place of the Kemways, and the Outside was open to anyone who wished to step into it. Life, in Neoma's opinion, would never be at peace until those doors were shut and a Kemway ruled again.

There would not be peace unless she forced it to happen.

Philippa sipped her cold algtea in the glow of the precious candles she was using to illuminate her sitting room, eyeing the other women without uttering a word.

Neoma flipped her bangs out of her eyes with a tip of her head, a haughty tick that harkened back to her childhood, a gesture all who knew her were familiar with. "Of course he's alive," she huffed. "I've never doubted it, no matter what the gossips say." Her lie was masked with a sniffing sound that mirrored the contempt of her gesture. "No one would dare…"

"You've seen him? Is he with you? How is he?"

Rather than look at Leslie, ignoring her over-eagerness, Neoma leaned forward and set her untouched teacup on the low table. "We have to be careful," she replied without directly answering the questions. "Dangerous people are looking for him…and we have a daughter to protect. If Ulynda's to assume the mantle of…"

"Ulynda's a lovely child," Philippa said softly, setting her cup down as well. "No doubt bright enough…but she will never be…"

Neoma's eyes narrowed just enough to drive her threat home as she countered, "There is no law…"

"No, no law…but there's precedent…"

"Haythem will reclaim power," added Leslie. "We all believe it. He will have another son. Nothing will be right until he does."

Something in her tone, in the notion of Haythem fathering children with someone young enough to bear them, made Neoma's mouth dry and her throat tighten, and pushed her to say something in response. But the words would not come, and Philippa spared her the need to cover the resulting awkward silence.

"Bring Haythem to the Uppers, Neoma…help us help him. You'll have the support you need. We'll make it happen. It wasn't right, you forced out the way you were…but we can change that…"

Swallowing the prickly burn of bile, Neoma uncrossed her legs with cat-like grace and stood, resisting the angry thoughts that pressed behind her teeth begging to be uttered. She had no proof to support her qualms, but the belief that both women had been part of her expulsion from the Uppers, if only through their silence and apathy rather than any expressed agreement with her eviction, persisted. The certainty that it was the support of Haythem's power they offered and not her and Ulynda, power that could benefit them in return, was driven home by the cool gazes that followed when the women rose as well.

They thought her weak. Vulnerable. The lack of the means to prove them wrong burned hotter than her offended indignation.

Perhaps she could convince Vanderwall to raid the Uppers. There were enough brako to attempt it. People like Philippa and Leslie would not stand a chance against them. If she could initiate an anonymous raid and then publicly be the one to negotiate its end, it would prove to everyone how strong and influential Neoma Kemway still was, could still be.

It was worth consideration.

"We'll be in touch when he is strong enough," she pledged in her best diplomatically satiating tone, a tone most often used to make promises she never intended to keep. Perhaps, as the pair escorted her to the door of the flat with polite smiles, stiff, false-friendly embraces, and handshakes of farewell, these women knew it too.

❧*❧

Nothing had changed in Prime Hall during his hours away from it, seeking answers he did not find, avoiding a confrontation he was loathe to have. The graffiti was still on the outside, the usual illumination of the Hall was absent, and his Talkers had, it seemed, gone out about their business. Only the absence of the debris, the dead, the wounded, and the two bound men now held in a locked room converted to storage after the Coup, hinted at the march of time. He knew the captives were in that room because of a solitary slump-shouldered, disheveled Talker with a confiscated popper leaning against the doorframe, not attempting to hide his boredom or discomfort. He scrambled upright, squared his shoulders, and tried to appear appropriately attentive as the Senior came into the corridor, but a weary wave of Kal's hand put the man at ease enough for him to slump back into place as the Senior passed.

He was not a soldier. He could not be expected to comport himself as one. He was only a man pressed into watch duty until a decision was made about the captive vandals.

Kal expected Grainger to send buggers for them eventually.

Eventually would not come soon enough.

"What did she say?"

Expecting his office to be empty, finding Bene there wringing his hands, was both unsettling and bothersome, but not enough so to prevent Kal from hoisting off his coat and pouring a much-needed drink to chase the chill from his bones.

"She?" he mumbled, placing the glass squarely at the center of his desk before dropping into his chair and rubbing his eyes with the heels of his hands.

"You found her, didn't you? Laertes?"

Kal's expression darkened at a suggestion he had not considered pursuing. Many had claimed over the last few years that the individual spearheading the Igraci was a woman, identified by her code name Laertes, but like most others, Kal had no proof it was so. People claimed to have spoken to her at Igraci rallies around the Levs, but they could not identify her. If her identity, her true name, her affiliation, were known to the bugorra, she had never been tagged as a person of enough interest to be hunted or arrested.

The Igraci were a nuisance but they had never been violent.

The Founder might have known her. Kal, however, did not. If they had crossed paths, he had not realized who she was at the time.

"Why would I...?"

"They were Igraci, sir, others are sure of it. Igraci and brako."

"Sure?" He swirled his drink in his glass and studied Bene evenly. The Igraci had perpetrated vandalism before; the tags on the outer walls might be their work. But he had never heard of them molying a building, killing anyone. Short of a handful going rogue from the group's primary tenets, Kal doubted this assault was their work.

Hearing the doubt in the Senior's tone, Bene shrugged sheepishly. "Sure as we can be. There weren't any masks...they were too organized to be civilians..."

"In case you haven't noticed, Crow masks don't mean anything anymore." The number of men without masks carrying out the work of the brako was rising every day. He had seen some of that evidence. Whether those men were Feena's or Neoma's, or if they were a different-affiliated third faction, he recognized the belligerent, bullying tactics aimed towards the same end.

Keeping Hebenon on the edge of fear's blade.

"Did those two say anything?" His head cocked towards the corridor and the direction where the captives were held.

"They're not talking. We thought she might come for them...that you'd find her and..."

And what, he thought bitterly? Have a lovely chat? "Wasn't looking for her."

Bene nodded, solemn but disappointed, and waited for the glass raised to the Senior's lips to lower again. "They're talking, you know…the others…that the Igraci want to displace us…the Voices. Since they opened the doors…people are listening to them more…"

The corners of Kal's eyes twitched. "Then we make our Voices heard. Reassert our relevance…"

"How? They blame us for kidnapping the Founder…people are saying it was you…"

Though not surprised that those very public suspicions had seeped into the ranks of his Talkers, this was the first evidence of it. Already steeped in the quest for means to prove the importance of the Voices of Faith, aware of those issues and others, he pursed his lips, paused, and asked, "Do you believe that, Bene? That I could walk into the Uppers without notice…walk him out of there…kill buggers and hold him without any one of you finding him?"

He thought, as the other man swallowed hard and shifted his weight from one foot to the other, that Bene would admit to believing it. That he would admit that he thought the rumors were true and that he thought the accusations by the buggers had grown into a much larger problem than they should be.

"So, what do we do?" was what Bene chose to say instead with a barely noticeable shaking head and downcast eyes that kept his thoughts hidden.

Kal grunted. The question had been his private struggle since the first accusations were made. The Voices were rooted, founded, in the infallibility of Kemway rule. The Founders' words, their voices, their laws and decrees, were never questioned, never wrong. Abducting the Founder was akin to heresy.

That foundation of infallibility was undermined by the revelation of an unpolluted world that was nothing like generations of Founders had touted it to be, and the Kemways no longer held Hebanthe Falls in their grasp. Despite Haythem's attempt to rally the people, it was unclear in the prods Kal had seen on his way through the Levs whether he was alive or dead, whether the footage was fake or, if real, if Haythem had gotten away from the riot safely.

It was unclear whether any in that crowd believed him anymore.

What was clear to Kal was that the majority of people would never support Neoma's claim to power based on her marital status. It was less obvious whether they might accept Haythem's daughter, a child, a girl, as the Founder in his place, even though she carried his blood. Whatever the path forward, the city would never return to what it had been. Scarecrow's Coup and the opening of the doors to the Outside made going back impossible.

There was still one chance for the Voices to regain relevance, a shred of influence, a trace of importance, regardless of the ongoing apocalyptic preaching of the Igraci.

"We find the dwarf, Enoch LeRoy."

In a dubious voice, Bene murmured, "Dwarf, Senior?"

Kal nodded, ignoring Bene's skepticism. "I guarantee you…you find him…bring him to me…find Founder Kemway…and you'll see. They'll understand then." He poured another drink and made a nod of determination. "Get everyone on it, everyone we can spare." As an afterthought, he added, "And if anyone finds Laertes, I want her brought to me too."

Bene hesitated, expressing confusion on his face that he chose not to voice. Instead, he nodded back and said, "At once," before scooting backward from the room.

❧*❧

It took Skelter longer to reach the kesfek than he expected, as the need to avoid brako looters and the bugorra who pursued them had redirected him through detours he had not intended to take. When he emerged from the head of the alley near his destination, he had waited more than thirty minutes as the cluster of buggers at Vapors' door grilled Maemi and Jonner about some matter Skelter could not hear. He remained hidden in case they were looking for him and lingered, spying, only to be certain that Maemi would not come to harm. The lack of raised voices reassured him and so he went down a half-Lev, moved around to the rear of the vindi, and then back up another flight of stairs to sneak inside Tox's workshop with the security passcard Zara had made for him, for herself, and for Rhyd, a long time ago.

Finding Zara with Tox in the secret workshop was never a surprise as the two often collaborated. They appeared to be involved in another project judging by the clutter scattered on the table before them. There were computer chips, modules, and hardware, solid metal plates of various sizes and shapes covered in the fine mesh Tox had fabricated for Rhyd when Scarecrow had been born, and a pile of wires and tools that Skelter took no time to study when he stumbled through the door. Using the passcard was the only reason neither woman aimed for his head with any of the assorted blades lying amongst the clutter. Both dropped what they were doing in the pale glow of artificial lamplight and aided the redhead in removing his coat and settling onto one of the metal-legged stools.

Neither asked what had happened. Neither scolded him for being out in the dark city alone. Zara offered a bottle of whiskey from the cabinet while Tox cleaned the wound and proceeded to stitch and plast the superficial shoulder wound left by a popper shot whose impact had been lessened by the coat he wore. The flesh was torn, bloody and purple around the edges where the hemplastic ball had dug into the surface meat of his shoulder, but the injury was not as detrimental as it could have been.

Removing it created less pain than the sting the cleansing alcohol left in its wake.

Now he was slumped on the stool, welcoming the alcohol numbness that eased the needle's lingering sting, with the bottle clasped between his hands as he watched Tox refocus her sewing skills to the items in production. Zara, careful to avoid the knee-to-knee contact both once would have welcomed, resumed the fine-tuning of the P1 Echo she was repurposing. Or maybe, he thought as he rubbed his knee with one hand, missing that friendly gesture, Zara intended to hack the Hub for information on the recent spate of unfortunate events. It would not be an easy task given the city's limited power but he trusted Zara would succeed.

He did not know enough about Echos to know their inner workings, but Zara certainly did.

Without the ever-running filt and climate systems, despite the absent glow of the forge that typically made the workshop unbearable, the room was stifling and stuffy. Tox's skin glowed with a faint sweat sheen, and Zara's pale blonde hair was damp, pulled into a long tail held in place by a fabric-covered twist of braided wire. They were details he noted absently as he pondered how much he should tell them about what had happened to break the silence left in the wake of the filts' absent hum.

Whatever he said, he did not want to provide details of his injury that would make the women in his life worry. He was going to get enough of that at home.

"Rhyd need new gear or is that for me?" he finally inquired with a nod at the mesh sections Tox was melding together. Rhyd always needed new gear, sometimes to replace damaged portions, sometimes to integrate the upgrades and changes Tox and Zara created that would, it was intended, make his work easier.

"Doesn't he always?" Tox's muted chuckle sounded awkward and strange. "Who says you're getting more?"

Skelter frowned and began to retort to the obvious but pointed teasing as he realized his question might have tipped his hand to his concern for self-preservation. The crackling audio of a prodcast that erupted from the Echo between Zara's hands as she twisted a bit of wire into place and attached it to the motherboard cut off what he had been about to say.

There was no video on the screen. There did not need to be. The clamor of the earlier riot, punctuated by the Founder's unexpected voice and a staccato double popping, lay the foundation for Kenneth Ximenez's plea for information about Founder Kemway and the attempted assassin's whereabouts.

"You were there," murmured Zara when the audio cut out, glancing at Skelter's shoulder as she tried to manipulate the electronics to provide the missing video feed.

He shrugged and tried to sound innocuous as he muttered, "One of those two shots hit me, yeah…"

"The other?"

"Wouldn't call it an attempted assassination for shooting you…" Tox set the torch aside and picked up a cutting tool. She doubted that, whatever the authorities knew, they knew anything about Skelter. It was doubtful he had remained on the scene long enough to be questioned.

"'specially since they don't know I was hit," Skelter confirmed. "Didn't know I was there." The Lieutenant, maybe. Rhyd. But nobody of any importance.

Before Zara could voice the worry in her eyes, Tox mumbled, "Was the Founder shot? Killed?"

"Don't know…don't think so…but I didn't see anything. Think Rhyd got him out of there before that happened."

"Rhyd or…?"

Not Rhyd. Scarecrow. Skelter nodded. "A cazzing mess…once Founder got up and things went dark…when the shots happened…"

The P1 was set down and Zara pushed away from the table. "I should go down." Vapors was one of the few places Rhyd might go if he needed help. He had not reached out over the comms but given the condition of the Hub, perhaps he could not. One of them should be in Vapors in case he came.

"Otta's probably worried."

Skelter let out a hissing breath and nodded. He knew Tox was right, but he was not looking forward to the anticipated confrontation awaiting him. "Should make sure everyone's secure," he agreed. He trusted Otta to take care of herself and the children, thought she trusted him to be capable of the same, but the growing uncertainty as each minute of darkness passed required assurances.

To Zara, as she pulled on her ankle-length crimson coat, Tox said, "You see him, send him up."

Zara and Skelter exchanged a look when the kesfek did not offer further information. Zara murmured, "I will," while Skelter clasped Tox's shoulder affectionately, wincing at the stretching of plast and stitches, and said, "Thanks for the patch."

Her request confirmed the purpose of the project on the workbench. Whatever it was, if something had happened to the Founder, Rhyd would need all the help he could get.

❧ * ❦

The first man he considered to be a potential ally was, Switz realized as the dark-skinned merc dropped a body over the edge of the platform, the last person he should be tempted to trust. The corpse, unbound, unwrapped, flopped and banged against the rails as it fell, and continued to flail as it struck the swirling current and was dragged beneath. It was thrown against jagged, submerged rocks and the thick pylons driven into the earth that supported the city's weight. Eventually, the body would be dredged by the straining nets, but by the time it was pulled out of the water, it would be so bruised, torn, and bloated that it would be unrecognizable. It would be equally impossible to identify the specific cause of death.

Maybe the person was alive but drugged and unconscious and would ultimately drown.

Maybe they were dead already, some impediment to be rid of, and the apparent flailing nothing more than a product of the river's flow.

Switz did not want to join them there.

There was already history between them. Switz wanted no part in the claims of murder lingering now that the Founder's face was being blasted on a loop throughout the city. For a time, he considered using what he knew to blackmail Blayd into protecting him. As the body disappeared and Blayd turned towards the place where Switz crouched in the shadows, the small man decided he did not have enough solid evidence to make a threat of blackmail worth using.

Blayd would blame him for the kidnapping unless Switz could prove he had been in the Core. There was a risk to that knowledge, as such an admission would require an explanation for his escape apart from the others rescued and registered from the Core's main door collapse. Blayd, or someone else, would make accusations. Blayd had connections. People like him always did.

Switz had no one. He had no defenses.

He pulled the hood of his tatty raincoat lower over his face and dropped his head so that, when Blayd passed, he would not recognize his accomplice there if he happened to notice the figure in the shadows. The merc might kill him anyway for witnessing the body disposal, but Switz thought his lowered head made him look oblivious and ambivalent to everything around him. If he remained still, Blayd might not even see him.

Rather than make any action that might suggest he had seen something he should not, Switz waited until Blayd was far past him, up the stairs and on about his business, before shaking the water from his coat and exiting his alley hideaway. He muttered loud enough for passersby to hear, the way Heb addicts often did, wringing his hands and playing with his fingers, staring at his shuffling feet as though unaware of his surroundings as he stumbled up a different flight of stairs in the opposite direction.

He did not look to see if Blayd was watching. But he did listen.

Continuing to mumble and mutter, he headed toward the sound of footsteps, waited until a passing pair of patrolling buggers happened by, and then trailed behind them as though attempting to ting a few ticks or the Hebbies officers sometimes confiscated and carried in their pockets. The buggers had not witnessed the disposal, would not see the body now that it had been swept towards the sea, and paid no attention to the Lev below them or the river beneath that. They only deviated from their patrol long enough to notice him and growl, "Piss off," to the strung-out tinger stalking them.

Switz gladly dropped back and turned down a side street towards another flight of stairs.

He had a new plan.

Maybe Enoch, Skelter, or Colyx would give him sanctuary. They owed him, after all, for risking his neck for those kids. Never mind that helping them escape the Core had been as much for them as it had been to gain his freedom.

If he had not made that choice, he might now be counted amongst the dead found inside.

That was not enough. What good was freedom if everyone in the city might come looking for him for a crime he did not believe he had committed?

It was only a stinger, after all. Nothing that should have killed anyone. Besides, the reports did not offer proof that anyone was dead. The prods were speculative. Switz had done nothing wrong.

Any one of those three could protect Switz long enough for him to track down Kemway, long enough for him to concoct a method of tagging Blayd as the villain, and maybe even earn a hefty reward for saving the Founder's life. As far as Switz could see, it was the only chance he had to remain free.

*

With hydropower stretched as thinly as it could be over every city system, most of the pneumatic doors in the Uppers, except those of private homes and prisoner cells, had been cut, leaving the doors open so that no one was trapped in an office, a lab, a meeting or recreation room, or vindi. The footsteps passing his office, the clicking of heels on tile, and the often-animated voices of people working as diligently as he was to resolve the situation before the hydros failed as well, had become an increasing distraction. Most hurried by without entering his office or speaking to him about matters he could not solve.

Those who did enter brought memos, handwritten or verbal to reduce the burden on the crawling Hub and comm systems, or else came seeking signatures on requests intended to be put forth to the Nau or meant to facilitate some action unit heads considered worth implementing on Hebenon's behalf.

They could have acted without his signature.

He suspected they wanted someone to blame if their efforts, or his refusal to allow an effort, resulted in further problems.

The set of steps that burst into his office now, staccato clacking he heard approaching long before they arrived, intruded on the short, eyes-closed break Grainger had taken to regain some of the energy a night of lost sleep had stolen. He knew before he opened his bloodshot eyes to meet hers that this visitor was none of those pesky bureaucrats.

"Why aren't you doing something?" snapped the thin woman in a piercing pitch that reached him before she reached the desk.

He wished the doors were working enough to have provided more of a warning or a barrier between them that might have locked her out.

"Mam…"

"I don't want excuses!" Her face was flushed with fury and the effort it had taken to travel up through the Levs to reach him. It seemed a long way, in his opinion, to go just to shout at him. "You didn't find Ulynda! Others had to do it for you! Now there's an assassin on the…"

"No one's been assassinated…"

Neoma stalked around the desk but stopped beyond his reach, her distance draining some of the threat from her actions and words. "That's not what Kenneth…"

Grainger snorted. "You can't believe everything on the prods…"

The city had been primed and beaten into believing every morsel, every rumor, every detail the Founders deemed worth sending over the prods for generations. Some had grown cynical about the claims of those living in the light of the Uppers, but many had never felt any cause to doubt the words of the Kemways or those the Kemways permitted to be shared…even in the waning years before the Coup.

It had led to sensational headlines and reports after the Coup without the Kemways there to moderate the output, fanciful prods tangled between truth and falsehood, that people devoured in their boredom, and gossiped about when there was nothing else to discuss. Neoma, more than most, should understand that not everything voiced on the prods was true or accurate.

Her husband had been a cog in that machinery, after all.

She pursed her lips and narrowed her eyes. "You think I'm a fool?"

Rubbing the bridge of his nose, Grainger resisted standing up so he did not have to look up at her as he spoke. Her looming did not intimidate him. "I think you're a mother, a wife, who's concerned about her family." While he thought her less concerned about their welfare than her own, he hoped his claim would assuage her rabid anger and dull the piercing edge of her tone. "We're doing everything we can to find…"

Her sneer remained. "Like you did to find my daughter? Like you did when he was taken the first time?"

"Got the brako running circles around what people I have down there looking for him. They're doing what they can while the rest of us work to get the lights back on for a hot evening meal and a long shower. It's the best we can do."

He did not, however, believe he was doing enough…on any front.

Before she could interrupt, he asked, "Ulynda's home? Safe?"

Her chin tipped up in arrogance and defiance. "Home and safe from that dirty, dangerous dwarf."

The corners of his eyes creased in support of the perplexed pursing of his lips. "What are you…?"

Neoma's retort was swallowed as she regarded his confounded expression, trying to ascertain how much he knew or suspected. Concluding the captain knew nothing about the recently uncovered Kemway heir and preferring that news be kept private as long as she could control it, she shrugged and cut him off with, "It doesn't matter. My people found her, brought her home."

"People?" Neoma did not respond. "If you have people, get them out there to find Haythem and keep the peace. Need all the help we can get. This will run a lot smoother, things'll get done faster, if there's more of us being helpful and less of us causing trouble."

Again, he noticed that her initial response was held back in favor of another haughty tilt of her chin and a shrug of her narrow shoulders. She smoothed out the front of her coat without looking away from him. "When they find him, Captain," she eventually said as though capitulating to a threat, "you'll regret the day you sat in that chair."

She marched from the room, carrying the unspoken realization that there would be no help for her here, no support for her anywhere in the Uppers, and very little in the Levs.

Behind her, Grainger silently acknowledged, not for the first time, that he already felt that regret.

❧Chapter 8❦

Despite his efforts, Tamner was unable to shake the trio of bugorra once they realized he was leaving the security of the Uppers to journey into the bowels of the city. The limited power, the absence of most street lighting, meant the increased likelihood of lawlessness and the doctor had proven too valuable to the relationship with the parah to risk his life on the foolishness of traveling down alone.

After a brief scuffle with two fellows in brako masks who tried to muscle the plain-closed, unmasked buggers and doctor for ticks or weapons or other items of value which resulted in the pair left comatose against an empty vindi's wall, Tamner felt begrudgingly relieved to have accepted the escort. He fretted with each set of stairs he descended, wondering how he would explain his destination if Scarecrow happened to be at the other end of the journey.

One member of the trio was selected to remain with the unconscious brako, zipping them to a crossbeam meant for the lashing of dog carts, to wait until backup arrived. He would escort the pair to the nearest bugorra field office before joining other duty officers in the search for Founder Kemway. The other two, one in front of Tamner and one behind, continued with him down one flight after another, complaining about the stairs as they went. They were law officers, he a man of influence; surely they could use the lifts. But Tamner chose to leave that expenditure of limited electricity to those with more urgent needs. He could not guess how urgent the summons was, given the delay in delivery.

Nor was he certain where the pinging signal would lead him.

It was wiser, if more draining, to approach that destination on foot.

He had not noted which Lev the protest and riot had occurred on, but the increasing bugger and brako activity as they descended suggested he was nearing the epicenter of both events. The signal's direction, however, prevented him from reaching the intersection. It pointed him down a barely-illuminated street, littered with crouching, unwashed streeter children. Spinks, he judged by the chirps, whistles, and clicking claps and snaps they used to communicate as Tamner and his escort passed.

He thought they would stop him. He expected Scarecrow, or someone else, to emerge from one of the vacant buildings to greet him or prevent him from going further. One child after another popped up in his periphery, their gestures and postures directing him to the haphazard lean-to guarded by a cluster of urchins standing disheveled with arms crossed in wide-footed stances of defiance. The Spinks that trailed behind, making the bugger behind him move nervously nearer to protect him, now circled in and maneuvered between the doctor and his escort, refusing to let the law keepers pass.

Tamner scanned the street, the lean-to and its blockaded entrance with a neutral expression intended to put the buggers at ease.

So, this was the place.

One of the buggers lifted his thumper and smacked it against his hand. Tamner shook his head and gestured for the man to put the weapon away.

"They're not going to hurt me."

"You don't know that, sir," the thumper-wielding bugger huffed, lowering his arm but refusing to return the thumper to his belt. "You don't know what's in there…what they want…"

"Probably Heb," snorted the other.

"Someone needs my help. Wouldn't have called me all the way here to hurt me." He was not called into the Levs often. A scientist first, he was not the sort of doctor who perpetuated a medical practice or offered medical aid as a rule, a man who studied biology and genetics and had dissected more than his share of cadavers. He knew the human body well enough to treat a variety of injuries, when the need arose, though the buggers likely did not know any of that. To them, unless the subject was a prosser or a city official, there seemed no reason for him to be in the Levs.

He wondered if Grainger, or a member of the Nau, had compelled the escort not merely to keep him safe but also to spy on his activities.

"Keep an eye out," he said, taking the offered hand of the boy in front of them. "You'll know if I need you."

The buggers scowled but he did not wait for their protests. The line of Spinks pushed them back as a skinny boy with red paint smeared across his eyes and down over his nose and mouth to his chin pulled Tamner forward. The clustered barricade parted as he reached the doorway, where he grasped the upper edge of the entranceway before ducking inside.

The comm signal pinged incessantly.

He had reached his destination.

Tapping the ICD's face, he shut off the signal so the sound would not serve as a beacon to brako, other buggers, or the curious inclined to investigate the source. Once through the second doorway, where the original door had been removed from hinges that hung from the frame as if pulled free, he recognized the big man with the leg braces waiting with his hands on the round hatch door on the opposite side of the cold, cluttered room. He might have been holding it open, preparing to slam it shut, and Tamner wondered who Colyx was expecting.

"You sent for me?" While certain it was Ballard's signal that let him here, the pair knew each other. Leaving someone else at the location in his place was not a surprise.

"No."

The shake of his head ended with a tilt toward the space beyond the partially open hatch. Colyx hesitated, the scrutiny of his raking gaze made sinister by the battery torch he held, but when a young woman's voice behind the door anxiously commanded, "Let him in…it's okay…" he grunted and opened the hatch the rest of the way.

"Not okay," he muttered, gesturing to lure the doctor forward.

Tamner swallowed and obeyed.

He expected Scarecrow at death's door. The man's body could only endure so many beatings before it succumbed to inevitable failure. No doctor, including Tamner, could prevent that forever.

He did not expect, as his eyes adjusted to the change in lighting, the pinched, unkempt visage of Hebenon's Founder on a sagging, threadbare cot, body limp and unmoving. Tamner had seen the SCAM footage. This faded man bore only a superficial likeness to the animated character who had recently railed at Hebenon's people from a platform at the center of the latest riot. His eyes were closed as though asleep, but a dark crimson stain spread across the filthy, rough-processed hemp fabric shirt worn by those less affluent than the Kemways had ever been. His chest did not rise and fall, and his skin was a pale, pasty shade Tamner had seen many times.

The unthinkable was true.

Tamner did not need to move closer to know it. The man's end did not surprise him.

The young woman beside the cot clenched Haythem's hand in a manner the doctor considered both endearing and heartbreaking.

"Did you…?"

Not allowing the man to complete the question, anticipating what it might be, Ginna defensively replied, "I'd never," as she assessed the man Scarecrow had sent to evaluate his trustworthiness. When Tamner stepped closer, she shifted on the crate where she sat to facilitate his examination, but did not rise.

Understanding her tone and answer though it was not to the question he had been about to ask, he squatted, removed his gloves, and pressed his fingers to the vein at the man's neck to confirm what he already knew. In a less pointed tone, without looking at her, he asked, "You didn't bring him here?"

"We did." Her gaze darted to Colyx and then back to the Founder's face. "Scarecrow and I. I was there when he…we needed to get him out of the crowd before…" Again, her gaze moved, although Tamner saw none of it as she beckoned Colyx and his light closer to aid in his examination.

Though not enough light for a thorough inspection, Tamner peeled back the fabric sticking to Haythem's chest to look at the place where the fatal popper pellet had penetrated.

It had not been a quick death. The Founder had likely lingered for several minutes, maybe longer, as blood filled his lungs to drown him. Another spot of blood at the side of his neck, encircled by a faint formation of bruising, suggested something else, but it was something that an autopsy would have to reveal and explain.

"He left me here to help Ilya at the…" Ginna whispered.

"Lieutenant Young?"

"My sister." She shrugged, embarrassed to admit it when Tamner looked up at her, and hastily continued to avoid further questions. "It was wild…screaming and shouting and running. He told me to stay until he came back…or until you did." She had not released Kemway's hand yet and used her other hand to brush his unruly hair from his eyes. "I was here when he…wouldn't have been right for him to go alone, you know?"

Whatever else Haythem Kemway had been, whatever so many in the city thought about him and the stranglehold the Kemways had held over them, he was still the Founder. Or he had been. The very last one.

He deserved the morsel of dignity and respect this young woman had been willing to offer in those last minutes of his life.

"Did you see how he got this? Do you know…?"

"I wasn't close enough. I was on the fringe, just arrived when he started talking. I heard the poppers, the screaming…I was trying to reach Ilya when I found Scarecrow and…"

"Sir?"

The bugger who made the mistake of getting past the Spinks bore the bloody nose to attest to his folly when he stepped through the open hatch and found Colyx's large hand around his throat. His eyes were wild with panic as the bigger man hoisted him to his toes and thrust him against the wall, and he tried unsuccessfully to pry the hand away so that he could breathe.

"There's a…" he croaked. "We're supposed to report to…" His effort to relay whatever command he had been issued was aborted when his gaze fell upon the cot. "Is that…?" One hand flailed as if in search of his popper but he was unable to remove it from his belt.

"Arturo…," started Tamner.

Colyx snarled but let the man crumple to the floor of the metal-sheathed room. One outstretched arm broke the bugger's fall as he rubbed his throat with the other.

"You're gonna arrest me, aren't you?" Ginna whispered.

"Don't think that's necessary." Was it protocol to arrest witnesses? This girl was not a killer, and Colyx was, as far as Tamner could tell, a brawler used to fighting with his hands, not with a popper. Neither was armed, unless a weapon was hidden in this room or had been discarded, and neither had a motive as far as he was aware.

But as the only witnesses to the end of the Founder's life, Tamner did not think he should leave them there.

"You should come up for statements," he finally concluded, his thoughts digging through the pressing need to transport the body through the Levs to the Uppers, to somewhere it could be properly examined, where the true cause of death could be determined, without sounding a public alarm or raising an unwanted fuss. "You should come up with me…"

If she had given Haythem something to hasten his demise, or if Scarecrow had done so, he needed to know that too. Until he could rule out unwanted guilt, there were only three potential killers. Two of those three would have to come with him.

"Colyx wasn't here…he didn't see anything. He only came when I sent for him because I didn't want to be alone…"

"May be true…but it will save the hassle of a summons if you come in and answer questions on your own…and I could use your help with him." He looked up from the Founder to the bugger who had finally pushed to his feet. "We can't let this get out until we know more…not unless we want another riot or coup. This stays between us here," he gestured around the room at each of them, "until he's examined and the Nau decides what to do. We'll need to move him without being spotted, not talk to anyone as we go up…"

"Blankets out there," grunted Colyx, motioning past the hatch into the main room.

Despite his skeptical expression, the bugger nodded and offered, "If we take the lifts up, will be easier…"

"And the Spinks can keep us a clear path," added Ginna.

As thin as the Founder had become over the last few years, particularly in the weeks since his abduction, Tamner believed he could carry him, but even with blankets and the Spinks' help, the trip to his labs and office would not be easy. He had avoided the lifts to conserve power. This time, he did not think he had a choice. "Alright, let's do this. The four of us…let's get him somewhere secure."

It was the best Tamner could do for the man he had known his entire life.

From the half-Lev above, perched on a roof with a clear line of sight to the lean-to's entrance, Scarecrow watched Tamner's arrival with the unfortunate escort and kept a cautious, scrutinizing eye out for the trouble he expected those bugorra to bring. Without the constant buzz and hum of city systems, with the mods incorporated into his mask and hood, he picked out fragments of the conversation inside the metal-walled room where the Founder lay.

Kemway was dead. Not a sham death this time, perpetuated for the populace. Not a living death hidden from the city in the care of physicians and servants. Truly dead. There had been little likelihood, after that popper shot, that he would survive, but Scarecrow had hoped. He had reason to hate that man but he found he did not. Now he only felt pity for him.

He had hoped Tamner would arrive sooner, might have been able to prevent the inevitable, that Ginna would not be the one to carry the burden of the Founder's dying breath, but those hopes had been slim.

He had left her here, aware of what was likely to occur. He should have returned sooner.

A summons for assistance by other bugorra on the opposite side of the city crackled through the air, emitted by one of the bugger's sporadically functioning ICDs. One of the two pushed past the Spinks, knocking two children to the ground, being struck in the nose with a thrown rock before stumbling past. Rather than follow him, the Spinks tightened their barricading line, trapping him at Colyx's mercy, daring the other to try to get past them too.

He thought better of it and maintained his post in the street.

Several minutes later, the bugger cautiously emerged, his hands raised as though to temper the Spinks' actions as he led Ginna and Colyx outside. Ginna spoke in hushed tones and hand gestures to the guarding Spinks who scattered moments before Tamner emerged with a shrouded bundle cradled in his arms. Some of the Spinks led the way, some followed as a protective barrier, others drifted into the shadows, all intent on creating a clear path for the group to reach the nearest lift.

Tamner had the appropriate pass credentials to use it. He could travel directly to the Uppers without anyone interrupting the lift's ascent. His burden appeared to be no more than the dirty, colorless blankets it was wrapped in, not something likely to raise questions, but only travel in the lift was going to keep this secret for now.

Eventually, word would get out.

Hebenon would have to know the truth.

Scarecrow followed, guided by their footsteps when he could not see them, monitoring their progress and the redirecting efforts of the Spinks when other foot traffic might intercept them, until they reached the lift.

The door opened.

Tamner stepped inside, turned to face the door, and looked into the face of the shadow on the rooftop near enough to leap down at them and dash to stop the lift if he chose to.

The crouched form did not move.

The doctor nodded, his expression grim, as others jostled in around him. It was enough to support what Tamner believed.

Ginna and Colyx were innocent of this death.

So too, he believed, was Scarecrow.

But his beliefs would not be enough to shield them if the city elected to lay its grief and blame on any of those people.

The door closed.

The lift began its ascent.

Scarecrow watched, and then listened to the lumbering whir of the gears that struggled under the strain of reduced electricity, until he could no longer pick out those sounds from the myriads of other environmental background noises Hebanthe Falls was accustomed to.

Someone a Lev above screamed in terror.

One more for the night, Scarecrow decided. One more, and then he needed to go home to rest.

He needed to go home to Jaron.

❧*❧

Prod transmission and reception were spotty, the trickle of hydropower and energy redirected from the Factory arrays barely enough to allow for the ongoing stream of prods intended to apprise people of the ongoing energy crisis, ways to conserve what power there was, and the work being done to restore the grid. There were directions and reassurances from Captain Grainger, the Ximenezes, sports celebrity Vittorio Oslo, and other familiar faces expressing the restrictions the Nau required to facilitate a smoothly running society until life could return to normal.

Smooth, but not smooth enough. Kal heard the endless grumbling complaints as he descended through his city after a tour of other Talker

Halls to see if they, too, had been assaulted as the Prime center of worship had been. Discontented rumbles and arguments about whether enough was being done, if the city was better off now or before the Coup, if going Outside was the best alternative. People disagreed about who was to blame, who might have attempted to assassinate the Founder…or if the target had been someone else…and speculation about how the man, missing for so long, happened to be at the heart of the latest salt protest. People argued about who should control the city instead of the bugorra captain, who many believed to be incompetent in the role he had been thrust into after the Coup. Better, many thought, that he returned to the bugorra full time and solve the brako problem.

By the time he returned to his desecrated Hall, Kal had formulated theories of his own. He stopped inside the door to stare at the scorched floor and carpet stained with blood, accepting that no one was going to protect him but himself. Not the Nau, not the bugorra, and not his subordinate Talkers. By the time he passed the fellow keeping watch over their captives, having listened to repeated requests for information about the would-be assassins, Kal decided there was no better course of action than to speak on his own behalf.

Thanks to years of carefully cultivated political relations with the Ximenezes and their predecessors, Kal had what was needed to insert his audio message into the repetitive queue of currently circulating infocasts. He had doubts about how long his message would be allowed to play before Grainger or the Nau ordered it removed, but once or twice in rotation should be enough to turn some of the wagging tongues of suspicion away from him, away from the Voices, long enough to allow him the opportunity to locate the missing Founder.

He cleared his throat and pressed record.

"The Voices of Faith have a long, glorious history of support for the people of our beloved city, for the cornerstones of our cherished way, and for Founder Kemway, his family, and his esteemed history. As it was from the beginning, so it remains today. It is no secret the

Voices and its leadership have come under unfair scrutiny, enduring accusations of treason and collusion against the Founder we hold sacred and against our city, things we hold too dear to risk such absurdities.

"What has not been revealed to you is that, upon my false arrest, no evidence was uncovered against me, against the Voices, and I was released to resume the holy work of providing succor to those who need it. Now, on the heels of evidentiary failure, a new accusation has been levied…the claim of attempted assassination. This is no coincidence.

"There are some in positions of leadership who want the Founder dead. Not only the Founder but also any who oppose those who have unlawfully usurped power. While we sit in dark homes, without heat, with lukewarm water, without the ability to cook, to filter our air, those in power sit in brightness as ever before, warm, full, and content. They offer inadequate, unproven reasons for our suffering, shutting us inside, shutting down the lifts, trapping us like rodents in a cage. What began as salt shortages will soon become a shortage of everything needed to sustain us.

"In short, they want us to bend to their will or die.

"Unlike the Igraci with their omens of doom and apocalypse, the Voices offer life. We believe all of us together can prove our mettle and worth. Unite. Bring this rumored assassin to justice or expose the lies. Save Founder Kemway from the enemies who have robbed him of power and seek to rob him of life. We can take back the future they are trying to steal. We will be strong again.

"This is Senior Driscoll. Faith and Forte to you all. Amen."

He clicked off the mic and sent the recording.

If he gauged the city's mood correctly, another coup would be born with the hosts of the Levs at his back. Whether the Founder was located or not, whether he was alive or dead, Kal intended that the Faith would make their move and recover their influence. Without someone level-headed enough to keep Hebenon strong, the city would continue its tumble down the slope toward human extinction.

The parah, he thought with a huff, did not count.

❧*☙

Scarecrow dropped the oft-removed grate into the empty room, closed it behind him after jumping silently down, and after removing the mask worn as often now as he wore his own face, shook out his sweat-damp blonde hair while absorbing the ambiance of his flat. The usual hiss of the filt systems was absent, with only a small wheezing of air being forced through the vents, denying his home the warmth he had looked forward to. The water systems failed to gurgle, reminding him there would be no hot water to shower or brew algtea, and with the barely detectable thrum of electrical current pulsing through the walls, there would be no cooking.

But there was food in his ice box to be eaten before it spoiled, cherries and carrots, goat cheese, and the dregs of hemp milk gravy and cooked sausage Jaron had last prepared. Edible, though not warm, and satisfying enough to ease the growl in his tight belly.

But no Jaron.

The staleness of the other man's scent suggested he had not yet come back to the flat. Despite the rational argument that part of his brain put forth, that Jaron was at the Archive working a double shift to make up for too many recent absences, Rhyd's too-honed sense of danger and the weight of lingering regret purported differently.

Without adequate electricity, the Archives would be largely inaccessible. There would be little work to be done. Some staff might be kept on hand to be available to resume work the moment full power was restored, but as unfamiliar as Rhyd was with Archive protocols, he did not think that possibility was likely.

No, he thought, bitterly chastising himself as he dropped his coat over the back of a chair, if Jaron was gone, there was no one for Rhyd to blame but himself.

With his meal set on the kitchen counter alongside the last bottle of Zaolei from his cupboard, Rhyd nibbled and sipped in between efforts to peel out of the upper portion of his suit, exposing bruised evidence of cracked ribs and sweaty skin to the cold air of the flat. The body armor had done its duty, protecting him from blows that could have caused more serious, even fatal, damage. The damage beneath the purple and black bruising, the ache when he breathed, was enough to make him wince when he moved, however, to occasionally stagger his breathing as he wrapped his torso with long lengths of elastic bandaging to stabilize the bones until he could seek professional medical care.

He should have asked Tamner, or his usual medic, to examine the cracks and set plasts if they were needed.

There was no time for it now, and Tamner had more important matters to address. As the darkness stretched on, more predators would emerge. The brako and other petty criminals would act. People typically disinclined to break the law would take advantage of this opportunity in the hopes of getting away with crimes they would otherwise not attempt. Hebenon needed Scarecrow. Skelter and Enoch and Ulynda, all at the scene of the protest, needed him. The others, Maemi, Tox, and Zara…he needed to know they were safe.

He needed to be certain Jaron was safe too, wherever he had chosen to spend his rest. Even if he never spoke to Rhyd again.

A brief respite, long enough to eat, to towel dry his damp skin and hair since there was no water for bathing, and he would return to Scarecrow's world. It was the safest place for Rhyd to be.

❧CHAPTER 9❧

Muttering obscenities that no one heard, Grainger switched off the sound of the offending prodcast Senior Kal had dared to issue, audacious accusations of sedition and incompetence that the captain resented even while knowing that, on the basest of levels, some of those claims were true.

Now, some of the Nau called for the Senior's arrest on multiple counts of treason, though Grainger doubted that had been Kal's intent. Others were less certain of that choice. How long it might take to sway them to a unanimous vote either way, Grainger could not guess.

But it was going to happen.

He had not been trained to rule the city. He was a law officer, a fighter, a peacekeeper, not a politician. Since the Lev uprising that had forced the contained metal city to open to the Outside world, his primary focus had remained on restoring peace and maintaining stability. Governance he left to the Nau. But it was his face the citizens of the Levs conjured when they considered who ruled in the Founder's stead. Used to a single, unifying leader, it was Grainger's face they would conjure when seeking someone to blame.

It was easy to argue that incapacitating the Founder, removing him from office, had been an act of treason, though no one other than Grainger and Scarecrow knew the truth of that night. If Tamner, if the Nau, if anyone other than the Lev rumor mill suspected that truth, it was rarely brought to the surface.

It would be now.

The restless citizens below, where change could be slow in coming, where the less affluent clung to rumors in the hopes of change, might be easily swayed by the Senior's barbed words. Just as some in the Nau were. One way or another, Grainger had to prove the Senior's hand in the kidnapping and prove the Voices' involvement. The limited evidence he held suggested it, but he needed more.

Turning his gaze from the window, he looked at the paused image on the Echo screen, the image that continued to demand his attention no matter how he tried to pull away from it. He rewound the footage, played forward a few more seconds, and then rewound it, scrutinizing each frame, looking for something he had missed, that they had all missed, during the explosion that killed the solar tech and robbed the city of its primary source of power. He compared every detail with the instructions uttered by the scrawny fellow with the prosthetic tongue who had provided both the parts and the schematics for the repair and directed the installation from the safety of Grainger's office.

The man was locked where he could not hurt anyone, where he would stay until Grainger had the truth, regardless of Tamner's claims about his virtue. Little by little, frame by frame, Grainger was forced to admit that Tamner was right. Lash was not the problem.

He watched the footage again. The assistant tech fumbled. Made a twisting motion with his fingers as though to tighten or loosen something. Stood up straight, nodded at the lead, and took a half-step back as the lead gave a thumbs-up gesture to those watching through the SCAMs. In that half-step, a loop of wire pulled taut between the assistant tech's foot and the array panel…and snapped in the millisecond before the burning flash brightened the screen.

It could have been a mistake. An accident. The action, the way the tech moved, the way his foot slid and pulled against the wire, made Grainger suspect differently. Now that he had noticed those details, he could not get them out of his head.

Until the tech was out of treatment for the burns he had received, Grainger could not ask questions.

But he could rewatch the footage again…just to be sure.

∾*∾

"You seen him?"

The hostel Maemi owned was a block away and two Levs above Vapors and Tox's home and kesfek vindi were next door to the bar, making it a short distance to travel in the murkier than usual streets with its heavier than typical mist rising from the river and the constant spray of the Five Falls. Alglamps' inadequate glow prompted Skelter, and others forced to travel, to do so more slowly, to cautiously watch their steps and listen for approaching or following footsteps, counting steps and Levs as they moved to reach their destinations without getting lost. It was easy to take the ever-present white noise of daily life and city systems for granted until they failed, to ignore the Echo prattle and perpetual glow of neon until they were no longer there. More than one person Skelter passed grumbled to themselves or to companions about discomforts they could not affect.

Scarves were pulled up over faces. Those with filt masks wore them unprompted. None of it helped. Heeding those he passed in case Molly erupted from the mist to finish what he had started, the furtively approaching steps did not surprise Skelter when they fell into place beside him. Only a voice he had not heard since their escape from the Core made his steps falter and made him look at the smaller man with a blink of surprise.

He did not know where Switz had been since aiding Enoch in getting the children out of the Core. Skelter had not cared to find him. He knew the wiry little man had separated from the group at the first opportunity, but Skelter did not blame him for that. Self-preservation was important. Switz had done what he had agreed to do. He had no obligation to any of them. And Skelter had none to him. It was why he was surprised to see him now.

He tucked his walking stick beneath his arm and against his body, continuing to fondle the head with one hand, using the seemingly nervous gesture to mask his ability to pull the blade from it if he needed to. "Good to see you too, Switz," he quipped, intending that his cordial and polite response would gain him more than hostility or apathy would.

They were not friends. They had never been friends. But he offered Switz a crooked smile and countered Switz's question with one of his own. "Might help if you told me who."

Stopping beneath an awning because Skelter was reluctant to reveal where he lived, Switz removed his hat and shook off the water before replying, "Enoch. Haven't seen him since…you know…and he still owes me. I wanna collect."

Skelter arched one brow. Enoch's business was his own. Whether Switz was referring to the escape or some other transaction between them, the redhead could not imagine Enoch intentionally leaving himself in a killer's debt. If anything, Skelter imagined it would be the other way around.

"Not in a day or so."

"Where's he stayin?"

Again, Skelter shrugged. "Not his keeper. He moves around…I don't keep track. Sure you'll see him eventually. I can tell him where to meet you when I see him if you can tell me where…

Face darkening, Switz muttered, "Ain't nowhere to be." Though a belittling admission, it was the truth. The Core survivors freed at the main entrance had been given houses, a bare minimum of goods to get their new lives started, a list of potential job assignments, and ticks to get by. Switz had gotten none of those things. Like Colyx and Otta, he had to scrape together a living now that he was in the city again.

Skelter was taking care of those two. Enoch had always gotten by inside the Core and outside of it. Switz, however, was on his own. Maybe, he mused, because Enoch had been the one to sneak supplies into the Core and provide to others that which they had lacked, it was why Switz felt the dwarf owed him.

"Somewhere he can meet you then? A flop or…?"

"That place you've always talked about…the bar where you…?"

"Not a good place for privacy," Skelter countered hastily enough to make Switz frown. For him, for Rhyd and his closest friends and associates, Vapors was the hub of many personal discussions. It was not the place he wanted Switz to be able to find him whenever he chose, not the place he wanted him to have unfettered access to, although he could not prevent him from finding it or drinking there.

Adjusting his hat and cloak, Switz continued to avoid eye contact and grunted, "Well, tell him I'm looking for him. I'll be around. Tell him it's important. I know a few things he'll want to hear."

"What sort of things?"

Switz refused to reply.

After a shrug, Skelter said, "Can't say when…but I'll tell him. Mark this place," he gestured at the awning beneath which they stood. "I'll send him here if he's willing. Good enough? That fair?"

Switz did not consider the open-ended offer to be either good or fair, an offer without the guarantee of a meeting, but it was better than nothing. Blayd was out there, probably looking for Kemway just as he was. Sleeping in the street was not going to be safe until Kemway was found or the merc was put out of business but maybe, he thought with a sideway glance at the door beside him, he could flop inside without anyone noticing. He might be safe enough here until he had Enoch's promises under his belt.

He would get no such guarantees from Skelter. He knew better than to ask.

❧*❧

The cadaver on the exam table was more emaciated than the last time Tamner had seen him alive, a detail both masked and accentuated by the ill-fitting castoff clothing he had worn. His waxy skin was mottled with bruises, some fresh, some faded to yellow. Those encircling his wrists looked to be evidence of a restraint system, cuffs sturdy enough to bruise if he struggled against them, but there looked to be no obvious indication of systematic abuse or torture.

In his previous condition and state of mind, unpredictable, rambling, incoherent, and mad, restraint had likely been necessary to prevent him from hurting anyone, himself included.

But that condition had not lasted. Tamner had heard the prod. Had seen the footage. While no less rambling, there had been a method, a message, behind the Founder's last words to the city he had been born to lead. It furthered the doctor's belief that, whatever had happened to his mind on the night the Coup had begun, Kemway had been gradually coming back to himself.

If only he had lived long enough to tell what had happened that night. If only he had lived long enough to tell them who had taken him from the Uppers, where he had been held, how he had gotten free.

As the blood processing unit whistled as it spun on the counter behind him, a use of energy Tamner deemed essential in this case, he completed the duty of washing the grime and blood from the deflated body so he could study the injuries more thoroughly. There was a multitude of injection marks on his arms, as though whoever had held him had deemed it necessary to sedate as well as bind him. But none of those was as fresh as the puncture on his neck. None of those bore traces of blood around the puncture point. Only a proper analysis would reveal what he had been injected with last and how much of it had been in his system at the time of death.

Even without that substance, however, the popper shot to his upper chest, where the hemplastic pellet was already removed from the hole where it had burrowed into his left lung, had been enough to kill him. With the tissue integrity destroyed, he had, as Tamner had earlier guessed, drowned in his own fluids.

He was no ballistics expert. He could not tell how far away the shooter had been or at what angle the pellet had struck its target. He could not determine the caliber of the popper used. Most poppers used the same size, a standard dimension that allowed for easy production. But some people fashioned their own poppers, their own shot. Some bigger, some smaller. Without a standard pellet on hand to compare it with, Tamner could not be certain what he had. The fatal, damning shot had been saved in a vial for Grainger's people to examine in the hopes that it could point them in the direction of the killer.

As far as Tamner could see from the evidence, it could have been anyone.

Knuckles popped against the door he had been certain to close when he entered in the hopes of preventing others from learning this truth before he was ready to reveal it. The voice on the other side called, "Sir? Mr. Nunn asks…"

"Tell him I'm busy," Tamner barked to the unfamiliar muted voice. Regardless of how important Nunn or any of the Nau members considered their business to be, nothing except the city burning could be as important as taking care of the dead.

Until he had the details necessary to put Founder Kemway to rest, everyone else would wait.

❧*❧

Jarred from his unintended nap by a sound against his door, Rhyd peeped through the lens, saw no one, and then carefully opened it after a second, more insistent knocking. Enoch. With a hasty glance up and down the street to be certain his visitor was alone, Rhyd pulled him inside with one hand and closed the door behind him with the other.

"Got her topside?" he asked the chattering, nervous man as he ushered him to a chair at the table. He glanced at the half-full bottle of Zaolei between them, debating whether to offer what would be difficult to replace in the city's current state, and then slid it closer to Enoch with a swallowed groan.

Enoch looked like he needed the drink more than Rhyd did.

"Not exactly." Enoch sank into the chair as if his bones were no longer able to support him, and he rubbed his face with both hands, temporarily ignoring the offering at his elbow. "You get him?"

Vanderwall.

Rhyd shook his head with a frustrated frown. "Things got complicated."

"Tell me about it," Enoch snorted. "You at least get Kemway out of there?" The name stuck in the back of his throat, making him cough, and his hand closed around the neck of the bottle.

"Was alive when I left him…but I don't think he stayed that way." Haythem's death did not feel to be the sort of detail Rhyd should be the one to share, even if his friend and the Founder were kin, but his admission opened the door to the likelihood without admitting it outright. "You know who…?"

Guessing by the question that Rhyd did not know the shooter either, Enoch shook his head. He also guessed, from Rhyd's words and those he did not utter, that the next news he heard about Haythem would be the announcement of the man's death. It seemed a peculiar, coincidental waste for them to meet one time only to lose each other. "Think it was Vanderwall?"

"Don't think he was armed by then." Unless he had tinged a popper from someone in the crowd, a bugger or fellow brako, Vanderwall had been unarmed when Rhyd had been forced to leave him. "But I got a look at him this time…saw his face."

Enoch's eyes lit up. "Good. That's something." Vanderwall's anonymity was one of the primary factors behind his success. The threat implied in Rhyd's admission was a sentiment Enoch and others supported. "Maybe you can find Ulynda when you go out again." Before Rhyd could question him, Enoch popped open the bottle, took a long drink, closed it, and pushed it towards Rhyd. "Got clocked by brako. By the time I came around," his shoulder hitched as his voice trailed off. "Probably expecting a reward from the Mam…but I haven't been there…and I wouldn't stake her safety on that."

Reward or ransom, either way, Neoma would be the place to start to make sure the girl was safe. Given that she had tasked Scarecrow with finding her daughter, something he had failed to do, approaching her would not be pleasant, but on the off chance the brako had been in contact with her regarding her daughter, or if they had returned Ulynda home, speaking with Neoma had to be done.

"I know where to start." Half-dressed, having not expected to doze off before completing the undressing process, Rhyd began to pull the suit back on. He had been idle long enough. Nothing would be accomplished by sleeping, except giving his body a healing respite. "Stay as long as you want."

As rattled as Enoch had appeared when he arrived, Rhyd assumed that lying low would be the dwarf's first choice.

Instead, Enoch shook his head and slid off the chair. He thought Rhyd looked weary, wary, haunted in a way Enoch had not seen him look since Venn's Vanishing.

He did not know what to attribute that look to this time.

"Need to get back, make sure Maemi and the others are okay." The statement ended on a questioning note and Rhyd shrugged.

"Haven't been there yet."

Enoch nodded. He had not expected otherwise.

"Be careful. They need anything…you need anything…"

"We'll let you know." If none of the others had summoned him, they were either secure or unable to reach him. Both men preferred to believe the first. He opened the door and pulled his hood over his head and down low over his face. "I'll be careful."

Though most would not know his face, would not know the truth, Enoch knew what Haythem's death made him.

Though not a burden he wanted to carry, it was his nonetheless.

❧*❧

The children, gathered around the alglamp on the table to share spooky and amusing stories from both inside and outside the Core, looked up when Skelter arrived. They nodded or bid him hello before resuming their game, less troubled by the darkness than the adults were. He removed his goat and patted the nearest boy on the head, noting that Otta was not in the room. Nor did she come from the kitchen or the corridor that stretched towards the multitude of sleeping rooms the hostel contained, a noticeable absence that Skelter felt before he closed the door. Fearing she was unwell, the only reason he could rationalize for leaving the children unattended, he fumbled down the dim corridor and peeped into the room they shared.

It was empty.

So, too, was the shower room.

He frowned and returned to the living room. "Has Colyx…?"

The children lifted their heads.

The door opened.

Silhouetted by the pale blue of the external alglamp and the one the children used, Skelter could see her disheveled hair, her torn, askew clothing, familiar evidence witnessed many times in the Core as the result of fights for dominance, peacekeeping, or amusement.

He did not think any of those things existed for her now.

"Where have you…?" he began, concern seeping into his voice despite his effort to hide it. She hated it when he worried. Just as he hated when she worried about him.

"Looking for you." She smoothed her hair, swiping water away, and started to remove her coat as Skelter crossed the room.

"I'm fine. You shouldn't have had to…" He assumed from her state that she had either made it as far as the intersection riot or else she had run afoul of brako or other troublemakers hoping to make a score who knew nothing about the woman they faced.

"I saw what they were…" They did not meet each other's gazes as he helped remove her coat but she noted the wincing grimace he tried to hide.

He immediately lowered his arm and shrugged. "Not like I knew that was going to go down," he protested, not asking how she had followed him to that same intersection. He shifted beyond her hand as she reached for his shoulder. "I'm fine."

She snorted and took her coat from him to hang it over the drip tray beside the door. "So am I." Voice low so the laughing children would not easily overhear, she asked, "You got caught in it?"

"At the start. Made it out before everything went to paso." His claim depended on the definition of many of the words in it, but as he looked uninjured, his hair still neatly in place, his clothes wet but not as mussed as they would have been from a fight, Otta accepted his claim. He had extricated himself from the riot without much of a fight.

She had thrown herself into it.

"Think it has anything to do with the power?"

"Don't know." Skelter steered her towards the kitchen where he offered her a glass of water. For the moment, there was enough water stored in the city's tanks and pipes to give them that. "Prods are giving instructions but not explanations. Maybe they don't know yet. Haven't had the chance to get feelers out; wanted to check on all of you and make sure you're…"

She pressed her hand to his cheek and her forehead to his after accepting the glass. "Everyone's fine." She was fine, he was fine, the children were fine. She did not know her father's whereabouts, if he was at Vapors or on his way home, but she trusted he was fine, too.

Skelter wrapped her in his arms and pulled her close with relief. "No more risks like that," he scolded with his mouth against her hair.

"You too, Ivan."

He nodded. His entire existence was a risk. Since returning from the dead and resuming business, there were many, clients and rivals alike, who would prefer he had remained that way, out of the way of their profit. But that was not the risk that she meant.

And he knew it.

❧*❧

"Better be good," Grainger groused as the pneumatic lab door was groaningly forced open. Tamner stood directly on the other side as if expecting him, blocking his entrance with a pained, sick expression that made the captain's frown deepen. The room was better lit than anywhere else Grainger had been today, a necessity if the doctor was to work on whatever matter of import had prevented him from going to the captain's office when summoned.

"Good…no…but it's important." Ignoring the trepidation that had to be confirmed, Tamner stepped aside and gestured toward one of the lab tables in the center of the room. From the angle of his line of sight, Grainger could only make out the top of the individual's head, his shoulders, the line of his nose, his bare toes. None were enough to confirm identification but they were enough, when coupled with the doctor's mien, to draw a tight knot of dread in Grainger's empty belly.

He entered further. It was only two long striding steps, but it brought him near enough to identify what his head was already telling him was true.

"How…when…?"

"Got a call…he'd been found…but he was already gone by the time I got to him." Tamner raked his hand through his graying black hair. "Reports on the prods are accurate. One shot…all it took…" he pointed to the now clean puncture where the pellet had entered, "but there was enough strychnine in his blood that it probably didn't help his chances of survival."

"Strych…where'd he…?" Another long step and Grainger stared into the face of the man who had been the boon and bane of his career.

Tamner moved beside him and indicated the puncture at the side of his neck. "Injector…possibly close up…or could have been at range…"

The injury had not been caused by the injectors he had given Scarecrow to use to temporarily incapacitate the Founder if he found him. There had been no strychnine in them. And it had not come from anything Ginna Young had been carrying as far as he had seen. Through certain channels, anyone could acquire anything, however. If the power was ever restored, they could poll the Source for sales but neither captain nor doctor expected to find answers there.

"There were two shots…" But there was only evidence of one, the hole Grainger reached to touch but then avoided doing so. Injectors made a different, softer sound, not likely to be detected in the uproar of the crowd unless it was near the audio recording device.

No one had yet claimed to be the source of the audio.

"Or there were two from the same shooter and the second missed," Tamner offered. "Lieutenant Young was on site when it went down; maybe she can tell us more when she's out of recovery…"

"Recovery?"

"Don't know the details. She was in surgery. I should know more about her condition in the morning, but I thought you should know about this now rather than…"

Grainger almost touched the hunger-thin man's face, but again his fingers fell short. Touching Haythem's cold skin would be a too-tangible verification of the visible truth. He had sought this man for weeks, looking for a kidnapper, trying to hold Hebenon together. His assassination felt like a stronger coincidence than Grainger cared to stomach.

At least the news about Young explained why she had not responded to his attempts to reach her.

"Your source have any connection to the Voices?"

"My…?" Tamner swallowed, not following the shift in topic and fearing that the question concerned Scarecrow.

"The solar tech without a tongue."

"Lash?" Tamner blinked, swallowed his relief, and shook his head, though he was still confused about the nature of the inquiry. "He has less to do with them than he does with any of us up here. He couldn't have done this," he gestured at Haythem, "couldn't have been involved…he was working for us…"

"But the Voices could have been…they could have done this." Regardless of the support the Voices had provided the Founders and their families over the centuries, Grainger would not put it past Kal or any other Talker to silence Haythem after he escaped their custody.

Especially if Kal could spin the Founder's death, once it became public, to make it appear that it had come at the hands of the bugorra.

"You got the shot?'

Tamner picked up the vial and relinquished it without a word.

"Can't let this get out…"

Though inclined to agree, Tamner sighed, "Can't hold it forever. We have to tell the Nau. City deserves to know. If the Voices did this, if we cover it up as we did his…that he was still alive after the Coup, it's gonna bite us in the ass. They're all gonna use it against us."

He might have used the word 'us', but Grainger heard what he meant. Failing to announce the Founder's death would be used against him and him alone. Spreading the grim news would, either way, result in further unrest.

"Then we let the Nau decide."

Whatever the fallout of the Founder's death, it was up to the elected officers to choose the time and place of a public announcement. The results of the revelation would fall on the head of the assassin and the Nau, not on Grainger or anyone else.

Whoever that assassin was.

Grainger refused to take more of the blame than was already his.

❧Chapter 10❧

The angle of her raised leg, held immobile by straps and cords, in addition to the plasts that would, if she was allowed time to heal, permit her to walk normally, created continuing flashes of pain from her knee to her hip and into her back already strained from the awkward propped-up position she had wiggled into. Her arm and head barely ached, but the throbbing in her leg prevented restful sleep, yet Ilya had continued to doze since the surgery that had reconstructed the shattered kneecap. There were vague, disjointed memories of being moved from the initial clinic she had awakened in, through dark, muffled streets, to the slightly better facility where she was now, a clinic she recognized through squinted eyes as a place where bugorra were brought for treatment of on-duty injuries. She remembered trying to prop herself up, moments of murky clarity when shifted from one gurney to another, but the meds given to dull the worst of the pain were enough to drag her under time and again.

There was an internal sense that this last period of sleep had been the longest, the aches in her body seeming to have diminished enough to permit mental clarity, and so she lay with her eyes closed evaluating her condition and trying to put order to her memories. She sensed the visitor's entry, the scent of cologne, and was aware of him standing at the bedside for several minutes before he pulled the room's only chair nearer and settled onto it. From his footsteps, evidence of his leg injury remaining in each dragging step, from the familiarity of the cologne and the sound of his breathing, she knew who he was without looking. She guessed he intended to wait for her to wake, to grill her about her part in the riot, to seek information that few others were likely to have. He would wait as long as he had to, as long as he could.

Captain Grainger was a patient man when he wanted to be.

The usual hum of city systems was barely audible. The buzz of neon was absent. When she cracked open her lids to peer at the bent-headed figure with his chin on his fists, the only light in the room came from the medical monitoring equipment and the dim luminescence of the corridor's emergency lighting beyond the silhouette of the captain's shoulders.

"Sir…"

Her voice was raw and crackling from too much shouting and an extended lack of water intake, but it was audible enough to prompt Grainger to raise his head to meet her gaze.

"Bad as it looked?"

Grainger sounded weary, a note in his thick voice that echoed a degree of defeat she had never heard in his tone before. With the burdens he shouldered, the struggling power systems, the recent fire, the missing Founder, and the increasing frequency of city-wide protests, exhaustion was expected, even if his lack of expressed annoyance was not. She began to reply, coughed, and choked on her dry tongue, and he shook his head before filling a cup of water from the bedside table.

"SCAMs worked well enough to show what happened…and someone uploaded an ICD recording to the HUB for prodcast. Heard the shots…saw the Founder…"

Licking the water droplets from her lips, she gave him back the cup and struggled to sit straighter. "We were chasing Vanderwall…" When the angle of her leg would not permit her to move any further, she stopped with a groan. "The protest was underway when I arrived. We saw Ulynda Kemway…but then there was the attempt to subdue Vanderwall…and the riot…don't know how the Founder got there, where he came from. There were Talkers…Igraci…brako…everyone rushing the platform to get him. We got to him just before the shots…"

"We?"

Without answering the question, she continued, "Don't know where he took him…but we had to get him out of the crowd…and I couldn't do it." She scowled at her leg. "Someone had to control the mob. There was blood, screaming…but he was alive when he…I swear it…"

Grainger nodded, assuming then that the 'we' she referred to was her and Scarecrow as they had been the two on the platform with Kemway when the shots were heard. Had he been chasing Vanderwall too? Grainger expected her to blame the vigi for both the brako boss's escape, the Founder's appearance, and the shots fired. He expected she would blame Scarecrow for the Founder's death when she learned of it. He knew better. If Scarecrow wanted the Founder dead, there had been opportunities before.

When such claims were not uttered, his brow furrowed, and the corners of his mouth drooped as he pinched the bridge of his nose.

"We found him with your sister."

Ilya tried to lurch up and fumbled with the bindings that elevated her leg, her wide-eyed concern prompting her to action that the captain's hand covering hers prevented. "What was she…is he…where are they?"

"Got her in a holding room for her safety while things are sorted. Doctor Tamner's with…" He paused, swallowed, and muttered, "him. You didn't know she was…?"

"I didn't see her." There were so many people in the throng, so much movement, it would have been impossible to pick Ginna's face out of the crowd unless she had been near the platform. Despite her efforts to steer her sister onto a safe, comfortable path, the girl seemed determined to live at the epicenter of Hebenon's troubles. It was less surprising, less troublesome this time, to know that Ginna must again have made contact with Scarecrow. Better that than to be complicit in the salt protest and its riotous aftermath. "So, he's…Founder Kemway…?"

Choosing not to offer any revelations, Grainger shrugged and repeated, "Doctor Tamner's with him. I haven't talked to her. Thought you should. But Doctor…" He sighed. "I believe him. Don't think she's guilty of anything except being with him…but we need an account. Think she'll be more likely to talk to you when you're ready."

"Soon as they let me out of this." She gestured at the contraption around her leg and again tried to pull free of it. As some of the buckles and ties were beyond her reach, she could not get free.

Grainger nodded, understanding the frustration of limited mobility and the desire to return to duty and work left incomplete. "What happened with the girl? With Vanderwall?"

"She was with a dwarf…he was taking her to safety, last I saw. They were told to come up to the doctor. We lost Vanderwall in the crowd when the Founder popped up…but maybe we tagged him." Assuming the man sought medical treatment, did not have a medic in his pocket, Ilya hoped he would be easy to track. "I'll find him, sir. I can do it."

Neoma had said something about a dwarf. Tamner had not mentioned the girl, but the finding of Founder Kemway's body had been an overriding priority. It would not be surprising if the other matter had slipped his mind. Grainger would have to discuss it with him later, but for now, he clasped Ilya's shoulder as he struggled to his feet as if the effort pained him.

"We've got other things to worry about right now, Lieutenant. We'll discuss it when you're on duty. Not sending you back out there until you're steady." He cut off her protest with a shaking head. "There's things you can do to help in the meantime. Do what the doctors tell you and see me when you're released. Glad you're okay, Lieutenant. I can use your help."

He needed all of the allies he could get.

Ilya nodded too. Help in any way she could was better than being stuck in her flat, in a bed, waiting for the lights to come on, waiting for Ginna to come home.

❧*❧

The air in Jaron's flat was icy and stale, a disturbing reminder, as Scarecrow scanned the single-roomed living space for any hint that Jaron had been here before his shift for a change of clothes or something else he may have wanted or needed. After watching the main doors of the silent Archive for longer than he should have, unwilling, as Scarecrow, to approach the few shift-change archivists who went in or came out, to risk revealing a connection between them that might put Jaron at further risk, he had come here, frustrated and increasingly concerned about the younger man's welfare.

He could have been there, beyond the closed Archive door, but Scarecrow had not been able to pick him out from the sparse collection of archivists on duty.

Zara could hack the Hub and learn if he was on shift if she could get around the city's brownout conditions.

There were two other stops he intended to make before Vapors, and examining this empty flat was one of them. A glass sat in the sink, stained by the traces of Zaolei it had last contained. Flotsam of first aid equipment was scattered across the table where Jaron had tended to Rhyd's injuries, and the oxygen tank he had provided still waited beside the sofa with the hose of the attached breathing mask draped over the cushioned arm where Rhyd had left it. There was a partial bottle of Zaolei there too, another in the cupboard that he tucked into his pack for his use, certain Jaron would not mind. They had been here before and were not evidence that Jaron had been here after being ejected from Rhyd's flat by angry, unnecessary words.

He had meant those words at the time. In some ways, he still did. The further Jaron was from Scarecrow, the safer he was likely to be. It seemed the only way to drive Jaron out of his life had been through cruelty; Jaron would not listen to him otherwise. He was too damned stubborn for that.

Just as Rhyd was.

The anger with which that cruelty had been hurled, however, had been unfortunate and unnecessary, and he now regretted it. The nagging sense that the precaution had come too late to protect Jaron continued to linger and grow.

Masked eyes scanned the room, mechanical ears listened for evidence he knew he would not find. Absently, he picked up the crumpled blanket from the sofa and brought it to his face. Unable to feel the soft, worn threads through his glove, he was able to inhale the intermingled traces of his scents with Jaron's that had seeped into the weave, scents made more potent by the mask sensors and memory. Behind the tinted lenses, eyes that could not be seen by others squeezed shut. His hand shook and he let the blanket fall.

Despite his failure to find him, Jaron had to be at the Archive.

Or he had to be with Grainger.

Anything else would be unacceptable.

The last option, Scarecrow growled as he left the flat through the filt grate through which he had entered, was barely tolerable.

❧*❦

There was no one else to talk to.

Years of putting his career above everything else had robbed him of any meaningful, personal relationships. His short-lived marriage had been cut short by the hand of cancer, and since then, Grainger had made no effort to fill that particular void. Two of those closest to being friends now, one a colleague, another a subordinate, could not be deemed the sort he could open his innermost thoughts and feelings with. The third, even when her voice unexpectedly responded to the comm call he had almost decided not to make, was abruptly discounted as a safe outlet.

Zara Peru was a lot of things to him, but none of them included the sort of relationship that permitted the revelation of secrets. There were too many external entanglements for them to make intimate sharing wise.

He had not expected her to answer his call. He had hoped, but he had not expected.

"Oliver?" Zara repeated, her voice soft in its velvet drowsiness. Assuming she recognized his comm ID, with a fleeting hope that she had tagged him in her contact list, he swallowed and cleared his throat.

"Did I wake you?" She sounded awkwardly weary, distracted, with the sort of slurring tone that followed on the heels of sleep. As the memories of her lying languid and beautiful beside him, her hands on his skin, her breath feathering against his neck as she dozed, Oliver toyed with the edge of his sleeve and closed his eyes.

He wanted both to block those remembrances and savor them at the same time.

"No."

The hour was late in the Uppers, but in the perpetual night of the Levs, late and early rarely mattered. He admitted, upon hearing her response, that he had no idea what hours she kept. He should have considered that when making this call, but he had never inquired about her personal life to know.

"Have you heard from Jaron?"

It was not the reason for his call. Hearing her voice, the soothing salve of it spread over his agitation, was the only reason he needed. But Jaron was the excuse he used, an honest question that seemed logical and innocent.

Jaron was his friend. Had been something more, at least to Oliver. If he could talk to anyone about Haythem, it would have been Jaron. He had to settle for talking to Zara about Jaron instead.

Because Jaron was no longer here.

"Not in a few days," she admitted, her tone fishing his inquiry for its deeper meaning. "Should I tell him you're looking for him when I do? Want me to let you know when I see him?"

Grainger hesitated, opening his eyes to look from his desktop towards the footsteps passing in the corridor. "Yes…do that. Thank you. How are…?" Dawn was beginning to color the eastern horizon visible through the windowed dome and his stomach churned, confirming the arrival of daybreak. Again, he frowned and cleared his throat before finishing, "How are things there?"

"Cold."

He nodded. "Working on that. Solar array's down; there was a fire in the warehouse. We need parts; we need techs…"

"I'm not a…"

"Know you're not. Not asking you to. I only called to…"

What? Have someone to talk to? See if she was available, if she would welcome his company.

Admitting what felt like deficiencies now that he thought about it felt stupid and weak, so he cleared his throat again and straightened in his chair, the act offering his next words a center of clarity and weight that lifted the tint of defeat. "I'm worried about Jaron…and you."

"Doing alright, Oliver," Zara said gently, the purr in her voice making him shiver. "Better than some."

He nodded a second time, realizing she could not see him. "Glad to hear it. If you need anything…"

"No favors, Oliver; it can't be like that."

"No favors," he agreed. "Just an offer to help from a friend, if you'll take it."

He could imagine her face behind his closed lids, the play of emotion across it, the sound of her breathing as she considered the offer. Were they friends? Did they know each other well enough for that? He doubted it now that he said it, and felt foolish for suggesting it based on their limited personal interactions.

When she murmured, "Friends," as if in agreement with his offering, he let out a breath he had not realized he was holding.

"I'll let you know when I hear from Jaron."

"Thank you, Zara."

The connection was cut.

Grainger did not open his eyes.

She would look for Jaron. Probably see him first. But it would not stop Grainger from also looking. There was no reason, as the bugorra went about their duties, that they could not look for Jaron too.

Looking might give him a chance to see Zara again, to see with his own eyes that her claims of well-being were as true as she said. It would be a distraction from weights he did not want to carry.

❧*❦

He could detect two people in the flat.

He had been here before, on this same rooftop, in these same shadows, when his search for this same girl first brought him to the place where he now listened to the sounds of childish fury nearing the end of its storm. The male voice that responded with agitated muttering and a sharp, "Shut up!" was unfamiliar but not, as far as Scarecrow could determine, a cause for concern. One of the Mam's hangers-on pressed into the duty of child-watching while she tended to some errand and the nanny, likewise, was elsewhere engaged.

Ulynda screeched back at him, rage without words, the sort of helpless anger Rhyd was personally familiar with. After Venn's Vanishing, before the birth of Scarecrow, that anger, and its accompanying despair, was all Rhyd had known. Something struck the wall of her room, thrown from inside to splinter into crackling shards that tinkled across the floor and rolled with a skittering sound.

He frowned. While he did not know if the man inside would harm the child, he knew her mother, now clacking across the grated walk in her hard-soled shoes with quick, perturbed steps, was not above lashing out for that insolent breakage. The woman paused with her hand on the latch, her tense shoulders suggesting that the noise inside her home was something she had little patience or desire to face, but she stubbornly slipped the passcard through the lock and pushed the door open.

Ulynda's raw-throated tirade paused at the sound of the door opening. Neoma stepped inside and it closed behind her. Again,

Ulynda threw something, something soft that struck with impotent outrage and rattled the bedroom handle.

Attempting to ignore the sound, Neoma huffed and muttered, "Permission to be here doesn't include the invitation to help yourself to my…"

"You try listening to that for hours," the man inside with her spat. "Didn't sign up to be…"

"You signed up for whatever I require, Mr. Netzer, or you're free to leave." The muffled sound of her arms pulling free of her coat and then the steady drip, drip of the damp pinging in the drip grate when she hung it up, followed.

Mr. Netzer. Someone Skelter knew. Someone from the Core. A member, he had said, of the Spades.

Scarecrow cocked his head and frowned.

"Seems I did you a favor," Netzer snarked back. "You owe me…"

"I'd say we're even. You dried out…waited out the brako…now I'm home. You can go. I don't need you here." He had served his purpose, briefly taking the edge off the blossom of her panic and remaining with Ulynda during the hours Neoma spent trying to coordinate her supporters. Before that, there had been Hebbies and ticks and a modicum of protection from Vanderwall in exchange for the prods he had created. Neither owed the other anything. She would prefer his irritating, rodent-like presence to go somewhere far away.

Hers were the only footsteps Scarecrow heard, movement to and fro inside the flat, setting her handbag on the table beside the sofa, turning down the volume of the Echo, and crossing the room. Liquid was poured from one container into another, bottle to glass, and then the bottle was returned to its tray. Ulynda pounded her door with both fists, but the sound was slowing, exhaustion eroding her ability to continue to express her anger, anger her mother ignored. Anger that covered something Scarecrow understood very well.

Fear.

Ulynda should not be here. Enoch should have taken her Up, to safety, though it had not been his choice to fail. The task had been taken out of his hands. Now the girl, an important political pawn, was home again.

The sofa creaked under the weight of someone sitting on it.

"You might still need me," Netzer grunted in a smirking tone that hinted that any such need, despite his verbal assertion as the refilling of Neoma's glass put her still at the bar, was primarily his.

❧*❦

"You okay?"

Ginna, having refused to answer questions after being deposited in this unheated, unlit holding room, dark except for a sliver of white that bled beneath the unevenly set door, had not gotten up for anyone who had come to check on her. She refused to move from the corner of the bench where she huddled, knees drawn to her chin to conserve body heat, staring at the shadow faces as she waited for anyone familiar to arrive. Founder Kemway's face was the only one she saw.

For her sister, however, when the limping woman with the wrapped arm and bandaged head shuffled into the room, Ginna made the effort to rise, give her an uncharacteristic embrace, and shoulder her weight enough to ease her onto the hemplastic bench.

The chains that supported the outer corners and allowed the bench to fold flat against the wall when it was not in use rattled when Ilya sank onto it and Ginna returned to her corner.

"It's nothing," Ilya replied, the minor annoyance of not being the first to voice that question set aside in favor of visually examining her sister in the light of the alglantern she placed on the table.

"And I'm here on retreat," Ginna snorted. "I know you were there."

"And I know you were with the Founder." Ginna looked away. Ilya continued, "What happened?"

"You don't know?" She expected that, by now, everyone in Hebenon must know the truth.

"Clinic just sprung me. Captain said you were here, that you were with him…but that's all he said. What happened? Why'd they bring you in?"

The younger woman sighed and leaned forward, her elbows on her knees as she focused on the finger of light from outside. Her clothes were stained from exposure to the Levs' perpetual dampness, but they were not torn and she did not look to have been part of the protest though she imagined Ilya believed she had been.

"Came by myself…they want to be sure I didn't kill him…"

"Scarecrow?"

"Like we could do that," Ginna huffed with an incredulous side-eyed glance.

"Founder Kemway's…" Ilya swallowed hard. The captain's peculiar word choice and demeanor made sense.

"I saw him on the stage with you…I intercepted them when Scarecrow helped him down and…I got them to a safe place. He was bleeding bad. I stayed with him while Scarecrow…until he…called Colyx to stay with me until…I didn't want to be alone there if the brako…and then Doctor Tamner came and we helped take him up."

Only then did she cast a desperate glance at her sister and mutter defensively, "I didn't do it. Didn't shoot anyone. Never have. And they didn't either. Neither one of them."

Colyx. And Scarecrow.

Ilya groaned and rubbed her face, "I know." That much, the innocence of those two people, she had witnessed with her own eyes. She had heard the poppers. She had seen the blood on the Founder's chest, on Scarecrow's glove.

"He didn't hurt you? What did he do? Where did he go?"

"To help…to stop the brako…same as he always does. Of course he didn't hurt me. That's not who he is."

It was not the first interaction between her sister and Scarecrow but the two finding each other in the middle of a riot, him leaving the Founder in Ginna's care while he pursued justice, pursued Vanderwall, was an unexpected fluke. Given the circumstances, there might have been few other options. He could not have remained there to be found out while waiting for the doctor's arrival. He could not have prevented the Founder from dying and stopping Vanderwall had been too important to set aside. He had at least had the respect to make sure the Founder did not die alone.

"You don't know that," Ilya muttered before she could stop herself. "He's dangerous." He had fought with her, had fought for her, and they had pursued and confronted Vanderwall together. He had exposed himself to the civilian crowd, to the brako, and the bugorra, instead of hiding in the shadows as he was known to do, all to protect Founder Kemway. He had removed the Founder from further threats and had made sure he did not die alone.

He had probably been the one to summon Doctor Tamner.

Yes, his methods remained questionable and fierce, his identity and actions suspect, but even as she uttered those words, Ilya wondered again if she had misjudged Hebenon's elusive protector.

He was, however, still a dangerous man. The number of injured Crows and brako left in his wake attested to that.

"No more dangerous than you. Less dangerous than the brako."

Sighing at an argument she could not contest, she clasped Ginna's hand, a sisterly gesture she had not offered in too many years, and chose not to comment or argue. Entwining her fingers through Ginna's with an affectionate squeeze, she said instead, "I'll get you out of here, get you home."

"Colyx too? He was only with me 'cause I'd called him to come."

"Colyx too." She did not know the name, assumed it belonged to one of the Spinks, some older streeter her officers had deigned to detain rather than release. "You'll go home. Tell me you'll go home. No more riots."

"No more riots," Ginna agreed. Her part in this one had been negligible, more accidental than intentional, and she had withdrawn before the worst of it ensued, but she had seen enough blood.

She did not, however, promise to go home. Or stay there.

Ilya recognized the omission but chose not to press the matter. Her sister had watched a man die. Had watched the Founder die. If she chose to retreat to the company of friends instead of sitting alone in their shared home as Ilya stretched her duties from finding a kidnapper to finding an assassin, the compromise seemed to be a fair one.

At least Ginna was safe.

❧*❧

He had never been here before. The opportunity had been there since his emergence from the Core, but despite Otta's coaxing and Skelter's encouragement, Colyx had resisted the unknown. His refusal to use the lev-chair had been an excuse. His braced legs had been another. His new position as a bouncer for Vapors had been a compelling third. But each had been just that, excuses, used to mask his discomfort about confronting this particular unknown.

Like everyone else, Colyx had grown up believing Outside was poison and dangerous, that going there was inviting an immediate, agonizing death to anyone other than the parah who lived there. Once sentenced to the Core as a much younger man, he had given Outside no thought. He had expected to die in that place, confined in a murky, underground mining prison that rarely gave up its captives.

Skelter had changed that. Skelter had set him free at the cost of the full use of his legs. A small sacrifice that cemented his faith in the redhead, but that faith had not been enough, when prompted, to draw Colyx Up and Outside.

The whispers of the Igraci outside of Vapors, however, their repeatedly intensifying claims of the future failure of Hebanthe Falls, had proven too tempting of a lure.

He could see the truth of their claims, even if others failed to do so. The city he had been reborn into was not the city he had left. The one he passed through now was in a state of disordered decay, a world that could never last. If his daughter, his grandchild, were to survive and thrive, they could not do so within the city in the Five Falls.

Colyx understood that he could not encourage them, compel them, out into a world he refused to see. He had to know if Outside was the wonder that Skelter, Otta, the Igraci, and others claimed it to be before he tried to push his family into it.

Released from the cell where he had been held and questioned only by the woman he knew to be Ginna's bugorra sister, finding himself in an Upper corridor he had only passed through when arrested before being sentenced to the Core, he glanced up and down the glaring white path illuminated by the glow of emergency lighting. People passed, dressed in the pressed, colorful fashions of the city's elite, looking at him with arrogance, contempt, or fear, but not speaking to him or pointing him to the nearest exit when he asked. This was not the first time he had been shunned by people of a higher station. He was not welcome here, their disdain enough to prevent anyone from helping him find his way out.

On the off chance that following someone would guide him to where he needed to go, he followed a pair of men chatting in animated voices as they passed the alcove where he leaned against the wall, shifting from one aching leg to the other as he contemplated his options. He could not read the signs on the walls as he had never learned how, but the arrows he noted made a clear path to follow after being turned this way and that, blocked from one set of doors by buggers and redirected from another by uniformed workers monitoring the Factory West One entrance. Eventually, his limping persistence and the path of the pair he trudged behind brought him to a community lounge filled with plush gray sofas, hard backless benches of scrolled hemp wire fashioned into floral patterns, and plain-fashioned high stools at tall tables meant for the communal sharing of work or meals or the games of the bored. There were people here, some reading T1 Echoes, some joined in muted, murmuring conversations, some engrossed in animated debates about the dilemmas facing Hebanthe Falls. A few heads turned to glance at him when he passed through the broad open arches but no one spoke to him. No one prevented him from entering.

No one asked why he was there or questioned his belonging.

It was brighter in this room than anywhere Colyx had ever been, lit not by artificial neon and alglamps but by the warm pink and amber glow of the vista beyond the windows. Once covered with a closed hemplastic shell and sheets of metal for the purported protection of Hebenon's residents, layered with a heavy cloth upon which digital dioramas had been continuously projected for the entertainment of those in the Uppers. The windows were now stripped bare to the glass so that everyone could witness the amazement of Outside.

Lured to the window where he pressed his big, scarred hand to the cold glass, Colyx joined others to witness the new joy of the rising dawn. The window faced the sea, with the parah village he had heard about on the distant left and nothing but water and the edges of the cliffs that constrained the river in place before him. The pulse of the surf he could not hear was soothing, the tiny white crests forming on its surface and then melting away as the tide kissed the shore he could not see. The colors of dawn chased the darkness west towards the top of the window's face and brought a gradually deepening blue at the edge of the horizon where the sea appeared to end.

Colyx had seen pictures. None of them compared to this.

"And we can go out to see it," he murmured incredulously.

"Before they locked the cazzing doors," snorted another man, one of the two he had followed here, with calloused hands and squinting eyes. "Now we're trapped again."

"Only 'til the power's back," said his companion, a smaller man with a bald head and sagging, wrinkled features.

"That's an excuse. They know they can't control us if we're out there and not here."

The smaller man chuckled, "Can't control most of us in here either, if you haven't noticed."

The bigger man guffawed and crossed his arms, refusing to be baited into a debate it seemed they had shared before.

Colyx was no longer listening. He was planning. He, Otta, and everyone they loved would never be trapped again. Not in the Core, not in a dying city. Not anywhere. He would get them out into that amazing world and set them free. Whatever it took to make it happen would be worth it.

❧*❧

He entered Vapors through the rear, through the shafts and vents he knew intimately, passing places where regular clothing was stashed to permit him to blend in with customers in a way that Scarecrow could not. This morning, Vapors was emptier than he had ever seen it, occupied only by the woman sweeping the floors of the debris left when the previous guests departed.

That had been hours ago, when the power had been cut and the free food and drinks ceased to flow. The counter, the glasses behind it, the dance floor, and all the tables and chairs had already been cleaned to pristine newness, the floors left until last. He could hear movement in the kitchen but could not see who was there, heard the sloshing of sink water and the clatter of items within it; since Maemi was untroubled by the sound, Rhyd assumed some other member of her staff was there.

Not alone at all. He was mildly surprised she had not waited to tend to clean up when the fullness of light returned, but this unexpected downtime was likely the best opportunity for a deep-clean Vapors had not had in too long.

"Wondered when you'd turn up," the dark-skinned woman said as warmly as her weariness and the stress of the night allowed. "Didn't have a hand in this did you?" She cocked her head towards the absent glow the lamps usually provided.

He shook his head no. "Was chasing down Vanderwall." With no customers on hand to overhear him and the person in the kitchen too far away, Rhyd did not feel the need for more secrecy than the softness of his muted voice.

"Get him?"

"Almost." He leaned against the edge of the bar and rubbed his sore shoulder.

"Soon," she encouraged. "Don't expect curlers today."

"I don't…but I could use a bottle if you've got one." He had dropped off the bottle taken from Jaron's flat in his own before coming here, but he intended to save that for later.

"Help yourself."

"Thanks." He circled the counter, examined the thin collection beneath it, found a single bottle of his favorite kept on hand for him, and selected a glass from the rack. With the lifts barely operable, if the power was not restored soon, Vapors and other vindis would find it too difficult to remain open if they could not restock. Maemi had a storeroom elsewhere, and he assumed she kept additional supplies there too, but that would not last indefinitely.

"All good here?" he asked as he cracked the bottle top.

"Good as can be. Heard about the protests and the Founder's speech."

"It was something," Rhyd agreed, revealing that he had been there when it happened without admitting it. "Things are gonna get ugly."

"You mean uglier?"

Rhyd nodded. "Zar?"

"With Tox, last I knew. Came down for a spell and left again. Hasn't come back through but I haven't heard anything from upstairs. Saw Skelter leaving a while ago. Looked okay. Enoch's not been by, but I imagine he's okay too."

"Good." If Zara were with Tox, he could check in with both women at once before resuming the hunt for Vanderwall and Jaron. "Tell Enoch I'm looking for him if he comes by…and put this on my account when the power's up. And Maemi?" He closed the bottle after draining the glass and tucked it back under the bar. "Keep your head down. Brako are thick out there…and I can't be everywhere at once."

She smiled, an expression both sympathetic and understanding, and said, "Colyx will be back soon, Jonner too. I'm good here. You stay safe, okay? Wanna see you back here by day's end, understand?"

Safe was relative and careful was subjective. There were things Rhyd needed to do, including being back on shift within a few hours. He would be safe enough until that shift ended. After that, he could make no promises to anyone.

❧Hyperion's Bier❦

❧Chapter 11❧

There was water, brought in sips on a soaked-through sponge, held to his lips long enough for him to suck the lukewarm metallic-tasting nectar past tongue and lips that the moisture was unable to satiate. He tried to resist, convinced he was being poisoned, but his body's needs demanded appeasement and he drank against his will. It was not enough to dull the thirst-swelling in his mouth, not enough to ease the cracking of his lips nor enough to ease the constant twisting in his belly that told him he had been without food for too long in this dank room.

How long it had been he could not gauge. There was only hunger and the periodic opening and closing of the door that brought the water and the wafting aromas of fish waste and decomposition. In the rational corners of his thoughts that fought to latch on to coherency, that fought against succumbing to surrender, he guessed that those smells put him on Lev 1 or 2. That was a big enough area, filled with twisting streets and stairways, filled with the rushing tumble of the river and the Five Falls and the clang and clatter of production those Levs were home to. The smells were not enough to lend support to the likelihood that he might eventually be found and taken from this place, taken home and away from his body's aches.

The scents only meant that, when his captors were done with him, he could be easily disposed of in the river to eventually be dredged when the nets were cleaned, picked clean by river denizens that would leave nothing but bones to find.

The last time, or maybe more than one time, that the door opened, his cotton-stuffed hearing noted the lack of industrial sounds. Not silence, as life in Hebenon was never that, but less filled with the manmade clatter of machinery and the systems that kept the city from collapsing upon itself in decay. When the door closed, he realized that the light on the corner of a building he could barely see, through eyes now accustomed to his prison's blackness, was also dark.

He chalked up both peculiarities to his weakening condition and his growing despair.

Time passed. His stomach churned as though it would devour itself. The room grew more stagnant, burning with the stench of his filth, his sweat, his fear…until the door opened again and the hulking shadow that entered growled in familiar disgust.

"Get some air in here," the gruff shadow-voice muttered.

"Isn't any," muttered a smaller shadow that lingered in the doorway and refused to enter as the bigger form grasped Jaron's chin and tilted his head to look into his face.

"And get this man more water!" He did not accept excuses. He expected results. His people had been given instructions, and it appeared they had not been followed. From the sunken hollow of his cheeks and swollen lips, it was clear this man had not been provided the water Vanderwall had demanded. Even if they had to illegally tap into whatever sources continued to offer water and power throughout the city, he expected his people to make it happen.

He wanted this prisoner taken care of. He would be no good to them dead…at least not yet.

Shuttering nervously, the second speaker chattered, "Yes, boss," before hurrying away, rattling the walkway in his haste, leaving his cohort to watch Vanderwall's back.

"Haven't told me why you did it," Vanderwall snorted, his tone and demeanor muffled by the cloth covering his mouth and nose in place of the Crow mask he typically wore, less rough and agitated than before as he released Jaron's chin so that his head dropped heavily against his chest.

Unable to reply without the speecher, the diodes at his temple failing to blink with the electronic translation of thought to audible words, Jaron only groaned.

Vanderwall tipped the man's head to the side to study the inoperable speecher, his expression behind the mask unreadable.

"You killed him, yes? Vanderwall?"

Jaron shuddered in his chains, a movement that shot searing pain through his upraised arms, into his shoulders, and down his spine.

Brako.

They were never going to let him go.

Rhyd would never find him before he died.

"Scarecrow put you up to it? Bugorra?"

Jaron's mouth moved as though trying to form words, but his head neither nodded in agreement nor shook in denial. Vanderwall circled him once, quiet as though collecting his thoughts or hoping to intimidate his captive, perhaps giving Jaron the time to consider the question and the likely results of capitulation or refusal to cooperate.

"Saw you on the SCAMs," the man muttered when he was again in front of his prisoner. "Denying it isn't gonna help. You know him. You did it for him. Where is he? Where can I find Scarecrow?"

It was not a yes or no question, thus not one the mute man could answer, but Vanderwall did not expect an answer. The man had not yet reached the breaking point. He stepped back, again contemplating whether spending the resources to repair the speecher would be worthwhile, since eventually the man would be disposed of, and then appeared to make his choice as he backstepped to the door. "You'll tell me what I need to know…or you won't. Won't matter. He'll come for you…for me…in time. You'll pay for the life you took…with the one I want. Don't think you won't."

Again, the chains rattled.

The door closed.

Jaron gave a weak, impotent cry past his swollen tongue into the darkness, the sound more of a breathy moan than a scream. He doubted Vanderwall, or anyone else, could hear him.

❧Chapter 12❧

The chip in Zara's hand, encrypted before Tox installed it in his body armor, took time to open and took even longer to download the collection of data files accumulated since Rhyd had last taken the time to purge it. Sometimes as Scarecrow, after the Coup when he had broken through the Uppers to Outside, the ICD connection was kept open to automatically dump its images into the database Zara had created. The record was meant to keep track of where he was, what he was doing, and who he encountered during each outing into the streets in the hopes that that data would permit him to triangulate Vanderwall's whereabouts.

It was also meant to be a safeguard for the inevitable day that Scarecrow fell. They both knew it, but neither admitted that out loud.

Most of the data never went anywhere and was never used for more than record keeping, redundant information he sometimes viewed with the intent of improving his fighting skills or studying his opponents' styles.

Most often, Rhyd did not bother to connect the link, to turn it on, specifically because he did not want a record of his activities that might be used against him, or those he cared about, if Zara's database was ever hacked.

This time, he was grateful he had the foresight to turn the recording on when he stepped into the streets.

"That's him."

Zara had synced the timestamp on his data records with that of the Hub and SCAM data that captured Kemway's emergence from the crowd onto the platform and Scarecrow's appearance with him. Little by little, she stepped the footage back until that one face appeared full frame, blurry but overall recognizable.

"Vanderwall?" Tox leaned sideways to get a closer look, setting aside her design project to witness the revelation that no one in Hebenon had yet been able to make.

Rhyd nodded. Though he was not the Vanderwall Rhyd had fought before, though he fought with a different style and hand, he had a similar physique and wore the yellow armband attributed to the leader of the brako.

"Thought he was dead," Zara murmured as her fingers flew over the Echo panel to clean the image of the pixelated interference inherent to Scarecrow's body cam.

"A title maybe…someone new taking his place. But that's him." Rhyd did not need to be closer to study the image. He remembered that face. He was certain of his assessment.

"Once I get this clean, I'll run it through the Archives and the Hub and find a match." Not every citizen had a Hub file, but most did. Unless Vanderwall was one of the minorities who had fallen through the cracks, the search was a place to start…so long as there was enough electricity to keep the Hub and Archive databases stable enough to allow access.

"I want his name."

"We should give it to the bugorra," Zara scolded gently, although delivering it to Rhyd first was a given. He had risked his life to get this shot. He deserved the opportunity to see this fight to the end. "Or at least to Doctor Tamner for the Nau to…"

"So they can botch a takedown?" Rhyd snorted and narrowed his gaze at the work Tox's hands were engaged in. He did not have enough fingers and toes to count the number of failures he had witnessed, nor the number of them he had not.

The bugorra were better at keeping the city safe under Grainger's leadership than the Crows had been under the Founder's, but in Rhyd's eyes, the difference was negligible.

"So you've got backup. I know this is…that you want…but you can't take on all of the brako alone…" Even though that was precisely what he felt he had been doing since the brako's rise to power.

"Don't need to take them all…just him." Without looking at her, Rhyd put a hand on Zara's shoulder to ease her fears. "Besides…with all this…think they've got their hands full…"

"With the grid? With Kemway?" Rhyd avoided Tox's gaze as well and did not answer the questions. "Saw you got him out of the riot. Everyone in Hebenon saw it…they've seen you now. What happened?" When he silently shook his head, she frowned and lay down the micro-welder. "Rhyd?"

"Called Tamner to come for him," was the evasive reply before he again squeezed Zara's shoulder and changed the subject. "Need you to break the Archives…make sure Jaron's on shift where he's supposed to be."

Zara's fingers stopped moving. "He didn't…?"

There was a strained sound in her voice that led to a tightening of the sour ball in Rhyd's belly that had yet to dissipate. "Know it's down…but there's people on shift, waiting for the grid to come on. Told him to go up, where it's safer…but I dunno…I don't think he…anywhere's safer than down here…"

He choked on his failed words as if the unfinished thought was too painful to complete. Having spoken to Jaron previously, she understood that something had happened between the two men, but she did not know the details. She did not need to.

Having spoken with Oliver as well, she knew Jaron had not taken Rhyd's advice.

"Didn't go up," she murmured, the corner of her eye twitching involuntarily. It had been hours since she had seen Jaron, more than a day since he had left her flat.

"How'd you…?"

"Just know." Rhyd was a smart enough man to figure out how she might know that, so she chose not to elaborate and voice a potentially incriminating truth. "You check his…?"

"His flat's empty. Mine too. Could be pulling a double…that's why you need to…" Jaron might even be pulling a triple shift if he was determined to avoid Rhyd and the brako-teeming streets. Some businesses had facilities that allowed long-shift workers to sleep on-site. Rhyd had done it numerous times in his years at the Shed. The only ways he would know if Jaron was there would be for Zara to crack the Archive records or for him to go inside and ask.

He was not going to do that. He was not going to make a fool of himself with unnecessary expressed worry or risk Jaron's life by displaying a relationship between them. It was better, easier, for Zara to look into it.

"I'll check," she said.

Her promise allowed his shoulders to relax and his hand to drop. "Send me what you get soon as you have it. And if you see Enoch, tell him Ulynda's home…and Netzer's there with her."

"The guy Skelter's…?"

"Assume so. Didn't get a first name. Don't know how he's connected to the Mam, but Skelter should know…Enoch too."

"We'll pass it on," Zara promised.

"Both of them," corrected Tox, "long as you're careful out there."

Retreating to the back of the room where the filt grate lay on the floor and the shaft led into the dark, Rhyd grunted.

❧*❧

"Isn't gonna be a better time," Jonner said ardently to the thin woman with bangs cut straight across her forehead in a look of exotic high-fashion. Eido was a difficult woman to track down, for good reason since the protest had degenerated into a riot. The shift might not have been her doing but there had been enough Igraci present that those looking to place blame were happy to use them as the instigators.

After hours of searching, of questioning one Igraci agent after another, he was finally able to crash this meeting uninvited and wheedle his way into a semi-private conversation with her.

As he spoke, he pointed to those beyond the windowed interior door, people leaning against walls with crossed arms and stern expressions or who paced the room speaking in animated voices as they gesticulated to punctuate the arguments they were making.

"They know it; you know it. We can proselytize. We can preach. We can plead. Or we can turn this accident into a boon…"

"Who said there's been an accident?" Eido's voice was evasively soft and coy.

Jonner's lips pursed before he spoke again. "The goal's to get out, not trap us inside." If the Igraci had a hand in the city's loss of power, or the plan to close the doors to Outside, Jonner had not been privy to either plan. He was new to the Players. Not everything Eido did or arranged was for him to know, regardless of his efforts and desire to prove himself vital to the Igraci's work. She had other members at her disposal, other actions to set into play, some of which had likely been planted before Jonner met her. He was but a small part of a greater whole. He would never know everything she intended to accomplish.

"It won't last."

He huffed. "You don't know that. With the power cut, the doors are closed until the Nau decides to open them…or someone inside or out forces them open."

She smiled softly. "You worry too much."

Despite that smile, he thought she looked worried too, based on the furrowed V that creased the bridge of her nose. If she was worried, however, she did not put her concerns into words.

"Get me what I need. I can do this. I'll scope out the best place, make it look natural. Once it's done, Hebanthe Falls'll be the last place anyone'll want to be. They'll see we're right…that you're right…and we get everyone free of this miserable prison."

Eido crossed her arms and stared at him long enough to prompt him to nervously turn his steady gaze towards an unexpected exclamation of outrage in the other room that resulted in one man punching another in the chest and knocking him off his feet. Jonner began to open the door, intending to break up the impending fight; people were already picking sides in the conflict. Eido stopped him with a light clearing of her throat that cut across his focus like a razor-thin blade.

"Make sure it'll work. Promise me. Give me a list…and I'll see what I can get."

He nodded earnestly. "It'll work. No way it won't." Maybe not all at once, but the cascading effect of his plan, once initiated, would have the effect the Igraci hoped for. He knew what was needed, including getting past the closed city doors, and Eido, having the resource of people throughout the Levs, could get those things for him. "I swear it will."

He chose to believe she would make this happen too. It was in her best interest that he succeeded.

❧*❧

"You're the kaheao, righta?"

Skelter blinked at the disheveled woman who caught hold of his arm as he pushed through the collection of people trying to get closer to a warming barrel a trio of herpa had set up at the intersection nearest Vapors. The reduction of electricity meant that waste disposal had dropped down the rung of immediate necessities because moving debris without the utilization of the lifts was too difficult. Numerous enterprising folks had placed burn barrels throughout the Levs to collect what needed to be disposed of, and some of what should have been recycled, to provide warmth to those who needed it. The barrels also provided light at the intersections where they burned, making travel throughout the Levs less precarious.

Skelter silently scolded himself for not being the first to come up with that idea. The few ticks he might have made from those who could afford the purchase of barrels would have been useful in helping someone else.

"A kaheao," he corrected, looking at the nearly toothless woman whose clothes smelled of the remnants of hemp handling that went into the creation of hemp cigs. The fingers hooked around his arm were stained yellow-brown by the processed juices and chemicals involved, and fringes of wiry, unkempt gray hair poked out beneath the elastic edges of the water-repellant rain cap she had snugged down over her ears.

He was used to strangers stopping him, seeking his help. Before the Core, there had been a certain segment of the population who had known him on sight, who had known what he could do for them. The woman who fell into step beside him as he continued past the intersection, however, was not one of them.

"Word is you can find anything…"

"For a price," he reminded her, despite knowing that she had little with which to pay. Sometimes his price was only the promise of future information. Sometimes it was ticks or an exchange of goods or favors. Sometimes he settled for a cup of hot algtea from a vindi if the client was amenable.

As chilled as he felt today as he pulled the front of his coat closed to ward off the misty damp, he would settle for algtea if there was any vindi with enough power to heat water.

She stopped walking, forcing him to do the same with her unrelenting hold on his arm. From the folds of her sack-like poncho, she produced a cig box that she unsealed and opened long enough to reveal the raw, unprocessed hemp crumbles ready for rolling.

Raw product was rare. Skelter nodded, accepting a negotiation for his help. "Know a few who'd appreciate that," he said, not asking how she'd come by it. Maybe it was her cut of production. Maybe she skimmed when she could to pay for favors or goods she did not have enough ticks to acquire. "What do you need?"

"Not what…who. It's a…need you to find my husband."

He withdrew his arm from her hand without taking the crumbles. "Not in the bounty business…"

"No bounty. He's been gone too long…without his medis…it's not like him to go without 'em for more than a day or two…"

"Make a report to…"

She, too, shook her head, a more violent, determined gesture than his had been. "Think the buggers took him, you know, like they used to. He always said they'd start taking people again…they always do." After an anxious glance to both sides as if expecting to be overheard, she continued, "Think he saw something, maybe did something they…he's a good man, but times have been hard since the Coup. He's always…afraid he's…I just know somethin's happened. Not like him to just…go. Not like him…"

"Might he have gone Outside before they closed the doors?"

Again, she shook her head. "He'd never…no…he wouldn't do that. Always said we would one day…but he wouldn't without me. Heard you knew someone who could help, someone who can find him…bring him home."

Skelter sucked in his breath between his teeth. Undoubtedly, whatever rumor she had heard connected him to Scarecrow. People had seen the fight he had been in, when Scarecrow had swooped in to protect him and Jaron. Maybe that bit of deleted SCAM footage after the Core escape, when Vanderwall had fallen, had been used to connect them. Or maybe people assumed a man like Skelter knew everyone of import in the Levs, Scarecrow included.

None of those assessments would be entirely wrong.

"Can't make promises," he muttered, pushing her hand and the box it contained towards her with gentle politeness. "Hold onto this for now. If I can…how do I find you?"

"Lev 3 hemper. Know it?"

He nodded. There were two hempers. One generated cigs and a variety of paper products. The other generated creams, lotions, pills, hemp herbal, and oil extracts. He could have guessed which one was her place of employment but he was not in the business of guessing.

Ballard would not want guesswork either.

"Name?"

"Wiffy Belder."

"Hold tight for a few days; I'll see what can be done. His name?"

She shook her head, her eyes narrowed, her lips stretched thin and tight. "Not 'til you say you can find him."

"Can't find someone without a face or a name."

"I'll give it to him if he helps; no one else. Not before. Everyone knows he's good for it. Everyone knows he can help. I trust him."

Skelter sighed and scanned the dim streets and alleys around them. "See what I can do, like I said. No promises. If he can't help you…I will. Wait for me to come to you; don't come looking for me again. I'll be in touch soon as I know something." He did not want to put her at risk. He had her name. In looking for her husband, maybe her name would be enough to work with.

"You're a saint. Thank you."

Skelter could not help himself. He laughed.

"Just a man doin' a job," he countered, pleased that his joviality put Wiffy more at ease. She nodded with a wan, weary, but sincere smile of gratitude and peeled away towards the nearest stairs without looking back. The city shift whistle whined. Routine continued; even though most production had ceased, the whistles still screeched as if nothing had changed.

Skelter stared up at the nearest horn atop its metal post and pondered what step to take first to help Wiffy find her husband.

❧*❧

Having expressed their annoyance at yet another meeting when there had not yet been time to generate a satisfactory resolution to any of the previously discussed issues, the Nau ceased their muttering grumbles with Tamner's announcement, words that supplanted the discontent of inconvenience with shocked, disbelieving silence.

"He is…" started Delora, wiping tears from her eyes with one hand while tucking strands of silver hair behind her ear with the other. Of those in the room, she was one of four to have known Haythem Kemway personally, one of those who had served the Founder's rule all of her adult life. Fahti's expression, while sorrowful, was almost blank, and Nunn's was pinched into a scowl of disapproval.

"I have him in stasis; I've done the autopsy," Tamner explained with a miserable sigh. "The reports are accurate. He was assassinated."

"We still don't know who abducted him from…" began Nunn.

"What does it matter now?" hissed Pearl through her tears, cutting his angry assertion short. "He's gone. How are we supposed to…?"

Fahti snorted, a sound both haughty and morose, and answered the question she presumed was being asked. "Same as we have been. We don't need a Founder to…"

"It matters if the assassin was the kidnappers," growled Nunn as Lydon said, "Hebenon's always had a Founder to…"

"Not since the Coup," Caminda reminded him.

Woster shook his head, his expression pensive and thoughtful as he rubbed his cheek absently. "We had a Founder through all of that. He just wasn't here to…"

"Does that make Mam…?"

"She's only a Kemway by marriage," Fahti replied to Caminda with a glint of disdain in her eyes and voice.

"The girl then? She's the only Kemway left."

Woster patted his brother on the back. "We don't need a Founder."

"Probably best we've moved past that," agreed Stace, smoothing his mustache and toying with his Echo stylus with his other hand.

"We could put it up to vote," Lydon offered.

"Can you imagine the chaos?" Nunn was barely tolerant of the vote that had filled many of the seats in this conference room, barely respected those the city had selected to lead by popular election. "There's upheaval as it is. We'll end up with this Vanderwall character in the Founder's chair."

"Or Scarecrow," offered Warren in a tone that suggested he was not averse to the idea of the protective vigi taking control of Hebenon.

Imagining what Rhyd would have to say about that suggestion, Tamner cleared his throat. "We should start by making this public…interring the dead…"

"Maybe," Delora suggested as the other heads around the table bobbed their reluctant agreement to Tamner's priorities, "we should appoint you."

Choking on his breath, Tamner shook his head. "I'm not Founder material…"

"You're the one the parah respect…the people inside too. We'll have to keep working with them, and you've got the disposition for it," Stace said.

"Doctor's right." The layers of distaste in Nunn's voice were ones Tamner and the others did not want to dig too deeply through. "There's ceremony, protocol, respect for the dead. Can't let rumor infect the chaos. We draft a statement, assign a day of mourning…"

"It'll take people's minds off their suffering for a short time," agreed Woster.

"Temporary salve, but better than nothing." Lydon bobbed his head. "We don't let Kenneth and Soleia break this; it'll be sensationalized out of proportion. People need details, the truth, not glamorized rumor and speculation. This has to come from us."

"They don't need details; that's not part of the truth. It's gruesome and invasive," Fahti protested, though she did not have the details of the Founder's demise on which to base that opinion. "They only need to know he's gone."

"Captain Grainger should do it," Nunn grunted.

Heads around the room shook in disagreement.

"Delora should," Caminda offered with warm sympathy. "You knew him best…you were his friend. He'd want it to be you."

"Me?" the older woman squeaked.

"You are more personable than the captain," agreed Pearl.

"Or most of us," Stace added with a half-smirking smile.

"Who's going to tell Neoma…before this goes public?"

No one answered Fahti's question. Gazes swept the room, moving from one person to the next as if seeking a volunteer, a confirmation of something they each understood and knew without saying. Eventually, their roving gazes settled on the man they had each grown, some begrudgingly, to respect even though he was not one of their elected number. He was not Nau but he was the best man for the duty. The only man the parah respected. The only one Mam Kemway was unlikely to dissect with her anger.

Reluctantly, Tamner nodded. It had to be him. There was no one better.

❧Chapter 13❧

Tamner stood with his back against the closed door, his face tipped into the mist of the Five Falls, eyes closed, listening to the glass shattering against the barrier behind him, a sound that broke the silent tension he had just walked out on. He had not seen Ulynda, only Neoma, the nanny, and a thin, suspect-looking fellow he vaguely recognized but could not identify. There had been a flash of panic on the stranger's face when the news was delivered, but given the company he was keeping, that discomfort was well-warranted. Neoma's face was stoic and blank as she nodded, and ushered the doctor out of the flat without any discussion or questions about how or where. She had closed the door on him as if he had done no more than deliver takeaway.

The veneer of calm had not lasted.

The fear and outrage that replaced it met Tamner's expectations and he was oddly grateful that she had waited until he was gone to release the tirade.

"Damn him!" Neoma ignored the shattering of the carafe, of the mess it made, and the man who cowered away from the wine-filled projectile that hurled past his head. Nanny stood at the kitchen arch, wringing her hands, looking at yet another spread of wine and broken glass, unsure if there were more carafes or wine to replenish the dwindling supply. Her pale blue gaze shifted to the child who opened the bedroom door with the closing of the main one. Ulynda stared at her mother with a morose look of victory in the silence that followed the shattering outburst as if to say 'I told you so' to a woman who never listened to her.

"This wasn't supposed to happen!"

Everything had been simpler before, when she had lived the pampered life of Hebanthe Falls' Mam, respected and lauded above all other women in the Uppers, in the entire city. The wife of the Founder, the mother of the heir. There should be no open Outside. There should have been no coup, no plague to rob her of her children. There should be no Nau and no banishment to the dismal Levs.

No abduction. No assassination.

In her upended world, there were many she could blame for the unending parade of disasters. Captain Grainger and the Nau, who held Hebenon's reins in Haythem's stead. Blayd, who had abandoned her and refused to come when she summoned. Feena Wulfe, who challenged her right to control the city in the only way she could. Kal Driscoll was the only man who could have stolen Haythem from under Grainger's nose and had, she was sure, the most to gain by removing Haythem from power.

If Kal thought he would outmaneuver her, he had yet to face her true wrath.

"Find out who did this!" she demanded of the only man in the room who scratched at the addiction ants eating his skin and stared at her with an expression she triumphantly interpreted as fear.

Good. He should fear her.

Someone had to.

She snatched her coat from the wall hook, paying no regard to her daughter except to call out to Nanny, "Clean this up…and make sure she eats. She doesn't leave this flat."

Now that Haythem was dead, many would seek to use Ulynda as a pawn. Despite her name, her blood, Ulynda had no more power than Neoma was willing to give her.

Neoma, the one with experience, expected that power for herself.

For all she had done on Haythem's behalf, she believed she deserved that much.

❧*❧

Every Echo in the city active when the array blew burst to life at the same moment, presenting Delora Carville's face to each home, vindi, walkway, and intersection where screens were operable. The unexpected flash provided illumination where there had been darkness and brought people to a standstill wherever they happened to be. Passersby braving the streets to acquire nessies without the power to operate tick card readers winced at the glare and stared, slack-jawed, in reaction to the words coming from the woman's downturned mouth.

Most knew Delora from past prods, when the Founder and Doctet had governed their lives. They knew of her, though they did not know her, but that minimal familiarity, her matronly features and heavy-pained voice, were enough to hold the viewers hostage until the words seeped from her lips into their heads, into their hearts.

"Dearest citizens…on behalf of the Nau and…" She paused to sip from a glass of clear liquid that might have been water, might have been something stronger, put it down out of sight, and then cleared her throat. "It pains me to report with great sorrow that our beloved…that Founder Kemway…has been assassinated."

She paused as though she could hear the gasps, see the shock and incredulity that surely rippled through her invisible, captive audience. She might also have been reacting to the flabbergasted expressions of Kenneth, Soleia, and the prod crew recording the announcement Lydon had arranged for. They had not known the nature of the requested city-wide prod; they had only known that the Nau had considered their news important enough to require immediate sharing.

There had been conjecture in the prod room, but given the gravitas of the city's current situation, the news could have been anything. The Founder's death had not been high on their list of expectations.

"At this critical juncture in history, we understand the need to grieve, to mourn…and to move our cherished city forward. There will be a Day of Remembrance three days hence, a day to honor the many accomplishments of our Founder, of the Kemway dynasty. Afterward, Faith willing…"

Her voice faltered. Her gaze dropped to something beneath her hand that could not be seen on the screen, and then her hand slid to the side as if sweeping whatever was there away.

"We are strong. We are mighty…the best of humanity. We have endured much during our many lifetimes together; we are survivors. We will persevere as we have always done…and we will survive this too. Founder willing…Hebanthe Falls will continue on the path of greatness that Duncan Kemway laid out for us. We will know the greatness he intended to be ours."

Delora dabbed at her eyes with a handkerchief, cleared her throat, and bowed her head. "Founder be at rest. Founder be at peace. Founder grant us our future. We will rise."

In the background of the prod studio, the voices of others echoed the phrases back to her, the ritual utterances of the Voices of Faith that had been offered at Duncan Kemway's death and the deaths of every Founder to have ruled since the city had been erected.

Throughout Hebenon, nearly everyone else, followers or supporters of the Faith or not, no matter their views on Haythem and the Kemway dynasty, echoed the sentiment as well.

For good or ill, the city's longest-standing historical tradition had reached its end. The Kemway dynasty could be put to rest.

∾*∾

At the base of the staircase, having returned home for a change of clothes and to see if Ginna had gone there as requested, Ilya gripped the rail tighter as the Nau's prod faded from the screen only to loop and begin again, the words no less shocking on the second hearing. It would continue to replay several more times until someone in charge deemed it likely that the entire city had heard the news. Then Kenneth and Soleia would begin the 'public service' of dissecting the announcement, picking it apart, splicing it with SCAM footage from the riot, weaving it with his final words and with unsubstantiated speculation about who the assassin was and why it had been done, about the nature of the riot and how it had begun, and likely Ilya's involvement in it.

She could already hear the questions. Why had she not acted sooner? Faster?

Why had she permitted Scarecrow to take the Founder from the platform and out of the crowd?

Had Scarecrow killed him?

Had she?

Were either of them in league with the brako to have this done? Had it been done at the behest of the bugorra?

The swirl of possible barbed questions created a stab of pain between her eyes. They had not even been asked yet.

There would be a hasty inquest through the Hub, through the Archives, for morsels of the past, Haythem's life, the lives of his father, and every Founder back to the city's erection. There would be a buildup of his importance to Hebenon that would be less accurate than it would be sensational, and the skeletons of his life would be kept largely in the closet until the period of mourning was complete.

Then the scavengers would pick clean the carcass of his memory.

What did it matter?

Ilya may have helped quell the riot but she had failed to keep the Founder alive. Had failed to find him while he breathed. Had failed to find his kidnapper. Based on the location and amount of blood on his shirt, based on what Ginna had said and what the captain had not, the man's death had been inevitable. Ilya believed she could have done more to prevent it if she had located him sooner.

She frowned, a memory bobbing to the surface of her thoughts as the words on the prod settled into a throbbing hum beneath them. Something Blayd had said…or something she thought he had said. His adamant conviction that Mam Kemway had been instrumental in her husband's abduction from the custody of the captain and the host of doctors who cared for him. While Ilya understood the Mam to be ambitious without Blayd's assertions and some of the comments Ilya had overheard her speak in the captain's office, she found it difficult to believe that the Mam would order her husband's death.

What sort of person would do such a thing? Did she want power so badly that she would do anything for it?

Blayd would be the only one who could confirm, deny, or suss out Mam's involvement. By the time Ilya reached the top of the stairs where she paused to rub her aching knee, she had made up her mind to reach out to the merc one more time. As before, her effort to reach him was met with no reply, only the same static-dead radio silence she was met with when trying to reach the captain. With the Hub reception spotty, there was no guarantee that the message she typed and sent would reach him, at least not in time to be of use. She would have to continue to hunt the assassin and the kidnapper on her own.

The weakness of her knee, as she came down off the final step, reminded her that such hunts would not happen soon.

Brownouts or not, the Echos continued to blare the unfortunate news. The Founder had been lost and Ilya was in no condition to do anything about it.

❧*❧

"You did this!"

Jaron's groggy effort to lift his head to the thrown-open door ended in the blackness delivered at the end of the fist that struck the side of his head, a blow that damaged any functionality the external speecher component might have contained. The diodes went dark.

The door slammed again, Vanderwall crashing out through it, knocking one of his men aside with such force that he collided with the handrail and flipped over it. Vanderwall paid no attention to the clatter, the crash, the impact made as the man dropped to whatever fate awaited him.

The other subordinates likewise did not attempt to determine their cohort's fate. They stared at their boss, waiting for his order, their mouths tight and eyes wide. This was not a mood they dared to cross. They were likely to meet the same fate.

If any brako had killed the Founder against Mam's wishes, it had been a matter of chance or had come at the end of a counter order made by the Wulfe bitch. Feena would never have sullied her hands with bloodshed, not even with a popper, but giving such an order and expecting it to be obeyed was the sort of thing she had a capacity for.

She had directed his precursor thus before. She cared little about the deaths of others. Frankle did not doubt she had made this order.

He did not personally care about the Founder's death. Beyond losing the reward ticks, it mattered little to him whether the deposed Founder lived or died. Nor did he care about the loss of name and status his death would cause his widow…and how that in turn would loosen her grip on power in the Levs.

His only care was how this murder and the events surrounding it were going to influence him and the business of his brako.

Scarecrow had seen his face.

By now, he imagined his description had fallen into the buggers' hands. If someone connected that description to any captured SCAM footage from the riot, the blowback of the assassination and the blame for it, for the insurrection, was going to fall on Vanderwall's shoulders. If that blame became public, if Mam learned he had been there, she would cast blame on him too. He would become the target of her wrath…and of anyone she still held sway over.

He did not think she could get to him and he had stayed ahead of the bugorra thus far. He did not think she could hurt him any more than Scarecrow had. Without the strength of the brako to wield its whipping fist, without the right-hand merc that Vanderwall had not seen in weeks, the Mam was no one to him. He was not afraid of her.

But the inconvenience of it was infuriating.

As was his inability to get answers from the man in the building behind him.

In the end, it all came back to Scarecrow.

The prisoner had to be his bait, his leverage.

All Vanderwall had to do was dangle the hook and let city politics play out without him. Until then, laying low was the best he could do.

Not having anticipated the ongoing brownouts and the difficulties they generated, Blayd did not know if the message he sent, via an accomplice he no longer had, was received or if the bugorra simply had too many pressing matters to contend with instead of exploring a rumored location believed to be the site where the Founder had been held captive after his abduction. Having checked the site off and on as other business allowed, seeing no activity or interest in it, he had decided that the Founder's sighting, his disjointed speech that thankfully had not called out Blayd or anyone else by name, meant his abduction was now less important to them than finding him was.

Now that his assassination was confirmed, news that eased his concerns about being outed as the abductor, Blayd could not say where finding a kidnapper, finding the site of his prison, would fall on the bugorra's priority list.

He considered dismantling the curated array of evidence he had put into place. He considered leaving another anonymous tip or adding some other stray bit of dubious evidence that might also implicate Switz in the plot. The little man had been useful, but now he was a liability, the only one who could incriminate Blayd if he felt pushed into it.

Blayd doubted Switz had the fortitude to do so without a push. He had not seen the coward in days. Switz was smart enough to stay out of his way and keep his mouth shut.

But there was always a chance.

Switz might not be looking for him, but according to the multiple messages that popped up on his ICD every time there was enough power allocated to the Hub to permit the sending and receipt of messages, Neoma was. He did not read her messages to learn what she wanted, having no desire to respond to pleas for help, nor tolerance for the ranting blame she had last hurled at him. The last message on his list, Ilya rather than Neoma, supported his suspicions that he was being sought as a person of interest, a witness at least if not a suspect.

He did not answer her either. If they crossed paths, he could blame not getting her message on the defective Hub services. Whatever she wanted, it would wait until their paths crossed or full power was restored to the city and she tried again, when ignoring her would make him look like the guilty man he was.

Watching a pair of fishermen pass with pails of dredged river waste destined for fertilization processing, listening to the prod loop begin again on an Echo he could not see, Blayd eased away from the window of the empty warehouse office across from his trap and decided to continue to lay low here for now. Once his evidence was found, if it was, the fingers of guilt and blame would shift off his shoulders to the places he believed it belonged.

On the man Neoma desired to implicate at all costs, who Blayd was happy to see fall.

On the woman who had disrespected and betrayed him despite his history of loyalty.

Maybe, if he chose to go through with it, on Switz as well, just to be safe.

Only then would Blayd be rid of this burden.

With it behind him, reaching out to Ilya, pursuing her affections, would be safe again. She would never need to know about any of the things he had done.

❧*❧

The news spread from one vindi, one shed, one home to the next, bleeding into the shafts on the whispers of each shift change crew he passed. The expected debates about Hebenon's future, the murmured worry and muted outcries of blame pointed to the bugorra, the brako, the Voices. Rhyd fought to focus on his shift duties rather than on those words and the direction they turned his thoughts. Such unsubstantiated rumors were inconsequential beyond their use in gauging the population's mood.

The filts, the pipes, the wires, and systems, would not maintain themselves. Some were easier to repair and maintain without heat, water, and waste flowing through them. Some components wheezed, fans, valves, backflows, meters, and diaphragms fought not to seize with the minimal trickle of usage or had already done so. Those that had failed, or were failing, needed to be repaired or replaced to be at full functional capacity when power was restored.

The shafts were congested with crews. It seemed to Rhyd that every bilger, heizer, spener, and skolper was called in on multiple shifts to keep the struggling city alive. They were accustomed to the dark in this place. They had weak generator lighting at shaft intersections, headlamps, and battery torches, all enough to function for several days, provided the capacity to recharge them remained. As the hydros whined, working to provide more power than they were designed to create or conduct, it was down to people like Rhyd and the maintenance crews to make it happen, to nurse the systems for as long as they had the parts and materials to do so.

He tightened the fittings between two sections of pipe he had replaced and tucked his wrench back into his tooler. He was torn about being here. He should find Vanderwall. Find Jaron. Many others around him could do the work he was doing now.

There was no one else to do the work of Scarecrow.

"Catch."

The pock-marked hemplastic ball removed from a broken valve was tossed his way, the warning spoken, the object released, before Rhyd could react. It bounced off his shoulder with enough stinging force to make him wince before clattering to the damp floor and rolling several feet until it met the resistance of an uphill incline in the shaft.

"Daydreaming?" his coworker chuckled.

Rhyd grunted and retrieved the ball. Many of his coworkers knew he collected broken things and delivered them to a kesfek who would find some way to repurpose them. The ball, like many other items he scavenged, was of no use for its original functions, and wasting potentially useful items was to waste materials that were often limited in supply. People could not afford to waste anything, particularly now that the lifts were closed to most residents and the flow of food and merchandise had nearly ceased.

The man who spoke, an andi capable of multiple shifts without requiring rest or food as long as his internal components generated enough power to sustain activity, was one of the better partners Rhyd could have been given for this extended haul. He preferred to work alone and usually did, his seniority giving him the choice assignments when he chose to utilize his prerogative. Shed bosses knew who worked best with whom, which pairs proved most productive, and if it came to a partnered shift, Rhyd preferred Hopper to anyone else. Indistinguishable behind protective gear and the prerequisite filt mask shaft workers wore, things he did not need but utilized to hide his nature from those of prejudice who might harass him, Rhyd knew Hopper by his voice. Knew him because they had worked together since leaving the Shed hours earlier.

Rhyd shook his head and shoved the ball into his belt pouch. "Wondering who's gonna be Founder now…or if we'll even have one." He did not care about the politics of the situation, but as the topic was on everyone's lips, it was a morsel of small talk he could provide to remain on friendly terms with Hopper. Being gruff, rude, or anti-social would mean he would eventually be stuck with someone else in Hopper's place.

"Think we need one?"

"No." Despite the growing pains after the Coup, Hebenon was better off without a single man clenching all the power in an erratic, iron fist. Shackled for centuries to the whims of one man, one family, he believed it was time to do away with the old ways. The shift had already begun. "But our opinions don't count for much, do they?"

"They don't," agreed Hopper, picking up his tooler from between his feet and shining his torch down the shaft. "Let's find the next one before you go off shift."

"Should get in more than one." They worked well together. So long as the next marked location was an easy fix, they should be able to keep moving before Rhyd clocked out.

One of the destinations on the T1 Echo map was an Archive Lev location. He hoped that, by making it that far, he might be close enough to locate Jaron before the end of his rotation.

And passing several more vent grates into alleys and into city paths, where streeters, tingers, and addicts congregated, where Spinks sometimes loitered for security out of the elements, might give him a current location for Vanderwall.

❧Chapter 14❧

"Hijo de puta!" shouted a deep voice from an otherwise nondescript figure dressed in waterproof gear who muscled past the white-robed Igraci standing near Vapors' door. The Igraci held a signboard proclaiming the end of Hebenon in neon red letters meant to enforce the need for those living in the Five Falls to leave their ancient metal home and return to the world of their ancestors. "Poq Gai! The doors are shut! No one's ever getting out!"

The belligerent speaker tried to push past Colyx's broad, cross-armed torso and wide-legged stance which blocked entry into the closed bar. The bouncer refused to move. His impulse was to swear, to take a swing, but when Colyx growled, "Verpiss dich," and narrowed his gaze, the stranger decided to avoid the confrontation and stomp away, muttering under his breath.

The Igraci, whose slight, youthful build was as indistinguishable in the white robes of the order as the other had been in his water gear, nodded to Colyx in gratitude as they picked up their sign and adjusted the hood over their head. Colyx nodded back, glanced at the retreating figure, and then left the awning's shelter to approach the first Player he had seen since his glimpse Outside.

Behind him, Vapors was devoid of customers, only occupied by a handful of the usual people he recognized, trusted, and counted as Maemi's friends, if not necessarily his. He was near enough to the door to prevent trouble from getting inside, but he wanted to hear more of what the Igraci had to say.

"Think he did it?"

"Who did what?" Ginna swiped the wet rag over the bar counter, its surface unused, the action meant to keep her occupied outside of her thoughts.

"You saw the SCAMs." Pietro put the last glasses he had cleaned and dried onto the bar rack. "Scarecrow…"

She growled and shook her head. "Scarecrow doesn't kill people."

"We don't know that." he shrugged with his hands raised and open in surrender. "Not blamin', just sayin'. Imagine he'd have as much reason as anyone else, maybe more, to do it though…if he had. Can't say I'd blame him. With all that's gone into finding the Founder…all the fights with Talkers and brako…dying might be the best thing the Founder could do for us."

Setting down her Echo and stylus, its dim screen lit by columns and rows of inventory numbers, Maemi clucked her tongue and took a light swat at her senior swiver with the drying towel lying nearby. "That's a terrible thing to say."

"True enough though," countered Tox coolly. She had left the inactive kesfek stall for a lukewarm drink and the handful of mixed nuts, seeds, and dried fruit Maemi offered. Her primary reason for coming had been the desire for company that might chase away the gloom of the deserted streets and an empty flat. "Weren't all bad over the years…they gave us a place to survive…but Haythem…his father…his grandfather…"

Remembering the torture she had endured, the people who had been Taken, her young assistant killed in the wake of the Coup, Tox shook her head. While Xiaodan's death could not be directly attributed to the Founder, as no Founder was guiding Hebenon at that time, all of the ills in her life, including the collapse of Rhyd and Venn's long relationship, were lumped together in her hatred for what the Founder stood for. Better that the Kemways were never allowed to regain control of Hebanthe Falls.

Pietro pushed the rack into place. "If not him, who do you think did it?"

"Could be anyone; best we don't speculate." There would be enough of that in the days ahead, and Maemi preferred not to be part of the gossip problem.

Movement in the doorway announced Colyx's return. He nodded at the woman who employed him. Maemi nodded back.

There was enough to worry about without trying to identify an assassin. That, she assumed, was something the bugorra and Scarecrow were already trying to do.

❧*❦

"He's not here, Mam," Bene stammered, less daunted by the reedy, thin-faced woman than he was out of breath from trying to keep up with her short, quick steps as she stalked the length of Talker Hall towards the corridor that led to the array of offices and teaching rooms that served the Senior, his underlings, and the people of the city. The Mam had been here before, though not as often as some of the Senior's other visitors; it was often enough since her eviction from the Uppers to make her face well known to the Talkers who served here and often enough for her to know where she was headed without a guide.

Bene chose to follow her anyway.

"Where is he?" she spat without looking to see how closely he was following, swiping the hood of her cloak back with enough force that the moisture it had collected sprayed into Bene's face.

He sputtered and wiped his cheeks, eyes, and lips as he caught up to her. "Business took him…"

"I bet it did. Better be cazzing important business…"

"I'm sure it is." He did not know where the Senior had gone. He had not been here when Kal had gone out and would not have asked the man's business if he had been. If he had wanted Bene's help, he would have asked or left a message. Some of the things the Senior did were no one else's business.

Some of that secrecy, however, contributed to the rumors about the host of accusations the buggers and others heaped on the Voices of Faith since the Founder's abduction. It would behoove the man, Bene thought bitterly as he quickened his pace, to be less secretive.

They reached Kal's office, and Neoma threw the door open as if she expected to find him inside despite Bene's claim. The empty wine glass on the desk in the dark office provided no clues about where he had gone or when, but for Neoma, it was enough to suggest he was still somewhere in the multileveled Talker Hall.

"You are welcome to wait for him if you will…" Bene began, gesturing into the corridor towards the sanctuary they had passed through, where it was customary for people to wait until summoned.

"I'll wait here." She pulled off her coat, hung it on the back of the door where other articles of outerwear hung, and then dropped onto the plush cushioned sofa with arrogant grace. The presence of other garments hanging there, though not the coat she most often saw him wear, offered no evidence of where Kal had gone, when he had left, or when he would return.

She would wait.

Bene looked as if he would protest her choice, his mouth pinched, his eyes creased at the corners, but instead, he bowed his head with a frustrated sigh. "Very well, Mam." Arguing with her was not worth the aggravation. She would pull the cards of rank and entitlement and he would be unable to change her mind. "I will let him know you are here as soon as he arrives. And please…" He swallowed as much of his irritation as he could stomach and lowered his gaze respectfully. "My condolences for…I hope they catch the person who…"

Without looking at him, Neoma hissed, "Oh, I will."

She did not believe that Blayd, Grainger, or even Kal would bring her the head of Haythem's killer. Any one of those men might be the guilty party. With no reliance on Scarecrow's aid either, she was going to have to find the assassin on her own.

❧*❧

He peered through the filt grates that should be blowing warm air in and sucking stale air out of this particular floor of the Archives, but of the more than a dozen heads he could count over the top of cubicle dividers, he was confident that none of them were Jaron.

He had never been inside the Archives and did not know how many people were employed in the multilevel structure of one of Hebenon's largest employers. He had never studied the layout or seen maps or diagrams and had no idea which desk, on which level, Jaron considered to be his. Having been given the Nau's blessing, bent heads poured over tedious data, less tedious now that they had an assassin to identify and locate via the endless SCAM footage they received amidst a backlog of data that needed to be sorted, tagged, and cataloged.

Unless Rhyd left the shafts and moved between the maze of desks, he would never find Jaron this way.

Men and women worked feverishly in the hopes that one of them would be responsible for bringing a killer to justice. One of them might see and identify Scarecrow, now that he had come out of the shadows. They expected a bonus at the end of their shift if they were lucky enough to provide something useful to the bugorra and the Nau.

As Hopper recalibrated the fan bearings they were here to replace, Rhyd contemplated excuses he could utilize to enter the Archive, some sensible reason that would permit him to move between cubicles, between levels, without rousing suspicion. Archive management would accommodate a shaft worker with the right credentials if it meant maintaining a comfortable atmosphere, but there was no reason Rhyd could concoct that would not make him look like a puerile fool.

He punched Jaron's code into his ICD, hoping to hear the other man's comm buzz somewhere in the room in front of him.

Nothing happened.

His scowl melted into a furrowed frown. It had been too long. Too long for Jaron to have been gone and too long for him to have loitered here. He needed to get the job done and get off shift. He needed to return to the streets if he was to find Jaron and bring him home.

❧*❧

"If not me, if not you, who was it?" Kal grumbled, watching Feena's fingers sift through a collection of passcards as if they were a playing deck, looking for something she failed to find. He was confident the assassin had been brako, for few others would have the nerve, the equipment, or the capability to make a distance shot through a crowded intersection as the killer had done. If not Feena's people, following her command in the hopes of installing a leader in Hebenon who was more to her liking, it left only those who continued to follow Neoma's dwindling influence.

There was no reason he could imagine that might prompt Neoma to be so bold. Not when it grew daily more obvious that people would never tolerate the Mam in the seat of the Founder. The city needed someone to lead them, not someone to control them. Neoma would bend towards the latter.

Ulynda was not old enough for either.

"He had enemies and detractors," Feena replied with an absent shrug. "I'm looking into it, but there were a lot of people there…and he might not have been the target. It was chaos."

"You were there." She had hinted at it during their previous meeting, and though she might have concluded the case based on the prods, Kal interpreted her tone and words as those of someone with firsthand knowledge.

"Passing on the fringe," she admitted.

He studied her neutral expression, compared it to her flippant remark, and scowled. "Tell me you didn't do this."

Feena eyed him with cool disbelief without deigning to reply. He knew her better than that. "There's only one chance for us if we want to move Hebenon forward."

He snorted and nodded. "We do it, he's going to need protection," he reminded her. "I can't give it. Not alone. Right now, any connection he appears to have to the Voices would be a detriment."

"You can't expect me to offer public support." Feena never did anything public that was not entwined with the wine business or the Den. It was why no one suspected her of wrongdoing…except for those who already knew.

"He doesn't want…"

"Doesn't matter what he wants. Hebenon needs its Founder, needs a Kemway, even if it's a security blanket for show. He's the only one who can do it. We can protect him if we join forces, but a statement from you, regardless of the current situation, should do a lot for the Voices' credibility.

"I doubt that."

"Give him another chance. Talk to him. See if he's on board now that everything's changed. If he continues to refuse, we can force him into it if we must. Just give me fair warning, whatever you do, before you do it."

Pushing away from the bar, weary of this repeated dance between them, he grunted, "I'm not doing anything, I told you."

"Someone has to…if he won't do it himself.

"Then you do it. I'm done." Kal could feel her burning gaze following him as he stalked out of the Den without looking back.

There was no reason for the dwarf to need him. No reason for him to feel compelled to accept his murdered brother's vacant seat.

To Kal, however, there was every reason in the world that he should, starting with the survival of Hebanthe Falls.

❧Chapter 15❧

The flat she called home was quiet, empty of everyone except the muted series of steps and mutterings that meant Nanny was going about the business of cleaning up the destruction Neoma had left behind. They were familiar sounds that made Ulynda look at the destruction she too had wrought in her fury. Much more, she imagined, than her mother had done.

How much like her mother she was becoming.

She pouted angrily and swore to herself never again.

She should clean her room instead of waiting for Nanny to do it. Unlike her mother, she understood that it was not fair to compel Nanny to sort out the mess just because she was the help and Ulynda had not controlled her temper.

It was not fair…but none of this was. Her father had been right in front of her. Touched her, kissed her, told her he loved her…and now he was dead. Not missing, not absent like one of the Taken she had heard about, but dead.

Assassinated.

There was no small bird of hope to tuck into her breast to nurse this time. No possible way that her father could come back. Father, brother, sister lost. Now there was only her and the woman who grew more loathsome every day. Her mother was wrong about so many things, and her efforts to shield Ulynda from the world, and the world from Ulynda, continued to generate deepening defiance.

She had been out there. She had seen life in the Levs with her own eyes rather than from the security of clinging to Nanny's hand on a nessies outing. She had seen people's hunger, their fears. There were shadows, but there was also light, light enough to make Ulynda long to see and know more. Light enough for Ulynda to long to see it grow.

Agnys had survived in the city streets alone before Scarecrow had found her. Ulynda believed that, given the chance, she could too.

Determined to see to the mess in her room after appeasing the rumble of hunger and thirst in her belly that she had ignored for several hours, Ulynda cracked open the door to peep into the common room. Nanny, having swept the broken carafe into a pile of sparkling shards, was mopping the wine stain from the uncarpeted floor directly inside the doorway. She looked at the creaking bedroom door and when their eyes met, cast the girl a sympathetic, matronly smile.

"Aw, qinai." She leaned the mop handle against the door and caught the girl as Ulynda flung herself into her open arms. Nanny had been with her since the Uppers, though Ulynda had never heard her true name uttered. As her life shifted and her world grew smaller and more claustrophobic, Ulynda did not think there was anyone she could trust as much as Nanny.

Not now that her father was dead.

"Do you want some algtea?" There was barely enough power to cook with, but the water from the sink was, for the time being, hot enough to create a lukewarm sweet algtea. The now unpowered cool box was stocked with fruit and cheese that would stay good for a while longer, the cupboard filled with seed bread, crackers, nuts, uncooked beans, and flour. The bread could not be toasted, but a little butter and preserves would make it palatable and better than no meal at all.

"He's gone…isn't he?" she sobbed, nodding in acceptance of Nanny's offer but refusing to release her. Her mother was not here, nor the strange little man with the quick, shifty eyes and jittery hands who made Ulynda uncomfortable. She could take her meal into her room to stay out of Nanny's way and to see to her cleaning, where she would be safe from her mother's return. What she wanted now was comfort and sympathy and someone who would treat her with the respect, affection, and honesty she craved. "I told her…I saw him. I was there…he was there…he said he loved me…"

"Of course he did, qinai. You don't ever have to doubt that." Whatever Haythem's faults had been, he had adored his children and had given them more of his time, his attention, and himself, than their mother ever had. As much as his duties as Founder permitted. Nanny had witnessed it every day, even if the rest of the world had not.

Gently, she pried the girl's arms from around her waist and kissed the top of her head. "Here now…sit at the window…watch the water. I'll bring you something."

Ulynda keeping watch at the window meant she would see her mother's return before the terrifying woman reached the door. Seeing her approach would allow Ulynda to retreat to her room before another confrontation erupted. Understanding Nanny's intent as she shuffled away with the mop, broom, and sweeping pan, Ulynda sighed and turned towards the window. Instead of sitting, she knelt on the window bench with her elbows on the sill, prepared to flee, her face pressed to the glass as she focused on deciphering the shapes of the world in the shadows.

The message received, Enoch risked the blooming dangers of the dark to find the place Ulynda called home, the location Rhyd had left for him along with the assurance that the girl who had been in his care had been taken there. He skirted the cluster of huddled Talkers that watched him pass with thinly veiled interest, the buggers knocking from door to door asking questions Enoch did not venture close enough to hear. He avoided masked brako breaking vindi windows, shaking down passersby who looked affluent enough to have something of interest or value, or the unmasked brako forcing streeters and tingers to give up any information they held about Founder Kemway, his killer, and the causes of the riot. More than once, he thought he heard his name on those brako's hidden lips without considering why they might be talking about him.

There were only two reasons worth anything.

Either they knew he was connected to Skelter and believed the kaheao had been involved in the riot…or they knew his true name.

Enoch did not have the time or interest to deal with either.

Having done his share of streeting over the years, having intermingled with the fringes of society since infancy, Enoch knew discontent when he heard or saw it. He knew fear. He knew the look of a runner afraid to go home. Ulynda, in the short time he had known her, exhibited those things. It was no coincidence that the brako who had jumped him had taken her to her mother. Likely they hoped for a reward. More than likely, he fumed with annoyance as noise tickled past his ears again, this time from another band of Talkers ducking out of the damp to share cigs in the faint light of a corner alglamp at the bottom of the stairs he started to climb, there was another reason he cared even less about knowing.

He paused at the top, breathless, heart hammering in his chest, and listened to the Talkers who moved away in another direction without following him, failing to identify the man of whom they spoke. Once confident he was alone, when his hands stopped shaking and he could breathe normally, he moved several feet forward until he could see movement in the window beside the door he was here to monitor. Expecting to make a hasty retreat if Neoma opened the door, he saw no faster route of escape than the path taken to get here. If Senior Kal knew who he was, if Haythem had realized the truth in that single, too-brief exchange, it was likely Neoma knew too. A confrontation, even if framed as an introduction, was unlikely to end well.

It was not Neoma who threw open the door. Rather, it was Ulynda who raced across the grated walk, barefoot and heedless of the damp, to embrace him as if she had known him all of her life.

"They didn't kill you!" She was not as alone in the world as she feared, and her hitching sob buried itself into his shoulder.

Stroking her hair, not knowing if the gesture would comfort her as he returned the embrace, he mumbled with thick emotion, "I'm good…I'm fine. I'm sorry they…I needed to see that you're…he told me they brought you home…"

"Father?" she sniffed hopefully.

Enoch shook his head and choked on the unexpected grief felt for a brother he had never known. "Scarecrow," he whispered.

Her surprise prompted her to pull back and look at the rooftops above and as far below as the darkness allowed hoping to see him. Maybe she could trust Scarecrow too. Three people to trust out of all of those living in the Levs did not seem to be a satisfactory support system against her mother but it would have to be enough.

"You'll catch death out here dressed like that," he murmured, stepping back to look her up and down with his hands still gripping her arms, masking his inspection of her well-being with the concern for her bare feet.

"I saw you through the window," she explained. "I didn't want you to go." She wiped her face with both hands, removing the mist and dregs of her tears. "I'd invite you in, but Mama would not…" Sighing, she dropped her gaze while casting it left and right. "She's heard about…and that he's gone…she…"

It did not matter if Enoch understood what she failed to say. He understood fear and understood that, whatever Neoma knew or intended, she would not want a contender for the title of Founder to show up at her doorstep. Pressing his forehead to Ulynda's, he murmured, "Listen to me. I'm here if you need me. There are people you can trust. Find the Spinks…the children…and they'll…"

"Shouldn't be here komeada." The familiar jeering voice trailed behind the rattle of footsteps on the stairs. They had not been enough to distract either Enoch or Ulynda, being the heavy sort of steps that ruled out the approach of the hard-soled clacking Neoma's shoes would make. But confronting Molly Netzer was unexpected, even though Rhyd's message had warned that the man had been in Mam's company here, at her flat.

Not so many weeks ago, Molly had come to him, bedraggled and wild-eyed, desperately begging for a score. Now he presented a haughty, chin-tipped sneering air that prompted Enoch to step away from the girl who had enough sense to flee back inside the flat and slam the door.

Another door slammed inside.

"Little young and high-class for you, don't you think," Enoch countered, avoiding looking at the door while listening to Ulynda's retreat to safety. He relaxed when he believed she was secure.

"So, I've made good," Molly huffed with a half-hearted shrug. "What's it to you?" He was surprised the dwarf had tracked him here. Or maybe, he thought as Nanny peered through the window to see who was there, Enoch finding him was accidental. Eyes darting around, he reassured himself that Enoch had not been followed and then strode around him to grab the door handle without losing his sneer, a passcard in his hand. Enoch was not going to harm him. He would not dare.

Enoch shrugged too. "Nothing to me so long as you don't hurt the girl. Live your life. Don't care. Didn't expect it, that's all."

With a note of defense in his voice and an indignant expression, Molly looked back and hissed, "I got skills, you know. My card's not been called yet. I've got things to offer. Just because Skelt refuses to die…" His mouth snapped shut and his lips thinned to a tight line before he hastily changed the subject. "Stay away from the girl…from Mam. This ain't no place for you. And tell Skelt…"

He opened the door, stepped across the threshold, and spoke again without looking back. "Tell him I'm coming. I didn't forget. Spades never do."

The door banged hard, rattling the walls and failing, Enoch could see, to latch. For several moments, he did not move. He heard nothing inside. No speaking, no doors slamming, no signs of reaction or violence. Nanny eventually came to the door, peered at him through the crack, and nodded once before closing it properly.

What in the name of the Founder was Molly playing?

Enoch would deliver the message to Skelter. Threat or not, if Molly was hoping to catch the redhead with his guard down, he would be sorely mistaken. Skelter had not forgotten either. None of them had.

❧*❧

"Sent for me?"

He was not as intimidating in size or stature as either Uriah Frankel or the original Vanderwall, but Tyrisi Balling was smarter and more dedicated to Feena than anyone else, her methods of doing business, and her perceived view of what was best for Hebanthe Falls. It was said he was enamored with the woman who was his senior by a handful of years, but he had never expressed such feelings to her or anyone else. She knew the rumors, however, and had done her best to prevent her lack of reciprocation from interfering in the oaths he had taken, the duties he had sworn to keep, or her treatment of him. Any preferential treatment he received came because of his steadfastness, nothing more.

Those around her likewise trusted him to carry out her wishes with fairness and unnecessary brutality…with enough sternness against any who failed her to prompt them, and others, not to fail again.

Her trust allowed him into the Den's back room, where Feena took inventory instead of delegating the responsibility to anyone else.

She glanced back when his footsteps stopped and nodded once. "Tyrisi. Get the word out; I want everyone to find and protect Enoch LeRoy. Protect him as if he's me and report his movements back to me. I want to know everything, and I want that man to stay alive."

"The dwarf?" Tyrisi blinked, the question sounding more like a request for confirmation than an expression of disbelief. Feena suspected the question contained a bit of both sentiments, but he would not dare to express doubts. "No more intimidation, is that correct?"

"No need for it. We've got a use for him, but for that, he has to stay alive.

Tyrisi did not ask who 'we' were. He did not ask the reason for the priority shift. If the dwarf was vital enough to warrant any order at all, then a change from the first to the second was to be obeyed.

"You want him protected from everyone? Buggers? Vanderwall?"

Feena stared, her eyes narrowed. "Especially Vanderwall." She did not believe the bugorra, under Oliver, would trouble the dwarf, particularly if Kal did what needed to be done. But there would be other enemies. Neoma. The beaked brako. Vanderwall. Once she and Vanderwall had been on the same side…until Neoma interfered. Then his loyalties shifted. Now things were changing again, and Feena no longer trusted the brute to act on anyone's behalf but his own.

"Nothing's to happen to Enoch."

Tyrisi nodded. "I'll get word out now."

His steps echoed through the Den as he left Feena to her inventory. Whatever Kal did or did not do, whatever path shaped the future, she could feel a change coming, see the proverbial graffiti on the wall. Whatever that change would be, she intended to be prepared.

❧*❧

"Didn't expect I'd see you again."

Skelter stopped at Vapors' door where Colyx stood inside, peering over his shoulder. With his hand on the beaded curtain, Skelter glanced at the woman loitering across the street, holding her water-cloak tight against her thin body, her head bowed but eyes watchful as if she was waiting for someone. He had noted her position without realizing who she was, but now that she crossed the path to grasp his arm with her bone-thin hand, he remembered her face, her voice, the color of her manicured nails.

"Looking for business?"

"Business is pretty rough, as you can imagine." He tipped his head towards the unlit neon sign that normally flashed Vapors' name. Without the lifts, with production slowed to crawling and the transport of product made nearly impossible, Skelter's services now involved more access to nessies than to the exotic, unusual, and hard-to-find products he was known to distribute. Ticks could not move, and goods for barter were less accessible.

"I have this." In her open palm, she unwrapped the cloth from the rectangular, boxy item she carried, exposing the contents to the dampness. Not enough light came from the doorpost alglamp nor bled from the generator lamps burning behind the beaded curtain to see it clearly, but the ornate, circular insignia stamped on the underside of the object, visible when Eido turned it over, was one any kaheao and many others would recognize.

Skelter ran his thumb over the stamp, wondering how a history teacher had possession of a block of gold as wide as her palm. He schooled his surprised expression and dropped his hand.

"Have to verify that…"

"Of course." She folded the dark oilcloth back to cover it again. "Take it. Verify it. Take my list. If you're satisfied, we can arrange for delivery. If you're not…" she shrugged with a thin, coy smile, "I have more. I'm sure you'll find some other use for that."

Less discerning people would accept the bar as real without a veracity test. The scarcity of gold would make such a payment a risk to take and a trade not to pass up. If the bar was fake, a skilled kaheao might pass it off to someone else in exchange for something of value he could use. He might even be able to bribe or own a few buggers for the perceived value.

If she had more, if the offer was made to further entice him or play off that she held the bar to be of little value beyond what she could get for it, it was worth the time to test this one.

Skelter offered his wrist; Eido presented hers so that the faces of their ICDs touched. The clicks and beeps of transmitted data took a few moments to complete, then she stepped back. "Tell me where, when…if I owe you more."

He huffed. "If you owe me, you'll know." But this much gold, if it was authentic, ought to be adequate payment for anything the Igraci leader wanted.

Unless it was a human life.

❧*☙

The Archive's daily duty roster listed Jaron as absent for each day he had been expected to be on shift but had failed to be, every day starting since the one when he had left Zara's flat to report in. For a man with a nearly flawless attendance record in all of the years he had worked at the Archive, absent only a handful of days when ill, but taking more than enough double and triple shifts to make up for it, this recent lengthy absence was troubling.

Zara stared at the data, looking for errors, hoping for a Hub glitch during the initial power outage that might have clocked Jaron in as someone else or might have failed to clock him in, any anomaly that might explain his extended absence.

She found nothing.

He had never arrived. Nothing meant, when combined with his absence from Rhyd's flat, from Grainger's suites, from his own, that something unsavory had happened or he had gone into hiding. Or perhaps he had taken Rhyd's advice and retreated Outside beyond the brako's reach. There were no rosters recording prossers and crossers, only data about the trade of goods made on an increasingly common basis before the brownouts had begun. There was no way to verify if he had gone Outside without going Out to look for him.

Now that the doors to Outside had closed again, if Jaron had gone there, there was no way to know.

What was obvious was that, unless he had intended to leave his archivist post without a word, he was at risk of losing his job.

For decades, citizens had Vanished without a trace. The hazards of Hebanthe Falls and the threat the Founder and Crows had once been to the Levs meant that most businesses had learned to leave a post open, unoccupied, for a handful of days or weeks before someone's position was considered terminated and vacant. It allowed ticks to continue to flow to needy families, made allowances for the possibility of injury or accident outside the job, and acknowledged the uncomfortable reality of people being crowed for no reason other than the Founders' paranoid whims.

The practice of crowing had ended with the Coup, with the deposing of Haythem Kemway, but the rise of the brako introduced a different reason for someone to fail to show up for their shifts.

Given Jaron's stellar record, Archive management might have allowed him several days, possibly several more, to report in. They might allow additional days before they considered his absence abnormal. With the Archives having endured the same shutdown as everything else in the city, before the need to hunt an assassin had sprung up, there had been days when his absence would have been inconsequential.

But she decided to remove the possibility of termination to give Rhyd long enough to find him.

A few keystrokes and it was done. Skim a few projects from other archivists so that they were tagged with Jaron's ID on days when the Archives had been open. Tamper with shift logs to indicate his arrival and departure, his attendance when there had been work to do. Her efforts would make any search Grainger or the buggers made more difficult, as it would for any but the most skilled haikara, but it would make Jaron appear to be where he should be, and protect him from everyone else except for whoever might have taken and harmed him.

Zara would get to the truth. As soon as she had it and saw Rhyd, he would have it too.

An Echo to her left beeped, its data search complete, and she swiped a finger across the pad to rouse the screen from slumber without looking at it. One more click on the Echo she was working on, one more saved piece of location data, and Jaron's job was secured.

His life, however, was less so unless she could verify if he had gone Outside.

She glanced at the other Echo and clicked on the top link her search provided. Five men on the screen, similar in features and yet not the same. Three men dead, one in a construction accident, one of heart failure, and another missing from the fisheries and presumed to have fallen into the river.

The two remaining, however, were of particular interest to Zara and would be to Rhyd as well. The first sported shaggy blonde curls and a cleft lip, another fishery worker with a record of disorderly drunk arrests and public fights with a multitude of Crows and bugorra over the years. Rhyd had not mentioned a noticeable birth defect and none was visible on the grainy bodycam images he provided. Rhyd claimed Vanderwall to be bald, a detail the bodycam shots supported, but hair was easy to change. Those two discrepant details were not enough to rule out the first face. Only Rhyd could do that.

Zara jotted down the man's name, his place of employment, the name of the hostel where he had last lived, and saved the file and photo to a passchip to be given to Rhyd later.

The second face fit the provided description more accurately but came without a residence, a place of employment, or any manner of arrest or personal record. It came only with a name and date of birth that she also recorded before saving the information to the passchip. She looked again at the man presumed missing, also bald, of similar build and age and expression as the still living man, and yet not the same. Curious if he, too, was Vanderwall, or had been, she included his information on the passchip before popping it out of the reader. It was tucked into a protective cover and into her pocket where it would remain safe until Rhyd came.

Any of those five could have been the original Vanderwall. There was no way to know.

Then she began to search again under a different set of parameters. Two faces. Two names. It might not be enough.

The man called Uriah Frankel was similar enough to the bodycam footage for Zara to believe they had their man. Any other details she could find would be included, and soon Rhyd would have every piece of information she could find.

Not long after, so would every bugger in Hebanthe Falls.

❧*❦

Neoma was the last person Kal expected to find in his office when he trudged in, his shoulders slumped but tense, his brow knit, and a throbbing pain shooting from one temple, around the back of his skull, to the other. Her piercing expression of accusation and the heaviness of her perfume, which had permeated the room and grown stagnant enough to indicate how long she had been here, did not help his mood as she lurched from the sofa and thrust a finger toward his chest.

He was already moving away to put the desk between them before contact was made.

"Afraid to face me?"

He sagged into his chair. "Why would I be afraid of you?"

"You assassinated…"

He realized before she spoke what her answer would be, and so he cut her off with a sluggish hand wave and snipped, "You know I did no such thing. Haythem was my friend. No one loved the Founder more than…"

"Me and his children…"

Kal held her gaze with a growing sneer and drawled, "If that's true, I'm the next Founder."

"You'll never be…" Neoma began triumphantly, only to realize that was the point Kal intended to make. The probability that she had ever loved Haythem was as unlikely as the possibility that the Voices of Faith Senior could rise to the position of Founder. He did not possess Kemway blood.

Nor did she.

Having passed through clusters of Talkers in the Hall, many eyeing him as he entered, others refusing to look into his eyes, he was reminded, as Neoma leaned over the desk to snarl in his face, that there were only three possibilities for leadership in the eyes of the Voices.

Neoma, who desperately wanted to cling to the power she had gained by marriage and increase it, despite having no blood claim to the position. She supported the Voices fiscally and vocally, or had in the past, and had the experience in politics and the willpower to force Hebanthe Falls to submit to her rule, whether they wanted to or not.

Ulynda, a child too young to have experience, but the only known heir left to take the reins. She was malleable and could, if married to the right person, produce a male heir who could join the Kemways and the Voices more intimately than they had ever been united. If not eventually bound by marriage, at least the youngster could be counseled by the Voices the way previous Founders had been and taught to make their tenets her own. Given the right guidance as she matured, she could be anything the Voices wanted her to be.

The final segment of Talkers needed someone else, anyone else, other than an untested child and a too-ambitious woman to fill the leadership chair. Someone to be Founder in name, if not by blood, who was not Oliver Grainger.

Feena was right.

Why not give those Talkers and the disgruntled people of Hebenon both of those things?

The dwarf, while bodily deficient by custom, could provide what the city needed. In time, people would accept him because he was a Kemway. As an untried leader who would need advisors, Kal's belief that the Voices could fulfill that need persisted.

Kal believed Enoch LeRoy was the Voices' best and only choice.

"Who did you hire?"

He also believed that Neoma was not.

"The Founder's of no use to us, to Hebanthe Falls, if he's dead," Kal countered.

"Only if he's locked away in one of your…"

"Told you, that wasn't us. Wasn't me. Ask Captain Grainger. If they had proof, they'd not have…"

"They arrested you!" She spat the words so that the spittle behind them struck Kal in the face.

He swiped the back of his sleeve across his cheek but did not otherwise concede the offense. His lack of reaction made her scowl. "I was released for lack of evidence. It's public record." Released, but he knew the captain had been reluctant to let him go. "Haythem's too valuable to the Faith. I loved him. He was my friend and…"

Neoma drew back with a snort and toss of her hand. "Haythem did not have friends." He had lackeys, servants, and staff. He had aides. He had toadies who followed and fawned and feigned loyalty and love to receive things they wanted or believed they deserved.

Those were not his friends.

Any more than she had been.

Duty done, children borne, Neoma had continued to perform the public duties of the Founder's wife and partner, but there had been little affection between them. She had been little more to Haythem than Kal had been. She knew it but did not have to admit it.

"He was my friend," Kal repeated. "I love him still…and will go to my death supporting a Kemway installed as Founder."

"But not me."

"You are not a Kemway."

Sucking in a breath between her teeth, she studied him, waiting for him to speak again, play his hand, reveal whatever game he intended to play, but there was nothing from him except the sluggish actions of a weary man pouring a drink to ward off Hebenon's chill.

"Ulynda then," she finally snorted with another toss of her head that allowed her hair to fall into place. "As soon as the energy crisis is resolved, I will bring her for indoctrination and appointment.…"

"I'm not the…"

"You are Senior; you're the only one with the authority to…"

"The Nau…"

"Corrupt sycophants that I would not trust to wipe my ass or chew my food." Not even the ones she had known who had previously served the Doctet. "Appoint Ulynda before Remembrance Day. Or during it. The Nau will listen. The people will listen. With their support, Grainger will be forced to relinquish his hold. Give Ulynda what is due…"

"And you?"

Neoma ignored the jab and cinched her jacket belt at her waist. He had not noticed her wearing it and wondered if she had worn it the entire time she had waited.

"If you love him so much, do what Haythem would have wanted, if you hadn't killed him before he could order it…appoint Ulynda…"

Rubbing the bridge of his nose, eyes closed, Kal muttered, "Please leave. Still time before the Remembrance…and the power's not going to be resolved tonight to permit me to do anything. I need to sleep."

Taking another step back, she repeated, "I'll bring her. You'll do what should have been done before…what you know is right."

The door thumped shut. Kal leaned his elbows on the desk and went from rubbing his nose to rubbing his temples, his drink untouched. Three days until the Remembrance. He did not know if the energy crises would be resolved by then to provide the celebration the Nau intended. But he would make sure Neoma did not bring her daughter to the Hall. He needed time. Time in those three days to decide the Voices' fate.

❧Chapter 16❧

It took longer than he hoped to track the Spinks who had aided Jaron before, children who would recognize his face if they saw him. He never knew their names, never learned the places each called 'home', but of every resource in the city at his disposal, the street children who had pledged themselves to Scarecrow's mission were the best chance he had of finding the missing archivist. He could not do it alone. One child after another was tracked and found until he was able to pass on his desperate request.

Then he was forced to wait.

He knew now that Jaron had not been on shift since before their argument. Zara had offered the reassuring possibility that Jaron could have ventured Outside as Rhyd suggested, a hope that Rhyd tried to latch on to, but the thread was too thin to be tenable.

Jaron had been to that door only once. He had not set foot Outside. Rhyd felt secure in the assessment that Jaron had not intended to make the venture into the world unless Rhyd went out beside him.

Perhaps, however, by pushing too far, Rhyd had broken that hope of unity and compelled Jaron to act alone. But he did not think so.

Or chose not to believe it.

Jaron had to be inside the city.

Having poked through the debris in the hideaway where Kemway had drawn his last breath, not sure what he expected to find, he was relieved there were no details there that could point the bugorra to him, except for Ginna. He trusted her discretion and returned to the epicenter of the riot, where the protest had turned deadly. He circled it several times, skulking from alleys to rooftops and back, always in the deepest shadows, before risking the empty intersection to crouch near the place where Kemway had fallen, trying to gauge from that line of sight where the killing shot had originated. Enterprising individuals wanting to reuse the materials had removed the platform as soon as the buggers left it unattended. Any other evidence had either dropped through the grates to the lower Levs, eventually into the river, or had been scooped up by the bugorra in their multiple sweeps.

Those bits of evidence did not interfere with his study. The shot had come from inside the crowd, somewhere in front of the platform and to the side, on the side where Haythem had joined, where Scarecrow had entered the fray, and where Enoch and Ulynda had been positioned on the half-Lev above. The shot had not come from any of the platforms, walks, paths, or rooftops. It had not come from above or below. The likely angle meant the shot could have been meant for the Founder, but might also have been intended for the bugger lieutenant. Or Scarecrow. Or anyone in between.

Kemway's death might have been accidental.

Such a shot into a crowd was reckless. Anyone taking it would know that. Accident or not, the shooter's culpability remained.

Though obscured from the few passersby who dared the darkness, the limping steps on the other side of the intersection announced Lieutenant Young's return to the scene, to see what she could find as he was doing. The cadence of bugorra boots, once Crow boots, was a sound Scarecrow knew well after so many years of hunting them, but her limp, her muttering voice, identified her before he saw her.

The bugorra were not his quarry. Nor was Young. But she could be an ally if she were willing. They could work together.

With his hand on the pocket where he had stashed the evidentiary passchip, he watched her actions, waiting to see if she would see him, acknowledge him, pursue him. Focused as she was on the details of her quest, she paused when she noted him in the shadows, a shape out of place. After a side-to-side glance, she crossed the intersection with stiff, struggling steps and when she reached the alley where he tensely waited, she leaned against the corner of the building so that her body position and long bugger cloak blocked him from anyone else's view.

Not a chase then. Scarecrow found that tentatively promising.

"What happened to Founder Kemway?"

Scarecrow did not reply. His head was cocked as if listening to something nearby and Ilya turned her head to peer in the direction he seemed to be staring.

Or maybe he was staring at her behind the tinted eyepieces in the mask that hid his face.

When she detected nothing of note, she continued, "Ginna said you got him somewhere safe. Where was that?"

"Ask her." If the location were a Spinks squat, he would not expose it to the bugorra.

Ilya grunted, her efforts to recognize his voice thwarted by digital filters, and crossed her arms, again scanning the intersection without turning her back on the vigi she did not fully trust. She trusted him enough to stand here in conversation, to not immediately try to arrest him or confront him in a fight she was not equipped to win, but the lingering years of 'Scarecrow as the enemy' habit she carried would not be easily overthrown. "Tell me one thing. Was he alive when you left him with my sister?"

"He was dying as soon as he was hit. Don't think anything could have saved him."

Ilya nodded and sighed. Ginna had said the same thing. "Think he was the target?"

Scarecrow cocked his head as if to suggest that question was more than one thing and Ilya scowled. He made a small sound that she interpreted as amusement before replying, "Could have been."

Huffing, she muttered, "Could have been you…or me." With the number of buggers at hand, the number of brako swarming through the crowd, the number of Talkers milling about, the target could have been anyone, but her assessment was a fair one, one she determined Scarecrow had likewise reached.

"Find anything?"

"No."

The dialog was as awkward for the one who had blamed the vigi for the city's ills as it was for the one who had few reasons to trust the lawkeepers who were once his enemies. For the moment, however, they were on the same side, hunting a pair of common enemies that presented as the assassin of the Founder and Vanderwall.

"Got a name for you though." The clatter of a tipped recycling bin on a side street and the scurry of two yowling cats turned their heads and kept Ilya from immediately replying.

When she was satisfied that the racket was not a threat, when Scarecrow did not continue, Ilya prompted, "Name?"

"Uriah Frankel." She was not looking at him, but he could read her disquiet in the tensing of her shoulders and the shifting of her arms. "Look him up. He was there, at the protests, just didn't know it."

The distraction the Founder presented had been enough to draw their attention away from the brako bane to a man who had been unaccounted for too long.

"We didn't…or he didn't? Who is he?"

"Got away from us…but he won't much longer."

Vanderwall. Ilya stared at Scarecrow now, her full attention on the vigi who had, it seemed once again, had success where the captain and bugorra had failed. "How do you…?"

Deciding not to give up the passchip just yet, he replied, "Search his name. You'll find him."

"If you're right…leave him for…it's not up to you…" In the distance, a short, shouted exchange made her look away from the vigi in the direction of the sound.

"If I'm right," Scarecrow growled, "if I get to him first, he's mine." He had done his duty by telling her what he knew, or part of it. He did not tell her about the soaper. Did not tell her he had seen the man's face. They could find Frankel's face on their own. What the bugorra did with the data was up to them. If they reached Frankel first, so be it. What Scarecrow did with the knowledge was up to him.

The grate beneath Ilya's feet shuddered. She did not need to look back to know Scarecrow was gone, into the shadows above her, into the darkness on a hunt of his own.

In the gloom beneath her, on another walkway in another alley, another shadow moved.

❧*❧

After his earlier rash, unrestrained blow, the speecher unit on the side of the prisoner's head was too damaged to connect to the translator he brought in the hopes of manipulating more than yes or no responses from the limp, exhausted man. The urge to cast the translator against the wall in frustration was tempered by the man at his side who muttered, "Should kill him and be done with it, sir. Keeping him's inviting trouble."

Vanderwall opened his mouth, but his retort was aborted by a signaled four-knock pattern at the warehouse door and its hesitant opening behind him. He recognized the bedraggled blonde intruder and spat, "Didn't I tell you not to…?"

"He knows, sir." The stammering fellow did not lift his head or make eye contact.

"Who knows what?" Already frustrated and irritated, Vanderwall did not have the patience for guessing games.

"Scarecrow…he's got a name…gave it to the buggers…"

"That's not…" Few of his underlings knew his name, his identity. Frankel had gone to extraordinary lengths to keep his name and face to himself. But Scarecrow had seen his face, and he had known it would not be long before the vigi dug down to the truth of who the brako boss was. Now this fellow knew his name too. Or thought he did. Curiosity might prompt him, and others, to seek a face for that name. As the other man at Vanderwall's elbow cocked his head curiously, Frankel knew that slip would have to be addressed.

The fellow at the door took a wary step back as Vanderwall's bulk filled the door. The chained captive did not stir or react to the mention of Scarecrow, suggesting he was still groggy from the earlier blow or unconscious from the electrical short-circuit signals the translator had fired into his brain.

"Heard him say it…" the messenger began.

Vanderwall's growl kept him from saying more. Whatever the brako behind him interpreted from the exchange, he only muttered, "Told you he'd be a liability…"

The sentry at the door remained silent.

Yanking that man outside the warehouse so that the door snapped shut, the translator dropping and cracking open on the walkway, Vanderwall barked, "Find me an empty warehouse."

"What good's that gonna do, sir?" He ignored the broken equipment he had spent so many ticks on, except to push the bigger pieces aside with the toe of his boot.

"Do it!" To the messenger, he snapped, "You too!"

He did not need to explain his orders. He had a plan, one that would solve a problem that had plagued the brako since their inception. His captive was exactly the bait he needed.

The pair scurried away, neither wanting to be on the receiving end of their boss's wrath. Once they were beyond sight, Vanderwall growled to the sentry, "Take care of them," before stalking away.

The sentry nodded silently. He knew what needed to be done.

❧*❧

Grainger slid the T2 across the desk in Tamner's direction, squinting away the pain between his eyes that made the doctor-scientist-turned-civic liaison indistinct around the edges. He wanted a drink but was doing his best to ration what stores of alcohol he had. There was no way to know when he would acquire more.

With a two-man crew creeping over the city's hull, making an effort to clear the burnt debris away and collect missed evidence, all that remained was the guessing. All the guessing in the world could be wrong. Until he had the opportunity to speak to the second tech on the shell at the time of the explosion, there would be few forthcoming answers unless the pair outside found something he could use.

"How's this a good idea?" He was surprised the Nau had agreed to such a plan and wondered which one of them had suggested it. The most likely answer to both questions was the man who stood on the other side of the desk and picked up the T2 with a half-hearted shrug.

"They haven't reached an accord yet. I told them I'd get your thoughts. Things are taking too long. As it stands, even if you put Lash to work solving the problem, planning, fabricating, and installing the parts will likely take longer than we've got. The hydros are struggling. If they fail, we'll have nothing. The more people we vacate, the less power consumption there'll be and the more time we'll have to complete repairs."

Grainger shook his head. "Some aren't going to want to go." He was one of them, but he chose not to admit that aloud. "And even if they do…some aren't likely to come back after they've had a taste…"

That was the crux of descent within the Nau as well, a potential shift in the center of population density that no one could foresee and might affect Hebenon's survivability. As Tamner saw it, either way, a reduction in the city's population was inevitable. Either they survived Outside, or they starved, froze, or were killed by violent unrest where they were. He shrugged again, his expression grim. "Not sure it's a bad thing in the long run…and I don't think we have a choice."

It would take decades or centuries to transform Outside into anything akin to the way of life that had existed inside of Hebanthe Falls since the collapse of the old world, but returning to the Outside was the future that Duncan Kemway had hoped for when he had shut this tiny fraction of humanity inside the fall city.

Having spent a significant amount of time in Marbordo, Tamner believed the move to Outside was in everyone's best interest. For those who chose to remain inside or return to it after the systems were restored, it would be their right to do so. One way or another, humanity would evolve, whether inside or out.

He would not have suggested the solution to the Nau if he did not believe it had merit. Their future, after all, was already in need of dire realignment.

"I don't trust him." Grainger leaned back in the chair, eyes narrowed. Whether his expression was because of his obvious pain or annoyance, Tamner could not guess.

"You already said it wasn't…" Tamner began with a frown.

"I know what I said…what we saw…but we don't have the truth yet. We need proof. He might not have been out there, but that doesn't mean he didn't have an accomplice. Until I'm sure…"

"We can't afford to wait that long. We need to act. He's our best shot. He can't work in a cell. Keep him up here, house arrest in the lab if you want, where he can work on getting this sorted out while you…"

The captain grunted again and swiveled his chair toward the window to watch the parah crossing back and forth between the hemp harvest underway in their vast fields and the collection of structures in which they lived. The demand for hemp would be high if they were to make necessary repairs. Their work was so crucial that many of the city's residents locked outside were lending their labor to the effort. Avoiding the issue of Lash and his importance to the array repairs, he changed the subject. "Think they'll cooperate?"

Watching the hemp farmers for a moment, Tamner finally replied, "I don't know…but I think so. They'll have to. We need to try."

Several more silent moments passed, both men weighing the pros and cons of the doctor's suggested solutions to the ongoing crisis. Eventually, Grainger nodded without looking at the doctor. "See what they say…if they'll agree…talk to the Nau again…"

He knew what the Founder would have said and done in this situation. What the Doctet would have ordered to preserve their centuries of upheld privilege and segregation. They would have rerouted as much power into the Uppers as they could and squeezed the Levs dry until all that remained was the bare minimum of workers to provide the food and nessies the Uppers relied on that they could not get from the Factories or the Outside.

But he was not Haythem Kemway. He had never wanted to be him. The Nau was not the Doctet. Together, they were the only ones who could make this decision. The choice to stay inside or go Out should jointly belong to every citizen in the city. Strongly encouraging them to venture Out, if that was what the Nau thought best, was not solely in Oliver's hands.

Only Lash's fate was. Only the array repairs were. And to that secondary, but primary matter, he gave Tamner another nod and reluctantly muttered, "Do it. Set him up."

❧CHAPTER 17❧

Lash ran his thin fingers over the stark white top of the lab station as he scanned the room he had been brought to without explanation. Better accommodations than the featureless four-walled, windowless cell he had been deposited in before and had expected to never escape, and better in many ways than the Lev flat he had called home for more than a dozen years. It was brighter than the corridor beyond the door that had closed behind him and with light being a luxury now, as he perused the equipment in the room, he suspected he was here to perform a very specific task.

It took no effort to guess what that was as Tamner turned and wiped his hands on the front of his shirt, leaving the Echo screen flashing its demand for a password in white against its black screen.

"Isn't much," the doctor said apologetically as he rose. His gaze strayed towards the mattress on the narrow wall ledge meant to serve as a bed he sometimes used when at work for too many long hours, the door beside it that provided access to the toilet room, and a corner now furnished with a micro-cooker, a small, square cool box, and a sink intended for the cleaning of scientific tools and lab equipment. A plate, cup, and single set of eating utensils sat on the counter beside it.

Many labs were similarly furnished, intended by previous Founders to encourage scientists, inventors, and designers to remain on task for as many hours each day as they could realistically function.

Tamner's lab was different. He had graduated, over the years, into a man with enough status and knowledge to warrant one of the best facilities in the Uppers.

This room was not part of it.

"Good enough." Lash examined the clean clothes laid out on the mattress without touching them.

"Yes, well, dire times and all that. He won't let you leave until the array's back at capacity, but so long as you don't…"

"At least he decided I didn't cause that." Or the captain had enough doubts about his participation to permit Lash the opportunity to prove himself and make the failure right. Compared to the fate the Founder had once subjected him to, this little lab was a luxury.

But he was a prisoner all the same.

"You've got power to work with, long as we have it, and I'll get you anything you need. So long as you can get us blueprints, plans, designs for new components, anything before the hydros shut down, you shouldn't be here long."

Lash nodded, continuing to evaluate the room rather than look the doctor in the eye. "Would help if I could see the damage…see what went wrong."

"I'll get you every image and as much data as there is, from the moment things went wrong. They agree…Grainger and the Nau…that the sooner we get this sorted, the sooner we get back to normal. Whatever you need…"

Side-eyeing Tamner, Lash reached the tiny multi-pained porthole window that had once been filled with an array of gases and particles between each pane to aid in the illusion of a poisoned Outside. The luxury of this window was a rare thing. He wondered what this room had been used for before. It only showed the sky and the top of the distant western mountains, but it was a welcome view.

"You don't expect normal, do you?"

"Not after all of this," Tamner concurred with a sigh and shake of his head. "Not after the Founder's assassination."

Lash met the doctor's gaze at last, his eyes wide. "He's been found? He's dead?"

"Popped up during a protest and got himself shot." Kemway had no hand in the shooting, as far as Tamner knew, but his frustration with the situation bled out in both word and tone. "Don't know why he was there, who did it…but it's done now."

The rule of the Founders was over.

Deciding it was time to leave Lash to his work, preferring to avoid an in-depth discussion about Kemway's passing, he stepped toward the door. "Password's there," he gestured to a card on the counter beside the Echo. "I'll let the others know you're okay…where you are, if you want me to."

Hiding something like Lash's whereabouts from Ballard, who would eventually notice his neighbor's extended absence, was to invite another raid into the Uppers, another potential Coup if it coincided with another spark with the already agitated population of the Levs. Hebenon had endured enough violence.

"Make sure Skelter knows. I'll need things if he can get them."

Though Tamner nodded, he said, "Captain's not going to let just anyone…"

"Best kaheao there is. I trust him. If you want this done right, done fast, gonna have to let me work how I want. Your…his…choice." Lash shrugged. "I don't want the hydros down any more than anyone else does, Doc. As you say, this isn't gonna fix itself."

Scarecrow trusted the kaheao, too. That was enough for Tamner. He nodded his agreement. "I'll see what I can do. Contact's on the card too. Send me the list…help us get Hebenon out of the dark."

❧*❧

Crime tips often fed into the hotline, details about missing persons, robberies, assaults, verbal and physical threats, and murders. Reports of suspect activity and criminal business practices, and, throughout the end of the Founder's rule, hit after hit of Scarecrow sightings that Grainger had been tasked to take seriously and investigate. None of those sightings had resulted in finding him, as the vigi continued to earn the popular support of those oppressed, marginalized, and victimized by Haythem's paranoid policies. The

Coup had not ended those sightings, nor had the rise of the brako and conversion of Crows to bugorra, but sometimes requests came in begging for Scarecrow's help as though the bugorra had direct access to the vigi who had fought against law-keepers for so long.

The Crows might have become bugorra, their bird-beaked faces now associated with the brako who had raided the law-enforcement stores during and after the Coup, and the Scarecrow's fight might have shifted focus to the same brako the buggers fought, but that did not mean they were allies. It did not mean they had access to him.

Still, the reports and requests came in.

Often, such tips were bogus, frivolous, or misleading, some too petty for Grainger's officers to deal with.

This particular message, forwarded to his dim Echo screen at an hour when he should have been sleeping, felt to be something more serious than frivolous.

Everything lately seemed to be serious.

It was too late to address it. The Founder was dead. Some would say that, under the circumstances, his abduction no longer mattered.

He read the message again.

The abduction mattered to Grainger.

The anonymous message might be a ruse, a distraction. It might be a trap set to eviscerate the bugorra's spread-too-thin force. But if true, if evidence of the abduction had been found, it was worth taking the time to pursue. He would not jump to the messenger's urgent tune, but he would investigate the scene himself. He would plan a force, bide his time to bypass a potential trap, and investigate what had been reported. At the other end of this message, at the address provided, he believed he would find the Talkers.

Kal would be there. Grainger was sure of it.

He shut the message and draped his arm over his closed eyes in the hopes of elusive sleep. He would bring the Voices down at last with the truth of their crimes, and if he was fortunate, this proof would lead to the assassin, too.

❧*❧

Off-shift but out of his protective Scarecrow shell, Rhyd was unprepared for the empty bottle that was flung past his head to shatter on something behind him. Long-honed reflexes allowed him to duck out of the way in the same instant that he realized he was not the intended target. Shouts of outrage erupted as the bird-beaked form struck by the projectile turned with his companions and launched into the collection of unmasked, but equally anonymous-looking, nondescript brutes shouting, "You killed the Founder!"

Rhyd shot out his arms and held back the coworkers exiting the shed behind him on impulse, preventing them from stepping into the thick of the erupting fray.

There were too many. Two dozen, maybe more. He could not count them as the collection of combatants met in a thunder of fists and boots and an assortment of knives, thumpers, poppers, and injectors. People from nearby vindis shrieked and ducked behind closed doors or stalls that were barely adequate protection against the weight of objects and bodies thrown against them or through thinly paned windows. Passersby caught in the commotion screamed and tried to scramble out of the way. Confident his coworkers were safe, Rhyd ducked into the crowd, grabbed the arm of a woman stumbling to avoid the kicking, trampling feet, and yanked her to safety, thrusting her back into the mass of his shift-change coworkers. A few of his fellow bilgers followed suit, doing their best to shield the helpless and drag them away from potentially lethal blows.

Something solid, a fist or a thumper, struck Rhyd's injured shoulder and spun him sideways as he released the woman's hand. She was sucked into the security of the Shed where crew less prone to engage in physical confrontation might protect her. He turned again and landed one fist into the nose of someone who had just shouted, "You killed Vanderwall!"

The words might have been intended for the beaked brako he was grappling with.

They might have been aimed at Rhyd, though only if the speaker knew his dual identity. For that to be true, there was only one sure way for that detail to be known.

His target stumbled, pulled to the ground by others wanting their turn in the fight. In the shoving and pulling, Rhyd was driven back as he fumbled in his pocket for the recovered hemplastic bearing. He was caught by one of his crewmates and dragged into the Shed.

But not before he saw that one man head and shoulders taller than everyone else.

He growled and tried to surge through the door. His aim was good. He could make the thrown shot and take Vanderwall down at least long enough, if he was lucky, for the bugorra to make an arrest.

The other bilgers blocked his way.

"You crazy? You can't take 'em all!"

Rhyd yanked his arms free, wincing at the renewed pain in his shoulder, but the pause the words and action inserted into his fury was enough to temper his impulsive instinct to fight.

Not even Scarecrow could fight so many at once. Six or eight, perhaps. Two dozen was suicide. Showing his hand, his skill, would be an identifying death blow.

If not for his coworkers' interference, that knowledge might not have prevented him from trying if his efforts meant reaching Vanderwall and putting him down.

He retreated, barely noticed, through the bilgers and rescued passersby watching through the doorway until he could disengage, retreat to one of the back rooms, and sneak into the shafts. There were other ways to get home, but home was not where Rhyd intended to go.

The brako were out of control. And now he had the first shred of potential proof that what he feared most was true.

Vanderwall had Jaron.

Jaron needed him. Hebenon needed Scarecrow.

If he were lucky, Vanderwall would still be part of this fight by the time Scarecrow emerged in Rhyd's place. If the bugorra did not arrive first.

❧*❧

Adjusting the brim of his hat so that the collected moisture ran down the back of his coat rather than the sides of his face and neck, Jonner studied the walk to his left and right before crossing to the alley across from Vapors and several doors away from it. Not that caution mattered. The entire city was veiled in shadow, having become a tomb that reminded him of every minute he had spent in the Core, a different sort of tomb he had been thrust into against his will.

He intended never to be trapped that way again. Not when there was an option to be free.

Not when he could make certain that everyone in Hebanthe Falls had the possibility of living the life humanity was meant to have, the life their ancestors had enjoyed before an eternity of environmental abuses had imploded upon their heads.

"You got it?"

Eido nodded and looked him over as if assessing him for a detail not readily seen, as if she thought he was hiding something. "Everything you asked for," she replied when satisfied with his honesty and veracity. "You can do this?"

Voice dropping, turning his back to the street to mask his identity and hers from an encroaching set of lumbering steps, Jonner replied, "It'll work soon as I can get out there. We do it now, before the array's up, then we'll have to leave Hebenon. Stayin' inside'll be the death of us otherwise."

"Will be."

Jonner looked back, wide-eyed, at the last voice he expected to interrupt him. He did not know Colyx well, despite their years in the Core. He knew him to be a brawler, a private man who most often kept his words and thoughts to himself. He knew him to be a protective man, particularly of his adopted daughter, Enoch, and later, of Skelter.

He knew little else about him.

"I don't know what you…" began Eido with evasive innocence.

"Colyx." He offered his hand but then, judging that she would not accept the offer, dropped it again. "I wanna help. Don't let these fool you." He tapped the leg braces. "I know what to do. I have a plan. I can help."

Jonner growled, "You left us to die." He was unsure how Colyx had escaped the Core, how Skelter and Otta had done it. He had not seen them at the door but that did not mean they had not been there. He was reasonably certain, however, that they had not been.

But he was certain of one thing as he scrutinized the bigger man's sincere face. They had both been in agreement about escaping their Core prison. They both agreed that escaping this prison was equally necessary, perhaps more so if humanity expected to survive.

Colyx neither nodded nor shrugged nor offered an explanation for the accusation Jonner made. He had done what he needed to do to survive, just as Jonner had. In the Core, survival was down to the individual. Here, now, survival was going to take a joint effort. Instead, he said, "No one's going to know me. I'm strong enough. I can do this. Give me a chance…hear me out. Let me help."

Jonner and Eido traded glances. Willing recruits were necessary if the Players were to succeed in opening the city to Outside and getting the population out into it. Trust was necessary, albeit harder to give. People willing to take risks in the name of freedom were rare. Could they afford not to hear what Colyx had to offer?

Jonner's head bobbed.

Eido smiled evasively and offered her thin hand.

"Welcome to the Igraci. Jonner'll get you caught up and take in your ideas. If they're any good, we'll let you know what's next."

Grinning like an excited child, Colyx shook her hand.

❧Chapter 18❧

The length of sterile gauze he wrapped around his hand had been reprocessed so many times it was now a faint yellow from the chemical processes, frayed at the edges and worn thin in multiple places but still functional enough to protect knuckles scraped raw in the unanticipated street brawl. The tensions between Feena's followers and those who continued to follow in his leadership, or some blind belief in Mam Kemway's authority, continued to escalate since his predecessor's death, with both sides blaming the other for events that held few facts. They had been thinly united once by the hunt to locate the missing Founder, each for their own reasons, but now that the man was dead, that cohesion was ripped away like an adhesive plast from a raw wound, removing any veneer of cooperation that could have held them together.

He did not dislike Feena Wulfe nor hold a grudge against Tyrisi Balling or any others who supported her. She had a good head for business; some might say too good, as she pushed back against the progress Vanderwall strove to generate. She might have been a worthy ally under different circumstances. Now she had nothing to offer him unless he worked for those things himself. He could not trust her.

His previously sworn alliance to the woman who had promoted him to the mythical status of Vanderwall in his predecessor's place meant he had to put on a show of loyalty he no longer felt. Now that Mam Kemway was without her husband's status to shield her, now that she had nothing to cling to but a name, she had nothing to offer Frankel either.

He preferred the idea of drawing all brako together under his leadership, without either woman at the helm, in his way, preferred to run the Levs himself, free of the interference of those who lived in the Ups. Given the animosity between factions, that was not going to be an easy goal to accomplish.

"Sir?"

Bristling at the interruption, he grunted, "What?" pushing aside the evidence of the death of two men he was relieved to have out of his hair. Men who had known too much. He was still debating the removal of that sentry too, but the man had proven loyal in carrying out this duty without question.

There was little privacy here in the relatively new soaper office. Braco went in and out every hour of the day. He should have gone somewhere else in search of solitude, but the first aid kit in his desk had been the closest he could reach and this had been the most convenient place to escape to, to regroup his thoughts, study his ledgers, and reformulate a plan to draw all of the brako from beneath the control of the women who wielded it.

He wondered if Balling had survived the scuffle.

He wondered if he could convince him to abandon Wulfe and defect to his unifying cause.

The flabby, bulging-eyed fellow who spoke wore a bugger uniform but he was no normal bugger. At least not through to his core, whatever he had once been. He was the only bugger ever allowed to pass unaccompanied into the soaper. Everyone recognized him on sight. He was the only bugger Vanderwall partially trusted.

But he was always careful.

"Think we should kill the prisoner…or move him…"

Vanderwall hissed his growing annoyance. "Not you too…"

The fellow shook his head, his fleshy jowls jiggling as he undercut his own words. "Don't mean that…but he's too close to…I don't have details yet, but there's a raid brewing, sir. A few doors away. Captain's looking for something…maybe your man. If he's got wind there's a hostage…or if he finds him before…"

His voice trailed off on an apologetic note.

Leaning back in the chair as he tucked the frazzled edges of the wrap into place to tighten it around his hand, Vanderwall grunted. The trap for Scarecrow was not yet complete, not yet set in motion, but perhaps a bugger raid could be used to his advantage. He might be able to pit the buggers against Scarecrow as it had been in the days before the Coup. That might get Scarecrow off his back. Getting the vigi arrested or killed would be satisfactory payback.

Afterward, once the captive was of no further use, there would be opportunity enough to be rid of him.

"Get me Ronson…and Lee, keep your eyes open. I want to know exactly where and when the buggers are planning to hit."

The heavy-set man nodded. "Soon as I know anything, you'll be the next person to know.

❧*❦

Ilya adjusted her uniform for the second time and tried not to look as nervous as she felt about being in the captain's office for the first time since the Founder's death. The passchip in her sweaty palm was turned this way and that as her fingers fidgeted with the tiny bit of plastic, circuitry, and memory chips. The office was illuminated by the light of Outside, making it one of the few places in the city where one did not have to carry a light stick, alglamp, or battery torch to see. On his Echo, she could not read the tiny blinking text, so she was unsure what he was looking at.

She had heard officers in the breakroom sharing rumors about the Founder's kidnappers, that they had been found despite the efforts she had made. They were speculating on the details, which made her more anxious as she came to stand before the captain. If it were true, he had not confirmed it. As focused as he was on the screen, she wondered if his failure to respond meant he was unaware she was there.

She assumed he was disappointed in her failures. With luck, the data in her hand would be enough to win back his respect.

When the search algorithm completed its slow slog through the struggling Hub files, she hoped that information, too, would help.

"What've you got, Lieutenant?" Grainger finally asked, his current endeavor reaching its end so he could focus on her.

Straightening her shoulders, drawing her heels together to stand straighter, she stretched out her hand to offer the passchip. "I thought you should see this, sir. I know there's rumors about the Talkers…and our evidence for the kidnapping has pointed that way…but we might have been wrong."

He frowned as he looked at her open palm. "What is it?"

"Just listen to it, sir," she replied, swallowing the anxiety his tone generated. "Hear it for yourself."

His frown did not dissipate as he reluctantly took the passchip and inserted it into the Echo's reader. The image of a man's face, grainy and brightly illuminated from behind so that he looked like a featureless shadow, filled the screen.

Grainger assumed, from the intensity of the light, that the message had been recorded before the array's failure.

"Didn't want to be part of this," the digitally modulated voice popped as some other burst of sound created feedback through the recording. "There's evidence here…a lot of it…but it's not her, no matter how he wants it to look…and it's not them. At least, I don't think it is. Bettin' my life on it. Awful lot of trouble to go to…but none of it's real. Don't know his name…just know him by…" The audio crackled again, the words he said next undercut by sizzling static, making them indistinguishable from the background noise. "…just in case…but look deep and you'll find him. Whatever he's doing, whatever he's done…this isn't about ticks. This is something else. Founder's life depends on it."

The words were ambiguous enough to mean anything, but Grainger, too, interpreted them to reference the Founder's abduction. "Who is this?"

Ilya tensed her shoulders to hold back the undignified shrug. What she thought she heard within the static was a word she did not want to believe. "Unknown, sir. It was on my desk in an unmarked envelope when I returned to duty. Desk sergeant didn't know who delivered it." She hesitated before adding, "I didn't listen to it sooner, with everything that's going on."

It had not been so many days ago when the salt protest had turned into a riot that resulted in the death of the Founder. The passchip could have been delivered at any time since that day, or hours, even days, before it, since the last time she had sat at her desk.

"This doesn't mean…" Grainger pinched the bridge of his nose, something he realized he had been doing more since the array's failure. The speaker on the chip had provided no locations, no names, or details that the captain could work with, nor any clues he could use. Even the prospect of a name was potentially lost to digital interference. Some vague implications and insinuations dovetailed with the details he had about a location where the Founder might have been held, but was it enough to serve as evidence?

"People are saying it was Senior Kal and the Talkers…and I know we both believed that…" The only evidence they had was the fact that the kidnappers had worn Talker robes.

"Next you'll tell me it was Scarecrow…or that this is." He waved a dismissive hand at the now black screen.

"It wasn't. It isn't." A few days ago, she would have believed wholeheartedly that the man behind digital voice mods and shadows was the one to submit this sort of evidence to taunt and mislead them. After her recent interactions with him, she believed that offering this evidence, whether real or fabricated, would be against everything the vigi was trying to do.

There was a chance that the speaker on the passchip was Scarecrow. She did not believe it was. She did not believe he was involved in any of this. His focus was on Vanderwall. He had, however, risked exposure and death to save the Founder's life. He had exhibited no fear in doing so.

The speaker on the passchip, male or female, was very afraid.

She could not prove the messenger's claims, but she could do something else. "May I order the nets dredged, sir? He says he might be dead after this…and it's likely been a few days…" There were other ways to be rid of a body if someone wanted the dead undiscovered, but dumping a corpse into the river was most expedient and common. In a few more days, a body beaten and bloated by the rocks and the river would be nearly unrecognizable. "If we do it now, we might find something we can use."

The process would be an inconvenience for the struggling fisheries, but such bugorra requests were common and the temporary cessation of work would be less of a hindrance than the darkness and intermittent availability of power.

Grainger drummed his fingers on the desk, his face pensive and thoughtful, his gaze on her face intense and unnerving so that Ilya was forced to make a more determined effort to appear unflustered by his scrutiny. Finally, he nodded. "Do it…and get this cleaned up so we can hear the rest." He handed the passchip back to her. "Find out who that is…where they are…get someone to mine the code for a time stamp, a signature…anything that might tell us something useful."

Relieved he did not appear disappointed any longer and pleased to have something more to do than sit immobile behind her desk, Ilya bobbed her head. "I will, Captain."

"And next time," he continued, "don't let something like this sit." Not that the data, the message, would dissuade him from his already decided course of action, but it might have some bearing on how he would proceed.

Maybe once the address he had been given was investigated, whatever was found there would fit neatly with this message to form a more accurate picture of the Founder's last days.

Maybe, after that, Grainger would have someone specific to blame for the hell Hebanthe Falls was going through.

❧*❧

Receiving Skelter's unexpected message while donning one of the sets of body armor he kept stashed in secret places throughout the Levs, curious to know what sort of person had reached out to him through the Lev's best kaheao, Scarecrow circled the Lev 3 plaza nearest the hemper for threats or traps that the redhead might unknowingly stumble into or might not be able to see without the assortment of sensory enhancements the suit afforded. He pinpointed the location of brako, of bugorra, of shift workers or shoppers, but none of those people appeared interested in the unilluminated plaza or those who chose to share off-shift banter or mid-shift meals on some of its many benches.

Now that some of the brako had forsaken the crow masks, however, determining all threats was more difficult.

He did not recognize the unkempt, stooped figure pacing from one side of the long bench to the other, but Skelter's white ruffled shirt, red leather trousers, the mechanized eye patch buckled with a strap around his head, and the ornate walking stick balanced against the bench by one hand made him easy to identify. He sat with his legs crossed, his other arm draped casually across the back of the bench, watching people around him with seeming indifference now that he had given up on encouraging the woman to sit and wait.

It was not the first time a streeter had gone to the kaheao for help or protection, for the return of property, or simply in the hope of something they thought would provide a better quality of life if only they could get it in their hands. More typically, the requests came via graffiti sprayed on wet vindi walls, the same way people often called out to Scarecrow.

This, as far as he knew, was a peculiar first. Someone reaching out to him via Skelter. Connecting the two men was a risk to both. But Scarecrow would not allow the risk to stop him from helping.

The little woman screeched in startled alarm when he dropped into the plaza from the half-Lev walkway above their position. The calm turning of Skelter's head, however, and his easy expression when he faced the shadow cut short the sound. Wary still, she inched closer to both Skelter and the one she had asked to see.

"Got my message," Skelter said casually.

"Was on my way out; Brako are stirred up tonight."

"Noticed that." None had troubled the redhead on his way here, but he had noted their increased traffic, heard the agitated, angry mutterings of brako he passed, and the distant cries of those they harassed, and he had made a point of staying out of their way as much as possible. If anyone recognized or noticed him, they left him alone.

"This is Wiffy…think you should hear her out."

"It really you?" Wiffy stammered, shuffling a step closer, wringing her hands around her scarf as she did so. The silhouette she could perceive against the dimness of the plaza's only glowing alglamp was barely discernible. She had never seen the vigi in person, only on the prods where, by now, everyone in Hebenon had seen him.

"Can I help you?" He tried not to frighten her, but his modulated voice was coarse and mechanical, making her wring her hands harder.

"Can you find my husband? Been gone too long, needs his medis."

Scarecrow skeptically shifted his gaze to Skelter though his head did not move. "I'm not…"

Wiffy cast a panicked glance at the kaheao too, afraid that Scarecrow would reject her request before she finished stating it.

"Just listen to her," Skelter repeated.

Scarecrow nodded and waited. It wasn't until Skelter gently cupped Wiffy's elbow that she haltingly began again.

"Melik's a good man…but simple sometimes. Falls in with bad sorts 'cause he wants people to like him…likes to be helpful. When he hasn't…thought the buggers might have him, you know…like they use to…and you know where they keep 'em…you've been there…"

Stories from the Coup had filtered through every stratum in Hebenon. Though few knew why Scarecrow had gone Up, what he had intended to accomplish by doing so, the fact that he had been in the Uppers, had found Outside, had freed many captive prisoners and test subjects spirited away by the Founder's Crows, was well-known.

Wiffy tried to steady her hands as she continued. "After the prods though, I think maybe…I don't think the buggers took him after all. I think Mel went to help…and now without his meds…"

"Help who?" Scarecrow asked as Skelter simultaneously explained, "He's a bleeder without his meds…"

A prickle ran across Scarecrow's shoulders and down his spine. Skelter nodded.

"Wasn't that he wanted to help…not like that…'cause he'd never hurt anyone…but with his medis, we're always short. He'd come to Mel before, wanting favors, wanting him to do things, so he wouldn't have thought twice…"

"Who?"

Wiffy shrugged and clenched her hands around the scarf. "Don't know his name. Mel never told me. Dark-skinned fellow with patterns in his hair." She let go of the scarf long enough to gesture as though drawing designs on the side of her head while gesturing with the other about how tall the man was. "They weren't friends. Mel doesn't make friends. He isn't…like that. Usually, he made Mel a runner and gave him Hebbies or…" She shrugged as though not wanting to complete the sentence, her voice trailing off evasively as if she was embarrassed or wanted to hide some uncomfortable truth.

She clutched the scarf again and stared at her thin, holey cloth shoes as water dripped from fingerless gloves thick with grime. "Been so long now. Saw them talking a few days before. Mel wouldn't say what he wanted, doesn't like to talk about his helpin'…said it was a job and he'd have enough ticks for a new dress…same as he always gives me on my birthday. I don't think…now that it's been…without his medis…he might not be livin'," she choked, "but I have to know that the buggers didn't take him."

Behind the mask, Rhyd closed his eyes. Finding a dead man would be difficult, but perhaps something Zara could find in the Hub records, in the Archives, could determine the missing man's fate. If the bugorra had taken him, arrested him for some reason, there should be a record.

And maybe the single clue she had inadvertently given, filtered through Skelter's words, would be a bigger clue to a larger mystery.

"What's his name?"

Wiffy shook her head, her mien wavering between defiance and fear, before she wiped her bare wrist over her teary eyes and choked on the name as though it hurt to say it. "Melik. Melik Tully-Belder."

Skelter put a comforting arm around her and drew her close.

"When did you last see him?" Even an approximate date or time would help. It was something Skelter could have asked and taken to Zara without Scarecrow's involvement.

Perhaps he had not done so, Rhyd thought with surprise when Wiffy responded with conviction and certainty because the woman had not been willing to share the last of her truth with anyone else. Or Skelter had thought it best he heard the details himself.

"Last time…he said we'd watch the big show together on the prods when he came home and I got off shift…that last one prodded all over the city."

The last major prodcast show of any sort before the announcement of Founder Kemway's death had been Venn's orchestral concert.

The night the Founder had been taken from the Uppers.

Skelter's half-smile at Scarecrow's reaction, unseen but still felt, was smug.

"Was he a Talker? Did he know…?"

Wiffy shook her head from side to side. "We've no use for those eblans…ain't never done anything for us."

He had not expected affirmation, but the question needed to be asked. "Do you have his pass? An ICD or…?"

Again, she shook her head no. "He didn't want Crows findin' him. Didn't want the Founder to take him. I told him he was being a payaso but…you know…having a blood sickness…he was lucky he hadn't been put out as a babe…lucky to live as long as he did. It was bad enough his name's out there on the registry…"

"Registry?"

There were multiple lists the Kemways had kept, meant to keep tabs on people in the Levs. Dissidents, criminals, troublemakers. Arrested addicts. Tingers. People who failed to log into the prods each day for mandatory indoctrination. Men, women, children. Andis. Those who could not work. Those too handicapped to be productive members of society.

Those the Founder and Doctet could not allow to breed if they were to keep Hebanthe Falls' population pure.

Wiffy sniffed and wiped her nose again. "Cut as a boy…the way we all are if they don't want us makin' little ones. That's one of the reasons he liked me…couldn't have children anyway." She shrugged without elaborating on why she had been selected not to bear children. The reason did not matter.

Scarecrow understood.

He was beginning to formulate an image, a timeline, with the pieces she offered, that suggested the answer he believed he would find at the end of his search for Melik Tully.

It was not a pretty one.

"Whatever I can find, he'll let you know. He inclined his head towards Skelter, the redhead having kept silent, choosing to observe and listen as he was most often prone to do. Once word of this meeting got out, as Scarecrow was sure it would, Wiffy would be the first of many unfortunates to seek him through Skelter.

He trusted Skelter could manage most of those requests or supply other resources as necessary.

As he retreated into the shadows, leaving the pair in the square, intending to seek the one person he suspected could offer answers, Scarecrow was unsure if such arrangements through Skelter, such entanglements between them, would prove to be a good thing.

Or if anyone would like what he found when Melik Tully was thrust into the light.

❧Chapter 19❧

ach vacant stretch of shaft felt wrong, sounded wrong. The familiar tingle across his skin, every expected hiss, gurgle, bubble, and crackle, was either absent or strained, barely audible to his sensory units. Pipes that usually glowed with infrared warmth offered only a pale shine. The increased traffic of crews scurrying to redirect power and water, to counteract the damage created by increased pressure on the hydros, to prepare the systems for the inevitable surge that would occur when the array was brought back online, kept Scarecrow's progress through the shafts at a frustratingly delayed crawl as he wound his way through them.

He had staked out the hemper where Wiffy worked and afterward followed her in the shadows to the dirty, windowless flop she called home, a place without running water and negligible power routed to it from a hacked tap into the city's main line at a nearby intersection pole. From the condition of the pipes and wires, when he examined them inside the shafts, the regulators and generators that should have kept the place at a functional, livable minimum, he doubted there had been adequate systems here before the brownouts began. The pipes were corroded, the power wires rat-frayed, looking as if they had lacked function for many years.

Why, he wondered, had Shed crews never been directed here for repairs? As an employed worker, Wiffy should have been supplied with better housing. The Doctet, in place when she had begun her hemper career, should have seen that such things were provided as intended for every productive citizen of Hebanthe Falls.

The possibility of Melik coming to the authority's attention, of being discovered as a man with his particular defects who had survived childhood, might have prompted a desire, from both Melik and Wiffy, to remain hidden, out of the Hub records, and might have prompted them to accept such meager housing.

It was likely this had been Melik's home before it had become Wiffy's, that she had given up the life she had enjoyed before to be part of his. If she had a better home elsewhere, allotted by the Doctet, it was likely empty or had been invaded by streeters and addicts.

She returned home after her first shift long enough to change from mist-soaked clothes into dryer, cleaner ones, to hang the damp ones across a wireline running through the single room flat to dry, before returning to the hemper for another with the wail of the shift change whistle. He waited until she was away, perched on the flop roof, before pushing through the broken, unlatched ventilation grate to look inside.

He could have asked for permission.

He did not think she would grant it.

He sought details in the life debris gathered here. Who Melik was. What he looked like. How he filled his days since he was not legally permitted to work or collect ticks. The single-room flop with its corner-curtained shower and toilet isolated by corrugated hemp board sheets, contained very little else. Against the rear wall where Scarecrow entered, where it might absorb some of the city's warmth from behind the wall when there was any to absorb, lay a filthy, hand-stitched mattress fashioned from discarded clothes and probably stuffed with the same. It was rumpled and flat, a cushion that provided less comfort for rest than protection from the sheet metal floor beneath it. Drab blankets devoid of their original color were bunched at the foot of the bed, partially draped over the lip of an open storage trunk where the flotsam of Melik and Wiffy's life had accumulated.

Assorted articles of clothing, most of them threadbare and faded to varying shades of gray and brown. A pair of shoes in need of a shoeman's attention. A rattling plastic sack with a script sticker pasted on the outside…the medis Wiffy had indicated Melik needed to control his blood disorder. A small image on the corner of the sticker suggested the medication had come via a herpa rather than a clinic, possibly the herpa Scarecrow had passed on the way from the hemper to this dismal place.

It might be worth questioning the herpa.

There was a hemplastic locket on a cord tangled with bits of hair, containing an image of a man so faded it was difficult to make out his features without enhancement. A beloved father or brother, perhaps, or else Melik. Scarecrow scanned it with the body cam and stored the images for Zara to retrieve, enhance, and study later. The locket was returned to where he found it. Whoever the man was, it was one of the few treasures Wiffy possessed. There was no need for him to take it.

Two plates and two bowls, two cups and two sets of utensils, all stained with age but clean, lay next to a cracked sink where the last washing waste had seeped onto the floor beneath, into a buildup of green and gray mold that had grown and been scrubbed away many times. Two jugs of water, one full, one nearly empty, sat beside the stain, out of the way of movement within the flop. Two stained cloths, one for washing and one for drying, hung over the basin lip and had also dripped onto the floor. He glanced at the portable heater by the bed, flat-topped with a cooking burner and a power cord that stretched across the room to connect to the wire strung in from outside.

Not safe, but functional.

A headless pipe through the wall would have served as a shower if there had been water to use it. The toilet, dark-stained with water rings and mineral deposits, looked as though it was flushed by a third water jug, larger than the other two, that listed against the wall as though the container had, at some time, sat too near the heater. Water seepage accumulated around its base, nearly dry now that the leaking contents had reached the level beneath a melted hole where it had been allowed to escape. The recycle bin beside it overflowed with takeaway containers and the wrappings of herpa-offered food, waiting to be set out to the street for incineration or repurposing.

The wide, shallow metal pail beside it was littered with ash from burning, suggesting that a good portion of the waste material was being burned for additional heat instead of being fed back into the city.

Upon the low chabudai lay a scattered collection of tiny figures and beads of plastic, river glass, wood, and metal, as well as the tools used to carve such intricate creations. A hobby or a means of generating additional income, something Melik could occupy his time with that could be bartered for food, water, clothing, and the all-important medis when Wiffy's earned ticks failed to be enough to provide for their needs.

Amid the figures set with care to one side to protect them from dings and scuffs, Scarecrow extracted a black metal disk stamped with the red double X of the merc guild. Not payment, but a marker used to indicate that someone was under guild protection or used as a badge to present to a member to summon the giver to the holder of the token.

It supported the claimed connection between Melik and a merc.

Not thinking she would miss the token, that it would mean little to Wiffy, and not wanting her to have access to people likely to take advantage of her as they may have done of Melik, Scarecrow tucked it into one of his pockets, sealed the flap to prevent loss, and then left the flop the way he had entered, closing the shaft grate behind him.

He would talk to Skelter about procuring Wiffy better supplies. A mattress, clean bedding, and a safer cooking heater at least.

Not that the heater would be of any use until there was power to utilize it.

In the meantime, he needed to get back to Zara. She would know what to do with the locket image. She could aid in locating Melik if he were anywhere to be found.

Scarecrow had other prey to hunt.

Like the Spades, mercs could be difficult to track. He knew one, and though Wiffy's vague description could indicate that same man, others fit it too.

Mam Kemway's man was the place to start.

With their ears so often kept to the ground, to the city's pulse and the need for those working outside of the system, that same man might have an inkling of Jaron's location too.

❧*❧

Like other Lev establishments, the Den was devoid of patrons, silent without the usual thrum of music and muted banter she was accustomed to. The Hub had been restored to sporadic, minimal function, allowing for tick transactions on a rotating schedule when the readers had the power to operate. But the tick system was down as often as it was up, preventing the accurate tracking of payment, and resupplying dwindling goods was a spotty endeavor. Nessies, too, were difficult to come by, and lines of desperate, hungry people formed in front of any vindi able to provide until their stock ran out. Herpa halls provided any aid they could, but they could offer only as much as they had to spread around.

Most places opened briefly and then closed again as abruptly as the ongoing wave of power cuts.

Feena had seen it. She had been forced to push past tingers and streeters with begging hands, seeing desperation grow in people's eyes with every hour that passed.

The Igraci were right. Soon, the protests and the increased activity of Neoma's unruly brako would be the least of Hebenon's worries.

The shelves behind and beneath the Den's bar were empty now as Tyrisi, sporting a newly acquired black eye, split lip, and fingers wrapped in a splint, tucked the last precious bottle of alcohol into a compartmented box meant for moving stock. The diminishment of her stock concerned her enough to prompt her to hide what she did have before some enterprising cretin decided to steal it to barter on the street. The crates were stacked in front of the bar, waiting for transport, and elsewhere, in the places where seeds and seedlings were stored that kept the Wulfe's Head label in business, the easily movable stores were being prepared for transport too.

All awaiting the inevitable end her contacts, her instincts said would come to pass.

The doors to Outside would open. They had to. Either the Nau and Grainger would do the right thing by allowing people to escape the stagnant city, or a second, more deadly coup would force the matter.

Even if the power was restored, there was no way of going back.

"Think that's all of it," Tyrisi said, stretching his strained back and choosing not to sit to catch his breath.

Feena nodded and murmured, "Thank you," before waving him away to other duties. He would not move it away from here. She wanted him close. But there was other work in the Den to be done.

To stay in business, Wulfe's Head had to adapt.

The winery, like her other business ventures, had to move Outside.

⊱*⊰

"Anyone seen Colyx?"

Vapors was empty of patrons. The andi dancers were perched cross-legged on the dance stage playing cards, while Ginna made a show of cleaning the unused bar of stickiness and grime it did not have. The kitchen was dark, the stove and oven unlit, and the shelves behind the bar were devoid of the majority of their stock. What stock Maemi did have was locked in storage to avoid theft and discourage loiterers from using Vapors as a hub of troublemaking.

Rhyd had been here and gone again, the restroom door at the back of the vindi still shuddering as it clattered closed. Whatever he had silently given Zara, seated at a nearby table with Enoch, was enough to push her into a frenzy of focused activity, prompting her to bury her nose in details that Enoch, too, seemed interested in as they murmured together and pointed at the screen of the battery-powered Echo.

There was little need for a bouncer, but Maemi would feel more secure if the big man she had grown accustomed to seeing at her door was present to discourage the unending stream of brako who passed and the pushing scramble of the hungry, the thirsty, the cold and bored who stuck there head in seeking offerings she could not give.

"Could send for him?" Enoch offered, assuming the man was home, catching Ginna's shifting gaze across the room. The biting edge of his suggestion revealed that he, like the others present, considered the idea of passing through hostile streets to find Colyx something he would rather not do.

"I can go," Ginna offered. With the Spinks as backup, she suspected she would be the safest one to travel to the hostel and back.

Maemi shook her head with a scolding, clucking sound. "No one's going anywhere." She could not prevent them from leaving if they chose; they had already come and gone and come again multiple times without incident, but she did not want to be the reason anyone got hurt.

On the tail of her words, the beaded curtain door rattled. A spidery man pushed inside and looked around, a curt nod acknowledging Ginna whom he remembered from the night of the Core escape, before eventually smiling at Enoch with undisguised but still nervous relief.

"Good…you're here."

The dwarf scowled and pushed out of his chair, intending to meet the intruder halfway across the room to discourage him from entering. He had not seen Switz since leaving the Core. The man had gone his way as soon as the children were safe. Hebenon was a big place. Switz's life was his own. Whatever life he intended to create, Enoch had not expected to cross paths with the shady fellow again.

"Switz."

"Think I can crash here for a bit? With you and…" his pleading eyes scanned the others in the room a second time, again lingering on Ginna, "just for a spell?"

Also scowling, knowing the man's name but not his face, Maemi set down her paper ledger pad and replied, "We're closed. No food or drink or…"

Switz shook his head. "Not looking for any of that. Just looking for somewhere dry to…"

"Who you running from?" Given the man's proclivity for finding and creating trouble as he regularly played one side against another to his benefit, constantly seeking the most advantageous angle he could, it was an easy assumption for Enoch to make that Switz was in trouble.

"Who says I'm running?" Switz scoffed, trying to push the squeak of anxiety down beneath a note of bravado that Enoch was familiar with. "Staying clean, staying busy…even earned a few ticks." He waved the tick card Blayd had provided in front of Enoch's face as proof of some new leaf he had turned. "Cold out…not even barrels burning in most places…and there's those Crows…"

"Brako," Enoch corrected.

Switz nodded. "…everywhere. I don't need…"

Unhindered by anyone at the door, paying no heed to Maemi's purse-lipped expression of disapproval, Switz made it as far as Enoch allowed, the dwarf cutting him off from reaching the table where the platinum blonde woman sat with her back to him, ignoring his arrival. Over her shoulder, Switz could barely make out dozens of tiny images flickering past on one side of the screen, while on the other was a face he had hoped to never see again.

"…that sort of trouble," he continued. The bluster sounded as though it was sucked out of his voice, prompting Enoch to glance back to see what he might be looking at.

Only Zara and the Echo she was studying. The merc on the screen.

So, Switz had run afoul of a merc. Or he had crossed paths with him long enough to be familiar. Enoch was not surprised.

"You heard her. Place is closed," piped Hiana as she put her cards face down on the platform and stood as if she would cross the room and confront him. The two with her did likewise.

"But you're all here…there isn't…" began his countering whine.

"We're employees." Nigel joined Hiana and crossed his arms over his chest. Ebenee stood with defiant hands on her hips. Ginna dropped the rag and came to the edge of the bar while Zara turned in her chair just enough to look at Switz.

"And he's my friend," Maemi finished with a gesture at Enoch. "Readers are down. Come back when we're open."

Switz's shoulders sagged. "When'll that be?"

The swiver shrugged. "Anyone's guess. Now out with you…or I'll toss you out myself."

Switz almost sneered at her, but he was a small man, unaccustomed to physical altercations if he could weasel out of them instead. The three on the stage did not appear to be a threat, but they, the swiver and girl behind the bar, as well as Enoch, meant Switz was outnumbered. Any one of them alone might have been capable of beating him. This was not a fight he could win.

Again, he glanced at the Echo. If they were interested in Blayd for any reason, if they sought, found, and brought him here, it was best for Switz to be as far away as possible. There was no benefit to staying.

"You'll regret this," he muttered, hoping the threat sounded persuasive as he trudged to the door without turning his back to them.

"Doubt that," Maemi grunted.

Stillness settled over Vapors again. The andis returned to their cards, Maemi and Ginna to the bar, and Zara to her Echo and the faces on the screen.

Enoch snorted, sank into the chair beside Zara, and continued to stare at the door, expecting Switz to return.

"Captain, I think I have a lead."

Ilya's hands trembled as the captain handed a memo to the young officer present when she had come in, noting her superior's weary frown and pinched brow that suggested another headache he was attempting to ignore. Having been here a few hours before, feeling that he had a continuing right to doubt her after her previous failures, she braced herself for the clipped words that accompanied his dour expression. "The killer?"

"No," she replied, wondering if the shifting of his eyes to the Echo screen indicated he had already located or apprehended the assassin. "The kidnapper…"

She had not thought about it before. Only the image that had snapped her awake, a face within a forgotten memory brought to the surface in a dream, made her question every lead she had previously followed, every hunch she had believed. It was a vision that made her angry enough to want proof she was wrong, proof that it was only a dream and not the buried recollection she suspected it was.

"We've been over this, Lieutenant. The Talkers…"

"Maybe in conjunction with them…but I think my source is credible. I won't know until I bring the suspect in for questioning. Do I have authority to…?"

She should not need to ask that question. Arresting criminals was part of a bugorra's duties. Her question fell off, dragged down by her uncertainty about this particular suspect despite her belief that he needed to be questioned. She had to follow through. Having churned over the dream, the memory of images and conversation shared, she had to rule Blayd out before she would sleep peacefully again.

He was, or had been, her friend. He had always been bright and resourceful, if impish and rebellious. It was difficult to imagine him capable, or willing, to pull something of this magnitude off. Even if done at the Mam's request. But they had been out of touch for a long time, long enough for her to become bugorra. Long enough for him to become a merc. Long enough for both to become something the other had not expected.

Grainger nodded. "Bring them in, notify me when they're in custody. I want to hear what you've got. If this is about Scarecrow…"

"It's not."

Another nod and a grunt of approval. "Good." The last thing he needed was a reignited feud with Scarecrow that his bugorra were unlikely to win. "Get to it, Lieutenant; I don't have all night. And stay off that knee. I want you back at full…"

"Yes, Captain." Squaring her shoulders, not asking how she should accomplish both orders, she hurried out before he could counteract them.

If Blayd was responsible for taking the Founder from her care, as the recollection of that voice above her in the corridor, moments before blackness came, returned to her, Ilya wanted to be the one to look him in the eye when he denied it.

If her suspicions were true, he would pay for making a fool of the bugorra, and especially her, for too long.

❧*❧

Colyx had not been back to this place, where the stripped-away shell was intended to limit the city's exposure to the Outside, the place where he had been pulled from the river, freed from the Core, and thrust back into Hebanthe Falls' dank streets after a lifetime of being separated from it. He appreciated this new freedom, appreciated the day of escape, respected what it had cost him, and respected the loss of life it had taken to make this opportunity happen. He valued the people who had planned and carried out the successful extraction that offered Otta a life outside of the Core.

But it was not enough. It was not enough to live in darkness and cold and constant anxiety about survival. His daughter, her partner, and their soon-to-be welcomed child should not live in a place, in a world, that was little better in some ways than the Core had been. Particularly, he mused as his gaze traveled up toward the first series of support beams driven into the nearly sheer earthen faces on both visible sides of the river, when there was a world of sun and clean air, sea and fertile green life, ripe and open for humanity's return.

It would not take much. Lev stacked upon Lev made the city heavy, its weight supported by stanchions and pylons, which continued to gradually settle into the eroding river bed. Likewise, it was supported by beams that spidered out like long arms on three sides of the city into the equally eroding cliffs. None of those supports had been intended to last forever. Staying here indefinitely had not been Duncan Kemway's plan. Even with ongoing upkeep, none of the city structures were meant to be eternal. Like the array, like the Upper's shell dome, the supports also required care, but unlike those things, the city's spine, arms, and legs were often easier to take for granted.

Out of sight of those above, largely out of mind. There was rust, there was erosion, details unattended as the last several decades of Founder rule had turned towards infrastructure neglect, towards controlling the increasing dissatisfaction of the decreasing population in the dim, perpetual damp.

Just a few blows would force the hand of those who ruled.

Colyx bobbed his head and muttered, "It'll do," as he watched the white-capped water bubble over rocks and rush towards the sea.

Wherever the river led, he would one day see it for himself.

❧*❧

"Don't see that there's another option," Warren said, the only face at the table, other than Tamner's, to lack the distress that Stace Sargin's suggestion had birthed. "By the time the array's…"

"He's working on it, isn't he? Your expert?" demanded Pearl, staring at the doctor who noted the look despite his squinted eyes and the rubbing of his fingers up and down between them along the bridge of his nose where the migraine he had been ignoring was settling.

He wondered if Grainger's perpetual headache was contagious.

"When there's electricity to run the lights, the Echos, yes. He's forced to do it by hand, mostly on paper, by alglamp. It takes time. The Hub simply isn't reliable enough to…"

"Then reroute power to…"

"We've rerouted all we can," Warren reminded Pearl. "Families are suffering. Little heat, little light…little power to cook…little hot water…it's worse in the Levs…"

The hydros had been rerouted to feed the Levs. The Uppers were forced to run on what power was available from the Factory arrays. None of it was enough.

Nodding, Stace added, "What food there is in storage can't get to people who need it…and perishables aren't going to last. If you think the salt protests have been bad…"

Tamner set his stylus down, the sound it made proving peculiarly interruptive as it drew everyone's attention to him. Continuing to rub his nose, he did not need to see their faces to know they were looking at him. "We'll have another coup, something worse, if we fail to act. This can't wait. As Stace…this doesn't have to be permanent. But evacuating Hebanthe Falls, at least long enough to secure city power and make things livable again…"

"No one is going to…" began Nunn with a grumbling growl.

Stace stared at him. "They will if we don't give them a choice. If we assure them, they can return to their homes as soon as…"

"What if no one comes back?" Fahti's question hung in the air, the completion of worried thoughts others were reluctant to ask.

Tamner was tempted to voice what he assessed to be the truth. Would abandoning the city in the falls be a bad thing, now that the Outside was safe? After centuries of forced residency, was requiring a return to the Levs after power was restored something the privileged families of the Uppers wanted to enforce?

"Going out at first is frightening," Stace agreed with a shrug, "but dying in the dark, cold and starving, is more so."

"It's not like they have to go…if they don't want to," Caminda murmured. "We need the shaft crews, the hydro crews…the dredgers. We need the Archivists, the bugorra. People to man the hothouses and the fisheries. But if enough of the rest go out to balance available power to the city's needs, until the systems are online…"

"That or we risk a lot of needless death." Delora rubbed her eyes and shook her head to erase the horrors her words deposited. "It'll be like before but worse. Friends, families. Some of us."

Thoughts turning to the Coup, to the plague deaths in the Factories, to the city-wide spate of conflict that continued to escalate with the rise of the brako, many of those at the table stared at their hands, at the table, or blank spaces in the air. Those from the Uppers who remained fostered enough of a superiority complex to bear an exaggerated fear of dying the way so many they knew had.

"So, we do this?" Woster asked, staring at his twin.

If Founder Kemway had been here, the Us versus Them attitude would have led to an extinction-level event in the Levs created by a choice to keep everyone inside the city. Those around him, Tamner thought with relief as first Warren and then others bobbed their heads in hesitant agreement, had a healthy dose of fear, if not compassion for the lives they governed, to be willing to do the right thing.

Tamner pressed the button on his Echo and turned the screen black. "Lydon, get the message out." Kenneth and Soleia, Tamner did not doubt, were eager to have something new and controversial to sprinkle into the ongoing regurgitation of more mundane, historical Kemway tidbits as they waited for the Remembrance Ceremony to air.

"I'll get Quincey moved somewhere he's got light to work by…power to work with…so he can get things up faster, get parts into production. I'll speak to the captain so he can coordinate officers."

Maybe by the time the array parts were fabricated and the repairs were complete, only a fraction of the population would have been moved. Maybe the delay would be significant enough that nearly everyone would have gone out. Grainger would be less happy to have one more responsibility piled atop his already burdened shoulders, but if the Nau agreed that this course of action was for the best, Captain Grainger would too. He would not have a choice.

*

Having ignored her messages in favor of keeping a low profile, this new message sparked his interest and prompted Blayd to resurface in the hopes of protecting his image and gaining his friend's sympathy and support. There was no need for elaborate alibis for the time of the Founder's audacious ranting public speech and ensuing assassination. With no sign of Switz, having already addressed his other weakness, Blayd agreed to her offer of hot algtea at a vindi granted a license to operate as it served one of the bugorra satellite offices in the Levs. Perhaps they could make peace. Perhaps he could glean some morsel of information about the ongoing crises that might benefit him.

Still, as he approached the vindi, he was wary.

He sat within sight of the primary Talker Hall, watching the jerky, furtive movements of wary Talkers skulking in and out of the Hall, cleaning fluorescent graffiti from the walls, curious about what had occurred and when. He wondered if the vindi was fortunate enough to have power to operate from the same feed that fueled the Hall, if it was the other way around, or if the Voices of Faith had enough authority still to demand power for their Halls while the rest of the city suffered. If that was true, he did not expect their privilege to last. Not when the bugorra found what he had left for them.

There was little foot traffic, few visitors to the Hall, and as it was the mid-shift hour, the bugorra were likely engaged with the sporadic shouts and screams and breaking of windows and more that echoed through the Levs.

The brako were busy. The buggers were too.

It might be in his favor to share in putting down some of the unrest. Apprehending a few brako would put him in the buggers' good graces, net him a few ticks, and show whose side he was on. It would also irritate Neoma, perhaps thwart her plans, a boon that would benefit him too…serve as part of the solution rather than part of the problem.

Steps echoed on the stairs across the promenade, and he looked up with his hands wrapped around the warm cup of tea to watch the woman he waited for descending from the half-Lev above. He set the cup down and began to rise to greet her as she reached the bottom of the stairs, relieved that she had come as promised.

The smile faltered as four additional masked buggers in their stiff black long coats followed behind, but he forced the smile into place and straightened his coat. Of course there would be others with her. The Levs continued to grow more unruly, the buggers more aggressive; buggers had increased the patrols to make their presence felt in every occupied corner of the city, the way it had been when Kemway was Founder. This was a place where bugorra hung out between shifts. Ilya, as second in command, was wise to travel with an escort, particularly as her limping gait spoke of a recent injury.

She would take her break from duty to share tea with him. There was nothing out of the ordinary here. The increased scrutiny of the Talkers from their hall on the other side of the promenade made an equally valid excuse for the buggers to be here and be watchful.

Blayde offered his hand with a welcoming smile and gestured to the other chair. "Glad you could make it," he said, ignoring her straight-faced expression, reading it as an afterimage of the duties she continued to bear. "Wasn't sure you would…"

"I did invite you," she reminded him, the friendly embrace he offered brushed aside in deference to a more professional demeanor in front of her subordinate officers. The four buggers stopped several paces behind her, hands at their sides, resting on their weapons, or else clasped before them in a formal posture. Slightly turned as they were towards Talker Hall, behind their masks, it was difficult to tell if they were looking at the Hall, Blayd and Ilya, or nothing at all.

"Sit then." Pretending the buggers' presence was irrelevant, choosing to set aside the uncomfortable prickle that raced down his spine, he waved to the vindi owner to join them and asked Ilya, "What do you want? Been a while, hasn't it? Lots to catch up on. I want to hear all about Ginna and…"

"I'm not here for algtea or a chat." Ilya tried to read his eyes, judge his expression, but he had always been good at feigning innocence and disinterest. She was not sure he was hiding anything, but she could tell her officers made him uneasy. Rather than force him into a corner where he might feel compelled to run, fight, or squirm away, she continued, "I'm here to…I need you to come in with me."

The swiver started towards them, but as Blayd's mien darkened and his hand dropped, and the four bugorra stepped closer, she retreated behind the counter and busied herself with an elderly woman seated there, both doing their best not to attract attention.

"What's this about?" the merc asked, his voice cool and sharp.

Despite that tone, there was that over-sheen of innocence again, a sincerity laced with offense. It was a tone Ilya had heard often when they had known each other better.

The edge to his words, however, suggested something else.

"You're under arrest for the murder of…"

"I haven't murdered anyone!" Blayd stepped back, gauging a way out of his situation without wildly shifting his eyes.

The four buggers came closer.

"You can keep talking…force me to drag you in…or you can come peacefully and talk about this somewhere less public…"

Blayd shook his head. "I deserve to know my accuser. I wasn't anywhere near the intersection where Founder Kemway…"

Ilya's brow crept up.

Blayd shuddered and snapped his mouth shut.

They stared at each other for several moments, assessing what had been said, what had not been said, and the implications of both. After a long, exhaled breath, Blayd picked up his still-warm algtea and drank the entire cup so as not to waste it as his thoughts continued to whirl. He did not speak again until he set the cup down with a thump.

"If Neoma's doing this…I'll tell you what I know," he agreed, hoping to shift any suspicion from himself to the Mam. "But not here."

"No," Ilya agreed as her officers frisked him, confiscated every weapon they could find, and took hold of Blayd's arms to propel him along before them. "Not here."

Whatever he had to say, truth or lie, she was interested in hearing what part Mam Kemway had to play.

❧Chapter 20❧

I don't care," Maemi growled, turning her back on the latest prod announcement that had begun to run on repeat on the Echo behind Vapors' bar.

"There's nothing here to…"

"They'll get the power back," Skelter countered with stubborn assurance, ignoring the look Jonner threw at him that acknowledged the faint note of uncertainty in the redhead's assertion. "When they do, people are gonna need my…"

"And he needs us," murmured Zara, glancing up from the Echo screen where her finger scrolled through the data that flashed there. For a woman whose work now consisted of Echoes, of Hub and Archive access, of supplying computer electrical devices and services to the Levs, she could not envision a life Outside where such things would be largely useless. And although the more diverse skills of a kesfek might lend themselves to survival in this new world, Tox too felt a deeper sense of purpose in remaining where she was.

Scarecrow could not continue to do what he did alone, no matter how he preferred it. He needed people to supply and maintain his tech. He needed people to fight with him, behind the scenes or at his side.

He needed them.

As a bilger, he would be permitted to stay inside the city. As Scarecrow, Rhyd would insist on it.

The Nau's decision to compel the city's residents to vacate might make his hunt for Vanderwall moot if the brako boss heeded that order, but the women were not the only ones to suspect the boss would remain inside. It might make it easier to find and stop him.

That meant Rhyd was not going anywhere.

"In the meantime?" Jonner snorted, glancing between Skelter and Maemi as Ginna washed the glasses that accumulated in the vindi sink during the last brief period of power Vapors had been allotted.

Patrons had come to drink, but only those still seated along the bar counter had stayed.

It was not enough to sustain a business with the meager stores Maemi had on hand.

She did not look at him, but her tone remained strong. "This is my world…not out there. This is my life…"

Jonner reached across the bar and covered her hand. "We can build a new one. You can start again…all of you…"

"No reason we can't come back after," Nigel offered. As dancers, he and the women seated to his left had even fewer skills with which to build a life Outside. They could be reprogrammed or upgraded, but doing so was to risk the core of the long-resident personalities and memories they had built over the years. They did not need the same sustenance, the same warmth, or shelter, that their human companions did, but they did need electrical power. Outside of the city, that would be difficult to come by.

They might have enough to function until the array was repaired if their internal generation systems continued to function properly.

Jonner pulled his hand away and wrapped it around his whiskey glass instead. "Might not be much to come back to at the rate things are going…and once people are out there…see what it's like…"

"Hebenon's not going anywhere," Skelter scoffed.

"Maybe not, but you think they'll not want to trade all of this gloom and damp for sunshine and clear skies?"

Gesturing to the room around them, Maemi said, "None of this will exist out there. Nothing will be the same. They're used to the way things are. People'll stay, or they'll come back…that's why I have to be here. They'll need places like this."

"Those who choose this life…who come back…will be fools…"

Her gaze shifted away from his face when she shut the Echo off and headed into the kitchen, where her last dozen eggs boiled in a pot on the stove.

Realizing the implications of his words, Jonner's expression drooped. "Maemi…I'm sorry. I didn't mean it like that…"

"Think you did," Skelter snorted. "Made it pretty clear you don't wanna stay…so why don't you go if you're so keen and let us be?

"Why don't you admit business is lagging…that we'll wither and die if we…" Jonner shot back indignantly.

Tox cleared her throat, cutting him off. "Lived all our lives here. You might have lost everything when you went inside…and I'm sorry about that…but this…this is all most of us know. It's what we have. Some of us prefer to fight for our homes rather than…"

Swinging to the side and sliding off the bar stool, Jonner sighed with a defeated, frustrated shrug. "Guess we all have to decide if the chance is worth it. I've been a prisoner too long…didn't come out to be a prisoner here too. Not the life I want."

Skelter, too, had been a prisoner, something he reminded Jonner of with a glance. He had not been in the Core as long as Jonner, but he had been there. He had also seen Outside. He believed he knew what he had to lose and gain regardless of the choice he made. But as long as Zara and Tox chose to remain inside Hebanthe Falls, he would stay. Like them, he believed Rhyd needed him too…even if his business got harder and harder to maintain.

At least Rhyd needed him long enough to find Jaron and take down Vanderwall. After that…

"We're not prisoners if it's the life we choose," he murmured.

Ginna listened to the others retreat to their philosophical corners, wondering, as the Nau's edict burrowed into her brain, what she would do if Vapors' door closed. What would she do if the city emptied and her sister went Outside?

Would her sister even choose that life, once duty no longer required her to stay in the Levs? Would a continuing base of residents require some of the bugorra force to remain inside?

Would Scarecrow stay in the shadows as long as there was a Fall City to live in, whether powered or not?

Was staying inside what Ginna wanted?

She sighed and closed her eyes. She had no answers…but the time to make that choice had come.

❧*❧

"Wasn't anywhere near the Uppers," Blayd huffed, the only sound he made that revealed his frustration with a question that had been asked in different ways multiple times since Captain Grainger joined him and Ilya in the sterile interrogation room. His wrists hurt from where the too-tight cuffs cut into his arms, though he did not deign to complain about that, refusing to appear weak before the man he did not fear. "Not that night, not any other…until now." He rolled his head around as though using his shifting gaze to indicate the room. "Switz'll tell you…and Tully."

"Where can we find them?" Grainger grunted back, his hands flat on the table as he leaned forward so that he towered over the other man with the table between them. "What's their full names?"

"All I know them by."

Given the adoption of anonymous monikers by streeters and tingers alike, this was not a surprise. Nor did it surprise Grainger that even a merc of Blayd's status might not dig deeper into accomplices' identities for his own protection.

"Why did you bring up Founder Kemway when I brought you in?" Ilya asked, the first time she had done so as she moved in and out of the room.

Rather than chide her for interrupting, Grainger nodded, seeming unfazed by the question as if that detail had been revealed before.

Blayd bit the inside of his cheek to prevent the scowl from forming. "Everyone's looking for the assassin. Word's all over the Levs. You said I'd killed…I assume you thought I'd…"

"Suppose this Switz and Tully are your alibis for that night too?"

Shaking his head, staring at Ilya rather than looking at the man who spoke, he said, "Don't have one. Don't need one. I wasn't there, at the protest…at the riot…"

"But you did participate in abducting him."

Ilya saw it, the flicker in his eyes, the slight shifting of his gaze that told her he was hiding something in the silence between her statement and the words he finally uttered. "Look," he grunted, "I wasn't here. Mam Kemway wanted him out, wanted him home. I know that much. She wanted me to bring him to her…when I worked for her…but I told her it wasn't possible. You'd have to know where he was…be familiar with the Ups…know a way in. Never been here. Told her I couldn't do it."

"A man in your business has resources." Grainger had worked with mercs before. He knew what they were capable of. He straightened his shoulders, not noticing the staring detail shared between the prisoner and his lieutenant but sensing that she was ruffled by something the merc had said.

"Man like me," Blayd spat, looking at Grainger with a sneer, "isn't stupid enough to try…and she never paid me enough to want to. Only one person I know has that kind of resources…and I'm sure he has the ego to do anything she asked if he thought it would buy a favor."

The corner of Grainger's eye twitched.

Blayd continued. "You know what I'm saying. Number of times she and Senior talked about bringing the Founder out, putting him back in power…how it would benefit her and the Voices. If anyone had the resources to try it…" He shrugged. "I was only surprised it took 'em so long."

Grainger and Ilya exchanged a look. He bobbed his head, but his expression did not change. Ilya frowned.

Taking a step back, Grainger said, "Make yourself comfortable." He took another step so that he could reach the latch of the closed door. "You're gonna be here awhile."

"You can't hold me! There's no evidence!"

Following the captain, Ilya said low and cold, "We have time to find it before we have to cut you loose…and you have time to reconsider lying to me."

She had the recorded, mostly anonymous confession she believed implicated him, but that was a card she was not yet ready to lay on the table. She had the dream the recorded confession had prompted, although that would never hold up as evidence. The Hub techs were trying to clean up the audio on the card, and she hoped to extract from it the names she believed the static contained.

So long as that audio was recovered while Blayd was in custody, she would not have to track him down. There would be no fooling him into a trap again. He would be more difficult to capture a second time.

If there was any connection to him at the secret location the captain was preparing to raid, a location he had not yet revealed to her, they would soon have that too.

Regardless of the lack of physical evidence, Ilya was certain she had her kidnapper. The question remaining to be answered was why.

Mam Kemway was the only answer she could see.

❧*☙

Shoulder aching enough to remind him that he was not at peak efficiency, when Scarecrow came across the eight brako looting an uninhabited vindi, he retreated into darkness on the rooftop as two buggers came around the corner and interrupted them with a shout. Shifting his weight on the lip of the roof, he listened to the ensuing pursuit, confident it would not last long. He expected the brako would get away with their crimes this time, as they so often did.

He did not expect, however, to tumble from the lip of the rooftop into a side alley, barely landing on his feet, to subsequently emerge into a street where a different trio of masked bugorra interrogated a disheveled, frightened-looking Talker. Two had the fellow pinned to a vindi wall by his arms while the third shoved the barrel of his popper against the man's neck so that he stammered and stuttered and begged for his life between their gravelly barked questions. Scarecrow's unexpected arrival made the buggers stop and stare.

The Talker believed he was saved.

For a moment, everyone stared at one another as Scarecrow drew up short, chiding himself for not hearing them, wondering why they were more interested in the Talker than the sounds of looting and the chase such a short distance away.

For a moment each of them was silent.

"You! Stop there!"

Choosing not to engage when he interpreted the odds to be against him, Scarecrow grabbed the walkway rail across from him and swung over it onto the rooftop a half-Lev below.

"Hey! Stop!"

The Talker was released and left on the ground, rubbing his neck, wiping his eyes, gasping with a blubbering sound as the buggers sped after the vigi. Relieved to have spared the Talker without the need for violence, Scarecrow was confident he could outmaneuver the buggers before they caught up with him.

One stumbled down the stairs. One ran along the walkway that followed Scarecrow's path. The third likewise leaped over the rail to pursue him across the rooftops.

Every bugger now had seen Scarecrow on the prods. Everyone had seen him remove the Founder from the crowd. Undoubtedly, many, after years of pursuing Scarecrow as the enemy, believed him to be the assassin. They might arrest him. They might kill him.

Under a braided wire overpass of power lines and sign chains. Into a greenhouse shed between rows of berry bush pots and miniature fruit trees. With one hand, Scarecrow yanked over a heavy potted shrub to block the path of his pursuers. One jumped over it. The other crashed into it, picked himself up, and continued running despite the time lost in his chase. The roof over their heads, designed to allow exterior moisture from the falls to drip onto the thirsty plants, rattled as the third bugger ran across it, warping and sagging with each step and threatening to fracture beneath his weight.

Workers less affected by the lack of city power screamed and stumbled out of the way.

The buggers continued the chase.

More agile and experienced in the Levs' shadows, Scarecrow was faster. He reached a rear entrance and swung around a post that held up one corner of the waterproof tarp stretched over tables, chairs, and benches where the greenhouse workers took their breaks. A hemplastic conduit along the side of the building carried unused water away so that the plant roots would not rot in standing moisture, and it was into that wide conduit that Scarecrow jumped, protected by the stench of fertilizer and bilge by the breather in his suit.

The slope of the current carried him away from the greenhouse, away from the buggers. Many who had fallen into the conduit were drowned or crushed in the river at the other end, but Scarecrow's coat and the soles of his boots slowed his descent enough that he was able to catch the edge of the conduit with one hand, shaded by structures above and to the left of him. Letting his legs and torso bob on the flow, he listened for the sounds of his pursuers, and when, confident he was alone, he hoisted himself up and over the lip of the conduit.

He dropped over the side and rolled beneath it and paused to listen again. The pipe was wide enough to shield him from sight when he crawled along the downslope for several yards, giving his clothes a chance to drip, assessing his location and his security. He did not hear the buggers. He did not hear anyone. The nearest buildings were silent, and the life systems he could hear were barely operational.

The roar of the blasting spray of the Five Falls into which he emerged could have blocked out all of those sounds.

But he believed he was safe.

The water, the mist in the air, were cold. The bellow of the falling water barely masked the churning growl of the nearby banks of the hydropower units stretching above and below him. Gripping the rail with one hand and rolling his opposite shoulder to ease the ache the conduit escape had created as he bumped along the pipe, he staggered as he followed the walkway on the right side of the conduit until he reached a set of stairs that led up and away from the falls. At the top, he found a hydro repair shed, empty now as the crews were deployed elsewhere to keep the hydros working. He scanned the walks around him, the other stairs and structures, and then ducked into the Shed and beneath a workbench tall enough to allow a person to stand and work without undue fatigue.

The Shed was not warm. It was not dry. But it allowed him a place to wait out the buggers, if they were still following, and gave him time to reconsider something he had put off too long.

He needed a medi. He was not going to be of any use to Jaron, or anyone else, if he did not tend to his injuries.

He would never take Vanderwall so long as he nursed those pains.

❧*❧

"You're late

Vanderwall ignored Neoma's acidic tone as he dropped onto the icy, tooled metal bench beside her with a look as though he had chosen this place not for a meeting but because it was the best place in the vicinity to sit and pull up the socks slouched inside his boots. He did not question why she suggested meeting here with the drip-drip from the overhang onto the grating at their feet and the wisping mist blowing across them from the falls to their right. The woman typically avoided such dismal, uncomfortable places, so he assumed, whatever the purpose of her summons, it was something she did not want her daughter and servant to hear.

"Helped right a tipped cart," he muttered with a shrug, not looking at her, furthering the appearance to others that this was no more than

❧247❧

a chance meeting of two people sharing the same bench and small talk. He could see no one from where he sat, and if anyone in the half-Lev above happened to peer down on them, their faces and identities would be hidden beneath cloaks, hats, and gloves.

Neoma huffed. She did not think Frankel to be the helpful sort, but in a time of stretched-thin supplies, making sure what there was got to where it was needed would be expected.

Or maybe the cart belonged to one of his people.

"What do you know about Haythem's…?"

"Nothing." Socks adjusted, he stretched his legs in front of him and leaned against the back of the bench.

She glowered at being cut off. "You were there. I've seen the prods. I saw you."

"Lot of people there, some just passing through." He paused as if to suggest he had been one of those people, and then added, "He was worth more alive than dead."

Again, she snorted at the reminder of the reward she had offered for her husband's return. "Your people didn't…"

"If they had, I'd know."

"I want security. They'll come for me next. You owe me."

"I don't owe you anything." Before she could retort, knowing what she meant without her saying it, he continued, "I don't have the people to spare."

She yanked his arm to turn him towards her and hissed in a squealing breath, "They murdered him! Ulynda and I will be next!"

Though he frowned at the hand of the only person who would dare such an act, who would dare to threaten him or deign to show him so little respect, her grip did not lessen, her hand did not move. The points of her nails, felt through the thick fabric of his coat and the sweater beneath it, did not have the sharpness she intended. After a pause and a few short breaths. "I'll see what I can do."

"You'll do more than see. Not paying you to…"

"Not paying me at all." With the Hub down, the tick system had ceased to operate reliably, and he was willing to wager that any ticks he had accumulated or had been granted by the wife of the Founder were already depleted. Or nearly so.

Without ticks, without her husband's prestige and power, she was no longer worth anything. She was not worth the effort he would spend to protect her or kill her.

The vacancy of power in Hebenon's leadership that Oliver was not fit to fill, the child, however, might be. For the girl, Neoma's demand for protection was worth consideration.

"You heard the prods. Not gonna be anyone in here to be a threat much longer."

"They're not going anywhere." Neoma spoke of herself if not for everyone else. The fear of Outside was deeply ingrained in the population by generations of Kemways. Those brave enough to venture Outside had likely already done so. She could not imagine anyone else willingly taking the risk to mingle in the unproven air with the uncouth, primitive parah.

One normal little girl or not.

"Are you?"

Vanderwall did not reply as he stood, adjusted his hood, and walked away from the woman on the bench. His business was inside the city. Everything he was building was here. Once people began to move Outside, Hebanthe Falls would be ripe for plunder, conquest, and claiming. Once people went out, they would only get back inside under his control.

Not Neoma Kemway's.

She did not need to know his plan to further the expulsion of residents. No one needed to know.

❧CHAPTER 21❧

Haldris Borne was a handsome, clean-cut young man of Asian descent in appearance, with the sort of bright smile and amiable mannerisms that fostered immediate trust and friendship amongst his coworkers. His fellow solar techs had nothing bad to say about him; when asked, they offered glowing reports of efficiency, diligence, and dedication to the duties he was assigned. He had served in that capacity beneath Founder Kemway at a time when repairs and upkeep of the external systems had been crucial, when being out on the dome had required specialized suits and gear to protect the workers from the reportedly toxic Outside environment.

He knew his craft thoroughly enough that he could have been promoted into one of the lead tech positions but he had never requested a promotion, choosing instead to fulfill his shift duties seemingly content with the life he led.

Grainger had met him before. There had never been anything to draw attention to Borne, never an inkling that something like this could happen.

Looking at the man through the one-way viewing glass, calm in his dull gray prison clothes, his face unreadable, his hands casually resting on the table in front of him without a hint of anxiety, Grainger now understood many things he had not before.

He did not, however, understand what had prompted Borne's final on-duty act.

"Captain." Borne's voice was cordial and warm when Grainger entered the room. His posture, his expression, did not change.

"Mr. Borne."

"Haldris, please." The corners of his mouth perked into an almost smile, the first change in expression Grainger had witnessed, which caused him to wonder about his captive's state of mind. He focused on the man's hands, where burned and blistered flesh should have been evident. Instead, he saw only the cloth patches he knew covered the blackened edges and exposed mechanical layers beneath.

If someone had not told him that truth, he never would have guessed it, although for as long as Borne had been at his job, his face never aging, someone should have.

Grainger wondered if the lead tech who lost his life had known the truth.

Such differences never mattered to Grainger, not enough to think about them. He could not say that Borne being an andi mattered to him. The only thing that mattered was the unanswered why.

He sat across the table and folded his arms over his chest to look more intimidating. Deciding that gesture seemed a more defensive posture than an intimidating one, he unfolded them and put his forearms on the table in a way that mirrored Borne's posture.

"Who put you up to it, Haldris?"

"No one."

Borne's expression did not change.

Grainger frowned.

Andis' baseline code was meant to prevent them from harming people. In his years as Crow captain under the Founder, he had encountered malfunctioning andis who behaved outside of their programming, in the same way as any other defective machine or mentally flawed or substance-addled human might. Those andis were contained, diagnosed, and reprogrammed. One might occasionally be decommissioned if it was determined the flaw or damage would be too costly to rebuild or reprogram. Grainger had only encountered a few intentionally altered to serve the illegal bidding of whoever had retained their services. In such cases, the person responsible was arrested and sentenced while the andi was repurposed for a more suitable duty.

Studying Borne now, Grainger ruled out a physical malfunction. There was little in his behavior, other than his calm demeanor and smile, to suggest faulty programming or the introduction of a virus-tainted processing unit.

Something like that would be more insidious and harder to detect.

The second possibility, now that he had Haldris' history, was the answer Grainger expected to find. Somewhere, someone was manipulating Haldris' programming to direct him to do horrific things.

"Was it Burton? Did he put you up to it?" As the lead solar tech, with Haldris as his favorite and most frequently paired subordinate, Burton was the obvious choice. It would explain Borne's failure to be promoted, explain Burton's favoritism.

Maybe Burton's death had been part of a larger plan.

With Burton dead, if he was behind the sabotage plot, this matter could be quickly put to rest. There would be no ultimate punishment, no one else to blame. There would be only the reprogramming of some portion of Haldris' core code and the rebuilding of the array to undertake. The problem would be solved.

Borne's response, however, was, "No."

Grainger's frown deepened. Could andi lie? "Then who? The Voices? The brako? The Igraci?"

Borne shook his head. "There is no one. It is time for us to evolve. Time for the next…"

"Evolve? Who? Andi?"

The vague smile took on a vaguely patronizing warmth. "All of us. We're not meant to stay inside the city forever. That was not Kemway's vision. Stagnation has already begun. It is all around us, every day. If we stay inside, if we do not evolve, we die."

This time when Grainger crossed his arms, he made no effort to disguise the shielding gesture meant to ease his discomfort. "That's not…someone must have…"

"I've heard the talk. We all have. You've heard it too. There's no need for alteration." Borne tapped the side of his head. "The truth is obvious. Duncan wanted something done…so I did it. Taking this step will prompt others to take theirs."

It was the sort of logical, progressive line of thinking that any person might have followed after introspection and the evaluation of Hebenon's deteriorating way of life. It was not irrational that andis, made to be human-like, would also be able to reach that same conclusion.

But from his understanding of the inhibitive programming installed in each andi during the single decade of their manufacture when Duncan Kemway had been Founder…long before paranoia ruled that 'as human as human' was a dangerous thing, the choice to seek and carry out a solution for humanity should have been impossible for an andi to undertake.

"We will have to run scans, you realize…evaluate your…?"

"Yes," Haldris nodded. "I know. It is necessary to analyze for defects." He did not question why that had not been done during the days he had been kept in holding. Like most andi, he inherently understood that his reality differed from the humans around him.

It did not mean he, or any other andi, accepted those differences, but Haldris did understand them.

"You know what will happen? Based on the outcome of…?"

Haldris could not be confined like other criminals. Such a punishment would not solve anything. What fate awaited him would depend on what was learned. And honestly, Grainger thought as his fingers twitched where they rested in that cross-armed position, what sort of punishment was 'death' to a machine?

Perhaps Haldris had been tampered with without his consent.

Perhaps he had a virus in his system that he could not detect.

Perhaps he had developed a malfunction or system failure.

There was no falter to his smile, no change of posture. There was only a slight twitch at the corner of one eye as he replied, "I do."

Grainger nodded, trying not to feel grim about what came next. "You will wait here while I arrange it…and someone will come for you." Here or back in his captivity cell, it would not matter. If his programming could be trusted, he would remain here without creating a scene or trying to escape until the evaluation could be ordered and completed. He had been in that cell for days. He had been in this room for hours. He had been silent and cooperative all that time.

Another hour or two of waiting was unlikely to change anything.

Just in case, Grainger would leave the buggers posted at the door with orders to shoot to kill if Haldris forced their hand. A rogue andi loose in Hebanthe Falls was a trouble he did not need.

"Of course, Captain. I will wait."

"Thank you." It felt an odd thing to say.

❧*❦

The stains on the front of his dull gray shirt looked as though he had dumped his last meal down the front of himself, and its wrinkled state attested to how many nights he had slept in the same clothes. But they were the only clothes Molly had, and he was too uncaring to try to appear other than what he was. He had been given this shirt, these now torn trousers, after the escape from the Core had ruined the clothes he had worn inside. At least his shoes were good, his feet dry and warm. Though supplied with ticks to buy more, to allow him to set up a modest life until his first salary was recorded in his account, that amount had already been depleted.

His initial allotment was spent on his first score of Heb. He had not bothered to seek legitimate employment to score more. Mam Kemway had offered him only enough to eat with for the prods he had made for her, and he was too proud to beg…either for ticks, food, or Heb. There was still enough of the handful of Hebbies he had pocketed to last him a few days and enough ticks in his account for a cup of barely warm soup if he could find a vindi selling it.

Cleaner, dryer clothes would have to wait.

Those waiting at the end of a trail of hidden markings he had followed would not care about his condition. Assuming he found anyone, they would not be interested in the state of his clothes. More than one struggling, suffering, indigent soul had succumbed to the lure of the Spades in the hopes of one last payout, in the hopes of providing something lasting for their families.

Molly had no one to provide for except himself.

Any payout he might get, when his card was drawn, would fall back into the pot for the next chosen cardholder.

"Help you?"

The opti looked up from the lens he was crafting to see who had jangled the bell above the vindi door when the person did not immediately speak. His puffy cheeks and wide nose were red as though from overexertion or inebriation, and his fingers were swollen and shaky, suggesting instead some manner of medical condition. Something incurable, Molly guessed, but not something that prevented him from continuing his work. Such a condition explained why the signs had led Molly here. Whether one of the Spades or not, someone had to maintain the place of meeting.

Who better than a dying man with nothing to lose and no reason to reveal secrets?

Afraid of contagion, Molly remained near the door and refused to move closer.

He held up the token for the opti to see. The man grunted and beckoned him forward. Warily watching over his shoulder, Molly inched near enough to put the token on the counter for the other man to pick up and study through the single-eyed magnifier he wore. The opti grunted again, set it down, and slid it back across the counter.

"It's fake."

"It's from the Core. It's real."

Eyeing him cynically, the opti muttered and resumed his grinding.

After picking up the token and stepping back, Molly did not move.

"Blocking the light," the man groused when he was forced to stop the foot-driven grinder a second time.

What little light there was came from an alglamp sconce behind Molly's head. He did not turn to look at it. "The one who's drawn the Ace…he's not following the…"

"Not one of ours. Not our business."

"There are rules," Molly protested.

"Not ours. Your lot need to sort it out…" Leaning forward, reaching across the counter, he pushed Molly to the side so the light again shone across the grinder. Molly, in turn, leaned across the counter too, forgetting the fear of contagion that had originally caused him to keep his distance. "We're the only ones left! Him and me! I'm one of you! I demand you call the card…!"

"Demand?" Unaffected by the little man's effort to intimidate him, the opti pushed him back from the counter with both hands. Not expecting the shove, Molly stumbled to the floor, wide-eyed with shock. "You're not one of us. Can't have two cards in play. Whatever you've got going isn't our business. Take care of it yourself. Anyone who got out of that place alive is damn lucky and deserves a second chance. More than most people get. Go away. I've got work to do."

He returned to fitting the lens into the frame at his elbow. Molly stared at him from the floor, unmoving. He had tried to address the matter himself and failed. He had expected the Hebanthe Falls Spades to follow the rules and claim the life that had been pledged.

He had not expected another Spade to encourage a member to live.

"I'll take care of it," he snarled, crawling to his feet to adjust his rumpled clothes and resume his dignity. "I'll take care of all of you."

The opti snorted and ignored the threat as Molly opened the vindi door and stumbled out.

The bell jangled twice as the door slammed.

The grinder resumed its hum.

❧*❧

"We don't have enough to hold him."

Ilya's fists tightened behind her back where the captain could not see the act of frustration, but her already dark expression was impossible to hide. "I know him, sir. I know what he's like. We have the recording. We should at least hold him until after you've…"

"I want to…believe me…" Grainger, too, was frustrated by the inability to locate the two stated alibis and by the nagging suspicion that he was chasing smoke ghosts. Between the merc and the andi, who was still under evaluation by coding techs, in addition to the increasing amount of brako activity and the slogging delays in restoring full power to the city, he felt like a rodent on a treadmill, running fast but not getting anywhere. "It's a recording made by a person we can't find. We don't know if it's real or…"

"The techs are working on it. They need more time. There must be a way we can hold him…"

Grainger shook his head. "Not enough. But…" His voice trailed off. "I have another idea."

Kal had already slithered out of his grasp, but as a public figure, finding him when the time came for an arrest would be relatively easy. They had no such advantage with the merc. But if he was involved in the kidnapping, in cahoots with Kal, Blayde might lead Grainger to the truth he expected to find. He might have answers soon if the merc tipped his hand.

"Tag him. Watch him."

"He's gonna know I'm there." And with her healing knee slowing her down, it would be too easy for Blayde to escape.

"Someone else. One of the coverts. Tag his ICD, his passcard, his clothes. If he's tagged, no one needs to get too close." A tag's reception was going to be spotty, given the condition of the Hub, but it was the best solution Grainger could offer. The chip in the merc's ICD would monitor his movement and if he thought he was being tracked that way, he would find a temporary comm to use in its place.

If he wanted to continue the façade of innocence, he would have to keep his comm on him and let himself be tracked.

Either way, they would learn the truth about his guilt.

He would know all of the tricks, just as Ilya did. But there were other ways to track someone, ways developed by the paranoid Founders' teams to monitor dissidents and presumed traitors.

The man in the cell behind the mirrored glass, set for release, pushed back his chair, rubbed his wrists as they were freed by the officer in the room, and glowered snidely as if seeking the hidden recorder that had to be there. He assumed, too, that there was enough electricity directed to those systems to watch and listen to him. He assumed one of the opaque panels was a window, though he could see nothing out of place.

Having not eaten a hot meal since the brownouts had begun, he gladly accepted the second meal he had been offered in this room, a bowl of potatoes and meat gravy and a cup of hot algtea. He chose to believe those meals were an apology rather than believe either or both were his condemned man's meals.

"Get someone to go over every minute of footage while he's been in here. Maybe he'll show us something, tip his hand."

"He's too smart for that."

Raising his brow, Grainger asked, "Questioning an order?"

Ilya forced her hands to unclench and her shoulders to relax. She took a breath, refocused on the window, and shook her head. There was a challenge in her old friend's expression. A certainty of position and success in whatever game he was playing.

Such smugness came with a cost and always hid a weakness. She was determined to find his.

"No, Captain. I'll see it done after the raid…"

"Now, Lieutenant. You're in no shape for that. I'll see to the raid. You see to…"

"Sir…"

"If both things are connected, if the kidnapper and killer are the same or are in league, we'll know. If not…we'll know that too. There's an assassin to catch too, you know. Your job is here. I'll take care of the raid. Tomorrow, we give Founder Kemway his due…then after…" He believed that due had already been given. Custom was not his to thwart. Haythem was the last Founder. The rituals had to be followed one more time.

It would be nice to have answers about his abduction and death before that hour came.

❧ * ❧

"Can't you get him a message?"

The Nau's decision to encourage emigration, temporary though it was, intended to reduce the strain on the life systems and the suffering of Hebenon's population, necessitated the opening of the doors long enough for Tamner to go Out to address the dire situation with the parah leaders. With the original opening of the doors, there had already been clashes in personalities, culture, language, and the access and use of resources, but the parah had, thus far, been remarkably accommodating to the strangers from the metal nest. The arrangement had come with the option for the parah to go inside if they wished to.

Only a few dozen had been curious and enterprising enough to look beyond the doors that their hemp carts had visited for centuries.

This change would be different.

A mass exodus from Hebanthe Falls would present problems not even Tamner could realistically anticipate or address until they arose. Without following through, many inside would suffer and likely die.

After a day's negotiation, lasting from the early morning hours after the sun crested the ocean horizon until the evening meal hour when it sank behind the mountains in the west, Tamner's persuasion and the parah's belief in the sanctity of life, as well as their concession that those trapped in the metal nest should not be condemned to suffer any more than their captivity had already caused, was enough to secure the treaty he had come for. A sizeable portion of territory was allotted to the people of Hebenon, a place for them to settle. Boundaries and rules for interaction between people would be ironed out over the next several days, but Tamner had enough to return to the Nau and allow emigration to begin.

The straining sound of machinery, the struggling hydros, and the life support systems forced to output and operate on the minimal amount of power available that Tamner listened to as he stared at the repair crews on the shell tasked with removing the damaged inverter and panels around it, reminded him of how critical his actions were.

Lash and a mobile lab would be among the first to come out. He needed more power to work. He needed light. He needed adequate equipment. There was no suitable place in Hebenon, none in the power-restricted, too-populated Factories. A tent structure adjoining the West Factory wall was being erected and would soon be supplied with everything lash needed to complete the plans for a new, and hopefully improved, inverter system that would last Hebanthe Falls for centuries to come.

The Factories were ready to build those needed parts, with hemp being processed for printing and the printers being recalibrated for mass production as soon as the drawings were coded. Within days, everyone hoped manufacturing would begin.

Tamner did not believe it would happen soon enough.

His son and Agnys loitered near the Table of Meeting, as had many of the parah, the prossers and crossers trapped outside as the future was debated, listening to the decisions being made. Some had drifted away to tend to daily business, some had left and come back. Most of the children, bored with rhetoric and arguments they did not comprehend and could not influence, had been amongst the first to go.

Cori and Agnys had stayed. So too had Venn, a silent presence in his worn-thin parah attire, loitering at the rear of the crowd. He was not the only person from Hebenon expelled into the Outside for crimes only the Founders had sanctioned. He was not the only one to have mixed feelings as the reality of Hebenon's state rolled toward them like an avalanche.

He was not the only one holding out hope that friends and family would abandon the dark world they had known to enjoy this new breath of freedom.

He was not the only one, Tamner suspected, who would be disappointed by the refusal of some to leave that old way behind.

"I can try." He did not have a direct line to Ballard, but since his first confrontation with Scarecrow, he had come to know some of the people who did have that connection.

Lash was one of them.

Rather than look at Venn, he busied himself with the T1 Echo and the assortment of handwritten parchments collected throughout the day, pages of notes and questions that would provide the Nau with details to debate. Nearby, Agnys squealed as she and Cori finally left the finished meeting to chase each other across the field, the children relieved that the day's tension was behind them. With the air filled with the aromas of the evening's communal meal, they were free to be children again.

Free was the best Tamner could offer his son.

Free was the best he could strive for, for all of them.

"She wants him here." Venn's strained voice carried a knot of distraction that affirmed that Agnys was not the only one hoping to influence Ballard's choice. "Out here…he doesn't need to do…what he does. He deserves to be free, too."

Tamner nodded, but his face was carefully schooled to the most neutral expression he could muster. "He does."

The vigi was not the only person to dedicate himself to the peace and survival of those in Hebenon. He was not the only one to give so much of himself to the fruition of a better life. But without Ballard, Tamner and many others would not be standing where they were now, beneath a sun and moon that no one in Hebanthe Falls had believed they would see. They would never have the chance for the ocean air in their nostrils, grass and soil beneath their feet, the evening air blowing across their skin, ruffling their hair, things not generated by the artificial life systems and Hub coding.

"I know he doesn't think…but she wants him to come home." Venn paused, the connotation of home bringing back memories of a very different place, a place where what they had been had come to an end with unexpected force on the day Venn had been Taken. Outside had become Venn's home after that. Rhyd's home had not changed. He was not ready to give that up. Venn knew it.

Despite the violent finality of their last exchange, Venn still hoped that Outside could be Rhyd's home too.

❧*❧

Watching Rhyd, attired as Scarecrow again, disappear through the vent shaft, after the unsuspecting medi treated his shoulder and other less serious injuries, Zara waited for her flat to reclaim its silence with her eyes closed behind the arm draped over them.

Rhyd was right.

There was only so much Scarecrow could do.

Finding the Founder's kidnapper, now that the man was dead, was no longer Scarecrow's priority.

Nor was he focused on finding the assassin that every bugorra in the city was looking for.

His focus needed to be elsewhere.

The information filling the Echo in front of her needed to be addressed, but that, too, was not up to Scarecrow to tackle.

Oliver would be glad to see it. It might even offer the man closure to failures he shouldered for crimes not yet solved.

Without lowering her draping arm, she tapped on the key as the echo of Scarecrow's movement faded.

The file was sent.

Zara had done her part for now as Scarecrow left to attend to his.

If Melik Tully had connections to the Founder, to the Voices, to Senior Kal, if the merc Scarecrow suspected did as well, it was up to Oliver and his bugorra to find out.

Zara knew if Oliver turned to her for help, she would give it.

❧Chapter 22❧

He jarred awake to the Founder Salute blatting from the wall Echo and rolled away from the brightness of the screen to bury his face in the sofa's back cushion. The effort did not muffle the sound but it spared his eyes for the several moments that it took his brain to shift from sleep to wakefulness. He had hoped to find Jaron's scent burned into those cushions, some trace of him from the last time the other man slept here. But all he found was evidence of the many nights the sofa had been his bed of choice, when anger and grief refused to allow him to sleep in the bed he had shared with Venn.

Now that he had slept in the bedroom again, however, though only once without consequence, there was no good reason to continue to avoid it. There was only the hope, when he had returned home, that Jaron would walk through the door, his body's beat-down exhaustion, and the pain meds he had accepted from the medi, taken with the intent of forcing quick healing, that kept him from moving those few extra feet into the other room.

The lack of effort had been wasted.

Jaron had not come back.

The shift in position exposed his bare back and shoulder to the cold room and the solemn, regal tune burrowed into his head, undercut by the persistent digital beeping that spelled the impending shutdown of the nearly depleted oxygen tank. Both were bothersome enough to prompt him to roll, swing his feet to the floor, and sit with aching slowness with the blanket dragged up to wrap around his upper body. Absently, he switched the tank off, wondering where he could get it refilled or acquire a new one, given the state of most city facilities. Skelter could do it, perhaps…or Tamner. They were his best shots.

Movement on the screen cut through his distracted thoughts, drew his eyes to the screen, and he squinted, then rubbed them to clear away sleep to focus on what had forced him awake.

He had forgotten the funerary prods would begin today.

The music continued to drone over the still footage of Haythem Kemway lying in state, to be viewed by everyone as he awaited whatever end was intended for him. Time and attention had been invested in trimming his unkempt hair and beard, in washing away the grime that would have attested to his time spent on the Lev streets. He was dressed in the formal white banyan he had worn for public appearances. His cheeks were sunken, his features gaunt, as though the byproduct of the illness it was claimed he had suffered after the Coup. By now, however, there were few in the city who would believe his death had been the product of illness.

The illness reported at the time of his abduction may have been real enough, but the vengeance hunt for his assassin had glossed over those old details to paint a new narrative.

Presumed dead, absent from the role of leadership for so long, there would be some who would reminisce and fondly mourn their lost Founder. Some who had conveniently pushed aside the memories of long-endured oppression at Kemway hands. There would be some who would discuss today, as past speeches played on prod loops for the city to hear, as Haythem's surviving acquaintances offered moving remembrances, as he was transported to the Hall where it was said every other Founder in history had been interred, whether, or if, it was time to elevate a new Founder and who that should be.

The debates, as the old world and ways decayed around them, would spark violence. Rhyd did not doubt it. Scarecrow would be needed. He would be there…but it would not be easy to keep his focus so long as Jaron did not come home.

The unspoken admission drove the acknowledgment of how much Jaron meant to him through his breast like a spike, robbing him of breath as he reached for the long-sleeved black undershirt worn as a second skin beneath Scarecrow's protective shell. He squeezed his eyes shut, gulped air behind the breathing mask he had forgotten to remove, and then ripped it from his mouth and nose as another voice, a startling voice, cut uninvited into the prod.

Given the nature of the day and the connection that had always existed between the Voices of Faith and the Kemways, that voice was not so unexpected. Permitting Senior Kal to speak a eulogy was the expected way of things, even if some believed that he and his Talkers were behind the abduction, and perhaps even the murder, of the man he was to vocally praise.

But it felt unexpected and out of place to Rhyd.

"Beloved citizens. We mourn the loss of our great Founder, Haythem Kemway," Kal began, the words as stale, Rhyd thought with a snort as he dressed, as any sentiment the Senior ever uttered. "Today, we remember greatness. Greatness born. Greatness lived. Greatness lost. We offer our thoughts, our remembrances, and our prayers, for Founder Haythem and all of the Founders who have gone before him, without whom humanity would not have survived the horrific ending of the ancient world."

Again, Rhyd snorted. With the opening of Outside, those words no longer rang so true. The fate of the world had seemed dire enough to prompt Duncan Kemway and a host of others to construct the protective shell of the city in the Five Falls, and other structures like it, but that threat, if it had been real, had passed. Humanity had survived. But maybe Hebanthe Falls had not been needed. The parah had survived after all, just as those inside the city had.

The parah had lost technology, but they had retained their freedom. They had inherited a more innocent world.

Perhaps Duncan and the Kemways after him were not the great saviors. Who could say if the enslavement of those in the fall city had been worth the exchange?

"This day comes on the precipice of a great tipping, when we look to the past and the future and weigh where our greatness will lie. Let us not abandon greatness simply by enduring what is. Let us look ahead, to the enduring greatness of humanity and to the continuation of the leadership provided by every Founder who has lived and led us to this pivotal moment."

Kal paused for a dramatic breath, a sound that might have been missed if the normal hum and hiss of life systems were operating at normal levels. Rhyd frowned and looked at the screen.

The image had not changed, and yet it seemed certain it would as the Senior's voice began again.

"The cycle of corruption, as ill-fated as it was, our beloved Founder pushed into unwise choices by the pride and folly of selfish, greedy advisors, has ended. A wife cannot bind us together. A child does not have the foresight, education, or wisdom to lead. But there is another. A son presumed lost. A Kemway found. Aldrich Kemway, hidden away under the name of Enoch, the dedicated one, hidden for his protection so that, should the inevitable day of judgment befall us, he would be here, the one to rescue and unite us as one people, the one to restore our city to the greatness Duncan envisioned in the days before the doors of Hebanthe Falls were shut upon our ancestors…"

Kal's voice, any continuance of his speech, was cut as though the prod-feed had been cut off either at the source or by controllers at the Hub. The Founder's March no longer played, though the image of Haythem's peacefully sleeping features persisted on the Echo screen.

Or maybe the sound continued, and it was only the name ringing in Rhyd's ears that drowned out every other sound in the room.

The chaos he had expected this day to bring had been magnified.

His stomach churned and knotted. His breathing became shallow, and for a moment, he felt light-headed as though he would faint.

There was no time for that. There were important things to do.

He retrieved his boots from their place by the door. His foot struck the nearly empty oxygen tank and knocked it aside with a clatter.

He had to go. Not only would Jaron need Scarecrow now.

Enoch would need him, too.

&Chapter 23&

"How dare they!

Neoma's face shone with outrage as she tore off the silk lounge robe, the meager morning meal forgotten in favor of storming from the kitchen to view the flickering, unstable image of her husband lying in state on the Echo, displayed for everyone in Hebenon to see. She had not seen such a peaceful expression on his face since before the parah child altered the fate of the city, had not seen him so regally dressed since before the Coup had ripped their world asunder.

Such public events had been so common, so similar, that she could not remember when the last event had been. Ulynda's introduction into society, perhaps? The vagueness of memory deepened her scowl and Haythem's serenity made her sad until the notes of the Founder's Suite pushed past her loss of focus and ignited her anger again.

"I'm supposed to be there!"

Nanny glanced at Ulynda who still sat at the table and covered the girl's hand with her matronly one. It would have been right, it would have been proper and fitting, for the Founder's wife and sole remaining child…the only family he had, to attend the rituals this day. Perhaps there was a reason the summons had not been received. Perhaps, because the lifts were not working reliably, someone had concluded Neoma would not deign to make the climb to the Uppers. But the day was young. Perhaps she and her daughter would still be summoned and brought to the place where Haythem was.

The Nau would not exclude them without cause…even if that cause was, Nanny sighed, Neoma's insufferable haughtiness.

It did not surprise Nanny that Neoma thought only of herself when the music began to play.

Ulynda accepted the offer of comfort with a sad glance of appreciation before sliding her hand free and leaving the table to witness the prod as well. Like other home Echos, this one had been dark and silent over most of the last day, allowing the preservation of the city's precious power so that today's long output to honor the murdered Founder could run uninterrupted. Today, every Echo in the city would be lit with the remembrances of the man who had led Hebanthe Falls all of his adult life.

Her father.

She blinked away tears as she stared at the man's profile on the screen. He looked different than the last time she had seen him, closer to the way she remembered from those brighter, lighter, happier days when she and her brother and sister had played in the Upper halls, when they had gathered at his side, at his knees, to listen as he read fanciful stories of exotic days when the world had been younger and human life had thrived in the world Outside. He looked as she remembered, but also older. Wearier. Smug and sad all at once.

The corners of her mouth trembled. Those days felt very far away.

Her mother stormed out of the living area and into her bedroom where the opening and closing of drawers and closet doors attested to an effort to find the right clothing to mark this day, something both noble and tasteful, befitting an official expression of grief for a man she cared little about.

Her mother might have loved her father once, otherwise, why would she have married him? But Ulynda was confident she no longer did, that whatever love there had been had bled away before her first memories had formed. There had been exhibited respect, attentive public acquiescence and deference, and there had been tolerant duty. But Ulynda could not recall witnessing any matrimonial love.

Kal's voice, overriding the melody that Ulynda knew from every public function her father had ever attended, made her frown and clench her hands into impotent fists before she understood why. His voice also brought Neoma, half-dressed in a cowl-necked blouse of gauzy black fabric and a starched stiff pencil skirt she struggled to zip, back into the room. Her panic-stricken, fearful stare made Ulynda's frown grow deeper and her fists clench.

It also prompted her to step away from her mother's reach.

The voice brought forth words that wrapped the flat in a deadly form of silence, a stillness that lasted only long enough for Neoma's face to lose color, for her to inhale sharply, spin as though to strike anything near to her, and roar so that the walls around them trembled. "Lies!"

Shuffling further away from her mother's outrage, Ulynda, too, gaped at the screen, at the voice without a face, trying to absorb the words that had been spoken. Enoch? The same man who had tried to protect her from the brako? A moment, a shared exchange when her father revealed himself, something that had passed between him and the dwarf that Ulynda had not understood, a moment that stuck in her head before it was buried beneath the avalanche of fear and pain that came after with her father's shouted words, the snatching up against her will to be dragged home.

Was it true?

That same man?

No images to support the Senior's claim were displayed, and no effort was made to undermine the respectful display of the deceased Founder the city expected to see. Ulynda could not be sure there was not some other Enoch of whom the Senior spoke, but her certainty in the odds increased with every splutter of outrage and jerking disgust her mother made.

Why else had Neoma threatened the dwarf and wanted to keep Ulynda away from him?

"It's him…" Ulynda whispered, keeping her eyes on the screen so as not to anger her mother by staring at her as she spoke.

"You'll go nowhere near him!" The zipper of her skirt snagged the back of Neoma's blouse, but she ignored it as she pulled on the fashionable shoulder wrap that hung over the back of a nearby chair, a black patterned piece long enough to mask the wardrobe mistake without her needing to take the time to correct it. She had no patience for that. "You will stay here and never…"

"I should visit Papa with you…" Ulynda was not familiar with most protocols of state affairs, but she understood that if this was a day of Kemway family unity, particularly as part of a public display, she should go Up as well.

"You will stay here!" Neoma screeched. If there was even a slim chance Aldrich would be there, that someone had located him, if the Nau was about to elevate him to Founder in Neoma or Ulynda's stead, she wanted her daughter nowhere near the scene that would transpire.

The dwarf would not contaminate her daughter any more than the parah girl had already done. Neoma would expose him for the defective, ill-fitted candidate he was and demand her rightful claim to her husband's position. She would do everything she could to protect her child while simultaneously fighting for her right to power.

She would protect Ulynda as best as she could…even if that meant sending the girl Outside, as far away from the dwarf, from the seat of the Founder, as possible.

Her hand slammed against the off button on the Echo's face and the screen went black.

"Mama…"

"Do not leave this flat. Do not…"

"Mama!"

"Stay here!"

The door crashed open, again shaking the walls, and then banged shut. Motionless, Ulynda listened to the receding clack of heels on the grated path, the ring of the woman's passage reverberating across the metal until the sound was no longer heard, her held breath of horror released in a whoosh of relief when the world grew still. Though she could try to find him, this uncle she had never known about, she understood that today of all days it would be unwise to venture into a city that might either hate or revere her…if she was recognized at all. For today, for the moment, there was nowhere to go.

Not even to her father's side.

She turned the Echo on after a glance at Nanny's stricken features to see if the woman would forbid her from watching her own father's funerary farewell.

Today, there might be nowhere else to go, but tomorrow, she could begin again.

If she could determine how.

❧*❧

Standing with the Nau and Doctor Tamner as the memorial broadcast began brought back memories of other occasions in this same room with some of these same people awaiting word from the man who, today, would be interred with the Kemway Founders who had gone before him. Founders were the only people in the city to be interred rather than processed through the electrical system for the brief spot of additional power their bodies could provide.

Most Founders, nearing the end of their lives, recorded a final message to the city they were leaving behind, words saved in the Archives to be read, listened to, and dissected by the generations who came after. Today, that final word would not come. The Coup had robbed Haythem of the opportunity to record any parting words so, at this day's end, when the images faded and the prods ceased to play, the last voice of the Kemways would be silenced forever.

There was his last, disjointed speech in a random city square, where someone was likely to erect a monument in his honor. Those words would be studied too, read and pulled apart for their meaning, but the Nau had opted not to play that speech today so as not to inflame an already disgruntled population. Maybe, Grainger mused with a stern expression that kept his impending scowl at bay, that incoherent ramble had been precisely the final word Haythem intended.

It was doubtful that Duncan Kemway could have foreseen the city coming to this.

The music droned, the expected viewing period provided so that the citizens had ample opportunity to mourn, those minutes creeping by for those directed to attend the entire hour in this room by customary mandate. In the Levs, some undoubtedly spent a few minutes staring at the image fed through every Echo the Hub could access, and then went about their business until the next phase of the funerary memorial began. For the Nau, as for the Doctet before them, for the captain and other city officials, this viewing was a duty demanded of them.

Every other duty was set aside, including the capture of a kidnapper, an assassin, and the interrogation of a saboteur.

Of the faces Grainger could see without moving from his position at the head of the table, standing behind Tamner who had been forced by the others with them into the seat where the Founder once sat, as many attendees displayed grief as they did solemn boredom. He doubted anyone in the room honestly missed the deceased man, except for perhaps Delora, who shed open tears and wiped her nose and eyes on an embroidered handkerchief. Nunn clenched and unclenched his fists, and Fahti dabbed at the corners of her eyes without any change in her neutral expression. The rest he could not see.

He wondered what thoughts were running through Tamner's mind, wondered if the men and women with them would choose to elect, or appoint, Tamner as the Founder now that Kemway was legitimately deceased. Tamner would protest, would resist, but in many ways, he was already being pressed into the role of leadership over the joint populations of Hebenon and Marbordo.

Grainger led by default, as head of the law. He did not want to relinquish that. He also did not want to shoulder the responsibility for all of the city's woes that continued to pile upon one another. He would be satisfied with Tamner taking those duties if it came to that.

When Senior Kal's voice hacked into the feed, some of the faces at the table wrinkled in distaste. Others expressed support for the man at the helm of the city's religious establishment. He had not been asked to speak, and most around him did not appreciate the intrusion. Grainger growled at the man beside him and muttered, "Shut it down."

"Let the Senior have his say," Fahti interjected sternly with a wave meant to prevent the officer from acting upon the order.

"Customary thing to do," Nunn agreed. Despite the suspicion swirling around the Voices and the Senior in particular, the man did have the customary right to participate, even if he had not been invited to do so, but it suspiciously appeared to Grainger that Nunn and Fahti might have conspired to allow the Senior this chance.

Heads bobbed to Kal's opening words. Faces expressed approval for the sentiments the Senior was wise enough to lay as the foundation of his brief ceremonial sermon. But his words seemed incongruous with the guilt Grainger was certain the Voices carried, an effort to exempt the Senior and the Voices from blame in the eyes of the only people who might protect him. Each bobbing head tightened the grip of uneasiness around Grainger's throat.

The sensation did not last."

"The cycle of corruption, as unfortunate as it was, our beloved Founder pushed into unwise choices by the pride and folly of selfish, greedy advisors, has ended. A wife cannot bind us together. A child has not the foresight, education, or wisdom to lead."

Gazes shifted as some turned in their chairs to look at their companions. Words of corruption made Nunn rub the back of his arms as though chasing an itch that would not be satisfied. They seemed to agree that neither wife nor daughter were a suitable replacement for the late Founder, but Kal's pause predicted words that none of them were interested in or eager to hear.

"But there is another. A son presumed lost."

Chairs creaked as the attendees shifted awkwardly.

"A Kemway found. Aldrich Kemway…"

Nunn lurched out of his chair. Grainger thought he would turn the Echo off, but Warren grabbed his wrist and held him in place as Fahti snorted, "That child's long dead…"

"…hidden away under the name of Enoch, the dedicated one, hidden for his protection so that, should the inevitable day of judgment befall us, he would be here, the one to rescue and unite us as one people, the one to restore our city to the greatness Duncan envisioned in the days before the doors of Hebanthe Falls were shut upon our ancestors…"

The audio feed fell abruptly silent as though someone at the Hub had disabled the hack without instruction. The silence that replaced the Founder's Suite and the Senior's announcement lasted only long enough for Pearl to back away from the table with a breathless exclamation of incredulity. "There is another Kemway?"

From his periphery, Grainger noted the tension that rippled across Tamner's shoulders but the doctor did not speak, only tipped his head forward to rest his chin on his clasped hands. He imagined the doctor's eyes were closed and suspected that, somewhere in the man's circle of Lev acquaintances, he knew the man Kal spoke of.

He might even know the man was the missing Kemway heir. Tamner was no fool. If Kal had uncovered this truth, others might have done so too. Unlike Kal, the doctor would be prone to take such a secret to his grave. He was unlikely to give up what he knew or suspected easily.

Later, Grainger would question him about how much, if anything, Tamner already knew.

"Aldrich died as an infant," Delora sniffed sorrowfully.

"Are we surprised the Voices would try to capitalize on communal grief by offering an imposter?" began Lydon, his snort accompanied by the pushing back of his water glass with enough force to tip it. Its contents dribbled a lazy river across the polished black surface. Caminda yanked her T1 away with a glowering glare, but Lydon's gaze shifted between Nunn and Fahti as though accusing them of inviting the Senior to participate and thus being complicit in his claim.

"There's no reason for them to…" huffed Nunn.

"Without a Founder, the Voices are nothing," Wooster reminded him. "Of course they'd try to extort us to install a puppet…"

Warren leaned back thoughtfully with his arms crossed over his chest. "Maybe it's true. Maybe he's right, and there is one…wouldn't be the first time the Kemways hid the truth and lied to us. Mom and Dad always thought there was something suspect about the kid's disappearance and reported death…"

The missing Kemway would be Warren and Wooster's age. They had grown up in a home where conspiracy and gossip and talk of political machinations in the forbidden Uppers were common. Their uncle had been Taken for such talk outside of the home, as had their grandmother and several cousins. Warren and Woster had been lucky to escape that fate.

Now they were here.

"Should bring 'em in, Senior Kal and this poser," Stace suggested.

"This is treason," Nunn challenged. "We'll have none of that."

"We owe it to Hebanthe Falls to learn the truth," Caminda reminded them, cutting off the tirade of the man across the table. "We owe it to Haythem. We should invite them to speak…"

"Not today we won't." Fahti's cold gaze settled on Tamner, a scathing scrutinizing look that strengthened Grainger's certainty that the doctor knew details he was not sharing. "Today is for Haythem. The Founder is yet to be interred. There'll be no talk of a new Founder until it is done. "After…" She looked around the room, meeting everyone's gaze. "We'll address this again.

"There's nothing to discuss…" began Nunn's bitter protest.

"We are nine…not one…" Delora offered. "The decision is for all of us, not yours. It can't hurt to talk to him, to test the veracity…"

"We don't need a Founder," Lydon snorted. Talking's moot. But," he sighed, "we should investigate the claim before someone else does…or the people turn on us for failing to learn the truth and seek out this man for our protection. We should see if the claim is…"

"It isn't." Nunn swiped his hand over his forehead and through his hair. "It can't be…"

Caminda shrugged. "Even if it is, there's no reason we're required to elevate him. No need to go back to how things were, now that things are so much…"

"Are they though?" Pearl whispered. "Are they better? We're leaving the city. The brako are everywhere. How is that better?"

"Evacuation's temporary," Warren reminded her, "until the systems are restored. Then things can go back…"

The door at the rear of the room opened; a young woman in a stiff, white, service uniform bowed and said, "The Hall is ready."

People glanced at the still image continuing to broadcast on the Echo, an image overlaid with the march movement of the suite rather than the Senior's voice. A counter ticked in the corner of the screen, reminding everyone that the next segment of Remembrance Day was about to commence.

"Tomorrow then." Delora was the one to voice the appointment that no one visually or verbally acknowledged as they stepped away from the table. The others did not agree, but each knew that the other would attend. It was the role they had agreed on when they accepted this nomination. Their gazes turned to Tamner as they passed, asking for, expecting, demanding his attendance too.

Tamner did not rise. Grainger was the last to reach the pneumatic door he reflexively tried to hold open, though the loss of power kept it open until someone manually came to close it.

"Doctor?"

Tamner lifted his head. He met the captain's gaze and sighed. There were too many questions to answer. As far as he was concerned, it was not his place to do so.

The curious captain, however, might not give him another choice.

❧*❧

Rain cloak pulled up to hide his face, Enoch skirted the corner crowd of off-shift workers gathered around an Echo. It had switched from showing the late Founder lying in state to the procession of the Nau, friends, and associates creeping behind the prone form and the stationary camera, offering their remembrances of the man to the listening public before shuffling to the dais on the other side of the room. Nothing but glowing, kind words that failed to express the hollow reality Lev viewers had experienced during the years of Haythem's reign.

The horror had not been entirely his fault, passing as it had from his father and grandfather, but he had done nothing to end it. That was fault enough.

Few Enoch saw appeared upset by the man's death. Most seemed not to care. Many who expressed emotion were distressed by the unanswered assassination and the electrical issues that made their future insecure. They watched the screen, a wide-angled shot of the room adorned with white and blue banners, and the window behind that provided many with their first glimpse of an Outside world they had yet to investigate or see for themselves. The staging suggested a gift given to his people when the truth was that this legacy, forever associated with Haythem, had very little to do with him and everything to do with Scarecrow.

But the strategy was there. Outside was safe. Outside was good. Outside was a gift Haythem had given to them, now moving there until power was restored was the greatest gift people could give back to Hebanthe Falls, the greatest memorial act they could surrender to their Founder's memory.

Those were the morsels echoing in conversation, the pros and cons of change, that Enoch heard as he passed, tidbits interspersed with the excited chatter debating the validity of Senior Kal's claim.

Jostled aside, Enoch pulled the cloak tighter at his throat with one hand to keep the hood from slipping. Thank the creator that his face had not been blasted all over that prod too. Those who knew his name would cluster to him soon, demanding answers, seeking advice, or wanting to prompt action from him that he did not want to give. He did not have answers. He was not a leader. He did not want his face, his name, to become the focus of other people's lives.

The choice had been taken away from him now. He would never be anonymous again.

"Hijo de puta!" He swore beneath his breath as he pushed aside Vapors'' beaded door curtain to be immediately grabbed by the wrist, snatched inside, and swept to a table by Skelter's guiding arm and the echo of the redhead's exclamation. The vindi was empty except for Nigel, who was diligently resurfacing the dance platform, and Maemi, taking inventory of her dwindling stores behind the bar. Judging by the pair of glasses on the bar, she had paused to share a drink with Skelter when he spotted Enoch outside and chose to drag him in away from the outside crowds.

"Did you give Senior…?"

Angry and unsettled by the abrupt action, Enoch dropped onto a chair and kicked the nearest one with one foot. It skittered sideways away from him but did not fall. "Cazzo…told the eblan I didn't want the responsibility…wouldn't take the…"

"Trying to take away your choice," Maemi interjected as she brought Skelter's drink and another for Enoch to the unlit table where the pair had settled. Nigel glanced at Enoch, nodded respectfully, and continued his work. "All they ever do."

Assuming he had heard the prod too, Enoch was relieved that at least one person in Hebenon was content not to make a fuss. Secrets were secret for a reason. Whatever the andi knew, he did not want to know anymore, any more than he wanted his secrets aired.

Mutual trust and respect made Vapors a haven. Enoch did not expect it to remain that way, so long as he continued to come here.

Hand wrapped around the glass, Enoch side-eyed Maemi's calm demeanor, the woman seeming to take this news in stride as though she had always known the truth or did not care about it. He bobbed his head, took a long swallow of the pungent, clear liquid, and muttered, "Choice is mine til I'm dead. Hebenon doesn't need a Founder. It needs a savior, someone with a head for this posa, and that's not me."

"Better you than Mam…"

Enoch snorted and emptied his glass. "Never gonna happen. Situation's too precarious. Nau's not gonna let her anywhere near that post…Ulynda either…and I don't want it. I won't take it. Suspect they rather like their power now that they've gotten a taste of it. They're not gonna bend for her, or me, or anyone else."

"'nough of us know your name down here…know your face," Skelter warned. "Word's gonna spread. Gonna be a fotz keeping low now, but if you need my help…"

"Dark'll help for a while, but yeah." He sighed and rubbed his face with both hands. The spotlight was going to be on him as soon as the first streeter pointed him out. Sooner or later, who he was would get to Neoma and she was going to send whatever loyalists remained to get him out of her way. He would not be able to hide from her indefinitely and he did not want to live as a fugitive.

Nor did he want to stand in the spotlight and embrace the side-handed destiny his name entitled him to.

He wanted to be anonymous, left alone.

That was not going to happen.

Maybe, if he could get close enough to Neoma, he could convince her he was no threat.

He had no idea how to manage everyone else.

❧*❧

"Power's diverted to the prods," muttered a nondescript figure trudging past as Neoma ran her passcard through the lift reader for the fourth time as if repeating the attempt would force the lift to respond. "Only gonna work if you're a bugger or a medi with the right code."

"Don't they know who I am?" she hissed, tempted to kick the screened door but resisting the compulsion to avoid looking entitled. The stranger raised his head to reveal a shaggy, salt-and-pepper beard and weary brown eyes, and though he met her gaze, he did not appear to recognize her. Neoma's eyes narrowed more.

"Doesn't matter who anyone is. All the same here. Only way to change is to go Out. You wanna go up, you gotta register, get a pass…"

"I am not," she emphasized as she shoved the card into her pocket, "taking the stairs." She was also not going to register for some list like a commoner. If she took the stairs, by the time she reached the Uppers, much of the day's ceremony would be over. The time for family would have passed.

The fellow shrugged. "There's a delivery trolley that takes supplies up," he pointed, "but might not be operating today. Could talk to the director there if she's around. Might make an exception if you offer something worth the effort."

He provided no further comment or assistance before plodding off to join a gaggle of similarly attired people beneath a pavilion in the middle of the nearest intersection, gathered to watch the mourners' procession on the Echo end with Captain Grainger assuming the Founder's podium.

Neoma could not hear his words, but seeing him in the place where Haythem once stood made her snarl. Perhaps the volume of the Echo was broken or turned down too low, or her proximity to the Falls' roar was drowning out his voice. This was his doing, the man who had illegally stolen the torch of leadership from her incapacitated husband. Captain Grainger, who had sent her to live in the cold damp of the Levs. Grainger, who had no right, no jurisdiction, to lead Hebenon.

His job was to restore and keep order. He was failing to do that.

And now he had excluded her from Haythem's final rite.

Or someone had. Grainger was the most convenient target.

Hissing through her gritted teeth, she turned in the direction the stranger had indicated where the commodities lift might function. She was no longer rich in ticks, but her name would buy her passage Up.

There was still time.

The ringing step of boots, the looming hulks of three shadows who slunk by her with disdainful glances of recognition, men she judged to be unmasked brako…and thus not hers, made her falter, stop, and stare after them for several wordless minutes as a shivering sickness raced from her head to her toes and back up again. Their gazes felt like daggers, pointed and deadly, and here she was alone, without Vanderwall, Blayde, or anyone to protect her.

Hebenon was no longer safe. There was no haven to be found here.

Her daughter, the most likely target if the brako took the claims of an illegitimate Founder to heart, only had Nanny to protect her.

Remembrance Day was no longer important.

Neoma needed another plan.

❧Chapter 24❧

Vanderwall sneered at the Echo images, drumming his fingers on his desk, seeing the moving forms but no longer paying attention to them as the door creaked open in response to his grunted summons.

"Sir?" squeaked the older fellow with one sleeve bunched up and tied with a cord at the stump where his forearm had once been. He was a big man, retired now but once a hatchery worker before his injury. The paradox of his size and meek demeanor meant that he was able to perform several functions on both sides of Vanderwall's business, from the use of brute force to diplomacy and spying, but none of those were what the boss needed today.

"It's time. Is it ready?"

"It is. Are you sure…?"

Disliking being questioned by subordinates, Vanderwall lifted his annoyed gaze from the screen to stare at the other man. "Not gonna be a better one. Whole cazzing lot's caught up in this posa." He gestured at the muted Echo. "Not going to pay attention to us. Get it done." The bugorra would be preoccupied, the rumored warehouse raid put off by the Founder's ceremony. The bait had to be moved far enough away from that place so that the buggers did not accidentally find their hostage. "Get me Tappy. Got something for him to take care of."

The older man nodded. "Right, boss. We'll get it done alright."

❧*❧

Retracing her path home but still an uncomfortable distance away from it, Neoma stopped at the stairs, her passage impeded by bothersome footsteps behind her and a dozen unarmed Talkers in front of her descending into her path. Unafraid of Talkers, her pensive frown morphed into a sneer as she looked from one face to another, expecting them to move aside to allow her to pass. She did not recognize any of them but expected them to recognize her and comply with her wishes.

"Mam."

They knew her now. Her sneer gave way to a tight-lipped, smug smile, but having no patience for small talk when she only wanted to return home, she snipped, "Step aside."

They did not move.

She thought they intended to take her to Kal, or maybe hold her hostage as they had done her husband to remove her opposition to the Senior's plan. There were too many of them to escape if they mobbed her, and going back meant risking the brako she believed were following her, so she stood her ground and refused to show the fear she thought they wanted to see.

But when the speaker started again, it was with an eagerness that suggested no dark agenda. "We hoped to find you before…"

"I have nothing to say to you or your Senior. Move or I'll…"

Their excitement could be a ruse to lull her into trusting them. Neoma did not want to take that risk.

The young woman, approximately half Neoma's age, shook her head so that her tendrils of pale brown hair shook free from her hood and stuck to the sides of her mist-damp face. "We're not here from the Senior, Mam. We…" she indicated those with her as she continued her greeting, "we heard what he said…the revelation about a brother…and we want you to know, we're with you."

"Senior's wrong," sneered another. "There's no lost Kemway."

"Does he?" The tone of Neoma's question made the group look at each other as though casting doubt on their beliefs.

But the previous speaker, cutting off their female spokesperson, replied with a continuing sneer, "Even if there's one out there…he doesn't have experience. Either as a leader or in the Ups. He has no right to the seat. Founder's daughter ought to…"

Neoma arched her brow and cocked her head, an action that cut the young, sharp-featured man off. The role of Founder had passed between brothers before, but it had never passed to a woman…or a child. She was curious about what had led this little group to their conclusions but decided against questioning an allegiance she could use. She needed backers, for safety and security, and information if nothing else, and any splintering within the Voices was worth the irritation she could wheedle into Kal's side.

"It is only you?" she asked with coy skepticism as her turning head raked her gaze from one side of the group to the other.

"There's more," the spokeswoman replied with an enthusiastic nod. "We've been building for a while…but today, everything's different. Hebenon's never going to be right without a Founder. It's in our creed. Everyone knows it. Without a Kemway…"

"And now they're trying to drive us Outside," someone else grumbled, "punish the Levs for the Coup while…"

"Trust me…" Neoma started, only to swallow her words and nod. If people believed the Uppers were hoarding the city's power as punishment, it was another morsel of dissension she could use. Rebels seeking a cause, for their way to make the city better, were people she could utilize. Maybe not everyone believed it, but Neoma only needed a spark to work with.

"We do," the young woman nodded. Others did too. "Tell us what we can do. How can we help?"

There were more footsteps of passing brako a half-Lev above, this time beaked faces that leered down at them without passing. They might be her people or Vanderwall's minions, but she no longer trusted them any more than she trusted the Talkers before her.

The disruption gave Neoma time to pull stray thoughts together before speaking. "I'm working on something. The objective is to protect Ulynda, keep her safe from the brako and other Talkers who think she's not fit to…and from Aldrich and his minions…whoever he is. From those who want to install an imposter as Founder. When I have the plan prepared, how do I find you?"

"Here." The woman tapped something into her ICD and held it out so Neoma could sync their devices and lock their communication codes into place. "Whatever you need…whenever you need us, call us. Tell us where to be, what to do. We'll come, however many of us can get to you as fast as possible."

With ICDs synced, Neoma nodded once and adjusted her sleeve without taking her eyes off the woman. "That will work." These might be pawns in whatever game Kal was playing, but the young woman sounded earnest and Neoma doubted she was as adept at subterfuge as the Senior. Neoma had to begin rebuilding. Whatever she did, she would not be able to accomplish anything alone. This was a start. "I will be in touch."

⇦*⇨

Things that explode were not his specialty. Colyx was a man who had lived by his hands, his fists, both outside and inside the Core. Once forced into the grim world of the mines, he had watched others work, miners who set charges to open new veins for extraction or men using smaller ones to break open stubborn streaks in the rock. He had aided those crews enough times to know how setting charges was done safely and for the best effect, though he had never done it himself. They were delicate, volatile devices that might be triggered before they were in place, that could kill him or anyone else before they were ready to be activated, but they were the only things powerful enough when in place and discharged to accomplish the goal he intended.

He brushed rust and grime away with his fingers and pushed the piece he held into the cylinder in his other hand.

He did not want people to die trapped within Hebanthe Falls, though some invariably would. As with the escape from the Core, sacrifices had to be made to ensure the survival of his family, the survival of as many people as possible.

He had not asked where the supplies came from. He was given the location of an empty warehouse, found the materials he asked for, and then moved everything to a secondary location where he could work without fear of discovery. Skelter would not know he was here. Otta would not know. Not even the woman Eido would know unless she had spies following him in and out of the original warehouse.

He did not think she would risk revealing a connection to him. It was best if she feigned no knowledge of his activities.

Colyx was doing this as much for her and the Igraci, for Hebenon, as he was for his family. He did not believe she would interfere. He had chosen this mission, presented it to her for her approval, and as his big fingers wrapped the exposed wires into place and set a third device aside on the dingy, scavenged table, his conviction remained.

Once this was done, there would be no choice but to leave Hebanthe Falls for good.

❧*❦

The alley shortcut he had chosen ended in a street where four beaked shades made it impossible to pass. Before he could choose retreat, before he could find another route or abandon the planned destination he remained uncertain about, the four heads turned as one to stare as if they could pick out his small frame from the shadows. Assuming that the tinted eye-pieces of what had once been law-enforcement masks were fitted with infrared, and the masks equipped with advanced audio detection tech, it was likely they had heard him before they saw him, likely they could see him now. Enoch did not expect to outrun them. Reluctant to turn his back, hindered by the alley clutter that made backward retreat awkward, it was only the shadow that dropped from above to land in a crouch between him and the brako that allowed Enoch to escape.

Instead of running, startled by the abrupt intrusion, Enoch cowered and watched with slack-jawed awe at the spinning kick that flung the front-most brako against a handrail with enough force to make the stairs rattle and ring and leave him limp and unmoving amid the recycle bins his fall tipped over.

"Where is he?"

Scarecrow's modulated voice growled the question as he wrapped an arm around the second brako's neck, turned, and caused the man's swinging force to trip the fellow behind him. The fourth dodged the third man's fall, but Scarecrow's drop to his knees propelled the man he held flat on the ground and caused the fourth to miss his target and roll over the vigi's back.

With no one between them, Enoch crabbed hastily away from the fourth brako. The man's attention, however, remained on Scarecrow.

"Where's Vanderwall?" It was not the question he wanted to ask. He had been to the soaper again but found no trace of Uriah Frankel there, nor any other brako, but he knew he would find the boss soon enough. His most pressing fear was one he could not voice, for he chose not to utter Jaron's name and give the brako leverage over him.

He did not want to kill anyone. He wanted Vanderwall to get word of this altercation, to know Scarecrow was coming for him. But he did not want Vanderwall to know the names of anyone he could use as pawns. He could not speak Jaron's name.

The man held in his elbow grasp snarled and thrashed. Scarecrow reached for the nearest item, a broken bottle, and hurled it at the man charging from his right. The beaked mask protected his face from the glass but the impact shattered one of the goggled eyepieces and was enough to cause him to stumble sideways with an arm raised too late to shield himself.

"I want his location!"

"Cazz you!" The third brako was on his feet again, and as the second stopped struggling in Scarecrow's grip, his air cut off long enough to render him unconscious, the third threw himself at his enemy. The comatose body was dropped; Scarecrow charged low and crashed, shoulder first, into the charging man's knees. The leather crop the brako wielded clattered on the grate as it fell, to be kicked away in the scramble of feet as one rolled to standing and the other barreled into his only remaining ally.

Scarecrow rolled his neck from side to side, gauging that Enoch remained safe, judging what the remaining brako intended to do. The one with the broken goggles, his hands bloody from his efforts to wipe his vision clean, swept left. The other dodged right, kicked off the tipped bins, and threw a broken chunk of hemp brick. Scarecrow ducked, allowing the brick to soar past, across the path the four had followed. It clattered from the rail to the walk to the rooftop on its way down toward the river. The visually impaired brako followed the brick, hitting the rail and tumbling over it before managing to catch the rail with his blood-slippery hand to dangle unaided.

Gloved fist catching the last brako in the throat below the edge of his cowl, Scarecrow jumped, straddled him, and pinned the gasping man to the ground. "I won't ask again."

The brako made a sound, like a spit or hiss of disdain, but it might have been an effort to breathe as he clutched at his throat. The edge of the mask and the collar of his coat prevented the blow from being fatal, but it would be a week or more before he could speak the words Scarecrow wanted to hear.

Behind him, the floor rattled as the fallen brako attempted to hoist himself back onto the path. One more blow and the man beneath him blacked out too, leaving Scarecrow as the only one to reach the man whose hands clutched and clung to the edge of the walk.

The climb up should have been easy, but the blood on his hands made his grip slippery, and the blood dripping into his eye was a distraction. It forced him to struggle to hold on with one hand while trying to wipe the blood away again as he pulled himself up with the other arm. With one eye visible through the broken lens, he looked at the looming shadow just before the vigi ground the heel of his boot into his fingers.

He screamed despite himself.

"Same offer. Only gonna ask once. Where's Vanderwall?"

"Dunno," he rasped, reaching for the bar above his head, but the effort was feeble against the grinding pain in his hand that prevented him from falling. "Never seen him. Most of us don't…"

Scarecrow loomed over him, his focus seeming to be on the brako though behind the mask he was judging the distance the man would drop if he fell, judging the likelihood of his survival. "Then give me someone who does!"

"I dunno anyone!"

Scarecrow growled, swiped the reaching hand away, and with the toe of his other foot forced the man's gripping hand to release as he barked, "Then you're of no use to me."

The brako fell five feet to land on the roof of whatever home or vindi was beneath him, the fall enough to briefly stun and incapacitate him but not, Scarecrow knew as he cocked his head to listen to the man's painful groaning, enough to kill him.

Forcing himself to stand, ignoring the squish of rotten food beneath his feet, Enoch emerged from behind the recycle bin where he had taken shelter but kept a supporting hand on the wall as his trembling knees threatened to give out.

"Think you enjoyed that."

Scarecrow grunted, watching the barely moving brako below before turning to face Enoch. "Gonna be more of that."

"You've heard." Enoch was not surprised. Very little of import got past Scarecrow for long, and the existence of another Kemway was news that spread like an oil fire throughout every corner of the city. Hesitant steps brought him to the vigi's side so he could look at the brako below them.

The other three were not moving.

"He gonna live?" Though the three behind him in the alley were silent, the rhythmic hiss of their breathers inside their masks indicated life. Scarecrow had never been averse to bloodshed, but he had, to Enoch's knowledge, been reluctant to kill.

As conditions degraded, he expected that aversion to change.

"Yes." At least he should. The sounds inside the building beneath him hinted that someone was about to emerge to investigate the thunderous ruckus on the roof, if the brako required medical attention, those individuals would see that he got it.

Or they would leave him there until he was recovered enough to slink away.

Or, noting that he was brako, they might decide to kill him.

Scarecrow opted to drift back into the alley to avoid being seen, leaving the fallen brako to his fate.

Enoch followed.

"What are you going to do?"

"Not sure what I can do. I don't want the job…I don't want to be a fugitive…but I don't want to be the center of attention either. Don't want to be a hunted man. I'm on my way to have a word with Neoma. Might not get everyone off my back, but maybe she'll call off her supporters and give me a little peace." He shrugged. "It's a start."

Scarecrow bobbed his head. His aimless path from one brako skirmish to another as he hunted Vanderwall…and Jaron…might as well include seeing Enoch safely to his destination and then somewhere else after that. With the possibility that Neoma had a hand in her husband's death, it would be worth hearing what she had to say.

"Got your back. Will dog you there, then get you somewhere secure after." He leaped over the stair rail and began his ascent to the rooftop, where he could easily follow Enoch without being noticed.

"Not sure there is such a place…but thanks." Enoch looked at the nearest brako at his feet and added, "For this too."

Digital distortion masked what he perceived to be a chuckle before Scarecrow replied, "A pleasure," and moved out of sight.

Enoch chuckled darkly too and left the alley, moving with more assurance now that Scarecrow was looking after him.

❧*❧

"Should have invited them."

The hours of ceremony were over, although Kenneth and Soleia would continue to prodcast snippets of the Founder's life, tales of his ancestors to elaborate the nobility of Haythem's eminent bloodline, outtakes of speeches the man had made during his tenure, and the final disjointed words he had shared with protestors shortly before his death, words that had been noticeably left out of the official doings this day. Grainger neither knew, nor cared, about the public's reaction to the color-blind prods. Any Founder fervor they spawned would last a brief season before the daily reality of a city quickly losing access to resources and power would take over their attention again.

Overall, it had been an uneventful day.

He did not expect things to remain that way.

"Couldn't afford the backlash. We let her get a foothold here and she'd never leave." Grainger set his glass down, the need for the alcohol burn to dull his nerves having lent itself to the judicious use of his dwindling supply. He was grateful Tamner had declined the politely offered glass.

More for him.

"Maybe…but for appearances, his family should have been here. It might lend a bad precedent." Not that precedent mattered anymore. Humanity was moving into a world without a Founder, a world Outside. Everything that had gone before would be relegated to tales of history and myth.

The future, the here and now, were what mattered.

Grainger grumbled, reached for the liquor bottle, but let his hand fall away before grabbing it. "Still not sure she's not behind this…his illness, his abduction, his…"

"You said you had new suspects?" There was still Senior Kal, but Tamner did not have, nor want, the details about the ongoing investigations. No charges had been made in any of the primary cases. Whatever the bugorra knew, the captain was playing his cards closely.

"I do. But I'm still bringing her in to…"

"You're arresting her?"

"Didn't say that. If I don't force her to come in, I won't get answers. She's gonna avoid every request I make. If she thinks I have something on her, or thinks I can be swayed to back the girl's right to rule over a claimed imposter…maybe I can get somewhere."

He glanced toward the wrapping window where the Outside sky shimmered over Hebenon's dome. Work crews with magnetic boots continued to salvage what had been damaged, now that Remembrance Day was over, despite the dimming glow of the setting sun. Though the fear of extreme radiation and toxic air was gone, the crews still required protective gear against the cold wind that made the darkening outlines of trees against their mountain backdrop bend and sway.

"Post's going out after I sleep off this pomp." An arrest, a raid, and hopefully some progress made in the restoration of the array. Tomorrow was going to be another long day. Grainger needed sleep if he was to face it with a reasonably clear head.

Tamner shrugged and sighed as he stretched and stood. Arrests were not his jurisdiction, but the rest of those issues were going to pile up on his plate in some fashion.

"How's those assessments coming?"

Briefly confused, Tamner paused, then shrugged again. "Haven't seen them. If they're done, I should have them tomorrow. What do you intend to do with him?"

Borne seemed an affable, likable, honest man. It would be a shame to terminate him for what had to be some fault in his coding. Andi did not simply decide to hurt and threaten humans on their own.

"Depends on the results. You'll let me know?"

"Soon as I have a look, you'll know what I do," Tamner promised.

"Good. Thank you." He gave in to the temptation and poured just enough brandy into his cup for a single swallow and raised the cup in Tamner's direction. "To your health."

"To all of ours," Tamner agreed before leaving the captain to his drink and another restless night.

The Founder was at rest.

If only the same could be said for the rest of Hebanthe Falls.

❧*❧

At first glance, Neoma thought the cloaked figure leaning against the doorframe of her flat was Ulynda, somehow locked outside or perhaps waiting, uncharacteristically, for her mother's return. Heart pounding with anxiety such a foolish risk created, with brako and buggers and more likely seeking them, and furious that her daughter had disobeyed and left the flat and could not now get back in, Neoma snatched the cloaked figure's arm to yank her towards her. Instead of Ulynda, however, as the figure pulled away, she stared into the bearded face of the dwarf she had never expected to meet.

He was undoubtedly a Kemway. She could see it in his eyes.

"You treat everyone like this?" Enoch grumbled, stepping beyond her reach.

Rather than answer the question, she barked, "You don't belong here. I don't want you anywhere near my…"

"Here to see you, not her, here to call a truce." He did not consider them to be at war but from her bitter expression, his assumption that she considered him to be an enemy seemed accurate.

"So you can steal my…"

"Yours? Don't you mean Ulynda's birthright? If anyone…"

"…daughter's…" Neoma finished, altering her tirade to suggest that his words were about to be hers, despite both knowing the truth.

They could hear footsteps, boots below them, but they could not see whoever was passing. Enoch was not worried about an attack, not with Scarecrow lurking nearby, but the possibility of this conversation being overheard by others was something he hoped to avoid. "We should take this inside…"

"You're not going near her!"

Enoch rolled his eyes. "Whatever Senior's plans are, believe me, I want no part of them. He's been at me for a month or more. Keep telling him no, but he doesn't listen. Don't know what he thinks this play will get him, but I'm no Founder. That's not me. I don't want it."

"I know him," huffed Neoma. "He's not going to give you a choice. He's got an agenda…"

"Then let him keep it. I'm not that easily manipulated. Besides, I'm sure you've got one of your own. Everyone does." Neoma hissed like a cornered cat as he continued. "You've got a beef with him, keep it between you. Don't punish me for what he's doing. Call your people off and I'll…"

"Keep away from Ulynda and I'll consider it." The haughty tilt of her head, the straight-backed elitist posture seen on hundreds of prods, gave Neoma an appearance of confidence that did not reach her eyes.

Rather than agree, Enoch crossed his arms and countered, "Whoever you've got on your side, keep 'em away from me, and I'll consider it. I don't want trouble with anyone. I don't want to be Founder. And if you hear anything about Vanderwall…"

"Why would I know anything about him…or care?" she shot back, the response erupting more quickly, with more venom than intended.

Enoch shrugged. "Presume you've got ears around the city…that you know more than…"

"Why does the brako concern you?" she asked indifferently.

"Because I want to keep him off me too. Tired of looking over my shoulder. Only a few hours in and everyone wants a piece…"

"Well, I don't. Know him that is," she corrected before her lips pulled into a frown at the way her words sounded. "Can't help you."

"Do what I ask and we're square."

He did not need to see Ulynda except to ensure she was safe and that whatever had forced her out of her home into the streets did not happen again. Enoch did not anticipate crossing paths with the girl after today.

With the twists his life was tangling, he could envision several scenarios, however, where they might.

Neoma huffed, pushed passed him into the flat, and slammed the door behind her. If Aldrich Kemway knew where she lived, she was no longer safe. Not if the brako and bugorra also knew.

It was time to rectify that situation.

Back to the door, she looked at her ICD.

An offer was made.

Accepting it would be the best opportunity she had to remain safe. "Ulynda!"

An offended shout from the neighbors at the shuttering clatter of the slamming door, and another of Neoma's shrill screeches faded into the Falls' roar, and Enoch looked up at the various rooftops, stairwells, paths, and shaft grates he could see. Wherever Scarecrow was, he hoped that one mole of detail might give the vigi something to work with in his hunt for Vanderwall.

Enoch was not sure he had gained anything at all.

❧Chapter 25❧

"**A**re the kids…?" started Skelter, his welcoming surprise at Otta's arrival at Vapors tempered by his concern for the Core children in this unsettling time. They were no strangers to the loss of electricity or darkness and were accustomed to shortages of food and commodities. To them, this was a common state of affairs. And they were, he knew, under the Spinks' watchful eyes. But Skelter could not imagine that this growing crisis was any easier for them, or the Spinks, than it was for anyone else.

"Ginna's with them." To Otta, that meant they were safe. Her concern was elsewhere. "Have you seen Father?"

Her question was directed at the woman behind the counter who shook her head. "Not scheduled to be here…said he had something to do. Won't be any regulars, so I told him to go ahead," Maemi said.

Skelter, likewise, shook his head.

"Won't stop the brako if they come ransacking," Otta muttered. While relieved that Colyx was building a life for himself, it was the first time he had gone somewhere without telling her.

She was unaware he had helped keep watch over the Founder's body or had been to the Uppers to see Outside for himself.

"Not much for them to take. Besides," Maemi laid the popper she kept under the bar on top of the counter. "They wouldn't dare."

Skelter snorted. The brako would dare, but at least the buggers were not likely to harass them. Wrapping his arm around Otta's shoulders, he bobbed his head towards what she carried and asked, "What's in the bag?"

"The few nessies I could wrangle," Otta sighed. There were too many mouths to feed and not enough on hand to do it right; the Spinks did their best to help with those supplies, but they needed to eat too.

Looking behind him at a room devoid of patrons, the floor polishing supplies Nigel had previously used abandoned at the edge of the stage, Skelter offered, "If you wait a bit, I'll walk you back."

Maemi waved dismissively. "Go on. Nigel'll be back, and Zara's upstairs. Jonner should be coming around soon…"

"Getting' on good then?" teased Skelter.

"We go way back…back to before you came skulking around my bar," she chuckled. They disagreed about what the future in Hebenon, or outside of it, meant, but neither wanted that to come between them. "Go home. I'm good here." She put the popper back under the counter.

"You got my number if you…"

"Get."

She swiped her cleaning towel as if to snap him, making him laugh as he took the bag of nessies from Otta. Their mutual laughter covered their uneasiness as Otta parted the beaded curtain so they could pass through it. Skelter's unrest was eased only by the sight of Nigel and Ebenee descending a nearby stairwell on their way back to Vapors. Nigel's yellow scarf, printed with beaded feathers and butterflies in shades of turquoise and green, stood out in the gloom like a siren's lure despite years of fading. He waved and Ebenee did likewise, a greeting Skelter returned before Otta's gentle tug on his arm guided him toward their hostel home.

"Don't know what he's been up to these last several nights," Otta murmured, pulling free of Skelter's arm to hike up the edges of her long coat as she ascended the stairs.

"Nigel?" Skelter tucked his walking stick under his arm.

"Father. It's not like him to go off without…"

"Wasn't anywhere to go in the Core…and we had to watch our backs. Maybe he's taken a second job…found someone…or's off exploring the city. Looking for people he used to know. Maybe he's been going Outside."

She stretched a hand back when she reached the top of the stairs to help him, her frown unchanging. "You think he'd say something."

There was a sound behind him, mirrored by a snarl on Otta's lips, that made Skelter pause and turn sideways to look. The movement was enough for her to swing past him and strike the individual who appeared abruptly at Skelter's back.

With her foot in his chest, the man fell flat to the bottom of the stairs with a squawk. The short blade in his hand clanged as it bounced across the grating and slid over the edge of the path.

"Aw, come on, Molly," Skelter scolded, preventing Otta from leaping on top of the prone man by offering a hand up. The shorter man was trembling, his glassy eyes wide, neither evidence of fear but rather of ongoing Heb use that did not surprise Skelter. "This really necessary? What've I ever done to…?

"Made a pact," Molly spat indignantly, slapping away the offered hand and sliding away from Otta. "You made a pact…"

"That was in there. This's here. New life. Doesn't matter now."

Molly climbed unsteadily to his feet, wiping off the seat of his pants as he did so. "Does matter. You pulled the ace. Oath's an oath."

Straining against Skelter's hold on her arm without enough force to break free and cause him to fall, Otta growled, "If you're eager to die, I'll give you an ace…"

"Isn't about me." Though the threat was enough to unsettle him, Molly continued, "Doesn't matter what I want. Doesn't work like that. He knows the rules."

"New life," Skelter repeated. "New place, new rules. Go home. Give this up and enjoy what you've got. Make something of yourself. Let that go, for crucksake. You're better than this."

Pulling Otta's arm, Skelter started up the stairs, insisting she follow rather than provoke Molly again. She snarled at the little man, pleased as he failed to keep his fear and frustration off his face.

He had no weapon now, the knife he had stolen lost. He would have to find another, something better, before he struck again. With Otta at Skelter's side, it was not going to be easy to get at Skelter again unless he struck when the redhead was alone. He might be able to take the lame Skelter in a fight but he knew he could not best Otta; he had seen her fight enough to know that. Now that he had failed a second time, with the woman as his witness, it would be more difficult to get a third chance.

Difficult, but not impossible.

"Hope they get you!" he snapped, pointing at a crow-beaked figure some distance away on another path. "You're a coward! They'll do it for me! They'll keep that oath for you. You'll see!"

Skelter rolled his eyes without looking back, pretending not to notice the far-away brako. Molly might be right. It was also possible that his Heb use was going to do Molly first. For Otta's sake, for their baby's, he hoped the latter would be true though he would prefer that Molly go on about his life and leave him alone.

❧*❧

From the hefty branch where they perched, Agnys and Cori had a broad overview of the parah village and the herd of small cattle grazing at the river's edge, where land was being prepared and filled by Hebenon's refugees. The river's sprawl tumbled swift and strong from their right to divide into five fingers and crash over the cliff edge, devoured by the metal nest, to be collected and eventually spat out again in its narrow race towards the sea. The river's chatter was fainter here where the pair hid among the leaves. Cori focused on his sketch of the tree in the book he frequently carried while Agnys watched an eagle soar overhead, circling the river in search of an unwary fish.

Unable to reenter the city with the doors closed, with only people trickling out but none permitted to go in, Cori was given refuge in Agnys' home as his father came and went, overseeing the growing refugee camp and monitoring the relationship between the parah and the nesters, intervening when problems arose. She treated him like a brother and spent much of her time trying to ease his fears about her world and the imagined happenings inside a city that barely glowed with life. Likewise, he sought to remind her that her friend Ballard, who had yet to come outside, would be okay.

According to his father, nearly everyone inside would come out.

Agnys continued to be amazed at the number that emerged.

Cori wondered where they would put everyone."

"They have to," he said, his drawing hand halting mid-stroke. "Until the power's fixed, they can't live inside."

"They're afraid of us. Some of us," Agnys glanced towards a cluster of field workers who watched the latest dozen refugees being escorted to the settlement. "Some of us are afraid of them."

Cori bobbed his head. He understood elitism and classism. He had lived with examples of both in the Uppers. Racism had not existed in Hebenon in generations, but out here, where the parah had always been viewed by the city dwellers as inferior, wild, and monstrous, he could see that such fears would take a long time to go away. Those from Hebenon were many. The parah, though he had been told that there were other settlements further up the river valley beyond Marbordo, beyond what they could see, were relatively few.

"Father will make it work." He did not know how, but he had faith in his father. His father had kept him alive when so many others had died. His father had saved many people from the plagues. He worked with the Nau to make the city better, with Captain Grainger to make the city safe. His father was even said to work with Scarecrow.

If anyone could protect the future, Cori believed his father could.

Agnys' face scrunched, her lips pursed, and Cori thought she was going to argue with his assurance. Instead, her gaze followed the eagle's path north, its prize meal secure in its hooked talons.

He pointed at a distant spot along the river's bank where it wound along a route carved into a stony hillock and changed the subject. "Is that someone there?" No crops grew on the too-steep bank, no herds or flocks grazed, and there were no trees to cut away.

"Hunter maybe?" The scrub on either side of the river made prime cover for rabbits and river birds. "Maybe looking for a lost calf or lamb…or someone from upriver." Whoever it was, they were too far away to see to determine what they were doing or who it might be.

"We could go see…go help?" Cori offered.

Agnys shook her head as the stranger squatted at the water's edge. "We're not allowed to go that far alone." The river, where it split into its two primary branches, was too tumultuous. There were wild beasts from the mountain and the mossy stones were hazardous.

"Won't be alone," he countered with a grin.

"We shouldn't."

Shrugging, setting aside the effort of finding a distraction since she was uninterested, he resumed his sketches. Agnys continued to watch the speck of a person, her curiosity distracting her from troubles she was too young to do anything about. If that figure needed aid, they were close enough to be heard if they shouted.

When they stood up again and continued walking, Agnys did not think her help would be required.

The pair of brako limped away, allowed the opportunity to rethink their deeds as Scarecrow herded the three Spinks, siblings he judged by their identical mops of black hair, towards a now-unmanned vindi cart. The owner had taken cover in the building behind him when the fight began and watched from that shelter as the vigi ran a tick card through the currently working reader and offered cups of mixed fruit to each of the children.

It was a rare gesture for him to make. Thankfully, Zara had generated that passcard so that such purchases could never be traced back to her, to Rhyd, or to Scarecrow.

The vindi owner nervously bobbed his head.

Scarecrow led the children away.

"You shouldn't involve yourselves with them like that." The brako were his fight. The Spinks doing anything more than spying and delivering messages continued to settle sour in his stomach. "You're gonna get hurt."

"Our fight too," mumbled the oldest around his mouthful of eagerly welcomed food. Guessing him to be around thirteen or fourteen, the boy had taken the brunt of the altercation before Scarecrow arrived. His face was bloody, his coat sleeve ripped away, and there were gashes on his exposed arm but he was still on his feet. As hungry as he was, he chose the food over cleaning his face.

"Better ways to help…"

The middle child of indeterminate age, shorter though his face bore nearly the same degree of physical maturity as his brother, asked, "How's that?" His cheek and knuckles were bruised and there was blood around his mouth from where he had bitten one of the brako and he sat on the rail as though his hip troubled him.

"There's a man, an archivist…about so tall." Scarecrow gestured. "Curly dark hair. Speecher." He tapped the side of his head. "Think the brako took him…"

"If they took him, he's probably in the river," the oldest said.

The youngest, a girl of around ten, kicked her brother in the shin. "Doesn't have to be," she scolded.

Scarecrow ruffled her hair, appreciating her reassuring words. "Think they're using him to get to me…they won't dump him so long as they can use him…"

It hurt to admit that, hurt to think what Jaron might be suffering in the interim, but it was better to believe that than to believe his life had already ended.

"Gotta be holding him somewhere. Somewhere they frequent. Somewhere not obvious."

Beaming at the affection she'd been given, the girl asked, "Want us to find him?"

"Want you to keep your eyes open…spread the word." He had already tasked some Spinks with the mission, did not doubt that word had spread. But there were a lot of Spinks, and since none had come to him with usable intel, it was worth tasking these three with the same mission. "Don't engage them," he scolded, "find where he is and let me know."

The oldest handed the remains of his fruit cup to his brother, who had already emptied his, making sure the boy got enough to eat rather than keeping it for himself, and nodded. "We can do that." It was a fitting repayment for Scarecrow breaking up the fight.

He might have entered that fight willingly to protect his brother, but he had no interest in dying at the hands of the brako.

"Good…now get on with you." He left them there, climbing onto the rail and swinging onto the nearest rooftop to disappear into the darkness. But he did not go far. He watched the three finish eating, murmuring amongst themselves as they argued over where to start their search, and after they dropped the empty cups into a recycle bin, they started down the nearby stairs.

There was no need to follow. The brako were gone. They would hunt for Jaron on their own. Just as he would.

Backside bruised, musing on Skelter's 'you're better than this' remark that Molly knew was not true, he opened the door of the small flat he had been given, still empty of most furnishings except for the table, chairs, and Echo equipment provided by Mam Kemway and Vanderwall for prod making. The smell of something cooking and the meager trickle of water running in the kitchen drew him to where a tea kettle warmed on a battery burner. Beside the kettle sizzled a flat pan of scrambled eggs and sausage crumbles, while on the counter, a plate of buttered bread waited to be served. He stared, confused, as the sound of hard-soled heels clacked in furious steps in the bedroom.

Unconvinced the intruder was not a threat, he patted himself down for a weapon he did not have and then scooped up the butter knife before creeping toward the closed washroom door.

It opened, nearly striking him in the face, and he jumped back with a squawk to stare at the matronly woman who emerged.

"Apologies, Mr. Netzer," Nanny murmured, her face red and damp, hesitating long enough to identify him with a contrite expression before bustling past to return to the kitchen. Over her shoulder, she asked, "Would you care for eggs and tea? It'll be bitter as there's no sugar, but it'll be warm.

Water bubbling from the kettle splattered and sizzled on the hot surface while she took four glasses from the oversized hempcanvas moving bag on the floor at her feet.

He had not noticed the bag before.

Nanny's presence meant one thing.

"What are you doing here?" he snapped at the other woman who emerged from the bedroom, dressed in the plainest, most non-descript outfit he had ever seen her wear, her hands tight on her daughter's shoulders to steer the petulant, reluctant girl to the table.

"You've seen the prods," Neoma said curtly as if that was answer enough. She pushed Ulynda into one of the two empty chairs and then pushed the table's contents, the Echos, SCAMs, and other production equipment, to one side so that there was a place in front of the girl for her breakfast plate.

"The Founder's Remembrance posa?" he began. Neoma's harsh glare cut him off and his shoulders hitched. "You mean about Enoch."

Neoma did not miss the note of familiarity in Molly's tone. She abandoned what she was doing to stalk back across the short room and snarl in his face. The heels of her shoes added extra height so that she towered over him as though he were a child. "You know him?"

"In the Core…"

"How…?" Was that where the miserable infant had been banished to? Was that why no one had been able to find him during the early months of searching? Was Aldrich the reason Haythem had wanted to close the mines…and why Grainger had worked to reopen them?

Had everyone known the truth except her?

When Molly started to speak, she gave a flippant wave and huffed, "Never mind." The answers she wanted were best not discussed in Ulynda's company as the child was already too attentively quiet, undoubtedly hoping for information about her newly uncovered uncle. Here in this flat, there was nowhere Neoma could send her to remove her from a private conversation. It was bad enough Neoma was forced to share the bedroom with both her daughter and Nanny.

"There are people…I need a place to…you will acquire a bed and…"

"Don't have ticks for that."

Certain he had ways to get what she asked for, not concerned about whether the others had beds as well, Neoma continued, "You'll profit if you provide…"

"When? Hub's down. Can't even get nessies. You think I can just conjure a bed?"

"I don't care how you do it. Do it and it's yours when I'm out of here. Just a few days, and then you'll have a bed of your own."

Molly scowled and side-eyed the girl's bowed head. There was no way to know when the Hub, or city power, would be restored. 'A few days' was a generous assumption and one he did not believe reflected reality. It had already been too many days as it was. If Mam thought her flat was no longer safe, if she thought someone was looking for her, thought coming to him was a better choice than seeking safety with Vanderwall, there was no way to guess how long he might be saddled with unwanted guests.

But this guest brought hot food, or the promise of it, something he sorely missed, and she was willing to pay for a bed he could keep afterward. Maybe he could move one from her flat and have it when she was gone. He doubted she would recognize it.

This arrangement might not be a bad thing.

Wasn't like he had been sleeping here anyhow. He did not need to stay or keep them company. They would all be happier if he did not.

He snatched the offered plate and cup of algtea from Nanny when she offered and devoured the contents, barely noticing the bitter traces that Nanny had warned about or Neoma's perturbed expression. He was finished before the Mam sat across the table with her plate.

He stomped to the door.

The child watched him with wary, judgmental eyes. Neoma did not lift her head.

"Deserve a medal for this," he groused as he yanked the door open.

"When this is over, I'll see you get one," Neoma promised offhandedly without looking at him, replying to words she was not meant to hear. "Maybe even two."

Medals he could sell for a score. The extra ticks would provide the Hebbies he wanted and replace the lost knife. Temporarily pushing the matter of Skelter aside, Molly left to find the bed she wanted. So long as Mam held up her end of the bargain and paid him, he would find the best fotzin' bed the Levs had to offer…even if it was her own.

❧*❧

Ilya rose stiffly from her desk to stretch her back, favoring her injured knee, keeping her gaze on the grainy enlarged image on the screen. She should go home, check on Ginna, and sleep. But the flood of calls trickling in after the day's replaying of the Founder's last words had brought the identities and names of nearly two dozen potential assassins. There were the expected accusations made against the Talkers who had been present, men she had witnessed charging the stage without noting any opportunity for any of them to shoot. There was the usual roster of finger-pointers who named neighbors, coworkers, relatives, or soon-to-be ex-friends, condemned by the assertions of slander and drunken, boasting threats of action possibly fulfilled. As with the kidnapping many weeks ago, each claim had to be investigated, and the bugorra, already overworked in their efforts to patrol the too-dark Lev streets, were stretched ever thinner as officers were diverted to test the veracity of every tip.

There were two suspects, however, that stood out to Ilya as she read the details she had found on each. A name that turned up only once in the Archive data that remained in the undamaged Hub, a name from the day the man had been disfellowshipped from the ranks of the Voices he had spent a lifetime serving. There was no mention of who he had been before that, no record of his birth or achievements made during his service, no details from his childhood or about what had become of him after he had left the Voices. There was only a single anonymous line of code in her comm box from someone suggesting that, if the bugorra wanted to know the truth about the Voices of Faith, they had only to follow that name.

If Reamon Folwell knew anything about Senior Kal, about the Voices, about Founder Kemway's death, Ilya needed to know more.

That meant a discussion with Kal, an interview she did not know if the captain, given his busy agenda, would permit now that they had released the Senior once. The message she had sent had been met with a 'user offline' response that suggested the captain was pursuing the much-needed sleep Ilya was unable to find.

The second person of interest existed only on the captured ICD image that someone forwarded to the investigation team, a small, spidery-looking fellow in the crowd with his arm raised, something in his hand that could have been a popper, an injector, or a recording device. Something aimed at the platform. The image was not clear enough to tell what he held, nor to make out his facial features from the side-angled shot.

But someone in the crowd must have seen his face. Ilya cropped the image to remove evidence of what he was holding to avoid false responses and sent it to Soleia with the request to cast it throughout the city, describing him only as a person of interest, a person with potential information. Not a suspect. She also supplied the image to her officers, especially those active on the protest Lev and the few above and below it.

With luck, the individual lived near the epicenter of the protest. With luck, he could answer questions about what he had seen on the day of Haythem Kemway's death.

❧*❧

"That's him! That's Kemway!"

Enoch heard the shout and skittered around the nearest unattended vindi carts to duck into the first open door he found. His short stature gave him an advantage in getting out of sight, allowing him to hide in places where most would not easily fit. The storage closet he selected was already occupied by two Heb-addled streeters and three older children, possibly the streeters' offspring, possibly Spinks. The children, recognizing his face from the previous day's prods, nodded, muttered, "Got this," and then dispersed into the street. With the constant pinging drip of falling water on the vindi's metal roof, Enoch could not hear what they said and could not see what they did, but the people who had shouted at him, eager for words or to offer adulation and support he did not want, did not come in.

One of the streeters, her stringy hair hanging around her face and over her eyes, looked in at him with a string of muttered phrases he did not understand. He nodded, he waited, he listened, and when he thought it was safe, he pressed an apple he had procured into her hand before creeping out of the closet. He made it to the vindi door, paused to listen, and then dashed to the nearest alley to make it to any stairs that would take him away before someone else recognized him.

❧*❧

Banished to the bedroom out of her mother's presence, where she preferred to be while the woman grumbled and cursed about the place she had brought her daughter to hide and Nanny did her best to make their refuge tolerable and livable, Ulynda sat on the floor in the corner, back against the wall, with her T1 Echo propped on her knees, pretending to pursue her school work as her mother demanded.

The most recent assignments had been completed before she had been dragged through the wet city to a small flat more cold, damp, and miserable than her own. She had not told Ulynda why. It was not the Ups, but at least the bedroom walls had been recently whitewashed to counteract the mold. An alglamp across from the window allowed a little blue-green light into the room. The plumbing worked, which was another plus, but nothing about this flat made her mother happy.

Ulynda sniffed and wiped her nose and eyes on the back of her sweater sleeve. Trapped here, unable to get past her mother, there was no way to message Scarecrow or reach Enoch. She had no ICD contact information to reach Cori Tamner and doubted that Agnys had an ICD of her own. Likely, the pair were Outside, enjoying the warm sunshine that Ulynda had never experienced.

But she did have another idea. Using the Echo, the process delayed by poor connectivity and too-frequent swapping between the search function and the study page of volcanoes that was part of the day's science lesson, it took nearly an hour of searching the Hub to access the government directory with its myriads of sub-categories of personnel, to find the name she wanted.

If the reports were true, if the dwarf was the same Enoch they spoke of, if he was her father's brother, then surely Cori's father and the Nau would know how to find him, how to get a message to him. And Enoch knew Scarecrow. One of those men had to be able to get her out of this dismal place. One of the three had to be able to prevent whatever her mother intended to do to Enoch.

Ulynda had not heard her plan. She had not heard that there was one. But she knew her mother. If Neoma perceived the dwarf to be a threat, if she thought the man who had saved her child's life from the brako would hurt them, she would do something about it.

Typing fast, Ulynda's message was brief. *Ask Enoch and Scarecrow to help me. Please. I am scared. U.K.*

There was a knock on the door. Ulynda hit send with one finger and raised her face with a trance-like stare to meet Nanny's warming smile. "I found a tin of biscuits in my bag. Would you like one?"

Her mother must have approved of the giving, or else had left the flat without Ulynda hearing her leave. She nodded with a grateful, "Yes, please," and clutched the Echo to her chest.

Nanny nodded too. "Be right back.

Ulynda looked at the screen. The progress bar was complete. The message was sent. She hoped Doctor Tamner got it and came to help her, even if she had no idea where she was or what he, Enoch, or Scarecrow could do.

❧*❧

The life of streeter children consisted of the daily effort to survive, scavenging, tinging, looking for handouts, moving from one herpa ministry hall to another in search of warmer clothing, food, and with luck, a bed or dry corner to sleep in each night. Some had fallen to the vice of Heb addiction, where the use, or the withdrawal, was equally likely to result in death, or into the use of alcohol or some other substance that would be just as likely to end their lives too soon. Some stole or plagiarized scrips for sale to those desperate enough to want them. Others accept scrap pay, food, or shelter in exchange for acting as couriers or messengers or as lookouts and snitches for the buggers, the brako, or both. Those with some education taught their fellow streeters in the hopes of gaining an advantage, where a few might succeed in apprenticing to a trade or a vindi owner in the hopes that the effort would lead to a home, a family, and stability.

Scarecrow's rise had given birth to another, growing subset. The Spinks dedicated themselves as the eyes and ears of the vigi who could not be everywhere and took their duties seriously. Because they wore no identifying emblem, it was difficult for anyone to tell the Spinks from other street children, but by now everyone knew they were there.

This new mission, given by Scarecrow, was one they took seriously so they moved through the too-dark streets following brako between Levs from one location to another whenever one was spotted. Tasked with finding the archivist Scarecrow thought important enough to save, they worked for Scarecrow's gratitude, for honor amongst their peers, and perhaps a few ticks or other favors in return.

The six children were on their way up from the fisheries where they had stolen a bucket of rejected fish destined for some other use than feeding people when they spotted four brako opening a warehouse door. Though the action was not particularly suspect, like anything brako-related, it was worth watching, and so the Spinks ducked into the shadows, hiding beneath the hemplastic ramp of another warehouse. They remained there, avoiding detection, avoiding the repercussions of their theft for as long as they dared.

Brako moved in and out of warehouses all the time. There were so many on this Lev, where growers and fisheries, food packagers, slaughterhouses, waste processing facilities, and other physical labor jobs abounded to keep the city alive. Or they had done so when the city had the power to allow them to operate. The brako and other shady types found it expedient to use abandoned warehouses to stash both legal and illicit goods. When the activity in one area began to draw attention, the illegal goods would be moved somewhere else before the bugorra came looking.

It was not boxes or crates, sacks or pallets, that were removed from this warehouse today. It was a single man, limp, possibly dead, carried between two brako while a one-armed fellow led the way. The fourth, with a bucket of brushes and industrial cleaning supplies, remained behind.

The Spinks looked at one another, communicating with hand gestures that sprouted a plan. The pail of fish was upended, its contents dumped to fall between the grates and back into the churning river. A delay in delivering the fish might have meant sickness if they died and began to rot, so it was better to let the creatures go. The oldest Spink, tall enough to fight if the brako spotted him, though malnourished and skinny enough that they might think him not worth their time, remained under the ramp to continue to watch the warehouse.

The other three split up to follow where the departing brako led, communicating with gestures, chirps, whistles, and claps as they moved. They expected to end at some easy-to-access point of Lev 1 where a dead man could be dropped into the river without notice.

Maybe, if he was not dead, they could save him before the current swept him away. Maybe they could get a look at his face to determine if he was worth the effort to do so or worth telling Scarecrow about.

What they did not expect was the speecher on the side of the limp man's head, partially covered by sweat-matted black curls.

One Spink whistled.

Another responded with a different note, a confirmation of probability. The third sought instruction.

The brako grunted and muttered between themselves, their dialogue muting the Spinks' exchange so that they paid no attention to it. Eventually, the one leading paused long enough to scan their vicinity for threats, his head cocked as if noting the bird calls. The brako might not know the signals, but they knew the Spinks used them to communicate. The children were well hidden, and when the men stopped moving, the only whistle-talk they could hear was far away.

The one-armed man grunted and motioned for the pair with the burden to continue.

One Spink gave the signal to wait, to see where the brako were going, to be silent to be suspected further. They continued to follow without a sound. The one-armed brako gave no further hint that he thought they were not alone.

The brako reached another warehouse door, rusty and dented, that groaned in protest when it was opened far enough to shove their wilted captive inside. He landed with a heavy sound of painful collapse. The brako made a show of locking the door when a herpa shuffled past, his footsteps slow at first but then short and hasty when one of the thugs glowered and growled at him.

"Make sure he's not gonna be a problem," the one-armed fellow said, his tone temperate despite the threat in his words. He pointed to the other and added, "You stay here for thirty and make sure no one comes, that we weren't followed."

One of the three peeled off to follow the herpa, uncoiling a short, braided whip from his belt while the other plopped down on the warehouse steps and began to pick at his nails with a knife, looking as though he had stopped to rest rather than as if he was guarding the door or the warehouse contents. The one-armed man started away.

Several minutes of silence. One whistle. One chirp. One clicking pattern that ended with the slap of a stick against the walkway rail. One Spink remained where she could continue to watch this new location. Another tailed the one-armed man hoping he would report to Vanderwall or someone higher up the chain of command than he was.

The last Spink scampered up and up from one half-Lev to another, chirping and whistling, calling as he climbed, sending the word out.

They needed Scarecrow.

Scarecrow needed to know that Jaron Rei might have been found.

❧Chapter 26❧

It was not the sort of message he expected in the middle of the night. From the digital time stamp, he should have received it earlier, before giving in to the sleep that had mostly eluded him since the solar array's sabotage. He hastily reread the message three times, rubbing his eyes between each read, struggling to force his brain into coherent thought instead of letting it succumb to panic.

What was Neoma up to that had her daughter so afraid?

He tried to send a message, instructing the girl to sit tight, assuring her he would do what he could. But the squawking error message indicated the Hub was down again, the message caught in a loop of attempts that was impossible to bypass. Growling, he got out of bed, dressed, and opted to visit the captain, hoping Grainger was there. Unsurprisingly, given the hour, he was not, and so Tamner left his message with the sentry stationed at the man's office door.

Whatever you're going to do about her, do it now.

He assumed the sentry would not know who 'her' was.

He assumed Grainger would.

The sentry, barely old enough to join the force and thus pressed into this marginal duty, promised to deliver the message as soon as the captain arrived. He would be stationed here all night until Grainger came and dismissed him.

Unable to send a message below, unable to reach Grainger without waking him, Tamner chose the only remaining option. He began the long descent into the black bowels of the city to find one or both of the men Ulynda asked for. Between the three of them, perhaps they could rout whatever plan Neoma intended to set into motion, or stop it if it had already been initiated, and protect Hebenon and the Founder's daughter at the same time.

❧*☙

There was no way for Tox to hide her actions, what she wore, when the grate at the back of her workshop popped open to allow Scarecrow to slither into the room and drop to the floor. She did not move as he straightened, as he looked her up and down, studying the form of the very similar body armor she was altering. He worked off his mask and raked a hand through his damp, blonde hair, a gesture that momentarily hid his scowl, before sighing, dropping his arm, and asking the inevitable question.

"How long?"

Tox sighed too, not in resignation or embarrassment but with the weariness her last several hours of work had produced. With her vindi unable to operate, she had allotted more time to a project she had been working on since the rescue of Skelter from the Core, since Scarecrow had rescued her and brought her home.

"Just after…you know…" After the Coup, she worked hard on her fitness and self-defense skills. Once more confident in those things, the production of body armor had begun.

Rhyd nodded. After her arrest by the Founder's forces. After her torture. He had known she was working out, gaining strength and agility. She often asked his advice, his guidance, about how to fight off something like that from happening again. He had trained and instructed her in skills he had honed during his years as Scarecrow. He knew she wanted to fight back to be ready, and he wanted that for her.

He had not expected what he saw now.

"And you're planning to…what?" She had not been on the street yet; he would have known if another vigi was out fighting for the people, cleaning the streets of the brako virus that plagued it.

"Was going to tell you when it's ready." Tox began to strip down to the bodysuit she wore beneath it. "It's not yet…but almost."

"You shouldn't…"

"You should be out doing this alone? Good as you are…" She glanced at him, knowing intimately what his physique was like under the body armor she had fitted and built and feeling no discomfort at undressing in front of him. "You're only one man."

He did not replace the grate but removed the damaged glove from his left hand and tossed it onto her workbench as he moved further into the room. "Should be working towards your pension, not this."

"Cazz the pension. No one's getting one…whole system's cazzed unless Lash gets the array up…and maybe not even then. Nothing's going back to the way it was now that Outside is open…especially not while Vanderwall and the brako…"

"Leave him to me." Untested on the street, though he did not doubt she could defend herself against one or two opponents, he did not believe she could stand up to Vanderwall. There were moments since Jaron's disappearance when Rhyd doubted his chances against the man who had nearly bested him before.

"You can't take on all of them…"

"Maybe not, but…"

A shrill whistle cut the silence in the street outside, a familiar summons that made Rhyd hurry to don the mask and hood again. Having tasked the Spinks with a pair of critical missions, anything they had to share was worth prompt attention.

"Here." Tox opened a wall chest to her left, pulled out a drawer, and selected a replacement for the damaged glove on the table without asking how the damage had occurred. He had other replacements stashed around the Levs, but if he had come to her, it was because he had been working nearby.

"Stay here," he ordered, his natural voice replaced by the ominous digitized intonations of Scarecrow. "We'll finish this when I'm back."

He jumped into the shaft before she replied. Her inner debate lasted until the sound of his movement gave way to silence.

As she had said, he could not fight the brako alone. Not anymore. She had a score to settle, and the body armor was nearly ready.

It was time for Tox to join Scarecrow's fight for the future of Hebanthe Falls.

❧*❦

Despite business being at a standstill as all products grew harder to acquire and the demand for basic nessies continued to rise, Vapors persisted as the place to gather, the familiar home Maemi's friends had always shared. There was nowhere else they felt secure, no one they trusted more than the dark-skinned swiver who sat with them, trying not to wring her hands with worry she did not want them to see.

Jonner had said something days ago about Outside. With the doors closed to all except exiting traffic without appropriate authorization that allowed the first wave of emigrants to leave the city, it was no surprise that he might not be able to gain permission to come back inside. With the increasing activity of the brako, Maemi worried that he had, instead, fallen victim to some less favorable fate.

Skelter's efforts to reassure her were thus far not helping.

"Don't think I have a choice," Enoch mumbled over the rim of his whiskey glass, the precious commodity more valuable at that moment than anything else…except his peace of mind. "I'm a target in here. They're not gonna leave me alone. Only reason the prods haven't plastered me everywhere, that Kal's not shouting my name every hour, is because they don't have a photo yet…and the Hub doesn't have enough power for it. Outside, parah aren't gonna care who I am."

"There's a lot of us out there already, people who would…" began Skelter, reminding him of the obvious.

"You should go too," Colyx grunted to Skelter and his daughter without looking up from the scrap of wood he was picking at with his switch knife. "Safer out there for you, too."

Skelter grunted back, "Got business to…"

Otta looked at Skelter pointedly. "What business? Everyone's hoarding. Nothing's moving. People come to you for things you can't get. With Molly out there…"

Stumbling footsteps at the door brought Colyx out of his chair with a warning growl. Though recognizing the skinny fellow made his shoulders relax, he did not sit as Switz staggered towards the table, exhausted and out of breath. There was enough ambient light in the room, created by the Echo screen over the bar that ran the newest prod about the ongoing hunt for an assassin, the alglamps on the corners of the bar, and the increasingly rare candle burning at the center of the table where the group gathered, to prevent him from running into anything. His movements were jerky and breathless as if he had been running for too long or was inebriated on Hebbies or alcohol.

Maybe both.

"Skelt…"

"Wondering when you'd turn up," Colyx muttered. Switz was the sort of man to seek the patronage of others when times got tough and ignore them at every other opportunity. With the conditions in Hebenon and his face now made public on every Echo in the city, few at the table were surprised that Switz came seeking Skelter's assistance. It was only a surprise that he had not come back sooner.

"Need a roof…a meal…somewhere to…" He gripped the back of an empty chair with both hands and leaned heavily against it. Pushed under the table as it was, it did not slide away from him.

Skelter, wondering if Switz had gotten what he needed from Enoch since he seemed to be ignoring the dwarf now, shook his head. "Make you think I've got…?"

"The kids…"

Otta huffed, "You're not a kid."

Indicating the Echo with a wildly shaking hand and wide eyes, he cried, "They think I killed him. There's a merc on my ass…"

"Did you?"

Enoch's question caught him off guard and he stared at the dwarf with wide, incredulous eyes. "Why the cazz would I do something like that? Never met the man, never seen him before the prods…

"Nor've most of us,' Otta snorted. But a lot of people would have taken the shot if given the chance."

Wiping his forehead with one hand, he whined, "Well, I didn't. Don't even own a…"

"Could've gotten one anywhere," Enoch challenged. "We don't need trouble from a merc…"

"How'd you even…?" started Otta.

"Look, all I want is somewhere to lay low til they find whoever…"

Skelter shook his head, annoyed that first Molly had come looking for him and then Switz. "Told you before, don't have…"

"You owe me," Switz snarled, looking from Skelter to Enoch. "Both of you…"

Disliking the anger and disrespect in the little man's voice, Colyx pushed him back with one hand. "No one owes you paso. Got you out alive. Your freedom for the kids. That's all you're getting. Should be enough. Plenty of empty…"

"Got nowhere for you," Otta agreed with her father.

"But he can…" The whine crept back into Switz's voice as he looked at Skelter but his plea was interrupted by the arrival of another man, tall, casually dignified, and dressed like a man of means. His was a face that many around the table were growing more familiar with although most in the Levs did not know him.

Waving the doctor to the table, favoring his company over Switz's, Skelter hissed, "Got nowhere here. Can't help you. Told you before…lay low. Keep your hands clean. If I hear of something…"

Switz grumbled, did his best to adjust the threadbare clothing he had piecemealed together as replacements for what Blayd had provided, hoping he would be unrecognizable to the merc, should they cross paths again, and anyone who had seen his picture on the prods, and said, "It's not fair…"

Grabbing Switz's arm, Colyx pulled him toward the door, passing the doctor with a nod. Switz pulled his collar up and his hat down as they reached the beaded curtain, hoping to avoid recognition by someone who looked important. Colyx huffed, "Nothin's fair." He pushed him out of the vindi and added, "Don't come back."

"Remember what I said." Switz threw another glance at the newcomer, relieved that the man did not appear to recognize him, and staggered away.

Colyx's grunt was his only acknowledgment.

Tamner half watched the exchange, only overhearing part of it as he crossed the room, drawn toward the collection of people by the man he had come here to see. He took the empty chair that Skelter pushed back for him, nodded at the only woman at the table he did not recognize, and then said with another nod to Enoch, "Just who I was hoping to find."

Enoch frowned. His hand tightened around his drink. "If you're here to drag me in front of the Nau…"

"Nothing like that…though you'll be called up sooner or later if they can find you," he admitted. Colyx returned to the table and sat, so Tamner decided to sit as well.

"Rather later than sooner."

"Don't blame you. Senior's got some nerve…"

"Thinks it'll make him relevant," said Maemi, pouring a drink in a glass she had brought in case Tox or Zara joined them and pushing it toward the newcomer.

"All he's done is paint a target," Skelter snorted.

"Imagine so." Tamner wrapped his hands around the glass to have something to do, being in no hurry to drink its contents though it might have dispelled some of the chill in his bones. "You're not the only one out there."

Enoch cocked his head, bidding Tamner to continue.

"Got a message from Ulynda. Neoma's up to something…"

"Course she is," grunted Skelter.

Reaching for the bottle to fill his glass, Enoch shook his head. "Tried to get her off my back, offered a truce, told her I'd stay clear of the girl if she'd…"

"Doesn't matter. Think she'll hold to it? Ulynda's scared. Something's happening and until the captain acts…"

Otta shifted her chair. "Think he'll do anything about anything?"

Tamner shrugged and swallowed his drink. The burn spread throughout his body and made him shudder. "Dunno what he can do. Maybe nothing, at least until there's power. But maybe our friend can do something."

"Kidnap a kid?" Skelter asked, knowing as the others did which friend the doctor referred to.

"Wouldn't be the worst thing." Enoch stared at the glass. "She was afraid before. Think Neoma hurts her…she's not safe where she is."

"You saying that because she's your niece and you want her safe or because you want her in place as Founder so you don't have to…?"

"We don't need a Founder," Enoch replied to Maemi's question. "Setting her up for it is putting Neoma in charge…and that's bad all around. She gets her foot in the door, she's not going to back out of it. Could turn on her kid to keep it. We thought Haythem was bad…" He shook his head. "Don't need that headache. Ulynda seems like a good kid. Doesn't deserve the pit of snakes she's been thrown into."

Tamner agreed. "If the captain…she's gonna need someone. Between us, there must be something we can do, even if it's letting her know she's got allies, isn't alone, until we figure something out."

"If I try to get close, Neoma's gonna have my head and give the rest to the fish. Want to keep it attached and get Outside soon as…"

The doctor stared. "You're going Out?"

"Think I'll be safer there. She and the Senior can't get their hooks in me, and the people who want to use me won't have a chance."

Steeping his hands under his chin, Tamner murmured, "Maybe we could get her out too." He doubted Neoma would ever go Out, not without being forced.

"Not with me…but yeah," Enoch agreed, "could try it."

Scarecrow had gotten one child Outside before. Maybe he could do it again. If he was willing.

"Might be able to get a message to her if you need me to," Skelter offered.

"Would have to act fast; if the captain jumps on this, we won't have much time."

Skelter stood up with a nod. "Come on then. Get me an address. I'll get things lined up."

"And get me a pass out of here, get us both one," added Enoch with a swallowed sigh. "Do that for us…and I'll talk to the Nau. Not offering anything, but I'll talk to them."

The unanticipated offer made Tamner hide his growing relief as he nodded. Maybe Enoch was more of a Kemway than he believed. Man enough, at least, to put aside his fears for the safety of a child.

"You should go Out with him," Colyx repeated with another pointed glance at Otta.

"Not without him and the kids." She met Skelter's gaze pointedly. She had doubts about their security inside against the brako who wanted their toughest competition out of the way, but there was one thing she could do to make Skelter safer if he insisted on remaining inside. She looked at the doctor and said, "You want to know who might have killed the Founder? Find Molly Netzer. Ask him where he was, who he was with, what he was doing during the protest."

Skelter blinked in surprise. "Molly?"

Guilty of assassination or not, Molly was undoubtedly guilty of something, given his persistent hunt for Skelter and his obvious return to a life of Heb addiction that made him as much of a danger to himself as anyone else. Picking him up for interrogation, keeping him in custody long enough to question him, might give him time to get clean again and afford Skelter temporary protection against the pointless Spades vendetta.

Otta's expression did not change. She knew Skelter understood she had no evidence against Molly. He understood why she was offering Molly up. "Ask him. Shouldn't be hard to find. "He's one of those who came out of the Core."

Perplexed but accepting the offered tip that would be piled up with the others the bugorra received, Tamner nodded. It was not his place to interrogate people about what they knew or did not know, or ask how they knew it. Her accusation might be nothing more than a Lev rumor or a personal vendetta. But he could pass the tip on to the captain and let Grainger run with it as he saw fit.

Tamner's concern, on top of the continued management of Hebanthe Falls and the relationship building with the people of Marbordo, was protecting a child who had asked for his help.

"I'll pass it on."

Skelter tapped his ICD and nodded at Otta. "Children are waiting. I'll be there soon as I can."

"If I can find our friend," Enoch added, making no effort yet to move away from the table, "I'll loop him in, have him check on her."

Maybe there was something Scarecrow could do to help, like scare some sense into Neoma. Or maybe he could not. But he needed to know if Neoma might be stirring a paso storm unlike anything Hebenon had yet seen, all centered on her daughter, her late husband, Senior Kal, and the dwarf she considered to be a threat.

❧*❦

"Mr. Folwell hasn't been with the Voices for years," Kal muttered to the lieutenant who stood on the other side of his desk, scowling at his cold breakfast with a mixture of antipathy and disdain, speaking as if the name Folwell implicated the Senior, the Voices, in whatever crime the buggers were trying to pin on Kal now. "Last I heard, he was off to be an economist." He dabbed the corners of his mouth with a cloth before finishing, "What's he done? Think he has something to do with the power? The Founder? What has he got to do with me?"

Ilya's frown did not change as she scrutinized him for some clue he was trying to hide. "You know I can't discuss active investigations. Just want to know where I can find him…and why he left the Voices."

Most people who joined the Voices remained involved for life. The managing hierarchy did its utmost to discourage anyone from leaving, from becoming an exposure risk for the secrets that existed within the organization. Belonging passed from parents to children, guaranteeing membership, even if that membership had begun to dwindle. Kal shrugged without shifting his gaze, and replied, "There's privacy concerns there, I'm afraid. We have to protect our members…"

"Yourselves."

"I can't reveal such details without his permission or a…."

"If it's a warrant you want, I'll return with one," she said coolly. "You know the captain will approve it. You might not like what we would uncover as we dig through your records."

Kal continued to chew on the cold gravy toast as he set the fork on the edge of his plate. Seeing through her threat, expecting that she, like her boss, thought him guilty of kidnapping, assassination, and more, and confident that he had nothing to hide, he swallowed his lukewarm algtea and shrugged again. "By all means, Lieutenant. Bring one. If Reamon is guilty of something, he should be brought in. But I will not, cannot, give you access to his files without a warrant."

She could go to the Archives. As bugorra, the second in command to Captain Grainger, she had that authority. She could demand access to every file to find enough information to make an arrest. Maybe she had already done so and was here as a courtesy, another ruse to maneuver him into admitting to crimes he had not committed.

Ilya adjusted her shoulders, her feet, and nodded. "If you know where he is, it would behoove you to tell me…because I will pick apart every Voices record if I have to."

Undaunted, Kal muttered. "Haven't seen him in years, I assure you. I do not know where he is…if he is even alive."

"For your sake," she grunted as she left him, "I hope that's true."

❧*❧

"What is it? What have you found?"

Ginna did not berate Scarecrow for the time it had taken to find her in the alley that ran from the walkway into a service shaft behind Vapors. Wherever he had been, it would have taken time for her message to reach him, to finish whatever he had been doing, to find his way to her. Regardless of the importance of her information, she believed that whatever he had been doing was equally important.

He dropped behind her from the catwalk above rather than appear from the depths of the shaft system, landing in a crouch that cushioned his knees against the impact and reduced the clatter the grate should have made when he landed. His clothes were damp from prolonged outdoor exposure, but she could tell nothing else about him.

She wondered, as she faced him with an arm protectively around the younger child who stood with her, how he managed to move so quietly through a largely metal world.

"Spinks found him. They believe they found Rei."

Recognizing the child as the youngest of three siblings he had recently recruited, he asked, "Where?" the digitizing speaker unable to mask the tremor and tension in his question. "Where is he?"

Ginna prodded the girl forward. "Warehouse on Lev One, near the gardens," the girl said, her voice timid though for different reasons.

There were many warehouses on Lev One, many used, many vacant but owned, many abandoned as the population of Hebenon dwindled. There was more than one garden there as well. Too many places to throw open one by one to expose their contents in the fury of seeking the quest he was about to undertake.

"Did you see him? Is he…?"

"I wasn't there…didn't see him…but I can get you there. He was in one place, and the brako moved him to a new one." Using the

Spinks' calls as a guide, she knew she could guide Scarecrow anywhere he wanted to go.

He swallowed. It was the confirmation of his worst fears. Scarecrow balled his fists. The shriek of the shift whistle punctuated the air, continuing to blat its periodic coded cry for those workers still able to conduct their jobs despite the deficiency of power. For the next hour, as workers moved to and from their jobs and homes and took comfort in whatever after-hours pleasures they could find, any action Scarecrow took would be more exposed. That would not stop him, but he would have to move more slowly and cautiously. But he could follow this child to the place the Spinks intended to show him, and his caution would be worth it if it meant finding Jaron.

If anything had happened to Jaron, if he had been harmed instead of merely detained as bait by the one Scarecrow expected was behind this, if he was dead, Vanderwall and those beneath him would suffer.

"Take me to him."

"Need us to…?" began Ginna, willing to mobilize the Spinks for any sort of diversion or assistance Scarecrow required.

"Too dangerous. But…" A distraction might be what he needed to get in and out of his warehouse destination without further risk to Jaron. He would not know until he found it. "Keep everyone back until…I'll let you know." He motioned the girl into the shaft. "Follow me. Then show me the way."

"Yessa," the girl said, unafraid to enter the world of the city shafts. It was Scarecrow's world, and Scarecrow was with her. No harm would come to her there.

Ginna whistled. Around them, on the streets and stairs, rooftops and alleys, other calls went up in response.

Scarecrow might need them.

They would be ready.

❧Chapter 27❧

Grainger did not need a signal to proceed. The walkway outside the address he had been provided was empty of traffic, devoid of nearby work crews or streeters who might interfere with the plan. This was the perfect sort of location, he mused, now that he saw it, for a kidnapper to hold a hostage or for a variety of other criminal activities to be pursued.

During his tenure as a Crow, he had walked these Lev streets. He had likely passed this building dozens of times. There had never been a need to make note of it.

He would have to see to an investigation of every warehouse in this quadrant, on this Lev, when the day was over.

With no illegal lock on the door, there was no reason for anyone to suspect anything unusual about the small two-roomed building. Grainger had studied the blueprints before coming here, a record in the city archives submitted by whoever had originally occupied it. Not every warehouse, vindi, or residence had been built before Hebenon was closed to Outside. Some had come after, sandwiched between existing structures, erected in place of something else that had deteriorated as time and the eternal damp ate away at the walls.

With so much Archive data lost after the Coup, he was lucky to find the blueprints.

Two rooms. Nothing unusual.

Three officers approached with him, two others stood watch on the walkway, and two more on either side of the steps as another used an A-Pass to unlock the door. The digital lock clicked, enough electricity supplied to the quadrant to allow locks to function without a manual override, so this raid could happen without interference. The officer pushed the door open far enough so that the captain could step past him and be the first to enter.

No one charged out, just as no one had answered the knock.

The interior was silent and dark.

No one was here.

Grainger took another step, turned on his body cam, and halted to take in the details of the room before anyone else had an opportunity to spoil the evidence.

A rare hempaper copy of a set of floor plans was spread across the desk, the paper distorting from the moisture in the air, its corners held down by a weighted disk embossed in gold with the Voices of Faith emblem, a T1 Echo left on and open for too long so that its battery was drained, an empty wine carafe, and empty crystal glass with evaporation rings around its clear, blue-tinted etched surface that matched the carafe and the stopper that was placed at the center of the print. Grainger had seen that glass pattern before, that color, and as he slowly approached the desk, he recognized that the placement of the stopper on the image was not as random as it first appeared.

It pointed to the place where Haythem had been while under Doctor Tamner's care.

He picked it up to savor the faint smell of alcohol on its beveled edge and frowned as he replaced it where it had been. Absently, he beckoned the officer at the door to enter as he stared at the map.

The officer shuffled cautiously inside. One of the two keeping watch moved into the doorway for assistance if he was needed.

There was an upright chest on one side of the room and a door that led into the second room, both held closed by padlocks that required keys to open. Not finding keys in the desk, Grainger nodded. One of the accompanying buggers broke both with a couple of well-aimed strikes of his thumper. Bugger uniforms tumbled out of the chest at the officer's feet, their haphazard stacking and the previous shaking of the city had shifted their weight against the door to promote their fall.

The other bugger pushed into the second room, his popper drawn in preparation for an ambush that did not come. "Captain, sir…you'll want to see this."

Grainger, rummaging through the desk to expose the typical array of items one would find…carbon styluses, passchips in a storage box, scraps of hemp paper with notes, clips, and takeaway condiments and cutlery, left his examination to follow the officer's summons.

Standing in the doorway, he scanned the room with a held breath.

Manacles hung from the ceiling on one side of the room. There were a variety of dents in the corrugated walls, as if something had been thrown against them or as if they had been kicked or punched…potentially old evidence from the room's previous usage, but it was equally possible that they were fresh. Even the manacles could be old evidence and could have been used for a variety of purposes. There was a down and hemp straw sleeping mat and a toilet pail, a hemplastic chair with a warped leg. Evidence of more takeaway, containers scattered around the mat with spilled food on the floor not yet entirely devoured by the mold that grew upon it.

And there was blood. Mostly spattered and concentrated beneath the manacles, dried but he guessed fresh enough. Some on the walls. Some just inside the threshold at his feet. Evidence that suggested torture, and when taken in conjunction with the traces of flesh and blood on the manacles, it was evidence that suggested someone had been held here.

Having seen the Founder's body, cleaned by Tamner, there had not been enough visible injuries to account for so much blood.

Unless it had come from his mouth or some other, less pleasant orifice. Unless the blood belonged to more than one person. He had not examined the dead man's corpse to know.

He assumed the doctor had.

He would need to see those reports. For the moment, he could not shake the first impressions left by the evidence.

"I want everything taken to the station. Power up that Echo, see what it gives us…what's on every one of those chips. I want pictures of everything the way it is…get prints off everything."

He would turn in his body cam as soon as he returned to his office.

"Should we find whose blood this is?" the officer next to him at the second door asked.

"If that much came from one person," another snorted, "they're probably dead."

"Could have been an animal."

"Why would anyone…?"

"Sample it," Grainger snapped. He had not told them why they were here, what they were looking for. He had not told them that the man said to have been held here was already dead. Speculation and rumor were not going to help. "Talk to everyone in the vicinity, nearby businesses, warehouse owners, streeters. I want to know everything about this building…and anyone seen going in or out of it."

He was confident of the property's ownership. He had investigated the deeds when the location had come to his attention. The Voices of Faith were the deeded owner, the property transferred to them, it appeared, before the Coup by the Founder. While the Founder often claimed ownership of abandoned structures until they could pass them to someone else, there were few warehouses recorded in the Archives as belonging to the Voices.

Those there were stored physical property, paper records, donated items of wealth, or personal belongings of the Senior and others, storage facilities most often located near the Talker Halls.

The passing of ownership did not implicate the Mam, but other things did, or could. If her husband had been here, if she had known, it was evidence of a conspiracy that had swirled through Grainger's mind since the night the man had been abducted.

But everything he saw in this place seemed too neat and too sloppy at the same time.

"I want every report you can give me on my desk by the end of the day."

The officers groaned. One muttered, "Gonna take us that long just to move it…and get the forensic team down to…"

Ignoring the difficulty of barely functioning lifts, Grainger grunted, "Then you'd better get started."

He might not hold the officers, the forensic team, to that deadline, but it gave them a goal to strive toward, a fire beneath them to prompt hasty, thorough action. In the meantime, he had some things to see to himself, including questioning Mam Kemway.

❧*❧

His palms itched and sweated within his gloves. Tightness in his chest reduced air and blood so that his head felt light, bringing a different blackness than what spread across the cityscape as it appeared through his enhanced lenses. The impulse to wipe them to clear his vision was prevented by the mask as the breather built into his body armor struggled to compensate for his labored breathing. Crouched in the alley beside the Spink left to monitor this place, having followed the street children's calls to reach it, Scarecrow stared at the unguarded door on the other side of the walkway, swallowing the bile in the back of his throat asking, "What've you seen?

The digitizer masked the choking quaver in his voice. The girl glanced sideways to acknowledge his arrival and inched away to make room for the vigi.

She did not know the memories Scarecrow carried of this same warehouse.

Rhyd did not believe it was a coincidence he was led here.

He was certain this was a trap.

"Not much. Brought a guy here and dumped him. One stayed on the steps for a while, but he left. Hasn't been any traffic 'cept a goat cart of recycles and bugger patrol." Wondering if she should have alerted the buggers to their suspicions, she paused to allow Scarecrow to listen for any sounds that might be useful.

"Did you see him?"

The girl shrugged. "Dark curly hair with a speecher. All I could tell except he was a limp fish when they dumped him."

Scarecrow scowled. There were no link locks or keypads to inhibit him, only the passlock he should be able to open. He fumbled in a pocket for the A-Pass Zara had long ago provided, a pass that gave him access to almost anywhere in the city he wanted to go. The SCAMs on the nearby building corners showed no activity, their red eyes were dark with the straining distribution of power. But that did not mean they were not recording.

Nor would that mean that any recorded footage was being transmitted, stored, or viewed.

Someone might see him crossing the street. How far away could an audience be? How long might it take them to reach this place? Who might come for him?

Maybe the buggers. More likely the brako.

It was a risk he would have to take unless he traveled a half-Lev up and dropped in front of the door.

Too much effort. Too much time lost. If Jaron was here, if he was alive, he needed Rhyd now.

"Watch the streets. Watch the SCAMs. Watch above. They're here. Send word to Doctor Tamner…tell him to go to the cat-man."

Tamner would know what he meant, just as the Spinks did. Tamner would know what to do.

Whoever was inside, so long as they were breathing, would need medical attention. There was no one Scarecrow trusted more for that.

He should have sent for the doctor sooner.

"Think it's a trap?"

Scarecrow nodded. Of course it was. If he was brako, it was exactly the trap he would have set. If he knew any similar weaknesses for Vanderwall, Scarecrow would have baited him the same way.

"Give me time…but get word out now."

"Got it."

The Spink whistled, a series of tones instructing others to do as Scarecrow requested. Others returned the instructions up and down the Levs, along the adjoining alleys, and along the Lev 1 walkway. Bugger, brako, or civilian, if anyone approached, Scarecrow would know it as soon as the Spinks did. Tamner would know his part, too.

Wanting a drink to steady his hands, Scarecrow plotted a course across the path, one that would take advantage of awning posts and recycle bins to block any spying SCAMs, and then he started across. He was not afraid of the brako or the bugorra. He was not afraid of anyone. He was only afraid of what he would find inside that building, where he too had once been held captive.

Maybe this would not be Jaron.

It could be anyone.

He crossed the walkway without incident. The Spinks' calls grew fainter as they moved higher through the Levs. At the door, he paused to listen, to gauge the other sounds of the day, the proximity of anyone in nearby buildings. He listened to what awaited behind the door.

A single, struggling, wheezing source of breath, too muffled by the falls and the door between them to identify a source.

He only knew it was a person in need of release.

The passcard slid through the reader.

The latch clicked and turned in his hand.

A flash of a red dot on a SCAM was noted out of the right corner of his periphery.

Then the street was dark.

He did not have much time.

One figure, huddled in the cold, lying in a twisted heap as though discarded, drawn into a ball in search of the warmth his own body could provide. Dark hair, damp with sweat and moisture accumulated when he had been moved through the streets to this place, clung to his skull, disguising the tousled curls Scarecrow hoped to see. The tattered remains of a maroon sweater barely covering his grimy back and held primarily in place by bruised, shivering shoulders, was a color Scarecrow remembered, although the pants he wore were stained to the point of no longer being any recognizable color. His feet were bare, bruised, and dirty, but it was the fingers clutching his shoulders as though embracing himself that Scarecrow recognized first.

"Jaron."

The younger man groaned as a gloved hand rolled him onto his back, offering no resistance to the forced movement. The speecher components at his throat and temple were damaged beyond use, his eyes swollen and stuck shut with sleep and tears and the bruising strikes he had endured, and his lips were cracked and puffy from thirst and further blows.

Despite those things, the hand that clutched Scarecrow's arms expressed words Rhyd did not need to hear to understand.

His chest constricted as if his heart would stop, would burst. He never thought he would see Jaron in such a state. He had feared he would never see him again.

This should not have happened.

"Course I came."

Frantic whistles in the street made him stand, pulling reluctantly free of the weak hands that clutched at him with accompanying pleading moans.

"Gotta take care of this. Then I'm taking you home."

Jaron shook his head and grabbed for Scarecrow's ankle. His painfully weak reach came up short.

One step. One turn. The flash of light momentarily overwhelmed the mask's sensors, leaving Scarecrow blind to everything except the massive black shadow in the doorway.

Blindness did not stop him. Scarecrow charged, head down. The yellow band on his arm was identifier enough.

Vanderwall, not expecting such a brazen attack, tumbled down the short steps when the blocking blow caught him across the chest.

Both arms came up, one to reflexively break his fall as he twisted mid-tumble, the other to wrap around his attacker. The hold brought Scarecrow down with him, but when the impact with the ground came, Scarecrow spun free.

Vanderwall bowled in the opposite direction.

Three Spink whistles.

Three more masked brako. Scarecrow noted their beaked faces as he rolled to his feet. He did not wait for his opponent to rise but charged again, fists closed, to catch him in the back of the head rather than landing the debilitating blow to the temple he had hoped for.

The body armor absorbed most of the impact, pushing it up his arm into his shoulder, preventing the breaking of bones in his hand and wrist but leaving a numbing pain in its wake. Vanderwall lurched away. The gestures given to his minions were meant to keep them away from this prey, but it was aborted by the instinctive act of catching himself with both hands on the walkway rail when he was hit again, preventing him from pitching over the rail into the river.

Several young voices cried out in unison as an uncertain number of Spinks jumped the three brako. The men shouted indignantly at the unexpected assault of children. The assistance they intended to offer their boss before his stay-back gesture was thwarted more by the children than by Vanderwall's demand to leave Scarecrow to him.

Another cluster of dirty faces appeared from the shadows to block the warehouse door. Their whistle calls continued to roll away and back like waves from a pebble dropped into a puddle. Spinks elsewhere responded.

Vanderwall turned sideways before Scarecrow's black boot caught him in the small of his back. The kick might have struck the rail, but the brako boss caught Scarecrow's ankle and twisted, dragging Scarecrow to the ground when he, too, stumbled.

There was no opportunity for Scarecrow to brace his fall. There was a grunt of pain upon impact, the ringing echo of the grate as his head struck the metal. The trajectory of his fall turned his leg out of

Vanderwall's grasp; that freedom was the only thing that allowed Scarecrow to twist out of the way of an impending body slam before Vanderwall's greater weight could crush him.

Once on the ground, Vanderwall lurched again, this time spasming unexpectedly beneath the blow of the hemp building brick that struck the back of his protected skull.

The Spink who stood over him grinned.

"Buggers comin'," he cried. "Get him outta here."

Warring impulses as he regained his footing caused Scarecrow to stare at the prone figure. He should finish this. Should end this now. He did not need the Spinks to win the fight, any fight, for him. Around him, the Spinks continued to torment the other three, a tiny mob like an insect swarm, each fist impotent without the cumulative benefit of their combined effort.

But the boy was right. If the buggers found him here, found Jaron, there would be questions, detainment, and interference from Grainger that Scarecrow preferred to avoid.

Getting Jaron to safety was more important.

If the buggers arrived in time, Vanderwall would not go anywhere.

The Spinks at the warehouse door parted to permit him inside. Jaron groaned again, this time in pain as he was hoisted from the floor. "Gonna get you out, get you up," promised a girl who scurried away in front of Scarecrow, following the direction of her fellow Spinks along a route that would avoid entanglements none of them needed.

One more glance at Vanderwall, the man unmoving. One strong kick would push him off the path, down, down to the river where he would never trouble another citizen of Hebenon.

The shrill shriek of a bugorra whistled closer.

There was no time.

This was not over, Scarecrow silently promised. Vanderwall had hurt Jaron. Even if he was detained in bugorra custody, Scarecrow believed he had enough cause to find him again and finish what they had started here. Not even Grainger would keep him from it.

❧Chapter 28❧

His flat was the only place Rhyd considered to be safe from the brako who had not, thanks to the Spinks' interference, pursued him away from the warehouse. Going to Tox, to Zara, to Vapors, or to Skelter would have been closer options but going to any of those places meant putting more people in danger.

The fragile, unmoving form in his arms was proof that Scarecrow had put enough of his friends in harm's way.

With the children's help, two of those individuals were summoned as he wove and climbed through shafts and alleys but only Zara met him at his flat, her custom A-Pass permitting her to open his door and stand in the open frame with her arms crossed as though casually studying the quiet streets. She handed something to the girl who had led Scarecrow this far, and after sidestepping to allow him to enter, closed the door.

No one had heard or seen them. Lash would not hear them through the wall their flats shared. The Spink would keep watch to make sure. If anyone approached, they would know.

Zara moved the blankets off the sofa, arranged the pillows, and stood to the side so that Jaron could be gingerly laid upon the aged, stained cushions. When Scarecrow stepped back, she bent over the injured man and began to work off the remnants of his crimson sweater as Scarecrow shed his gloves and mask to see Jaron with his own eyes, touch him with his own hands.

The moment he reached for him, however, tempted to push the damp curls off Jaron's face, his scent washed over Rhyd like sweet perfume despite his unclean condition. Rhyd's breath caught. He froze. His trembling fingers fell short of their objective and were hastily pulled away.

He couldn't do it. He could not touch him again. Not now.

Not ever.

So much bruising. Dried traces of blood, though not as much as Rhyd had feared there would be. Much of the damage, he suspected, was internal, hidden from view. Swollen features revealed blows to his tender face, and his chest, his ribs, and his stomach were laced with so many bruises in an array of mottled newness that Rhyd could barely tear his eyes away.

He had done this as surely as Vanderwall had.

"Can you…?"

Zara glanced at him as she began to unfasten Jaron's stained pants. The sound in Rhyd's throat startled him enough that he retreated with hasty steps to the kitchen to fill a bowl and his kettle with water for heating without Zara repeating her request.

The burner beneath the kettle glowed faintly. It was going to take too long to get warm water.

"I'm not a doctor," Zara murmured, ignoring Rhyd's awkward discomfort and unshed tears when he returned with the bowl and set it on the low table beside her. "He needs…"

"Doctor's on his way," he muttered as he retreated to the kitchen for towels and anything else Zara might need. He needed to keep as much distance as possible between himself and Jaron, despite the compulsion to join him on the sofa, wrap the broken body to his, and never let him go.

Tamner would come if the Spinks had gotten the message to him, as long as he could break away from whatever duty occupied his time.

Eventually unable to resist the lure of Jaron's face, Rhyd peered over the counter to take passing glances at Zara's work after tossing the towels to her, puttering in the kitchen as the kettle struggled to get warm. He took the bottle of Zaolei from the cupboard, the one he had taken from Jaron's flat, started to open it, but decided to wait. Instead, he wiggled out of the top portion of his body armor and his undershirt to wipe his skin with a cold-water towel, dry himself with another, and then pull his shirt and the body armor back on.

There were bruises on Jaron's bare calves and shins, some on his knees, a few across his thighs. There were binding bruises on his wrists from whatever restraints had held him, and his dirty feet were cut and scraped. It was impossible to know whether every dark smudge was a bruise or if it was dirt or his own filth. Until Tamner arrived, there was no way to be sure which bruises announced broken bones and internal contusions and which were the results of assault on the tissues alone.

Only when Zara covered Jaron with a blanket from the back of the sofa did Rhyd gather the courage to return with the bottle of Zaolei. He paused at the sofa table where she sat and handed the bottle to her.

His stomach was too knotted to drink it but there was no reason she should not. He was sure that if he took a drink, he would vomit.

"Is he…?"

"Breathing's shallow…maybe in shock. Gonna keep him warm until the doctor comes."

After gesturing to the nearly empty oxygen tank he had yet to refill, making a spur-of-the-moment decision that might not help Jaron but would make Rhyd feel better, he picked up his gloves and pulled them on over the black and purple bruising enveloping his knuckles.

"All there is, you're…he's welcome to it. Don't let anyone in except Tox and the doctor 'til I'm back…"

"You're not going out again?" she asked with a scowl. She did not voice any perception of need; reminding him that others needed him, especially Jaron, would drive Rhyd away faster.

He did not look at her or Jaron again. "Vanderwall's down there. Might still be there if the buggers haven't…I need to end this."

By now the buggers would have broken up the fight between the brako and the Spinks or else the brako would have retreated to take their boss with them. Maybe they had barred themselves within the warehouse. Maybe the buggers were dragging Vanderwall to the Ups.

A trapped quarry, or an in-transit one, would be easier to take care of than one who had escaped into whatever hideout he called home.

Angry with himself, furious with Vanderwall and the brako, action was the only emotional outlet Rhyd could take advantage of. He did not want to face the results if he stayed with Jaron another minute. He had to go.

"He couldn't be in better hands," Rhyd added, the forlorn melancholy in his voice the sort of blanket over an internal ache that had been omnipresent since the day Venn was ripped out of his life. Zara, like others, had hoped that ache was gone, that those days were behind him, that Rhyd might one day be happy again.

She was beginning to believe that happiness for any of them was no longer possible.

Despite the questions she could have asked, Zara nodded as Scarecrow's mask was cinched into place. He did not see it. Footsteps outside of the flat were accompanied by the scraping removal of the shaft grate. There was a knock and Tox's voice was underscored by the traces of shuffling knees and elbows within the shaft. By the time Zara opened the door, the grate was closed and Rhyd was gone.

"Molls?"

Switz had done his best to avoid the Core survivors except for Skelter and Enoch, and by extension, Colyx, Otta, and Jonner who had, for a time, come and gone from Vapors with clockwork regularity. Hoping for another, more beneficial shot with Skelter, that the redhead would rethink giving him lodging and protection if only for a few days, Switz had loitered near Vapors for hours, weighing his options, his opportunities, with every face that passed.

He could have gone back to Blayd and begged for security, but he was certain the merc would turn him over to the buggers as an assassin, a kidnapper, for the personal gain that would bring. If he were Blayd, Switz would be out looking for the only man who could expose him…the same as Switz would be doing if he thought he could conjure some means of overpowering or trapping the bigger, stronger man. The best Switz could hope for was to offer Blayd to Skelter in exchange for protection.

Maybe Molly was here for protection too. More than likely, Switz assessed as he clasped the other man's trembling hand, Molly was hoping the kaheao could hook him up with a score.

"He's here, isn't he? Skelt?"

Switz shrugged. "Haven't seen him."

"You're lookin'. Not gonna protect you." Molly shrugged off Switz's side-eyed glance. "Seen your face all over. Everyone's looking for a piece of you. If I were you, I wouldn't trust him."

The reminder prompted Switz to scan the street in case Molly had brought buggers with him and intended to turn Switz in for the reward.

"Didn't do anything," he mumbled, knowing that was not entirely true. "You're on there too, you know."

Molly pouted and ran a hand through his sparse, dark hair. If Switz had seen him there, it was only a matter of time before someone else picked him out of that protest footage, too, the popper in his hand intended for Skelter. He hoped that, in the ensuing chaos, his face, his presence, his actions would be obscured, overlooked, and forgotten.

He hoped Skelter had not pinned the popper shot in his shoulder on a man he could not be sure was there. He assumed a man like Skelter had a lot of enemies. That shot could have come from anyone. It could have been an accident.

"Just cause I was there, I didn't do anything. Was just tryin' to get through. Doesn't mean…there aren't some who…men like us are always targets of the powerful."

Switz shrugged again, knowing that to be true. Sometimes men like them brought this sort of scrutiny down on themselves, regardless of their intentions.

"Worked for Mam Kemway briefly, now she…" Molly shrugged off the disbelieving stare he expected. "I got skills, you know. Never met an Echo I can't hack. Helped her out, got her hold up where she can't be found, protecting her back…"

"How're you gonna protect anyone if you can't protect yourself?"

What were the odds of someone like Molly doing business with a Kemway? His surprise brought with it a new idea, a new plan, one that crept like ivy through his thoughts before his head began to nod with a low whistle. "Think she'll…I know a few things she'll want to hear…about what happened to the Founder before he was…think she'll have my back too?"

What could be better than having Mam Kemway as an ally? Who could offer better protection against the buggers and Blayd than the one the merc had betrayed?

After a few moments of scrutiny and a few more of watching the junior swiver arrive and disappear behind Vapors' beaded curtain, Molly shrugged too. They had known each other for a long time. He and Switz had been on the lowest rung of the Core hierarchy. They had rarely worked as allies, had most often fought over the same scraps of food and favors others tossed their way, but out here, in the city, being hunted like animals, Molly did not think he could find a better ally than Switz. Not even the woman who had invaded his home and treated him with the same contempt she treated everyone else. Switz might even be able to help get his hands on his next score in exchange. "Worth a try…for a price."

Molly stretched out his hand.

Switz snorted.

"Nothing on me…but I know where we might get something, long as we have a deal. You keep my back, I keep yours."

Molly's hand did not drop. He did his best to keep his nervous, twitching gaze focused on Switz and said, "Deal."

Switz shook his hand.

❧*❧

Tox was picking through the collection of material spread across Rhyd's dining table, looking for replacement parts that might allow the repair of the damaged speecher components, when the next knock sounded on Rhyd's door. She looked up as Zara ushered the flustered, out-of-breath doctor into the flat and nodded at the increasingly familiar man before returning to the intricate work that required magnifiers and needle tools to complete.

Tamner, having taken the time to complete other visits after leaving Vapors, working on behalf of the Nau to encourage influential residents to evacuate the city until the power was restored, was grateful he had not yet begun the long trip to the Uppers when the Spinks found him. Hearing no one else in the flat, his steps faltered when he noted who was in the room and who was not. He had expected to find Ballard in need of care. But it was not the vigi lying battered upon the sofa.

"Vanderwall…" Zara said as if that explained everything.

Tamner nodded, although the word hardly answered the questions that banged around inside his skull seeking a way out.

"If you'll stay with him, I'll get a few things…maybe we can replace the speecher so he can tell us what happened." Zara had been the last one to see Jaron healthy and vibrant, if broken-hearted. That had been days ago. She did not blame herself for his condition the way Rhyd did, but she did want to know what had happened.

Rhyd and Oliver would want to know as well.

"Evaluation will take some time…then time to treat him, so go on. But be careful," he added without looking up from the medical bag he placed on the sofa table beside a collection of dirty, bloody cloths, a bowl of dark water, and a partial bottle of whiskey. Used to clean his injuries, he judged, based on the pungent aroma on one of the cloths and the red irritation around some of the visible cuts and scrapes he could see on Jaron's arms.

"Always am," Zara assured him.

The brako were out in force. They would be looking for Scarecrow anew. She preferred to avoid revealing a connection to the vigi that could get either of them killed. She nodded at Tox and left the flat.

Tox continued to work without a word.

❧*❧

Seven bloody, unconscious brako later, Scarecrow stood at the threshold of a place he had never wanted to see again, fighting the compulsion to tear it down with his hands. The street was empty as he had expected, no Spinks, no brako, no buggers. No Vanderwall littering the walkway with his malignant poison. The warehouse door was closed and locked, and it was only when discovering it that he realized that he had lost the A-Pass. Maybe he had dropped it inside or during the fight with Vanderwall. Maybe it had been lost during the climb through the Levs to go home or dropped in his flat.

The loss was an inconvenience but barely mattered. With his enhanced hearing, with every sensor in his body armor that he could manipulate and utilize, uninterrupted by brako or bugorra, he evaluated the vacant space behind the door to verify that the brako had not taken refuge here or locked any of the Spinks inside. At least not any who were alive. He wondered where they had gone. He wondered if the Spinks had followed.

The only Spink here was the girl who had kept watch before.

Waiting for his return.

"See where they went?"

The girl shook his head. "That way…but I didn't follow. Too many buggers chased 'em off. Stayed cause I thought you might wanna see where he came from…where they had him before they dumped him here. Maybe it'll tell you something?" She added the last in a hopeful, praise-seeking tone.

"Show me."

The shift whistle wailed. Those people fortunate enough to continue working flowed in and out of the packing plants, gardens, laundries and recycling facilities, fisheries and warehouses, as the girl guided him through back passages that kept them out of the public's eye. When they stopped, the Spink pointed to a warehouse adjacent to another that swarmed with bugger activity as officers carried its contents out in crates marked, "EVIDENCE" on the sides. Scarecrow's attention was torn between what he wanted to inspect, where he wanted to be, and Captain Grainger's efforts to direct the work of others with increasing frustrated annoyance.

When the captain glanced at his ICD, his demeanor changed.

"Noel, keep at it."

"Captain?"

"Somewhere I have to be. No one leaves until it's empty?"

The officer called Noel, nondescript behind the bug-faced mask that allowed him to breathe easier in the overwhelming mist and spray ejected by the Five Falls and the river, bobbed his head. His words were lost behind the shouts of rowdy off-shift workers passing by. Grainger's marching steps took him to the nearest lift where his political rank and position allowed him the luxury to utilize what few in the city no longer could.

Scarecrow frowned. "Follow him. Let me know where he's going." Maybe the call was unimportant, something that was none of Scarecrow's concern. But sending the girl on that mission meant removing her from harm's way if things got ugly here. Whether it came to a confrontation with the buggers, if they found him here, or with the brako whom he would resume hunting once his curiosity was satisfied, there would be further bloodshed today.

Enough people had been hurt because of him.

He would not risk a child as well.

❧*❧

"Scarecrow found him. Jaron's alive." Zara paused, swallowed a hitching breath, and added, "You should come."

The box in her other hand contained the speecher set Skelter had previously obtained for her, a rare commodity she had not expected him to locate so quickly, given the conditions in the city. She had meant to give it to Jaron the next time she saw him, to replace the already malfunctioning piece of the unit he wore. She had not expected to need it like this.

She was grateful she had acquired the entire set even if it did need adjustments and finishing touches by Tox to make each part operational.

She would thank Skelter for it later.

She closed the box and snapped it into her pack of gathered tools, components, and materials, and two of her Echos that would be needed for the technical work that lay ahead. Ideally, replacing a speecher should be completed in the sterile environment of a medical center, not Rhyd's living room. On the off chance that the brako would come for Jaron, however, or come for Rhyd, she concurred that it was best to contain the violence to a place where innocent people would not pay the price.

The ICD caught on the zippered edge of her pack as she closed it and she paused. The message left for Oliver would be painful, would be bitter, would be difficult to hear, but he would never forgive her for hiding this news from him. She was not sure she would forgive herself for doing it.

She did not consider what Rhyd would think about what she had done. It needed doing. If Rhyd was not at Jaron's side when he awoke, if he awoke, it would be good for Oliver to be there.

❧Chapter 29❧

The echoing stomp and clatter of bugorra emptying a warehouse in an obvious raid made Feena scowl and pause to watch from a safe distance, debating, as Captain Grainger hustled away, whether she should find a way around the commotion or inquire about the substance of the raid…or if the matter was any of her business. Grainger's face was pinched and furrowed, the corners of his eyes creased with concentration, the look of someone she was not interested in disturbing. He did not appear to notice her brightly colored umbra of pink and lavender and blue, did not notice the men with her, as she tipped it slightly forward to shield her face as he passed.

It was not worth interrupting the captain, but the warehouse, possibly one of hers, was worth a handful of questions before returning to the empty Den. She gestured for Tyrisi and her escorts to stay a discreet distance behind, and casually sidled up to the nearest bugorra officer taking notes on his T1 as objects were removed from the structure, presented to him, and then crated to be carried away.

To Feena, nothing she could see looked to be hers. Nothing looked important. Making note of the desk and chair visible through the open door, the room lit by portable lamps to aid the buggers' work, she guessed that someone had used this warehouse for an office rather than storage. When the note-taking officer looked up, she offered her most alluring, cordial smile and asked with convincingly feigned concern, "Has someone died?"

Such an explanation would support the emptying of the building, though not the presence of the bugorra, unless the death had been a murder, one of enough import to drag the captain down from the Ups.

Murder was a good reason to bring the captain to the Levs. So too would be finding a stash of illegal goods.

"Stay back, ma'am. Official business. It's not safe here."

"Is there a bomb? Is it," she forced a shudder, "the brako?"

"Who else," the officer muttered as if scolding himself for his ill-spoken admission, while the drawer contents were emptied into the crate at his feet. Second-guessing his too-hasty, he shrugged and waved her back. "Best move on. Like I said, not safe."

"I don't think anywhere in Hebenon's safe," she countered with a gesture that beckoned Tyrisi and the rest of her escort forward.

"Right enough," the officer said, looking at the men joining her. They were big men, nondescript in their water-protective suits, but their presence meant that the woman he did not recognize was someone important enough to warrant such attention. He half-bowed apologetically, reversing his terse tone, and added, "Should get somewhere safe ma'am; if the owner comes looking…"

Feena did not see anything important in the nearest open crate. Business items, takeaway packets, utensils, and more. Someone came out carrying a chair, taking it away for processing. Two others began to maneuver the desk through the door for similar dispensation. The objects of primary interest had likely already been removed. Someone with print and DNA swabbing kits squeezed past the pair jockeying the desk and disappeared into a darker back room.

A murder then…or at least a death.

"Good luck," she murmured to the note-taking bugger, clutching her bag to her side as though afraid it would be stolen and shifting the angle of the umbra to block a gust of cold mist that snaked around the building's edge and pushed past, sucked toward some other building where an opening door had generated the slight pressure variance.

It was time to recheck the books. If this was one of her warehouses, she wanted to know what it was used for and by whom.

If it was not, she wanted to know what Neoma and Vanderwall were up to.

❧*❧

He lingered long enough to mark the bugorra's arrival, to note Captain Grainger among them, then Blayd retreated to the nearest herpa hall, to a place where the expected canvas awning had been damaged and removed, a place where he could hear the buggers' movements and monitor their actions without being seeing. He wanted to be certain they took everything, wanted to assess the captain's evaluation and first impression of the evidence left for him.

Blayd was grateful Ilya was not here. After the way she had looked at him when he was released from bugorra custody, she no longer trusted him. That was his fault. He expected she would have ratted him out if she had come to the warehouse, found his connection to it, and followed him to the herpa hall, no matter how well he tried to hide.

That bridge had been burned. Until the business with the Founder, his kidnapping and death was settled, blame and guilt pinned on the Mam and Senior as Blayd intended, Ilya was not going to believe anything he said.

So, he waited.

But the captain said very little during the search or spoke most of his words so softly that they were muted by the echo of heavy boots and the rise and fall cadence of Soleia's voice on the street Echó that continued to broadcast snippets of the Founder's Remembrance Day, his last incoherent speech, and the Nau's ongoing request for citizens to relocate to Outside until the power grid was restored.

Some businesses had begun to heed that urging. Some people likewise. It seemed that many, however, were inclined to suffer rather than brave the unknown they were conditioned to fear.

Barked orders to empty the building, to take everything inside for processing, marked the captain's departure. Blayd frowned, wondering if the ICD message the captain received had come from Ilya, if she had found something that put him at risk. Or, he thought with a narrow-eyed glower at the herpa moving about the room dispensing food, drinks, clothes, and blankets to those who had come for such nessies, one of these people here recognized him, suspected him of mischief, and revealed his location.

There was no reason they should, no reason they would, but Blayd decided not to take the chance.

He finished the cup of water as he ducked through the cloth-covered doorway, stood up, and went into the street. He would not be trapped here. He would not be caught like this, accused of crimes he had not committed, or ones that he had. Side-glancing at the barely lit Echo on the building across the street while he adjusted his cloak and collar, he frowned again at the still ICD image taken from the protest footage on the day of the Founder's death.

The day…the hour…the minute.

A figure in the crowd, circled in digital red, a familiar face that drew Blayd across the street to stare more closely.

That mierdita, he muttered quietly enough that the pair who passed did no more than glance at him for talking to himself.

He had trusted Switz to keep Kemway safe. To find him, to bring him back. He had never thought the little man would stoop to murder. Or maybe it had not been murder; it was impossible to tell the nature of what he held in his outstretched hand.

Whatever it had been, whatever he had done, if the buggers found Switz first, he would undoubtedly narc to save his skin. It was the sort of thing men like Switz did. Nothing about him had suggested loyalty without something being paid for it, only a desperation to save himself. That desperation had bound them briefly, for as long as Blayd had something to offer him, but it would never keep Switz loyal without some ongoing patronage.

Any more than it had kept Blayd loyal to Neoma.

He had to find Switz before the bugorra found him. Before Switz found him. He did not need the truth from the little man. He did not need answers about what he had done. Blayd only needed to keep Switz quiet before he ruined everything.

✶*✶

Such squats were common, though, since the Coup, the availability of structures left empty by the massive death toll that violence had generated meant that people homeless by circumstance or choice could claim any vacant property they wished as their own. The dysfunction of city systems and lack of adequate heat and running water brought many of the less fortunate together into huddled throngs to share body warmth and stolen food. Sometimes fights broke out when someone chose to horde rather than share, but this particular cluster she had been directed to was currently peaceful, calm enough, except for the soft chatter of friends and families and the incoherent mutterings of the mad addicts among them.

"We're looking for Mr. Folwell," Ilya called from the door as two officers wheedled people aside to inspect their faces, and two others stood with her to detain any who tried to leave. "Reamon Folwell."

"Ain't no Folwell here," a woman answered from somewhere near the center of the room. The speaker did not lift her head or reveal herself, and there were too many people in the area where the voice came from to identify which of the huddled bodies it came from. There had to be three or four dozen people clustered here, possibly more. Determining who the speaker was would take more time than Ilya wanted to spend.

Instead, she directed her officers to converge on the approximate location of the voice as she asked, "We need to ask a few questions."

"Know what happens when buggers ask questions," someone snorted.

"Gonna take us all in? Send us Out into the poison…?"

"No poison out there," someone else barked. "Get your head outta your tooter…"

Someone else shrieked, "They've got poppers!"

"Of course they got poppers!"

The exclamation, and one bugger yanking some nondescript individual up by the arm, induced panic. People lurched up, scrambled to collect their belongings, and began a crushing push towards where Ilya stood. The officers were swept along with the massive movement, and as the pair by the door tried to hold them back, Ilya was thrust from the doorway against the walkway rail so that those spewing from the flat could flee left and right like roaches driven by the light.

The guarding buggers were forced to let many of them go.

One officer's waving hand, a gesture in one direction that might have been random as he tried to avoid being trampled, was enough to propel Ilya off the rail and push through the escaping throng. Her gaze swept the heads of the mass, of those still trying to exit, and those still huddled inside with their heads covered by anything they could use as protection from the dripping damp. One was taller than the others, less stooped, his movements less jerky or panicked. He allowed himself to be swept up in the tail of the crowd, following their flow where their pushing and shoving meant he was gradually shifted nearer to the outer edge of the group…until Ilya was able to reach him, grab his arm, and yank him out of the mob.

She thrust him against the wall as he lifted his head.

"Reamon Folwell," she huffed with even sternness, confident he was the man she sought. "You are under arrest."

❧Chapter 30❧

One beaked brako fell.

Another.

Ilya noted each location on her ascension through the city with her quarry caught in her tight-gloved grip, ignoring the growing ache in her weak knee. She did not think this was the work of other brako as the two factions battled each other for dominance. They most frequently left the bodies of the vanquished where they fell as a warning to the other side or else disposed of the evidence by dumping the dead into the river, into vats of cleaning solutions, lye, recycling chemicals, or else dragged them into the nearest empty structure so that the dead did not clutter the streets.

Unlike the majority of the brako's victims, these men were not dead. Broken, unconscious, in need of medical attention, but not dead.

At least not yet.

Nor was this the work of fed-up citizens acting in self-defense, as the strength of most brako, and the fear of retaliation, was too much to give most vindi owners, streeters, or anyone else, a chance to win.

If anything, Ilya mused as the lift door groaned shut, closing off the three twisted beaked forms heaped amidst recycle bins, this had to be Scarecrow's doing.

She wanted to be angry with his lawlessness and disregard for the constraints of society. But the bugorra were stretched thinner with each hour the city suffered limited power, with each assassin tip that crackled through the hotline, with every brako fist that came down on those struggling to survive. The bugorra could not counter the brako's reign of terror at the rate things were spiraling out of control.

For the first time since Scarecrow's rise to prominence, for the first time since the Coup, Ilya was grateful the vigi was there, doing the things he did. Sooner or later, the last brako would fall. Or the city would die. Sooner or later, Vanderwall would be stopped.

When that happened, perhaps Hebenon and Scarecrow would finally find peace.

The man before her did not shift or utter a sound. Her officers kept their thoughts to themselves. What Folwell thought of those bodies, the brako, whether they believed them alive or dead, Ilya could not tell. She hoped seeing them made him reconsider what he had done.

Sides heaving, breather straining against the gradual depletion of oxygen in the tank and the struggling of filt systems that fought to expel waste created by heavy breathing and exertion's sweat, Scarecrow watched the lift door close, remaining out of the lieutenant's sight. It was not Vanderwall in these bugger's custody. The individual with Ilya, for all his dirty clothes and unkempt hair, appeared to be a respectable man, or a man who had been so once.

Scarecrow did not care who he was or what he had done. He had business to address. He needed another breather tank for the suit. He needed a replacement for home as well.

He should be at Jaron's side.

There were flashes of memory, bruises and blood, the sound of quick, shallow breathing. Wet curls clinging to his face. The feel of his skin beneath Rhyd's fingertips. Things that choked him with his too-rapid heart rate, things that blinded him with fear and outrage and a sense of impotence because they were things Scarecrow could not correct or resolve. Things he could do nothing about. Things he was afraid to confront.

He did not like to feel afraid.

The brako was an enemy he could face down. A force that hit back with physical blows that Scarecrow found easier to endure than the emotional clawing that raked his heart. He could not go back home.

Not yet. But he could make damn sure the brako suffered for what they had done, for the side they had chosen. He could find his way to Vanderwall through them and make that man suffer too.

For Jaron, for Hebenon.

Making sure Jaron was safe was the best Scarecrow could offer.

The only thing.

❧*❧

"Where'd he…?" Grainger tried to push into the flat the ICD message directed him to, not recognizing the address, finding it little different on the outside from any other flat in the Levs. Flats varied in size, by the number of bedrooms, and by the personal tastes of their residents, but there was little room for individuality.

There was little individuality in Hebanthe Falls if he was honest.

Zara blocked his entrance, preventing him from barging in, pushed by the rage and fear that drove him, but he could see beyond her to the dark-haired kesfek Kemway had once tortured, bent over the cleaning of delicate tools and the collecting of items into the open pack on the table. He saw Tamner drying his hands on a towel, meeting his gaze with a look that expressed both surprise and no surprise at once.

And he could see Jaron, pale, clean now of the blood of injuries and surgery he had endured, drying curls falling toward the pillow on which he slept. The gentle rise and fall of his chest, covered by old blankets in a room that smelled of Zaolei, sweat, damp clothes, and anxiety, meant he was alive. One arm was exposed, the needle that had coerced him into unfeeling sleep to allow for the replacement of broken speecher components now pumping hydrating, healing fluids into his veins to aid in recovery. The bruises across that arm, around his wrist, spoke of captivity and beatings, prompting Grainger to start forward again with a growled hiss as Zara stepped aside and allowed him in with her hand hooked around his bicep.

He barely noticed it was there.

"Scarecrow found him," she began, repeating that part of the message she had sent. "We don't know how…or where…or what happened…but he's safe now."

Grainger snorted. "Where's…?" he began again. Was this Scarecrow's flat? It was obvious someone lived here. Possibly the dark-haired woman. Possibly Zara.

He did not think it smelled like her, however.

Guessing at the incomplete question, Tamner said, "Doing what he does best." Though he thought the other man should have remained home, he understood the impotent helplessness that a man like Ballard must experience while pacing the room as someone else worked to stabilize Jaron's health, repair the speecher, save the man's life. Ballard needed to do something to feel useful. Wherever he was, he would be doing what he was best at…hunting down those responsible for this violent crime.

It was better than his being here making Tamner's job more difficult. Better that he was not here while Grainger was.

"I've got to get back up…"

"He needs you here," Grainger growled, pushing aside the table's contents to sit beside the sofa and stare at Jaron's pensive face. Some of those items fell to the floor. He did not seem to notice.

The bag under Tamner's hand snapped shut, and the oxygen tank he had delivered was toed to the side so he could escape without climbing over the captain. "He's stable. He's resting. His vitals are as good as they can be, given what he's been through. No damage done that'll kill him. Nothing more I can do now. He'll sleep for several hours…and the Nau needs…"

"Hell with the Nau."

"They're debating the andi issue…and I'm told the tests are back. You want answers?" He frowned at Grainger's scowl and glanced at Zara as if to express information he could not speak aloud. She might not know the details of what he referred to, but she understood enough.

The fate of the andi was a frequent political debate. In the Uppers, the rumors swirled about the andi currently in custody. In the Levs, it was common knowledge that the andi were often the scapegoat for the city's ills. This time was no different. Andi were always at risk.

"I want…" started Grainger.

"We'll stay with him until he wakes," Zara promised, thinking about the conversations she would need to have when she returned to Vapors. She laid a hand on the captain's shoulder and gently squeezed. "The doctor will come back when he's…"

"If you need me, or in a few hours. Remove the needle when the bag's empty, bandage the insertion point if it bleeds. I'll come back as soon as I can."

"So will I," Tox promised, hoping to sound reassuring. Her evasive eye movement and the quick zipping of her bag expressed her nervousness, a mood most understood. Grainger had been there. Grainger had seen her torture. Remaining in the room with him any longer than necessary was a torture of its own. "Take this stuff back, bring you the test unit you wanted."

Zara nodded. That was reason enough. She would not want to spend a minute in Tox's shoes.

Alone in the flat with the two men, after another squeeze on Oliver's shoulder only acknowledged by his bigger hand briefly covering hers, Zara busied herself by emptying the bowl of bloody water, cleaning it, and putting it away. She returned the sterilizing bottle of Zaolei to the cupboard, tossed the wet, stained towels into the laundry bin, and collected the medical gauze to be cleaned and sterilized and, eventually, repurposed for another injured soul. She sent a message to Skelter, requesting more Zaolei and another oxygen tank on Rhyd's behalf. She picked up discarded clothes, the handful of items Oliver had knocked to the floor, and put everything back where it belonged. She watched Oliver as she worked, as she brought a glass of water and a plate of seed crackers to the table in case he was hungry…the only food now left in Rhyd's cupboards…but she did not interrupt his brooding time with the wounded man.

If not for occasionally sensing his following gaze, it would have seemed he did not know she was there.

He tucked Jaron's curls behind his ear. He traced the unlit speecher at his temple, tapped it softly as if to rouse him, and pulled the blanket down enough to study the bruises across his ribs. His eyes traveled lower as he contemplated allowing the blanket to follow his gaze, but instead, he tucked it back around Jaron's shoulders, covered the arm with the fluid line as best he could, and finally, after squeezing Jaron's hand, sat back and let it go.

"I'm sorry. Shouldn't have let this happen. Should have found you sooner."

There was no way he could have. They both knew that.

There had been no clues to follow. No proof of any foul play except for his absence.

And Grainger had been so damn busy.

"I have something for you."

The spell between them was broken by Zara's voice. Oliver turned, not objecting to the distraction of the T1 she retrieved from the low table and repositioned on the dining table where she had put it during her movement around the flat. He looked at her, glanced reluctantly at Jaron as if wary to leave his side, but then rose with a stiff ache to sit beside her at the table.

"He saw him the day of the protest. Took time to dig through the Hub and Archives but…" She turned the screen toward him, waited as he studied it, then added, "Vanderwall."

His lips pursed. His eyes narrowed. "You sure?"

Though Zara shrugged to express a degree of uncertainty, she also replied, "He is…and I trust what he says." She opened the ICD footage captured by Scarecrow's bodycam, a dangerous thing to share with the bugorra captain, and placed the images side by side. If Oliver had been unsure before, as he examined the likenesses on the screen, he trusted Scarecrow's certainty now.

"Think he did this?" He motioned toward the sofa without taking his eyes from the screen.

"He believes so…" Zara nodded. "I do too."

If it was true, Vanderwall was a dead man. Jaron might no longer be an intimate part of his life, but Oliver still cared for him, more deeply than he thought he should. He would gut Vanderwall like a fish…if Scarecrow did not get to him first.

He assumed the sentence Scarecrow would mete out would be much worse.

"Can you send it to…?"

The double chirp in the room made him spin around, expecting to find Jaron in distress or awake, to see that the medication bag was empty or the delivery needle had pulled free. Jaron's eyes were still closed as he slept. The next chirp was more recognizable once the initial panic subsided, and he tapped the ICD with a perturbed expression as he glanced back at Zara.

"Grainger."

"Captain." It was Ilya's voice. He blinked, having forgotten the daily details of bugorra business the moment he entered this flat. "Need you to come up. We've got our suspect."

Though she did not know which suspect they had captured, the perpetrator of which crime, Zara's eyes lit hopefully.

Oliver, however, muttered under his breath. No suspect, no crime, could be more important than Jaron.

As though hearing his thoughts, without knowing where he was, Ilya continued, "Think we've got our assassin."

This time, he side-eyed Zara to assess if she understood what was being discussed. He would think it was obvious from Ilya's choice of words. Zara, however, appeared focused on transmitting the images of Vanderwall to Oliver's account. He saw no visible reaction.

This was good news. The best he had heard in days.

If only it turned out to be true.

"Soon as I can…I'm in the middle of something. Keep him cold, don't let anyone else talk to him. No visitors. When I can get away, I'll be there. Good work, Lieutenant."

He thought he could hear the smile on Ilya's face when she replied, "Yes, sir. Thank you, sir."

Cutting the call, he shifted on the chair to look at Jaron again. "I should stay…he should be…"

"He won't be alone, I swear it," Zara promised. "I'll be here as long as I have to be." Sooner or later, despite his disjointed emotional state, she believed Rhyd would be here too. Only then would she leave, until he needed her again.

It was not the fear of Jaron being alone that buoyed Oliver's hesitancy to leave. It was the aching desire to remain with the man he had failed in too many ways to count. The man he had not yet let go.

Zara sighed. Whatever she was to Oliver, whatever he was to her, it was not the same thing. So long as he pined for what had been, it would never be anything more than what it was.

Whatever that was.

"Go. I'll be here."

He kissed her mouth, tender hands on each side of her face, burying her melancholy with something of his own he could not name, and then released her to leave without looking back.

He did not look at Jaron.

He had the impression, with the closing of the flat door, that live or die, he would not see Jaron again.

❧Chapter 31❧

"Have you seen this man?"

Shifting gingerly in the plastic-covered chair to avoid contact with the soiled fabric underneath, Neoma leaned forward to stare at the image Kenneth displayed in the digital frame at the side of the prodcast, first in wide-eyed disbelief and then, as his false-bright voice droned, with narrowing scrutiny when the keywords of his dialogue began to puncture her thoughts.

She knew the man had been at the protests. He had not hidden that. It had been the reason he had fled to her for protection. He had already claimed he was a suspect in Haythem's assassination but had sworn his innocence. A small man with empty hands and empty pockets, he did not seem the type to assassinate a man so far above his station. Her choice to believe him, borne out of the expedience of mutual need, had eroded as her need for the services he could offer did. That attrition had not yet been enough to drive her out of this cold, filthy flat, not enough to risk returning to her own when she, too, was hunted. She had offered to protect him in exchange for shelter, in exchange for any other service she could conjure.

There were things she could not do alone.

But their arrangement no longer seemed beneficial.

As a Core survivor, this flat had been provided by the Nau for Molly's use. Somewhere in the Hub, in the Archives, Molly Netzer's name was attached to this address. A manhunt would eventually bring the buggers here. To her.

She would have to explain their relationship.

Haythem's death would be cast at her feet.

This haven was no longer safe.

It was time to go.

Her head came slowly up until her gaze pulled away from the screen. She glanced at the ICD. There was only one potentially good option. Only one place she might be able to anchor her trust.

Ignoring the too-prominent silence from the bedroom where Ulynda spent her hours, the message was sent. Her daughter might despise her, but Neoma had to protect the only link to a future she had.

In time, the girl would understand this was all for her own good.

꙰*꙰

"Think he's guilty?"

Grainger stared at the man behind the one-way glass where the merc had been hours before. The suspect's untidy, torn clothes, his mussed, greying hair, and the grime smeared over a handsome face and once well-manicured hands, were an odd juxtaposition against his dignified posture and nearly impassive face. Of the last three to sit in this chair, the merc had been the only one to exhibit any trace of suspect morals. Grainger was beginning to doubt his perceptions.

The intensity of this man's stare, as though he could see them through the glass, suggested purpose and confidence. A blood sample had been drawn, proving he was no andi, so maybe not in league with Borne, but Grainger could see why Ilya had difficulty determining the man's angle and state of mind without talking to him.

Grainger was having the same problem.

Ilya shook her head and shrugged simultaneously. "He's got a record…theft, disturbing the peace, public intoxication…but I don't know if there's motive. I haven't talked to him…"

Grainger grunted. "Think he did it?" he asked again.

"Senior Kal says…"

Again, Grainger snorted. He trusted the Senior's words only as far as they protected the man's self-interests. "What's the evidence? Weapons? Identification? Did he have anything? Say anything?"

"No," she admitted, the queries deflating some of her confidence and forcing her to exhale between her teeth, "But if you read…"

"No time for that now. Something else I need you to…"

"Sir," she scowled, reminding him of words he had said earlier. "We can't hold him indefinitely. If we're going to charge him…"

"We have time. He just got here. He's not going anywhere yet. See that he gets food and water, then meet me in my office."

Although Ilya nodded and muttered, "Yes, sir," before departing to see to the assignment, Grainger could see her annoyance in her quick, clipped steps. He expected the evidence against this streeter, with some claimed connection to Senior Kal, to amount to something that equally implicated Scarecrow, and as he nodded at the bugger guarding the interrogation room and returned to his office for the first time in hours, he wondered if there was any connection between the streeter and the Founder at all.

It did not seem plausible.

He needed a shower. He needed to conserve hot water. He needed a meal. He needed to save the power it would take to prepare anything to eat. He needed to talk to Tamner about Borne's results that still brewed on the bag burner, taking too long to get into his hands.

He settled for a shot of brandy when he sank into his desk chair, and for the hum of his Echo screen as he pulled up the information Zara had provided.

Real evidence, not rumor. Evidence Scarecrow had provided.

The empty glass was returned to the desk drawer before Ilya entered his office, her lids drooping wearily and her mouth and the corners of her eyes creased with frustration. Despite her limp, more pronounced in her exhaustion, her movements were as crisp and formal as usual. Without looking at the duty roster, he guessed she had been on the job as long as he had. He sighed and motioned for her to come around the desk to see the screen with him.

"I'm sending this to you. I want you to study it, find out everything you can about this man. His name. Where he lives. Where he works.

His history. His family. Anything in the Hubs, the Archives, we don't already know. Get this picture and any pertinent particulars to every officer in the Levs. Find this man."

"Think he's our killer?" she asked tersely, wary that his response would undermine her arrest of the man in holding. Perhaps this was why he was in no hurry to interrogate Folwell.

Grainger shook his head and pointed to the second image taken amidst that deadly protest. She would recognize the setting, the location, as she was seen in the shot. He hoped that seeing it would jog her memory, that she had seen this man on the scene as well. When he looked at her, her mouth had tightened into an even thinner line.

"Vanderwall," she muttered.

Grainger nodded. "So, you saw him."

Sucking in a breath, she shook her head. "Not without his mask, but we, Scarecrow and I, were pursuing him before the Founder…and later…Scarecrow gave me a name…"

The captain arched one eyebrow.

"It's running through the Hub. I haven't had the opportunity to find out if the search is complete…to read the results…"

"What's the name?"

"Uriah Frankle."

He did not know it, but nodded and leaned back in his chair. A face, a potential name. It was more than they had ever had to identify Vanderwall before.

It all came down to Ballard. To Scarecrow.

"See what you can find with this…get the word out."

Despite her elation at contributing something useful to the hunt for Vanderwall, she said tersely, "I will, Captain. Once we interrogate Mr. Folwell, I'll lead the hunt for Vanderwall myself."

"He's not going anywhere." Whether Folwell was guilty or not, the Founder was still dead. His potential assassin could wait. Getting Vanderwall off the street, after what he had done to Jaron and so many others, was, for Grainger, the bugorra's top priority. "Get researchers on this, get word out, then go home and get some sleep."

"Sir…"

"When was the last time you slept, Lieutenant? Went home?"

She frowned. "I…" She could not say how many hours she had been on duty, as they had bled together in her memory. It felt as if there were too many essential matters, too many details more important than going to an empty flat to find her sister, to dwell on Blayd's involvement, to dwell on the pain in her recovering knee.

"One of us needs to be on point at all times with these things, Lieutenant. We both need to be sharp. Eat something, get eight hours in, then we'll see what Mr. Folwell has to tell us. If we're lucky, maybe someone will have caught Vanderwall by the time you clock in."

"And you, sir? Are you going to take your own advice?"

Protest and denial died on his lips and were followed by a choking sound of defeat and resignation. "Got one more thing that needs addressing, then I'll take some downtime.

"Swear?"

"You're not the one giving…?"

"Someone needs to look out for you, sir. Hebenon needs you."

Beginning to believe less and less in those words, he nodded grimly. "Good night, lieutenant."

❧*❧

The raw evidence of pain drew Jaron near enough to awareness to assess his surroundings without the need to open his swollen lids. Muted voices streamed in a whisper somewhere behind his head, as if someone was reading aloud, the words too soft to identify despite his head-aching effort to do so. His face and one arm felt cool, exposed to the ambient temperature of the room, but the damp chill he recalled was replaced by the softness, the thickness of the well-used blanket that covered him from neck to feet. The weight of the fabric, a time-worn weaving of spun hemp, lay directly against his bare skin, announcing that the torn clothes he had worn had been removed, and beneath him, the lumpiness of the cushions supported the gradually building knowledge that he was no longer a captive.

His wrists were free.

The salve on his cracked lips tasted of mint as the tip of his tongue passed between them.

He remembered.

"Rhyd!"

The word was meant as an exclamation muttered as his eyes snapped open. But his muscles ignored the signal to move, his vision offered only narrow slivers of the room dimly illuminated from behind him. The force of the thought, broadcast through a speecher he recalled being too damaged to function, was loud enough to fill the central room of the flat, bleed into others he could not see, and draw hasty footsteps out of another room to his side.

"It's okay, Jaron. You're safe."

Not the hand he hoped for, but a welcome, comforting one that did not strike him or bring pain. After placing a pair of loose gray pants and a stretched-out black undershirt on the table beside him, Zara clasped his exposed hand and pushed his hair from his forehead, noting that it was no longer damp and that his skin was no longer warm with fever. With the general weakness of his condition, the exposure and injuries he had suffered, there was still a danger of complications, but for now, Jaron was as sound as a torture victim could be.

"Where's…?"

"He'll be back."

Rhyd had been absent for more than twelve hours, seeking whatever therapy Scarecrow's fists could offer. He was afraid for Jaron, afraid of himself, and angry enough at those fears and the man who had created them to prompt a renewed intensity in his hunting. Zara knew these things without being told. Sooner or later, he would come home, even if he had sought temporary rest in the Shed, in Tox's workshop, or slouched over a table in Vapors during his absence.

He would come home because he would need reassurance that Jaron had survived.

"Looking for him, isn't he?"

The production of lucid phrases was evidence that the deeper intracranial mechanics of the speecher had not been damaged, a concern that Tamner had expressed but was unqualified to address, particularly in the flat's less-then-sterile environment.

Again, Zara squeezed his hand, this time to assure herself too.

"Wouldn't be Rhyd if he didn't try…"

Rhyd's devotion to his self-assigned mission was part of what drew Jaron to him, but for once, he felt a flash of shared empathy for Venn in wanting Rhyd to set aside his vendetta-seeking and settle down. The medicated dripline attached to the fluid bag tugged as he brought his hand up to finger the repaired speecher unit at his throat, and his swollen eyes shifted towards the bag stand as though just realizing it was there.

"Helping you sleep, replacing fluids…helping you heal. It's safe. The plasts should have set by now, but you're gonna hurt for a while. Doctor Tamner recommends you stay off your feet for a day or two."

"Can't…I should've…I already missed…" Again, he wanted to rise, to sit, to do the things he believed he needed to do. Whether it was something in the drip bag or his muscles' wisdom in obeying the doctor's directive, his body refused to obey his wishes.

"I've taken care of the Archives. You're good…at least until the grid's restored. You have enough off-days accumulated you don't need to worry about it."

Was that the reason for the dim lights and barely audible system hums? He had thought something was wrong with his hearing, or that the sounds were muted to reduce the pressure and pain in his head. How long, he mused with a yawn, had the city been this way? How long had he been here? How long had Vanderwall held him captive?

Instead of asking, Jaron weakly nodded and settled into the security this room and the sensory reminders of Rhyd it offered. Rhyd had come for him. Had saved him. Rhyd was not here, but after the last words they had shared, those actions were comforting. Choking on the trembling emotion in the back of his dry throat, he murmured, "Tell him…come back…tell him…I need him to…"

Thankfully, his eyes closed and his breathing fell into the measured rhythm of deep sleep before Zara was forced to make a promise she could not keep.

Telling Rhyd that Jaron needed him was the surest way to prevent the man from coming home.

*

Eyes darting to the side, the prodcaster's voice still burrowing into his ears, Molly slid the passcard through the door lock. It answered with a beep more garbled than he was used to and the tiny green diode flickered and went dark. The door remained locked. He tried twice more, shoving against the door simultaneously and turning the latch each time before patting his pockets in the hope that, despite having no memory of doing so, he had picked up some other passcard somewhere and was using the wrong one. A handful of Hebbies, a hemp cig, packets of condiments collected to make his tinged meals palatable…but no other passcard was found. A fourth attempt to open the door produced the same results.

Pounding on the door with one fist, Molly glanced around to be sure no one could hear him before pleading, "Come on…lemme in.." as his focus shifted to the nearest unlit intersection. Maybe the brownouts meant that door locks were not working as they should.

Or maybe, he groused as he pulled the hood of his too-big jacket up to block his face from the owner of distant footsteps, those who were looking for him had changed the lock code or disabled his passcard to drive him into the streets.

They were looking for Mam too.

Perhaps the hunters had been here and now she was gone.

There were no sounds from within and the Echo was black. The mam and her girl could be asleep. Nanny too, but he was sure one of them would have heard his pounding, his plea, his effort to force the door open if they were here.

She needed him, too, after all. She would not have locked him out of his home.

She would not have the means.

It had to be the bugorra. They had come for her…or they had come for him and she had fled. Either way, Molly was exposed. He slid into the nearest alley, waited to see if he would be followed, and then left the flat with a pang of regret. The first place he had ever owned…lost.

Switz. He had to find Switz. Switz would hide him. They would beat the buggers together. They would clear their names.

They would never return to the Core, or any place like it, again.

❧*❧

The two men had known each other for years in the service of the Founder, the Doctet, the city. One had been born in the brightness of the Uppers' gilded white prosperity, the other in the Levs where he remained until his service to the Crows elevated him to prominence. Despite their origins, for the majority of their professional lives, they had crossed paths often enough to be familiar with the other's mannerisms, speech patterns, and points of view on many topics. They might not have considered the other a friend, but neither had held amity or grievances against the other.

The Coup had forced them into a closer working proximity, had meant that their paths crossed more often each day, producing added familiarity that permitted Grainger to identify the doctor's disquiet in the defensiveness of his posture. The crossing of his arms over his chest hid the nervous twitching of his hands and served as an emotive shield. His crossed ankles were drawn back so that his feet were beneath his chair as if he would fold in upon himself and disappear. His gaze focused somewhere to the side of the captain's face, on something on the wall, the empty air, or something Outside, and his shoulders shifted between thrust-back tension and stooped surrender before any word more than a greeting command to enter was uttered.

They were details Grainger had seen in the guilty, in the fearful, in those trying to hide something, or the bearers of bad news.

He could not recall seeing Tamner afraid. He had never seen him look guilty. Tamner was an honest man, as far as the captain knew, and so he attributed the evidence of his eyes to the promise of news he would not like. Hoping it was not bad news about Jaron, that the young man's health had not taken an unfortunate turn, Grainger paused to straighten his jacket as the door creaked and groaned as it closed.

Pulling a chair to the desk where Tamner sat, sitting beside him hoping the stance of equality would put the doctor at ease, he asked, "What've you got?" in the most passive tone he could muster.

"Evaluation's complete."

"Borne?"

Tamner nodded without looking at him. "There's no evidence his code's been overwritten or tampered with. He's got the same program he was initially given. They've done every diagnostic available. No evidence of a virus, mechanical defect, or failure."

"What does that mean? Aren't they constrained from…?"

One hand escaped the cross-armed shield to run back through his hair before he tucked it into place to speak again. "In theory, yes. They're given a base program, modified for whatever job they're to be given. Most get reset…reprogrammed, at least once in their lifespan. He never was. Maybe that's the problem…maybe he should have been reassigned and retrained. The AI coding…their ability to learn, to remember and adapt to their surroundings to serve better…"

"You saying he's developed a conscience? Is that it? Wouldn't a conscience keep him from killing anyone…"

"They don't believe killing was his intention. You talked to him. He's been exposed to…highly influenced by the Igraci in the flat next to his…prompting a desire to do something that might elicit an exodus from the city…the way Duncan originally intended. Turning off the power to encourage that was a logical means of doing it."

"So, they all have the capacity to be terrorists." Grainger's frown deepened, and it was his turn to cross his arms over his chest.

"We all do. What I'm saying is…like any of us…he…maybe all of them, if allowed enough time in one programming mode, appear to have the capacity to expand beyond their base…"

Grainger dropped his arms and leaned forward, his elbows on his knees. It did not matter why Borne had sabotaged the array, now that he knew it was no error, fault, or someone's intentional hacking. What mattered was what came next. "What do we do? How do we fix this?"

"It's not like counseling or punishment or…" Tamner began. "We wipe him…reprogram him…or…it isn't up to you or me."

The captain heard the strings of the doctor's conflict begin to ping.

Tamner continued more softly. "We need them. Sentience has the right to grow…but only the Nau can…"

The grimace on Grainger's face deepened as he imagined multiple scenarios the Nau could recommend, none of which, given the state of the city, would satisfy everyone or solve anything. If Hebenon evacuated, the andi could be utilized to keep the systems functioning until the city was safe and the citizens could return. But Tamner was right. Once the decision would have been made by a single man under the advisement, though not always in agreement with, the council that offered its varying views and suggestions.

Hebanthe Falls no longer operated on the whims of one. The Coup had demanded a more diverse voice. The Nau was several who worked as one. In moments such as this, Grainger was uncertain which method of governance would be best equipped to make this sort of choice.

At least when the Nau decided, their choice would not be blamed on him. It was his only solace and, it seemed, Tamner's as well.

"I'll take it up with them in the morning," the doctor said, sounding weary and defeated. "Wanted you to hear it first. Reprogramming's best I think but, whatever they do, if they decide to do anything, you'll be their instrument of implementation. You deserve to be ready for that."

Grainger stood. Perhaps he would not be kept clean of this after all, regardless of who made the decision.

Ulynda did not ask why she was forced to bundle the meager belongings she had been allowed to keep, did not ask where she was being dragged to this time by her mother's tight hold on her wrist. Her mother would not give her an answer or would respond with some trite, patronizing remark that would not be an answer. She struggled to keep up with Neoma's furious pace, grateful that Nanny bustled along behind to pick up anything dropped along the way and protect her from anyone who might come up behind them. Nanny did not ask questions either, did not speak, but her troubled expression suggested that she, too, thought Neoma was afraid of something.

It was that fear that drove their flight through the too-dark streets.

Ulynda hoped they were going home. She missed her bed, even if it was not as comfortable as her bed in the Uppers. She missed her toys and the comforts of familiarity she had learned to appreciate since being forced out of the white-walled world above.

By now, they had climbed enough stairs that Ulynda concluded that her second home was also a place of the past. If she was lucky, they were returning to the Uppers.

She did not believe in luck anymore.

Distracting herself from anxious questions by watching the doors and windows they passed, peering into alleys and side streets in the hopes of seeing Enoch, Scarecrow, or the Spinks there to rescue her from her mother's madness, Ulynda was the first to recognize the group of towering bird-masked figures wielding Crow confiscated weapons that marked the brako on the stairs a half-Lev above them. She tugged against her mother's hold to get the woman's attention, afraid to speak or draw focus to herself.

"Stop," Neoma scolded with a turned head that revealed the men descending the stairs with steps heavy enough to rattle the walkway. They were masked and thus should have been hers, but the stiffness of their approach bore a menace that made Neoma stop so abruptly that Ulynda ran into her. Though Neoma growled her annoyance, her gaze left the brako only long enough to hiss, "Back," to those behind her, and, with a shove, thrust Ulynda into Nanny's arms.

She would have to find another way.

"He wants to see you."

Forcing a tone of contempt and bravado, ignoring the threat in their demand, Neoma barked. "Good. I demand to speak to him too. Tell him to meet me at home. I demand to know the meaning of…"

Hands reached for her from the intersection.

"Mama!"

"You there. Stop!"

Faces turned toward the pair of buggers barreling out of the side street. Uncertain who the demand was directed toward, Neoma pushed Ulynda and Nanny at a run back along the street they had been following. The brako dispersed, some charging up the stairs while others fled along the third arm of the T intersection.

Prompted by her mother's pace, Ulynda did not look back. If they were being chased by the brako or the bugorra, she could no longer hear their shouts or footsteps. She only heard her mother's hard-soled shoes on the slick path, Nanny's heavy, panting breath, and her own pounding heart.

❧Chapter 32❧

Tamner left the meeting chamber to the sound of Andre Nunn's fist-pounding exclamation as the man tried to drive his point home with the side of his hand. "We should have terminated them decades ago. We don't need andi to…"

"But we do," started Caminda defensively.

"That might have been true before," Stace said over her retort, "but the Coup's impact has left too many positions unfilled…"

The glass at her lips did not mask Fahti's sour scowl nor muffle her muttered, "What if they started that? What if Scarecrow's one of them? It would explain…"

"Come on…you know he's not…"

Warren's disbelief was the final comment Tamner heard before the lift door shut the argument away. Once Hebenon had relied on andi for many of the less pleasant jobs, as supplemental staff in the ranks of shaft workers who kept the city at peak efficiency, and as hooks, dancers, and entertainers that neither suffered from the cold and damp nor from exhaustion. At the height of human population, there had been less need and the arguments for decommissioning them had begun, though many preferred to keep those they considered to be property or family. Each population decline after that, however, each need for the dangers of repair and expansion that required exposure to Outside, won the andi a stay, but each time their future came to a vote, the margin of support in their favor grew narrower. Weaker.

Thankfully, the andi had the Founders on their side.

The debate would rage for hours, perhaps days, a distraction from the slow progress made on the solar array repairs or hydro upgrades undertaken to boost their efficiency. Lash had promised schematics today. The Nau wanted an update, making the perfect excuse for Tamner to escape an argument he did not want to be part of.

The Nau was as frightened of the future as everyone else. Now they smelled synthetic blood in the water and, wanting someone to blame, to punish, they turned their fears to the andi.

Tamner believed that, if Lash failed to hold his promise, synthetic blood would be had. No amount of rational argument would save the andi this time if Lash failed to follow through.

He did not want to be part of their termination. He had argued for forced reprogramming as a compromise, but he did not know if the compromise would be accepted. What he did want now was to see his son. He wanted blue sky, non-circulated air, and good news from Lash before he returned to the Levs to check on Jaron's condition. For him, the choice of his future was already forged. It only required waiting for circumstances to permit it.

The sentries at the door nodded as he flashed his passcard and allowed him to go Outside. The door growled open.

Today would not be that day.

"Mam. Please…come in. Sit."

The young woman with the ash blond hair pulled away from her face with ivy-leaf clips put an encouraging hand on the woman's back and ushered her deeper into a spacious room littered with mismatched chairs and enough blue and green glowing alglamps to allow for a hint of warmth and welcome that Neoma had not expected to find from these people. Leaving Nanny to steer Ulynda toward one of the few sofas available, she made a slow circle of the room, clutching the bag she carried that contained a change of clothes and a collection of items she thought it best to keep close.

She barely listened to the woman talking to her. Instead, she assessed the other Talkers, their array of ages, their awkward smiles, and the wide-eyed respect of people who continued to believe in everything the Cult of the Founder stood for.

Neoma did not relish the company of fanatics, but for the moment, their support was necessary. In time, she might be able to mold them into a group she could tolerate and better utilize.

"We have eggs in the cool box…crackers and cheese and some milk. A crate of Wulfe's Head wine." Making note of Mam's glare, the young woman hastily continued, "We can try to get something else." Acquiring specific items was getting more difficult, but Neoma had few doubts that these eager, smiling things would do their best.

Kal and the Voices probably had an assortment of commodity stashes around the city. Whatever she wanted, these people would first try to get it from there. Stealing from Kal made asking for difficult and impossible items tempting.

"I need a new ICD…and a new T1 for her." She cocked her head toward the girl sleepily curled up on the sofa with her head on Nanny's lap. "Something that can't be traced." She had people to reach out to, and forcing her daughter to continue her schooling would be enough to keep the girl from getting underfoot. Having her and Ulynda log in from a Voices system might be enough to further implicate the Voices in the Founder's death. It was worth the risk.

She did not feel safe continuing to use their own devices. Molly had sworn that his tinkering made them untraceable, but Neoma no longer trusted his word.

Someone had sent the buggers after her. Someone had enabled the brako to find her.

Vanderwall had a lot to answer for.

"A change of clothes, too," Nanny interjected, hanging Ulynda's socks off the edge of the low table in front of them where one of the alglamps stood. "She's got some, but it isn't enough." She had no reason to trust so many Talkers, no experience that would support the claims of their innocence. But these people seemed friendly, better than that horrid little man who had provided them shelter, better than the brako Mam used to invite into the flat.

If Mam asked for something, these people seemed willing to get it. The luxury of clean clothes did not seem too much to ask for.

"Of course. Petey will take care of that, and I'll find some systems you can use. We've got eyes on the door, above and below, and Cyrus will stay in case you need…"

"We need to be left alone." So many attentive eyes might be meant as protection, but their presence also made Neoma feel as though she was a captive in this place. A prisoner in her own city. Ulynda deserved better. Ulynda needed to be out of the way, kept safe, while Neoma devised a new plan, but even she deserved something better than a prison. And Nanny…the woman was a necessary irritant she would have to endure for the foreseeable future.

Neoma had ideas, but none of them, yet, felt better than the others.

"Are you sure? You said the brako…"

"Better he stops them out there," Neoma shot an icy look at the one called Cyrus, "then wait until they get in here. They get inside, you're not doing your job."

The young woman flushed and bowed her head, motioning the other Talkers to the door. "Alright…you're right. He'll be outside with the others…and I'll be back soon as I have everything you need."

Neoma's response was a dismissive grunt and wave before the door closed after her retreating captors.

Captors. Saviors. It was all the same. Neoma hated being beholden to anyone.

❧*❧

"Here! Up here!"

Their short respite at one of the few vindis offering hot algtea, sizzling fish kabobs, and salted biscuits, was cut short by the arrival of a cluster of a half-dozen buggers. The vindi had been crowded, feeding the waxing and waning line of shift workers desperate for a warm meal they could not prepare in homes without power, people who paid little attention to the pair of men at a fringe table watching them come and go, neither speaking to each other nor anyone else.

The buggers fell into place at the end of the line, the conversation muted and vague to those in front of them who shuffled forward, or to the side, when their uniforms and bug-faced masks were noticed.

Molly saw them arrive. A kick beneath the table made Switz turn on his damp stool to look too, enough of a movement to make a few of the buggers notice them. They did not think they stood out. They were quiet, careful, and respectful of those around them. And though elbows and clipped words and a thumbed gesture in the two men's direction might mean nothing, Switz was not willing to take that chance. He scrambled hastily to his feet, tipping the stool, an action that pulled one curious bugger out of the line. Molly's mirroring abrupt rise drew another, and their quick retreat from the vindi, with glances over their shoulders, prompted others to pursue them as well.

Outside the vindi's perimeter, Switz began to run. Molly was right behind him. When Switz slid down a staircase rail and landed on his feet at the bottom, Molly's efforts resulted in a tumble to the platform at Switz's feet. Though Switz reached a hand back to help him up, the shouted commands to stop meant that he turned and dashed away before Molly could reach him.

Molly was fast enough to scramble to his feet and be away before the buggers reached the stairs, but he was bitter about being left.

Bugger masks meant the alleys and streets were not as dark for the officers as they were for their prey, but Switz took the risk of ducking into a littered alley of recycle bins and delivery crates, stumbling over each, until he reached the grated dead end that loomed unexpectedly out of the mist. The grate hung loose from its top hinge, its outer edge curled back as if someone had pried it open. Braced by a wide section of hemplastic pipe wedged between the top and the rattling platform, it looked safe enough to climb to the platform above that continued left and right a half-Lev between shuttered vindis and occupied flats.

Switz jumped, latched clawed fingers onto the grate, and braced his feet into the barely wide enough openings to climb to the top while Molly, having entered the same alley, hoisted himself out of the tripping clutter before the buggers emerged at the head of the alley.

"Help me!"

Switz hesitated. The gorra were coming fast. Soon they would be in popper range and Molly, if still in the alley, would be nabbed. He should run. He should leave Molly to karma.

Molly snarled as he continued the frenzied struggle to climb.

Muttering under his breath, knowing he would be exposed if Molly was caught, he extended his hand so Molly could clutch it and be pulled up. One heave and push, and both tumbled onto the platform.

"Come on," Switz grunted again.

He might have helped Molly out of the alley, but he did not help him to his feet, choosing to dodge the resounding ping of a popper shot instead.

Molly scrambled, swearing under his breath, ducking the shot, and followed.

When it came down to it, Switz would sell him out, regardless of their shared history. Just as he would do to Switz if circumstances required it. Shared history or not, they were both in this partnership for themselves.

Offers and promises to have each other's backs aside, he did not trust the smaller man, even if Molly believed in keeping to oaths made.

Switz, Molly knew, did not trust him either.

Shielding his eyes with one hand, wiping his other muddy one down the front of his nondescript blue-gray shirt, the sort that many shift workers wore every day of their lives, Jonner watched the pink and amber and dusky purples that painted the eastern sky as another dawn arrived in Marbordo. Sunset and sunrise awed and inspired him with an array of colors never witnessed in the city and never imagined in the Core. The parah were beginning to stir, their day's work in the fields of hemp, grain, squash, and beans about to get underway. The exterior lights of the factories were no longer lit, the conservation of power making the exterior lighting unnecessary, and the few wide windows that edged the dome were dark as the rooms behind the glass awaited the waking of those trapped inside.

But not for much longer.

He listened to the river's main tributary's rushing roar at his back and stomped the thickest mud off his boots. Thank the creator for the recent rain that left the spring fields muddy and difficult to traverse.

The work behind him was complete. Everything was in place. As long as the device functioned as he expected, the need for the centuries-old prison of metal, hemplastic, and glass would be no more.

It was almost time.

❧*❧

Unable to sleep once the nightmares of Jaron's screams propelled him out of his otherwise empty bed, Grainger came here, to three long tables strewn with scavenged relics from the raided warehouse, seeking a distraction to drive those imaginary sounds out of his head. The eight hours of sleep he demanded of his lieutenant and expected of himself had, after a shower, a meal scraped together from the dregs in his kitchen, and a glance through the daily logs he was remiss in following, been no more than four before the nightmares had come.

Four hours were better than none.

Being here was better than being alone to face restless, thrashing dream visions he did not want to have.

The Echo was absent, sent to the techs for a thorough evaluation, but he had already seen the preliminary report. Lifting an errant floral scarf from the collection and pressing it to his nose, he frowned. He knew that perfume.

It supported the trail of warehouse ownership he had previously found. But it did not make sense.

"Good morning, Captain."

He looked at the woman in the doorway and returned the scarf to its designated place on the table. His initial impulse to scold her for not taking the eight-hour ordered rest died in his throat as he motioned for her to join him. He could hardly hold her to a demand he, too, had been unable to satisfy.

"What do you see, Lieutenant? What does the evidence tell you?"

Ilya stopped beside him and scanned the table's contents before her gaze settled on a single, out-of-place shirt button. "I've read the reports…" she began.

He nodded for her to continue. The reports had just begun to come in an hour earlier. If she had already read them, she had been awake and on duty at least as long as he had.

"Someone was held there…"

"Someone?"

She shrugged. "DNA suggests Founder Kemway…and possibly one or two others." Blood evidence could have been planted by anyone who had access to it, but the blood on the manacles was consistent with the bruises she had seen on the Founder's forensic photographs. Combined with everything displayed here, in the ICD images taken of the crime scene, everything appeared neatly in order.

"There's no SCAM footage to place Mam Kemway on the scene or…" she traced a gloved hand over the bugorra uniforms folded near her, "Senior Kal. There's these…but no trace of unusual bugorra activity in the area. No signs of anyone."

Which meant that someone might have hacked the SCAMs.

"Spotty proof at best," Grainger nodded. Archive footage from every SCAM in the area from the moment of the Founder's abduction to the time of his assassination was being collected. No SCAMs pointed directly at that particular warehouse, however, and as frequently happened in the lowest Levs, there were periods of SCAM blackouts, times when mist or river spray obscured the sensors and lenses or caused a SCAM to go down. There were few reliable ways to determine whether a SCAM outage was deliberate without system techs combing the records. Many details of Lev 1's day-to-day movement did not exist.

It remained to be seen what the techs could tell them. Scratching his chin, Grainger wondered if Zara could create an algorithm to make such searches faster and more thorough.

"Is it hers?" Ilya gestured to the scarf.

"Could be, but it's not like her to be careless."

"And that?"

He glanced at the hemplastic rondure stamped with the Wulfe's Head logo he was flipping between his fingers, from one knuckle to another. Such a relic only meant that someone with a fine taste in wine had been in the warehouse. The Wulfes had a long history with the Voices of Faith. The Senior had a bottle of Wulfe's Head on his desk or the shelf behind it every time Grainger had been in the man's office. But that, too, was not evidence enough to warrant an arrest.

He shrugged and dropped the chip on the table as if his fidgeting had been no more than absent nervousness.

Ilya picked up the button and held it in her open palm. "I think this is the evidence we should focus on. The rest feels staged, but this…"

"Your source said it was staged," Grainger agreed.

The source. The recording that accused Blayd.

She nodded. "It matches the ones on the coat the merc wore when he was here." It was evidence enough for her. Blayd had been in that warehouse. She did not need further proof. "Should I bring him in?"

Grainger glanced at the time on his ICD. Tamner was due to report on the solar project, and he expected the Nau would have come up with an order regarding the future of their andi scapegoat and all others like him. Another few hours of combing through this evidence might allow the forensic teams to find more they could use, something more solid than their hunches.

"Think we have an interrogation to see to first, don't you?"

"Yes, sir," she nodded with a note of excitement. "I do."

❧*❧

The water-tight satchel clattered on the walkway as the fist connected with the side of his bird-masked head, a blow that pushed him sideways over the rail. Flexing her gloved hand, the other masked figure leaned forward to watch him fall, registering each crunching thump he made as he bounced and rolled between buildings and walks before finally coming to a heavy, soggy-sounding thud three Levs below. Heads popped out of windows and doors to watch him fall, greeting the body with shouts of surprise and alarm, but by the time they looked up to assess where the fall had originated and how it had happened, there was no one there to see.

It did not matter what was in the satchel, but she was sure it was something illegal, something expensive. Something she or Skelter could use. She snatched it up as she made a limping retreat, deciding it was time to go home. Despite the blow-absorbing body armor material and the hours she spent training, her body, after barely an hour of activity, ached in as many places as it had when she had been released from the Founder's torture experts.

How, she wondered as she climbed to the nearest rooftop and made her way toward the kesfek, did Scarecrow do this night after night for hours on end?

No wonder he drank so much.

❧*❧

"You ever come in through the door?"

Rhyd stopped, vent grate in his hands, analyzing the vitals of the weak man on the sofa through every sensor his body armor possessed. His heartbeat had seemed slow and shallow before the grate was opened, and so he had thought the other man was asleep. Now, as they looked at one another across the room, Jaron's heart beat at a weak but quickened pace as if he was trying to win an unexpected race. He was seated, slouched, his upper body bare to expose welts, contusions, and cuts that made Rhyd's chest ache. He had not expected him to be awake, not expected words to come out of the damaged speecher, but he knew he had been away from the flat longer than intended, long enough for Zara, Tox, and Tamner to have worked this miracle.

Returning to Jaron's suffering had seemed unbearable before.

Finding him awake, after the last words they had shared, was just as frightening.

The vent grate clattered out of his hand. Zara lifted her head from her arms, her bleary eyes revealing she had fallen asleep at the table. She was the first to speak so Rhyd would not have to answer the teasing, uncomfortable question.

"Good. You're back. Any luck?"

Freeing his head from his hood and mask, Rhyd shook out his damp hair and chose to look at her instead of Jaron. "Not enough. Didn't mean for you to have to stick around…"

"Someone had to."

Rhyd huffed and swallowed the initial annoyed snort. There was evidence that Tamner had been here and gone again, including two new oxygen tanks, and the scent of Tox's favorite soap lingered in the air. He might not have asked her to stay, but if he had returned to find Jaron alone, unprotected, she knew how perturbed he would have been. He had taken advantage of their assistance, especially Zara's.

It was not the first time.

There was another smell too, darker, heavier, that made Rhyd stiffen and scan the room as Zara took the mask from his hand and put it on the table where her head had been.

"Find him?" she asked.

"Getting closer."

Closer, as she helped him out of his body armor, was limited to a brako body count that they might or might not hear about on the daily prods if the Nau and Ximenezes deemed the news important enough to spend their daily limit of power on.

Rhyd could feel Jaron's gaze, undoubtedly assessing the new bruises against the old, as he stripped down to black shorts and socks drenched with sweat. The unexpected self-consciousness prompted him to pick up the discarded clothes and mutter, "Gonna clean up," still without meeting Jaron's gaze.

"I've gotta check in with Skelt; told him I would when I left. He'll be by again with takeaway later if he can find any…maybe whatever Maemi's got on hand."

"Don't need to," Rhyd said from the bathroom doorway.

"No, but Jaron needs to eat," she teased, smiling at the man on the sofa. "It's no trouble."

Whatever Scarecrow had been up to during those hours away, she was sure he had not stopped to eat. She guessed it was more important than her usual work, which could not be undertaken without power enough to operate multiple Echos. Being here with Jaron had given her something to do. Now it was time to leave Rhyd and Jaron to words that they were not likely to share as long as she remained in the flat.

⧽*⧼

"Ready as I can make it." Lash uncoupled the T1 from the primary computer and slid it across the folding table erected as his workstation Outside against Factory East's external wall, where the sun provided light for the majority of the day, and a power feed that had been created from the Factory allowed him to work uninterrupted. Watching the parah farmers, watching children play, or simply watching real clouds float across the sky had made his focus difficult at times, but knowing people depended on him kept Lash mostly on task. There were dark circles beneath his eyes, and his cheeks looked pinched and sunken. Though a cot had been set up here for his rest, Tamner suspected Lash had slept or eaten very little since being set to this task.

He likely felt the weight of Hebenon's survival as keenly as many others did.

"Let's hope it works." Tamner pocketed the T1 and snapped the pocket flap closed.

"Long as it's made to specs and installed right, it will."

"Want to do it?" Lash could operate the printers and assemble the components. But knowing how did not mean he wanted to.

Lash stretched. "Would be best if I did most of it…but I'm not fit to go up there…and I don't think they want me in their factories." Grainger, at least, would not trust him to both manufacture and install the new array himself. He only marginally trusted Lash to generate the drawings that the fire had consumed.

Lash did not know the details of the fire, of the sabotage, of component failure, of whatever had prompted his arrest and brought him here to address this project. But he knew his job, work he had performed until Kemway had taken his tongue as punishment for speaking out against his policies. He knew what it would take to get the array online before the hydros failed.

Tanner's ICD beeped. He glanced at the incoming message, noting the sender with a groan, and started to respond.

The sky roared. The ground bucked and trembled.

The walls of Hebenon shook.

❧*❧

Tox's hand slipped free of the rungs as the shaking thrust her backward. The satchel dropped. She dropped with it. The heavy rattle of its contents struck the rooftop first. She landed on top of it with a painful exhalation of breath.

The world went dark.

❧*❧

"You were going to leave me for them!" Molly shouted, shoving Switz backward…before the floor bucked and buckled and tossed both of them against the walls of the tiny public toilet where they had sought refuge.

Molly's head struck the door handle.

Switz's back cracked against the sink.

The receptacle broke free from the wall. The barely trickling flow of water seeped from the exposed pipe onto the floor.

☙*☙

One more set of stairs was all that stood between Enoch and the Uppers, his effort to climb this far repeatedly thwarted and slowed by buggers, brako brazen enough to come this high in the Levs, and the random cluster of Talkers who somehow seemed to recognize his face. Or thought they did. He had not seen his image aired on the prods but it could have come while he slept, or else some ICD image was circulating so that he could be found, detained, manipulated, killed, or twisted to someone's advantage.

To his memory, he had never been this high, except in the early hours of the Coup when the siren lure of Scarecrow's journey prompted him, Zara, and others to make the same journey. He had never walked the gilded white halls, had never enjoyed the light and warmth reserved for those some past Kemway had deemed more significant than others, important enough to lock away from the dismal, drab existence of the Levs. Those halls had been dangled before the population as a reward to keep them striving for a life most would never attain.

He had been born there, but regaining that life had never been one of Enoch's desires. He had never belonged there. He did not belong there now. But Outside felt to be the one place where he might escape the destiny the Talkers and others wanted to foist onto him.

To go Outside, he had to go through.

The stairs were there. The lift was there. Reaching either would take him to the door. He hoped his face, his name, his bloodline would be enough to grant him an escape. Enough to set him free.

☙392☙

For once, that name might provide something other than misery.

Or it would mean his arrest.

"Is that him? Is that the Founder?"

"Has to be…"

"Aldrich!"

Struck by the words of a cluster of unemployed men and women, people unable to seek refuge in bars, deks, or vindis, shocked by their recognition, Enoch hurried on, relieved that they at first returned to their gossip and complaints rather than chase him as the gorra and brako would have done.

He hugged close to the vindi walls; he watched for open doors where he could hide if he needed to. The thundering, jumping chatter of the walkway suggested a change of heart, a stampede on the cusp of following him that pitched him onto his hands and knees. Their screams of confusion and panic, however, revealed that rather than chasing him, they, too, were knocked off balance by the quaking.

Hoisting himself up by holding on to the nearest alglamp post, Enoch glanced around long enough to choose a clear path, long enough for the walkway to stop shimmying, and began to run.

❧*❧

He detected the shudder, the rumble, the quaking of the entire city in the briefest moment before it struck, in the moment before he was pitched forward, head into the mirror, the moment before Jaron yelped in distress from the flat's main room. Rhyd dropped the wet cloth in the sink and, without pulling a towel around his bare waist, charged into the short corridor between rooms.

"Jaron!"

The memory was there. His door blown open. Crows charging in, dragging Venn from their shared home. The crashing end of one life and the beginning of another. Not yet realizing the extent of the shaking, he expected to find the same sequence of events, his door ripped open with explosive force, men in beaked Crow masks dragging Jaron away.

But the door was closed. Jaron was pitched forward off the sofa across the table, his arms spread as if to brace his fall. Cupboard doors in the kitchen were flung open, the meager contents ejected onto the floor as if thrown. Other items were shaken askew or knocked from shelves in the wake of the quake, which had been much more than the breaking down of the flat door.

Jaron looked up, startled, questioning.

And then the world was still.

❧Chapter 33❧

Hebanthe Falls was silent.

For the first time since the walls were erected and the doors had closed humanity inside, the roar of the Five Falls ceased.

Not all at once, but gradually, over the handful of minutes it took for the last of the furious water to dribble to a trickling halt after the initial forced surge.

Metal stanchions creaked, a sound ever-present but always masked by the growling rush of water that helped keep Hebenon alive. Rivets popped, strained by the shaking. The weakest links gave way to the quaking assault, causing the ends of some walkways to drop, pulling some structures down with them, ripping open portions of the shafts that had not been open to the outside air in centuries.

Below Lev 1, the river ceased its rumbling race to the sea, taking the splash and crash with it, foundering fish and debris upon the exposed river bed as gravity bled the artery dry.

Mist rose towards the Uppers, gradually dissipating, clearing the air. The vestiges of moisture dripped from every surface or poured free from the pools that the shivering metal exposed. The echoes of the assault, the echoes of screams and shouts, the cries of terror and wonder, seeped into the drippage and were stolen away.

Hydros that had provided the city with an ongoing flow of electric power since Duncan Kemway's grand plan was set into motion whined and growled. Without the Falls, without the river, the extended screeching wail echoed through the walls of the nest as the mechanics of power ceased to operate with its last, dying gasp.

What light remained that had not been stolen by the damaged solar array, what light that did not emanate from alglamps and battery-generated sources blinked out.

From Lev 1 to the city's domed shell, Hebanthe Falls was black.

❧Chapter 34❧

The ground shook. The air shook. Tremors stretched east and west from the epicenter of the distant explosion so that Tamner was not the only person knocked off his feet when the shaking began. People screamed. Children cried. Animals fled the stronger shaking as if to escape it but there was nowhere to go until the earth stopped moving and the rumble in the air fell silent. Thankfully, that did not take long. He stood, wobbled as he reoriented himself, and turned his gaze to follow the pointing arms of those who indicated a plume of dirt and steam and what he thought looked like smoke that appeared to erupt from the earth into the pale, early morning sky. Some people ran towards that source while others, early risers, gathered at the nearest tributary's edge to fish and collect the day's water, screamed with flailing gesticulations and words that Tamner understood more fluently than others as his exposure to the parah grew.

"River's blocked," he muttered to the man beside him. The realization turned his attention immediately to Hebenon's doors as he listened to the shivering pop and strain of its metal skin against internal damage he could not see.

It was there, Creator help them, even if he could not see it. So were the majority of the population, trapped in the dark abyss.

The Nau would be in a panic. The captain and his bugorra would be thrown into chaos by the need to help the frightened and injured. The Factories appeared to retain power from their solar units, but that would not be enough to support the entire city.

He had to get Lash's plans into Nunn's hands. The efforts to manufacture the replacement components had to begin immediately.

The programming, the manufacturing, would be slow, but it could not wait. Every hour it took, Hebenon would die a little more.

"I gotta get in there."

"Cazz," Lash swore at the same time, releasing his hold on the Echo he had pinned down at the onset of the quake. "I'll get out there…see what's happened…see if we can fix it."

"Be careful." Whatever had happened, unblocking the river would probably be as dangerous as getting back inside Hebanthe Falls, both for those trying to clear the debris and those trying to salvage the hydros, which would have seized as the flow of water stopped.

Whether the rivers began to flow again or not, the water would find a way to the sea. In the water's path, Marbordo might be doomed. Without power, so was Hebenon.

❧*❧

"Screaming's not going to help," Neoma snapped at her daughter's frightened wail and sprint out of the bedroom. The frantic staccato banging on the door did not help. Nanny dashed out of the washroom, following behind Ulynda, caught the child with one arm, and pulled her towards the door, stumbling over tipped chairs, fallen lamps that refused to throw light without electricity, and an array of other items tossed about by the tremors. The shaking stopped as the Talker named Cyrus reached the door and threw it open.

So, too, had the familiar roar of the Five Falls.

For several heartbeats, no one made a sound. Only Nanny's panting, Ulynda's choking, frightened sobs, and the heavy panicked breathing of the others cut the silence.

"Are you hurt, Mam?" called one of the Talkers posted as a sentry outside the flat. Up and down the walk, on the Levs and half-Levs above and below them, people stumbled out of their homes, their businesses, seeking answers, seeking safety from walls that might no longer provide it. Echos that had continued to stream pleas for aid in catching an assassin, tidbits of direction to aid troubled citizens, and recommend relocation Outside were dark again, as was every light or machine not powered by generators or the long-cultivated fluorescent blue and green algae.

Sporadic as those alglamps were here, there was barely enough light to provide safe passage through the maze of walkways and stairs.

The lifts had stopped.

The stillness left by the absent roar was punctuated by drizzling drips and the usually masked creaking and echoing pops of their metal home. When Neoma pushed past the woman clutching her daughter and attempted to thrust past the Talker in the doorway, he refused to allow her to leave.

"Stay inside, Mam; it's not safe."

"No more dangerous than in here."

"Safer not to panic, to stay put until we know what's…"

"It's obvious!" Neoma swept her arms wildly about, gesturing to the silent city before dropping them to tap frantically on the ICD on her wrist. The screen indicated her message had been sent, but there was no guarantee it would be received before the Hub, too, went down.

It had to be down. Any power remaining, fed from the factories or battery systems kept on standby for brief outages, would be routed to medical facilities and any other resources the Nau deemed crucial. Factory power to the Levs would be cut.

Once, that would have been the entirety of the Uppers.

Now, Neoma did not know what the priorities would be. With water no longer falling as it had all their lives, even those backup systems would not last.

"Stay here. We'll find out…" Cyrus ordered.

"I'm going up. Ulynda, get your shoes. Get your things."

"Mam, it isn't…"

She thrust her finger into the man's chest. "You'll lead us up or stay here. I won't stay. I have somewhere I need to be. Lead the way or get out of it."

The Talkers looked at one another and at Nanny and the child who had yet to obey her mother's demands. After a nod to Nanny and a sigh of surrender, one of the Talkers handed over a battery torch so the woman could steer Ulynda to her room to get her belongings.

Nothing had been unpacked. They had not been here long enough.

"Five minutes." To his companions, Cyrus said, "Get the others; we're gonna need them."

The brako, those not trapped or injured by the quake, would be out in force, using the enhanced vision of their Crow masks to take advantage of the situation. The Mam would not be the only one scrambling for refuge. She and her daughter would need protection to reach the Uppers unscathed.

❧*❧

The one-way glass continued its shimmying rumble for several seconds after the tremor ceased beneath their feet. Ilya clung to the edge of the table, but Grainger, who had just entered the room, was thrown against the door he had just closed. The man on the other side of the table pitched forward, striking his head against its smooth surface. With his hands bound by the manacles, he was unable to wipe away the trickle of blood that meandered toward the corner of his eye from the fresh gash across his forehead. Ilya pushed her chair back to help the captain to his feet, but he brushed away the assistance with a snort. "We need to find out what's happening?"

"What about him?" She gestured to the man they had come to interrogate as Grainger pulled her from the room. Rather than risk being overheard, possibly instilling more fear and confusion, he closed the door again, rubbed the back of his throbbing shoulder, and adjusted his stance so that the ache in his leg was less pronounced.

The officer on watch was not there.

Behind the door, the prisoner frowned and fidgeted with the cuffs that bound him.

The corridor glowed with the same emergency illumination that had operated for days. There was no hint, from where they stood, that anything was any more wrong than it had been, but the nature of the quake and the peculiar silence of the comms that should have been screeching with damage and injury reports and requests for assistance was worrisome.

A glance at her ICD indicated there was no Hub connection.

The manual door lock clicked into place. Without power, it was going to be difficult to open again.

"Whatever the cazz this is, they're gonna need us out there. Send him some medi-attention if they can get in, get that wound cleaned up. Check in, see what needs to be done…let me know. I'll talk to Tamner, the Nau, see what they know."

Folwell's prolonged incarceration could not be helped. If this was an emergency, he was safest where he was. If this turned out to be no more than one of the tremors that periodically rocked the city, waiting a few more hours for interrogation would not hurt anything.

He needed to check in with Jaron, with Zara, and assumed Ilya would want to check on her sister. Such needs among so many, would have to wait.

"Keep me updated…use your best judgment. Meet me back here in six hours."

Ilya, rubbing the throbbing knee she had banged on the table as she stood up, nodded, "Yes, sir." Six hours seemed excessive, but he was right. Duty was duty, and getting into the Levs was going to take a long time.

Interrogation would have to wait.

❧*❦

"I'm here. I'm okay."

Though thrown from the sofa when the flat tossed every unsecured object to the floor, Jaron felt no additional injury or pain as he elbowed into a sitting position and clutched his aching ribs. Beyond the existing pain, the only thing he felt was heart-pounding shock and the hands that unexpectedly cupped his face out of the darkness. Hands that abruptly pulled him into a crushing embrace of reassurance and relief that he did not resist.

"I'm okay. I'm okay," he murmured, the words muffled and distorted by the speecher at his throat covered by Rhyd's damp, bare skin. He hesitantly returned the hug, worried that doing so would compel Rhyd to retreat, but instead, the effort prompted a tighter hold as days of bottled fear gave way to uncorked release.

He could smell Rhyd's favorite soap in the droplets that trickled down his neck. He gulped in the clean skin and wet hair smells he had missed and clung to throughout his captivity. Rhyd's muscles were hard beneath Jaron's fingers, the rapid rise and fall of his chest mimicking his anxious heartbeat. Whether Jaron had experienced these things before or not, it felt like the first time, and he squeezed shut his swollen eyes to shut out every external stimulus, to bask in this moment for however long it lasted.

Instead of saying more, Jaron pursed his lips to prevent impulsive words from spilling out.

He could have said it then.

He believed he was wise enough not to.

Rhyd listened to Jaron's uneasy breathing, felt the shifting of cracked bones mending beneath the still-setting plasts. He absorbed the texture of Jaron's hair beneath his fingers as they tangled in the dark curls. He listened to the slight squeaking of his wet skin sliding across dryer skin. Jaron's skin. His breath caught, too, and he squeezed his eyes shut against the overpowering compulsions that warred within, the need to stay where he was, the need to kiss the man he had believed lost, the need to speak of emotions he had never imagined he would feel or be able to voice again.

The muted tones of the room, the loss of every familiar hum, water gurgle, air hiss that had been an everyday reality, provided something to focus on that prevented him from saying what he was sure he would regret. He listened to the external, focused on what he expected to hear but did not, the straining system sounds that spoke of impending, catastrophic system failures, without pulling out of that comforting embrace. He was content, for the moment, to share himself with the man who seemed to need Rhyd as much as Rhyd needed him.

That external focus, however, was eventually noticed and Jaron reluctantly eased back enough to press their foreheads together so that he could look into Rhyd's whiskey-brown eyes. Before Jaron could order his disorganized thoughts into words, Rhyd sighed and murmured, "You shouldn't be here…you need to go Out…"

Jaron shook his head, creating a tingle of electrifying friction between their skin. "I'm not going anywhere."

"Jaron…" Rhyd pulled back and wiped Jaron's hair away from his face. "Whatever's going on out there…they need me."

"I need you."

Rhyd swallowed hard to abort his first impulsive words and said, "I can't protect you . Not until I stop him…and I can't do that if I'm worried about you. From what I can hear," he gestured toward the shaft with one hand and the world outside the flat where the roar of the Falls had ceased with the other, "there's gonna be no lights…no water…no heat…"

The pair of gestures meant that his hands left Jaron's body, and the younger man pursed his lips to hide the frown that tried to settle on his face. Without the crash of the Five Falls, a noticeable lack he became aware of now that there was no distracting physical contact between them, there was no telling how long Hebenon could survive. Without knowing the damage the quake had caused, there was no telling if the city even could.

"You need to heal…and I need to end this. There are people out there who will…"

Jaron shook his head, grasped Rhyd's wrists, and held them with gentle firmness. "I can't just leave you to…"

The plea in his voice, in his eyes, was enough to break the spell of shared intimacy and force Rhyd to retreat from Jaron, from himself. He picked up the first piece of undergarment he found, realizing his nudity then and his body's response to Jaron in his arms, and then hurriedly scavenged around the room for the rest, for the pieces of body armor he needed to protect himself from every threat, everyone.

Jaron included.

"I'll find Skelt, Zara, Tox…they'll get you out. When it's done, when it's safe…when the power's restored…but not before. I can't worry about you and do this. Promise me…"

One by one, the pieces of armor were drawn on, the shield he relied on to face the world. Jaron watched as Rhyd disappeared and Scarecrow took his place, but he did not speak until Rhyd began again.

"Promise me you'll stay right here until they come. Don't let anyone else in…don't leave…until one of them comes."

The plea to stay was a far cry from the previous command to leave. Jaron sighed, scowling, but neither nodded nor shook his head. "I'll stay here," he promised, the only assurance Rhyd would get. Outside this flat, he was a target, particularly if he went out alone. He was in no condition to fight, to protect himself, or to resist Rhyd's plea. Remaining in this flat was the only place he wanted to be. If he stayed, refused to go with Skelter or someone else, sooner or later, Rhyd would come back to him.

He could claim that his injuries, that physical weakness, prevented him from going up when Rhyd found him here. He could feign exhaustion or a relapse. He did not intend to go anywhere without Rhyd ever again.

Rhyd hesitated, his mask not yet in place, and turned his face towards Jaron in the hopes of dismissing the irrational feeling his interpretation of the man's tone inspired. Deciding his assumption was just that, irrational, he nodded, fastened the mask and hood, and pulled on one glove.

His bare hand hovered over Jaron's head as the internal battle waged, and then with a groan, he gave in to the urge to place it against the man's black curls. "Please, Jaron; be safe. I won't…I don't want…I cannot lose you again."

It was the only admission Jaron was going to get.

It was enough.

"You won't," Jaron promised. "Be careful…and thank you."

Rhyd nodded. The vent grate opened. Jaron closed his eyes. The grate closed.

Rhyd and Scarecrow were gone.

❧*❧

The combined effort of people inside and outside of the barrier finally pried the door open to reveal a darkness that Tamner had both expected and feared to see. Wet and bedraggled, with an expression of wide-eyed confusion, Enoch grabbed the doctor's hand and allowed himself to be pulled into the morning light as those inside continued to push the doors open further, allowing more light to get in.

"Enoch?"

Squinting, one hand raised to shield his eyes, Enoch croaked, "Doctor? What…?"

Tamner cut off the expected question with a gesture into the distance, an unnecessary one as it appeared that the majority of the parah were running north toward the river's edge.

Most of the dust cloud had dissipated in the morning breeze. "See if you can help. I gotta get to the Nau."

He might have been talking to the uniformed people at the door who blinked at the brightness of Outside and stared at the man the doctor had exposed. Or he might have been directing Enoch. The dwarf, noting the swarm, deciding that Tamner was speaking to all of them, began to run in the same direction. Tamner elbowed past the sentries and pushed into the city as they, torn in two directions, either remained at the door or chose to follow the revealed Kemway heir.

❧CHAPTER 35❧

Panting, Enoch stumbled and doubled forward with his hands on his knees when he finally reached the banks of the empty bed where the river branched into the separate flows that created the Five Falls into which Hebanthe Falls had been built. Older parah and children scrambled through the mud, scooping up stranded fish, while others gathered, shouting and pointing at the place where the edge of the plateau flanking the western bank had collapsed into the path of the water. The chasm banks behind the obstruction were growing fuller, the level swiftly reaching the point where it would spill over into what had once been its own tributary and flood the now fertile northern fields. Eventually, parts of the village might also flood as the water sought a new, low-lying path to the sea.

Parah were already hard at work to create a wall between their homes and the threatening water.

"What happened?" Enoch sniffed the air, the settling dust and moisture, trying to identify something but failing to put a name to it.

"I was coming to fish and it just…the earth shook and…" Jonner stammered, kicking aside the pole and spear at his feet and laying a hand on Enoch's shoulder as if to keep him upright.

With the way the river was slowly eroding the plateau, such a collapse was inevitable. Aided by the quake, the failure would have occurred on its own. Once destabilized, any shaking of the earth would have hastened a collapsing slide. If this had happened during the final days of Haythem's rule, the people of the city would have been trapped in darkness. The timing of the disaster, with solar power not yet restored, would have the same result if they did not react quickly.

"Has happened before…long ago…but never like this," an older parah said, a man bent with age who would be of little use in the building of the manmade dam. Slides from the plateau had pushed the river east in times past and had cut off what had once been a sixth tributary in the months when Hebanthe Falls was being built. There were mentions of that in Hebenon's history books, and a study of the landscape revealed the evidence. The violence of this slide, and its location, had created enough damage to cut off all five remaining tributaries. Even as they accepted the inevitability of such an event, the parah appeared, in their mortified scrambling, to find it unusual.

"We could dig it," offered someone.

"No!" Heads turned toward Jonner's adamant exclamation. "I mean," he stammered, "clearing the collapse is one thing. But if it isn't done right, when the water pushes through…people down there are going to die." He pointed towards the city where the water's path should have flowed.

"People are going to die when those banks are breached," countered Venn from the midst of the gaggle with whom he had just arrived. He was no engineer, was barely a farmer, but he could see the inevitable, the same as everyone else could. He just happened to be the one to voice the obvious. "We have to protect the village and the crops and…"

"…and too much at once is going to wreck the hydros," Jonner continued, ignoring the voices of contention, "if they aren't froze up and wrecked already. We can do this…but we gotta do it right."

"And fast," said someone else. People followed her pointing arm to watch the parah hard at work to protect their homes.

Enoch continued to scan the rock and mud collapse, noting places where the water was trying to trickle through, where the earth seemed softest, more mud than rock. He nodded as he pushed up his sleeves, his breathing even enough to undertake whatever effort was required. "Tell us what to do," he said to the elderly parah, putting more stock in the parah's knowledge of his village, the river, the land, than in

Jonner's professed engineering knowledge. There were people inside depending on them, people he cared about who would die if Enoch did nothing. People out here who might as well. This was no time for him to lean on a claim of entitlement or a lack of ability, no time to resist involvement in something bigger than himself. It was time to act.

"Do what they're doing," the old man said.

Jonner grunted, nodded, and gave one last long look at the collapse before following the parah with a determined huff. There were things they could do to get the tributaries flowing again, but the longer they were distracted by the work of protecting Marbordo, the more likely it was that those within Hebenon would be forced out. The plan was working as he had intended…although he admitted to himself, as someone thrust a shovel into his hands, that he had failed to take the threat to the parah sufficiently into account.

❧*❧

"We have a problem…" Tamner began, sinking into the empty chair nearest the door that the Nau most often left empty for him. Though concerned about the ICD message that continued to rattle at the back of his thoughts, the Nau and Hebenon's future needed to be addressed first.

"Of course we do! They did this! We must arrest every one of them and take them offline!" Fahti exclaimed as Tamner reached for a water glass. Once they discovered that the doors would not open without manual force, once they saw that the corridor was as dark as the room, they chose to stay put. The alglamps Tamner carried in each hand provided light for them to see by, and Lyden, who was closest to him, snatched one and took it to the other end of the table where he had been seated.

"The andi didn't do this," Tamner began, passing the other lamp to Warren so that, with light at both ends of the meeting table, they could see each other to allow a normal conversation. The light was enough to enable some to relax, enough for them to appear to forget the quake and resume their debates as if nothing else had happened. "River's been…"

"They're not out there," Stace reminded the woman beside him.

"We don't know that," Pearl chattered, wringing her hands.

"Doesn't matter." Fahti glowered at Tamner and grunted. "It has to be done."

"No, it doesn't. We're going to need them to…" hissed Stace, glowering back at her, his eyes narrowed in challenge. From their expressions, Tamner gauged that Warren and Stace were the primary holdout votes pushing back against Pearl, Lydon, and Fahti. The remaining four were undecided, knowing the andi had their uses, seeing both the advantage of workers who neither needed to sleep nor eat and could not be injured or die in the traditional human sense…and the threats such individuals might pose for those very same reasons. There were a few hundred andi remaining in the city at most. The primary reason they might prove a threat was that they could be anyone. A friend, a neighbor, a coworker. No one would ever necessarily know. If andi were developing beyond their original programming, what did that mean for the unsuspecting population?

With the state of things, did that even matter?

Tamner considered joining forces with Grainger and the bugorra to stand against the impending, seemingly inevitable decision the Nau would make. Taking a page from the Founder's old playbook was the only way to take action against the governing body.

He did not want to do that.

At least, for the moment, the andi question appeared to have reached a stalemate. He hoped he could get a word in about the city's newest problem. "I need you to listen…"

"But we have decided," Nunn added, turning his pointed gaze at Tamner, cutting him off, "all of the miscreants from the Core are to be brought in and…"

"The Core?" Tamner blinked, confused by the body's abrupt shift in focus and annoyed by being cut off again.

"One of them's responsible for assassinating the Founder."

"Might be responsible," Warren interjected with a wagging finger at Pearl, adjusting the collar of his shirt as the temperature in the stifling room continued to rise.

"We don't know what they want," Lydon explained. "They were in there for a long time…criminals…for a reason. Could have been plotting this all along. If they're involved…if they're the cause…even one of them…we need to bring them in for questioning…find out what they know…who knows what."

"It can't be all of them. They weren't all murderers going in." Stace crossed his arms and looked around the table, daring anyone to challenge the well-known truth of the Kemway law, Vanishing anyone who disagreed with him, even though those arrests might be enough incentive to cause someone to long for the Founder's death. "We can't make a mass arrest. It'll make us no better than…"

"Doesn't matter what anyone knows…we know enough. One of them killed…"

"There's no evidence, Andre," Warren snapped.

Tamner sighed. There were too many changes in Hebenon in too short a time, many of them life-threatening, and if he did not intervene, these debates would last for hours.

"We have a bigger problem. We need power." He handed the T1 Lash had provided to Nunn. "Those'll get the array up if you can configure the printers to…"

"Of course I can," Nunn remarked contemptuously as he accepted the Echo and swiped his finger over the images and code on the screen.

Irritated by being cut off again, Tamner growled. "Then you'd better get on it. You've seen that," he pointed into the dark corridor. "Gotta be like that all over the city. River's dammed up. Falls are dry. The hydros aren't running. They're out there working on…"

"The hydros aren't…?" started Warren.

"The falls aren't…?" squeaked Delora.

Tamner waved his hand to silence them. "Quake blocked the rivers. That's what I came in to tell you if you stopped to listen." He did not allow any of them the chance to apologize or speak in their defense. "Not going to be any power for anything…except in the Factories, until we get them back on…until the array's repaired. Batteries will only last so long…if we don't evacuate the clinics and get everyone Outside…"

Caminda looked pale. "Evacuate the city? We'll have a riot. Aren't we already…?"

"Evacuation's been voluntary," Delora reminded her before looking at Tamner. "We don't have the resources to…"

"Without reliable power, there's no choice. I wager a lot are already on their way up…scared, panicked people wanting an escape."

"It'll be a damned stampede," Woster muttered.

"There'll be trouble Outside if we dump everyone at once," Fahti reminded him as if that was reason enough to prevent an evacuation from happening.

"We do our best to keep people segregated…expand the camp like we're already doing…"

Lydon side-eyed Warren. "Gonna need more land. Gonna be harder to segregate everyone…there'll be trouble."

"I'll deal with the parah," promised Tamner. There was already trouble. Expecting high emotions, fear, and tension, he knew there would be volatile incidents and distrust. But there was no other choice.

"What about the Hub?" Lydon asked. "The Archives? We can't lose those…"

"How do we get everyone out without lights?" interacted Woster.

Delora spread her hands on the table. "We evacuate the clinics to the under-Factories. Move Hub and Archive systems there too." There would be an inevitable loss of data from the periods during the blackouts and data might be lost during the move. There would be unrecorded history as the Archives were taken offline and relocated.

But the people to operate those systems would have to be funneled out of the city, too.

They were unavoidable losses.

"Without the lifts, we'll never…" Fahti began.

"There's no choice but to try," Warren interrupted, reiterating Tamner's earlier words. "Bugorra can direct evacuations if we set up emigration checks…move food production and…"

Stace shook his head. "Food's the last of our worries." He oversaw the city's food production and fretted about the lost resources, but he was clear-headed enough to realize that there was an entire world of food outside Hebenon's shell. They would need to learn to grow and cultivate it, but the resource was already there. "We take out the seeds, the animals, and make due."

"Barebones," Tamner agreed. "See to what's needed, to your families. Warren, Woster, inspect the systems, see what you can do for lights with what we've got. See to the systems' integrity…how badly the quake hit us…what can be repaired and prepped for power restoration. Delora, Lydon, see to the Hub and Archives; coordinate the evacuation of all patients and medical personnel. Get communication working for the buggers and see that Ken and Soleia…even Vittorio…get the word out of an ordered evacuation. We want to avoid as much panic as possible. Caminda, you and I will coordinate the emigration process."

Finally, relieved to have gotten the Nau on task even if it meant he had needed to take the reins of leadership to steer them, he sighed and looked back and forth between Nunn and Fahti. "It's up to you two to get those parts and panels made, installed, and online…to accommodate whatever changes are needed in the Factories to make it happen…and to make plans for the medical staff. Pearl, lend them a hand. The sooner we get the parts made and installed, the sooner we can get the city back to normal."

Lydon met his gaze with unsettled eyes. "Think there'll be anything normal after this? Anything to come back to?"

Rather than share his earlier assessment of their situation and voice his concerns, Tamner muttered. "We survived the Collapse, found refuge in here. We can do this. We have to believe it if we want everyone else to. There's only a chance to survive if we get out and do something…and make everyone believe they can do something too."

"And the andi," Fahti reminded him tenaciously. "We will make a decision when this is over. When you talk to the captain, remember the andi and the Core survivors. We can't let them…"

"This isn't the time," hissed Warren.

Over those words, Stace added, "If we're doing this, questioning anyone suspicious on their way out, then it's time we get Senior Kal in for an interview. The Talkers have a lot to answer for."

Most of the heads around the table bobbed in agreement, the first time in Hebenon's history that the governing body seemed prepared to stand united against the Cult of the Founder. Tamner had no idea what dialogue had led them to that position, nor did he want to know.

All three matters, as far as he was concerned, were the least of Hebanthe Falls' worries. They could not spare their meager resources to address those issues. But he nodded grimly and followed the others, two groups carrying the alglamps, out of the meeting room. Without the Hub, without comms and ICDs, tracking the Core residents, the andi, and even Kal, was going to be nearly impossible.

That, he believed, was a good thing. Better that the Nau kept their focus on getting their people to safety and restoring power. The future of the andi and the people from the Core would take care of itself.

Senior Kal and the Talkers were something else. As were Neoma and Ulynda Kemway.

*

That was his signal.

Eido had said he would know it when he saw it, when it happened.

This had to be it.

While not an educated man, Colyx knew he would recognize the right points when he saw them, the places the shaking had weakened, the vulnerable places that would require only a small force to break them free of their joints. As he passed those seeking the nearest accessible paths up and out of the darkness, people choosing to take evacuation seriously now that the falls and the river had stopped flowing, led by the bobbing fireflies of alglamps and battery torches or the remaining charge in portable Echoes, it reinforced his certainty that this was the time for action.

It would take time to set the parts in place. It would take time for people to migrate out of the prison Hebenon had been for too long. They had a fresh, clean world now, where his grandchild could be born, grow, and thrive beneath the sun instead of here in the gloom. Otta deserved it. Skelter deserved it. The unborn babe certainly did.

If Colyx could do one good and meaningful thing with his wasted life, this would be it.

He had the supplies. He had assembled what he needed. The rest, he thought with a scowl of determination as he bumped past another scar-faced, sour-expressioned, burly man he thought was surely brako despite not wearing a mask to prove it, was up to him.

❧*❧

He hurt. Too much, everywhere. The medics who had treated him reported fractures, internal bleeding, burns, and possible brain damage. But he had lived. He could sit up and he could walk. The fractures had been plasted, the internal bleeding repaired, and though it was too soon to tell the full extent of the damage the head trauma had caused, he was alive.

Not that Vanderwall had come to check on him after the shove that sent him over one of the Levs' many railings.

Not that any of them had.

He heard about the mandatory evacuation and was aware of the preparations to move the most critical patients to a temporary staging area in one of the Factories. It was his best opportunity to act. Against medical advice, he scooped up a bottle of pain meds from the bedside stand, staggered out of the clinic when the staff was otherwise occupied, looked up and down the path before him, and staggered off to the right, clutching his ribs, wheezing with each labored breath that squeezed out around bones that would need time to fully heal, and decided on his course of action. If his fellow brako wanted him, they might come looking for him here, to silence him or drag him back into the thick of things where he did not want to be. They had not come for him yet, but if they wanted him and thought he lived, they would look in all his usual haunts, so those were out of the question. Vanderwall was like that after all, knowing where his people lived, knowing who they loved, knowing their weaknesses.

But anyone he had loved was gone, taken during the Coup. His second family had become the brako he associated with. Though Vanderwall might interrogate his cohorts to find him, he typically did not care if his minions lived or died…they were expendable pawns for wealth and power.

He was tired of that life; near-death had erased the wish to go back.

A word on the prods, more talk about the ominous evacuation provided his answer. Outside. Outside was his best chance to avoid Vanderwall or anyone else he knew. By the time he lay low for a few days, allowing time to heal more, the doors would still be open and he could find his way out. Vanderwall would never think to look for him there, if he looked for him at all.

For all of his bravado, Outside was one thing Vanderwall feared.

Outside was the one place anyone wanting to escape the brako could go to be free.

❧*❧

The hand that closed on his shoulder as Zeb and Rabia Faure hurried frantically away, their concerns either neglected or soothed, caused Tamner's heart to pound as he spun to face the shadow of a man towering over him in this dimly lit section of the corridor, a primary thoroughfare through the Uppers where residents of influence jostled in their haste to verify the safety of their loved ones. Work crews banged and pried at the hydraulic doors at the end of the hall, working to open this one and each of the others in the Uppers, probably in the Levs as well, to free anyone trapped inside or to open the stairwells for those who now needed them.

He did not think the Nau's message to the city had been prodcasted yet. There had not been enough time to generate it or route the power to the prod point to send it out. Yet it seemed that the Nau were not the only people to sense the wisdom of seeking immediate passage Outside. The lines forming here would continue to grow, the pushing and shoving continue, with fights breaking out as tempers rose. The chaos was building at every Lev intersection, at every exterior door out of Hebanthe Falls; without checkpoints and crowd control, soon there would be another type of disaster.

Finding Grainger was a relief, even if the hand on his shoulder had startled him.

"Just who I'm looking for."

Grainger's frown did not change. "What's going on? The hydros?" The two officers with him tried to redirect the flow of people past them as the captain and doctor talked.

"Quake collapsed a landslide across the river; dam's not letting water through. The parah…Lash and others…they're working on it, but it'll take time."

"He's supposed to be…" Grainger started to huff.

"Plans are in Nunn's hands. He's coordinating manufacture…but it will take time too."

Looking as though he wanted to punch something, the captain growled, "Why didn't this happen when the Founder was still…?"

Tamner shrugged, sympathizing with the frustrated sentiment. "Nothing to do with leadership. Natural disasters never do. Nau's issuing an evacuation notice…"

"Looks like they already did." A dozen people, a family with their arms loaded with personal belongings, pushed past, ignoring the men there. "Gonna need crowd control, especially at the doors and stairs."

"Hoping you could help with that." His passage through the Uppers to get information, through the flow of people seeping with pushes and shoves and hurried steps toward the nearest Outside doors, or in the direction of the Factories where light and warmth still existed, was troublesome enough to prompt the buggers and others he was able to recruit to take action. But people were going to ask questions that the volunteers, and Grainger, did not have answers for.

Thankfully, Tamner did.

"Folaw's getting a prodcast online, audio only, I suspect. We're moving the Hub, the Archives, and all medical services into the under-Factories. The Pissos are checking for system damage, putting crews on what they find. But the Nau wants something from you in return."

Bristling at the way Tamner's voice trailed off, expecting they had requested his resignation or the public execution of whatever scapegoat they chose, he narrowed his eyes. "Don't have time for…"

"I know it…but maybe we should make the time. They want the andis rounded up, decommissioned, the Core survivors arrested…and Kal taken in for questioning."

"Surprised they don't want Neoma's head too."

The mention of the Mam prompting a glance at his ICD was an action Grainger did not question. Time was a luxury they had very little of. "Didn't give them a chance. I don't think any of this is a priority, but maybe we can pull them aside as they evac. Might save a manhunt later."

Most andi, he imagined, would be working in the dark to keep the city from dying. It would spare them an arrest for a little while longer.

"No one's hunting anything down there… not even the brako." Most available light sources, other than alglamps, would not last long, and any light bleeding through the crevices in Hebenon's ancient shell where the water used to flow would not be enough to illuminate the Levs, particularly when the sun went down.

"We're gonna need comms. I need to get orders out. Lieutenant Young is taking command down there…but reaching anyone's going to be a fotz…"

"Nau's on that too, as they're working to keep cargo lifts operating for medical transport. Even so, this is going to be tedious."

Grainger grunted. "You just make damn sure the parah know what's coming." With his primary questions answered, he stomped away to fulfill whatever duty came next without waiting for the doctor to speak again.

Tamner's nod was unseen. He had sent a message to Venn, to Lash, to the Parah leadership to warn them what was to come, but going Out to facilitate this transition would have to wait.

Reaching Neoma to learn what she wanted would be just as tedious but saving Ulynda from the chaos seemed important. Neoma might not be a Kemway by birth, but she was the mother of one. Getting the two out of the city felt like a priority, whether anyone else agreed or not.

❧*❧

Stairways throughout the Levs were clogged with bundled figures shoving to go up in the initial post-quake panic, their arms and backs laden with personal belongings, pets, or small children at risk of being shoved off the walkways, beneath handrails, or back down the grated stairs. Disgruntled, frightened voices intermixed with the shuffled ringing of footsteps and cart wheels had replaced the customary rumble of the falls or the river's gurgle. Shouts came from those trapped behind doors as the hydraulic and electronic systems failed. Children cried and animals whined and protested their confusion.

Every intersection he passed over had become the territory of someone in Igraci white, with glowing sign boards that announced the rise of Hyperion and the end of Hebenon, signs that encouraged humanity's rebirth into the world the way the sun and moon had been born, claimed the way mankind had once claimed Hebanthe Falls. He was unsure if those signs were helping or if they were inducing deeper fear into already troubled people, but he had seen some of those white-clad figures leading others to less crowded stairs, helping the handicapped, making an effort to keep the peace where the absence of buggers and the indifference of others left disorder to erupt unchecked. A few scattered Talkers were on hand to help, but none, he noted, in the robes of those at the top of the Cult of the Founder's chain of command. Spinks flitted in and out of the crowd, retrieving dropped items, aiding the infirm, distributing the food and drink offered by corner-positioned herpa to those who had been trudging the longest.

It had been a few hours at most. The process was likely to take days. At the rate the resources were being handed out, without more to replenish the offerings, Scarecrow guessed the stores would be depleted by the first day's end unless the decision was made to raid homes along the way.

Few of these people, by that time, would have found their way into the Uppers, where they were likely to be bottlenecked if Hebenon's leaders refused to let them pass.

This was turning into a nightmare.

Scarecrow wondered if that was where he needed to be, at the top, compelling the elite to allow the less fortunate to escape.

Forced to move along the rooftops as the shafts teemed with work crews inspecting everything in the hopes of preventing catastrophic damage when, if, the power was restored, Scarecrow made a rolling leap from one roof to the half-Lev below and came up short next to a maroon-clad figure perched on the edge of Vapors' rooftop.

The other figure turned its head slightly, acknowledging Scarecrow's arrival before pointing at a cluster of scrawny streeters ransacking a vindi at the head of a shaft alley and then throwing broken bottles and pieces of debris at the pair of bilgers who tried to emerge.

A squad of Spinks came to the rescue and drove the streeters off.

"I should be in there," Scarecrow muttered.

Like his, her voice was modulated, distorted, and unrecognizable, but he knew who she was. "They've got this. If you want to be inside, I've got things covered out here, but I think we need you more here."

Scarecrow nodded. Professional duty might demand he pick up his bilger tooler and aid with the inspection and repairs, but inside the shafts was not where he felt obligated to be. "Think so too." The Spinks could chase away streeters and unruly addicts, but they would not fare as well against the brako, even if some had done so before. The tilt of his head indicated the structure beneath them. "Is she…?"

He might have meant Zara. He might have meant Maemi.

Tox shrugged. "This might be enough to get them out, but they're as stubborn as you are."

"So are you."

Again, she shrugged and chuckled darkly. "Got things to take care of. People to keep safe. Especially those who refuse to leave. You know how it is."

"I do." Once the population thinned, the remaining brako might be emboldened to plunder homes and vindis as the streeters were doing, if the refugees did not pick everything clean along the way. If Vanderwall was one of those who chose to go Out, he would be forever beyond Scarecrow's reach.

Scarecrow did not intend to give him the opportunity.

"Need someone to get Jaron out."

"Otta? Maemi?"

"You."

She shook her head. He could not see her scowl; he did not question or judge her silence.

Instead, he huffed. "Goin' down; goin' in. Keep an eye out."

Tox nodded. She knew what he meant.

"Find someone. Don't want him in here. Want him safe."

"Do what I can," she promised, though she was not confident of her success.

❧CHAPTER 36❧

Glass rattled in the recycle receptacle as Ginna emptied the dustpan of bottles that had fallen and broken in the shaking. The shelves behind the bar were empty, the few bottles that had remained there now spilled over the floor. From the kitchen, Maemi's frustrated swearing echoed off the mirrors and walls lit only by alglamps that had not broken. Such globes were typically made of stronger material that did not break easily. The pole in the center of the dance stage had popped free of the bolts that fastened it to the ceiling, and its weight, as it fell, created large cracks at both the uprooted base and the point of impact where it struck the floor. Ebenee and Hiana held the pole so that Nigel, tooler in hand, could try to fasten it temporarily into place.

It was a futile effort, Zara thought without watching. Unless the damage above and below was repaired, the pole would not stand. But the three needed to do something, to be useful in this time of crisis, so she did not discourage the attempt. Intending to see to Maemi's welfare after leaving Rhyd and Jaron, she changed into warmer, less wrinkled clothes and came downstairs, only to enter Vapors as the quake struck. Unable to reach Skelter or Rhyd on her ICD or the small Echo on the bar near her elbow, she focused her attention on righting tables and chairs.

She jumped when her ICD finally chirped and turned towards the back of the room, where Scarecrow unexpectedly appeared. The three on the stage stared in surprise, perplexed by the vigi's wraith-like arrival and that he was appearing before them at all. When Zara's only reaction was a glance and Ginna's was only a wide, surprised grin of awe, the andi looked at each other curiously.

It was as if the man born of shadow belonged there too. And yet none of them knew who was behind the mask.

Zara scowled at the persistently chirping ICD and brought the screen to her mouth, watching Scarecrow as she spoke. "Captain. This isn't a good time." Addressing Grainger first seemed to be a prudent move. Whatever Scarecrow wanted, there might be news at the other end of the call.

She ignored the looks that begged to know why the bugorra captain was contacting her.

More broken glass clattered into the bin, and the broom banged as it slid against the counter and fell to the floor.

"Are you okay? Are you hurt?"

Breath hissing in relief that his primary reason for calling included his concern for her welfare, she replied, "I'm…no; I'm fine. Some damage down here, but no one I know's been hurt."

"Good. Good." He sounded genuinely relieved. "How's Jaron?"

"I don't…" She resisted eyeing Scarecrow, feeling his gaze narrow without seeing his eyes. She did not want to be the reason the dancers learned Scarecrow's identity. "He's good. He's safe. I'm not there now…but he's good."

The breath on the other end caught differently this time and was followed by a conflicted-sounding sigh.

"At least he's safe."

Thinking it best to change the subject, Zara asked, "What's with the power? The falls? Everything's down here…"

"We're on it. Quake caused a landslide that's blocked the river. Working on clearing it, but have to redirect the water away from the village first. Got the plans for the array parts; they're in fabrication, but it could be a while before they're ready, before they're installed. Nau's ordered evacuation. You should come up. Bring Jaron."

"I…" They could hear the trudging of passersby on the walk in front of Vapors. They had peered out to see the growing lines of those trying to reach any stairs that would take them up. Evacuation had been optional before.

No one had ever thought it would be mandatory.

Though she shrugged, he could not see it. "Don't know if that'll be any time soon. There's too many already heading up."

"We've got evac points, refugee camps. I can make sure you've got priority but…" There was a long, uncomfortable pause. "Might want to leave your dancers."

"I'm not…"

Behind her, the women looked at each other with concern as Nigel muttered, "Like paso."

Hearing the man's voice, Grainger explained, "Andi sabotaged the array…started this mess…some in the Nau don't want to let them out…want them arrested. If they're tagged at the evac points, they'll be held…maybe decommed if they have their way. Safer they stay where they are until the power's back, until the doctor and I can talk the Nau down from this asinine idea."

Still holding Nigel's defiant gaze, Zara said, "I'm not leaving them…and they're not being decommed."

"I can try to get you exemptions…get them tested to prove they're not threats…but I can't guarantee it. Even though we've got enough to worry about with the power, you have to think about…"

Movement at the end of the bar. The beaded curtain rattled, cutting through Grainger's words, but it was Ginna's too-loud, "Come to check on me, sis?" that made the captain fall silent and cut the feed without a goodbye, guilty of offering exemptions perhaps, or reluctant to reveal his familiarity with Zara, or maybe the loss of connection was due to the loss of power as it was redirected from the comms to something deemed temporarily more important. With Scarecrow ducked down so that the bar counter was between them, Ginna again picked up the broom and met Ilya at the door as though unwilling to allow her inside.

The vindi was dark, the place where Scarecrow had hidden from the mirror's reflection darker still, but she did not want to expose him to her sister. This was not the sort of place the vigi typically visited…indoors with a collection of people.

"Wanted to see you're okay," Ilya began, glancing at Zara with a cocked head and perplexed expression before looking into the mirror as if expecting to see something there.

There was nothing except the reflections of everyone in the room except Scarecrow.

"Things going to hell out there…"

"Why I'm staying put," Ginna shrugged, trying not to fidget with the broom handle. "Making sure people have a safe place to…"

"Nothing's safe…and it's not your responsibility to…"

"But it is yours? Just because you're gorra?"

Ilya frowned. "Because I'm your sister."

"You can't tell me they're gonna let the kids out when there's Uppers elite and vindi owners and celebrities to get out first. None of the kids are gonna matter until the very end…if then."

"Everyone matters," Ilya countered, although she, too, harbored suspicions about the Nau's evacuation priorities. "Long as the power's out, until the city's evacuated top down, it isn't safe for anyone to…"

"Top-down. Of course. You're all more important up there," Ginna spat with a grumble.

"That's not what I meant."

"I know what you meant." The broom switched hands. "I'm staying until they're allowed out. You don't have to worry about me." She looked through the service window at Maemi in the kitchen. "We've got each other here. If they're staying…until they and the kids can go…I'm not leaving."

Ilya met Maemi's gaze too, hoping the older woman would offer advice that would prompt Ginna to reconsider, but Maemi's expression was more tenacious than Ginna's. "You should all get out." Her gaze shifted from one face to the next. "All of you should."

She did not appear to know that the dancers were andi, or else she had not gotten the debated decomm order. "Things aren't going to get better. Only going to get worse…for a while at least."

"We can manage," Maemi countered. "It's all the more reason to get the ones who need it most out first. We're fine where we are."

"I'm not taking a priority pass just because you're my sister," added Ginna. "When it's time…if it's time…I'll go."

Ilya adjusted her uniform coat and tried not to groan. At least that commitment was something. "Stay put here then. Don't go out there. I'll check in later." It had taken priority pull to utilize the lift to get down this far into the Levs, using her command and the need to get to the bugorra office to her advantage. The lift had free-fallen between Levs, with jarring stops at each where she reached out to every officer she could find. Doing so saved power, but the abuse of the brake gears would take its toll. Now that she was here, everything else to do would need to be done on foot. She doubted she would be allowed to use the lifts to return to the captain.

Ginna was as safe as she could be, and so long as she took Ilya's advice and remained in this bar, there should not be any problems. Ilya did not have time to linger and try to change her mind.

She had few doubts that the moment she was gone, Ginna would be out in the streets mobilizing the Spinks.

"We're not leaving you," Hiana promised Zara as soon as the woman in the bugorra uniform was gone.

"And I'm not leaving you," Zara reassured her with an outstretched hand that Hiana rushed across the room to clutch.

"Should all get out while you can."

Nigel shifted in his squat to look at the vigi he had never heard speak, had never seen up close, before.

"Not if they're going to…" Zara began before Nigel could speak.

"The Spinks need…" started Ginna.

"Vapors' all I got," Maemi added. Now that Jonner had stopped coming, might even be dead, she felt even less compunction to leave her vindi behind.

"I can get them out." The fastest way up was through the shafts, even as they swarmed with repair crews and inspection teams. There were underused, underserved passages to closed-off sections of the system where parts of the city had been abandoned as the population dwindled. Using them would mean avoiding the amassed horde of frightened people clogging the stairs and streets. The only potential obstacle would be getting anyone through the Outside door unhindered and undetected.

Scarecrow would do whatever he had to do to make it work.

"And you," he pointed to Ginna, "need you and the Spinks to do something…bring someone safely out if we do this."

"Someone you can't take through the shafts?" Ginna could not see behind the mask, but she guessed the vigi was frowning.

"Too many at once will move too slow…and he's injured." He ignored Zara's pointed stare. "Know they've got ways up…and I need them, and you, to get him safe…get all the kids out."

"We can help here. They're not going to want to…"

"Try." It would not take every Spink in the city to move Jaron, and Ginna would know that some of the youngest Spinks would be ineffective for whatever came next. Trying was the best anyone could do. "It's not safe for the little ones. Not safe for anyone."

Maemi, too, stared at him, snorted without arguing, and returned to her puttering in the kitchen.

The andi looked at each other and Zara, asking unvoiced questions before she finally nodded at Scarecrow in agreement. She would not be able to guide him through the higher shafts this time as she had the last. Once he made it into the shafts with her friends, they would be entirely in his care.

There was no one she trusted more to see them to safety. Especially if she was not going with them.

Scarecrow nodded too. "Get your things, important things, whatever you can carry easily. Three hours. Stay out of the buggers' eyes. They might leave you alone…but they might not, so don't draw attention. I'll meet you here."

"Zar," groaned Ebenee in protest. "Won't you come?"

"I've got to get to Skelt…make sure he's safe…that things are okay. Do what he says. I'll meet you out there when I can."

The andi set down their tools, the pole they had been holding upright returned carefully to the floor where it had fallen, and embraced Zara hard. Scarecrow watched, waiting until Nigel, the most stubborn, nodded his head, left his flamboyant scarf on the stage, and led the women into the changing room where they could sneak out to their flats unseen.

To Ginna, he said, "Get the Spinks to the cat-man's house. I'll meet you there. And you two," he looked between Zara and Maemi, ignoring Zara's skeptical gaze, "Stay safe."

❦*❧

Drawings made in the mud with sticks and fingers were scuffed out with the toe of Enoch's boot as parah and prossers hurried to fulfill their responsibilities. Trees felled and trimmed for home construction were being cut and sized to be set as a retaining wall to prevent further failure of the eroded bank. If they could force the flow to continue in the furrow of the original sixth tributary, the village would be spared and the water would be directed away from Hebenon until the city was ready for the falls to flow again.

Barriers of wood, hemp bales, and any other material that could be foraged, including sheets and bricks of hemplastic brought from the factories and the wagons used to transport trade products in and out of the city, were being repurposed and packed around with bags of soil to add to the barrier that would, it was hoped, spare the village from the rupturing overflow that was steadily eroding earth to reach them.

Though Jonner tried to spearhead the project, often clashing with the parah leadership about the best way to proceed, it was Enoch giving directions, directing the work as though born to do that sort of thing. People listened to him. People responded without time-wasting questions.

Some now knew who he was. Maybe that was why they listened. Maybe it was some natural charisma that had kept him alive, had won favors and friendship from people inside the Core and out. Whatever it was, Jonner was mostly content to let things be the way they were.

Hebenon's doors were open. The exodus had begun. No matter how long it took to clear the river, no matter how long it took to get everyone Outside, upon seeing the benefits the open world had to offer, he was sure Hebenon's population would never choose to go back. If the other half of their plan worked as Eido anticipated, whether the hydros functioned or failed when the tributaries flowed again, the rest inside would follow him out and remain here.

There would be no life to go back to.

Maemi would come. She would join him here, beneath the sun, and they would be happy.

Jonner had done his part.

Nature had taken the blame.

❧Chapter 37❧

Men and women scrambled within the Factories at the Nau's direction to shut down every machine, every system that was not involved in the printing of solar components, provide electricity to the medical equipment as it arrived, and operate the barely functioning Hub and prod systems. The members of the Nau gathered around the wide window to the Outside in the community room, using the light of day to discuss the logistics of moving people up and Out as quickly as possible, evacuating one Lev at a time to shut down more power usage as each was emptied and opening up multiple checkpoints and exit desks as the lines grew longer.

Kal did not know this as he raised his hand to silence the accumulating mass of Talkers crowding into Primary Hall, frightened faces that expected him to provide answers he did not have. The crowd provided body heat to the room, and the scattered alglamp glow from the lanterns dotting the perimeter provided relief from the darkness, but those things were not enough to provide the hope they expected their Senior to give.

"Listen, Sons and Daughters. This won't last. Whatever has happened, the Nau is aware and working to…"

"They want to drive us out!"

"They want to kill us!"

Grumbles of agreement and dissent washed through the crowd. Kal banged his hand on the podium and waited for their attention to shift back to him. "Nonsense." He forced a chuckle intended to disperse tension and fear, but from the looks on some of the faces nearest to him, he concluded that some of his Talkers interpreted his response as belittling derision.

"The quake has affected the rivers, the falls. It's a natural event, not caused by the Nau." He felt confident in his claim, though he had no evidence to support it. "The blockage is being dealt with. The falls will flow…"

"It's not enough!"

"They're forcing everyone into the poison…"

"They want us to die!"

This time, Kal held up his silent hand as Bene knocked the bottom end of the ceremonial Staff of Office against the floor twice, jangling the array of different-toned bells affixed at the top. The sound stilled most of the crowd, but pockets of unsettled voices continued to murmur and mutter.

"The order isn't just for us in the Levs; it is for the Uppers too. Do you think they'd risk going Outside if it isn't safe?"

The ongoing voice-only prods adjuring evacuation of all residents might be a ruse. But without workers, those in the Ups would have no access to the luxuries, to the foods, to the systems the Levs provided. What luxuries they had could not last. Emptying the Levs would ultimately mean stagnation and starvation in the Uppers.

Kal had few doubts that those closer to the top were being forced to leave their centuries of security, just as those in the Levs were.

He did not intend, however, to go see it himself.

"This order does not negate our sacred duty. We must help our people. We must find Mam Kemway and her daughter, see them to safety…and we must locate and secure Aldrich Kemway to…"

"They could already be outside if they're so important…"

Growling and scowling at yet another interruption, Kal cleared his throat. "They could be. But you've seen the lines, the crowds. With the lifts…every stairwell is congested or barricaded. They may be out in that. With the brako afoot, if they're still here, they're not safe."

"Thought we're supporting Aldrich over…?"

"He's a hoax," shouted someone else, prompting another scramble at the center of the room as some fought to pull the arguing pair apart before they came to blows.

"They're all Kemways," Kal reminded them. "Whoever is elevated, it is not up to us. It is up to the people to choose. For now, we find and protect all three."

"And if Outside is poisoned?"

Better we die a quick death than linger, suffering, in the cold darkness, he thought without saying the sentiment out loud. There were more rumbles of discontent. "No one is dying," he reiterated. "Not today. Not tomorrow. Not from evacuation. I promise that. Now…" He took the Staff of Office from Bene, who stooped to pick up a bag at his feet that rattled and clattered as its contents shifted.

"Everyone will approach and select a marker." He gestured to the digital signboard propped on the podium that boasted three symbols and the fate each symbol represented. He pointed to each consecutively as he continued. "Some of us will go Outside and seek the Kemways there, see to their safety if found. Some will seek within and, if they're found, will escort them Outside. The rest will provide succor and comfort to those working their way up. If you find any of our brothers and sisters who are not here with us, you will compel them to fulfill whatever lot you have drawn. Afterward, when the power is restored and the falls run again, we will return to this hall, stronger than before…for we will have the Kemways' gratitude to sustain us. Come…make your selection and begin."

The Talkers filed past, reaching into the bag, drawing out a hemplastic token of the sort used to cast policy votes. They paused, compared the token to the symbols on the board, and then gathered in three groups around the room following the lot they had been given. Some of those groups moved out of the Hall in pairs, in units of three or more, some loitered as the room emptied as if to stay the fates. Kal did not speak, did not intervene, or question his Talkers, trusting that they would do what they were instructed.

When the last Talker made her choice, as those remaining began to shuffle towards the rear door, over the charred floor, from a room growing increasingly darker with each departure, Kal called after them, "Founder and Creator be with us."

The sounds of footsteps faded.

Bene and Kal stood alone.

"And us, sir?" Bene asked, a muted voice in the near darkness.

Kal pulled two battery candles from the shelves at the rear of the podium and lit them. He handed the first to Bene. "See to the distribution of our resources to those who need them. Secure the treasury…and then you will go up too."

"Sir…"

"Do your duty, Bene. One of us must lead from there as the other leads here. The Founder requires…"

"Your duty?"

"When it is done, when the Kemways are found, when the city is secure, I will join you."

Bene pouted and set the bag of tokens on the podium. "This is not a sinking ship, sir. You don't need to…"

"I know my duties, Bene…you have yours." He tapped his ICD. "Imagine they're going to keep these open as much as possible so Captain Grainger can direct the bugorra. Keep me abreast of the progress and let me know when they're safe."

Though he sighed in resignation, Bene nodded. "Very well, sir. If you're sure you don't need me to…?"

"I'll be fine."

The brako would not dare enter here. He had battery candles and a few boxes of dried food stashed in his office to last for several days, for however long it took to free the city from the clutches of destruction. He had a little running and bottled water still, and the evacuation meant more and more of Hebenon's reserve would be available for those who remained inside. And he had multiple bottles of Wulfe's Head wine. For now, he was fine. He would go to the hub of the Talkers' evacuation…

…and he would never admit that he remained where he was because he was too afraid of going into a world he had been raised to fear. He did not fear the dark, starvation, or the brako nearly as much.

❧*❧

For the first time in recent memory, Neoma bit her tongue to swallow the scathing retort that pushed into the back of her throat. The spotty ICD reception was no more his fault than it was hers. She had never known him well, but she had always thought him a conscientious man focused on whatever duty Haythem assigned. She understood that the Nau was pushing him into a position of prominence he did not appear to want, although she did not know the details. If he was half the man she thought him to be, he was doing his utmost to solve the city's electrical crisis.

Utmost was not good enough.

"We need to meet," she repeated, voicing the unanswered message she had sent to him before.

She could almost hear him scowl. "This isn't the time…"

"Ulynda's not safe. I need you to get her Outside…see to her welfare until things are better."

There was a long pause, long enough for Neoma to believe their connection had been cut. "Doctor…"

"You know the Nau wants you to come in for questioning?"

It was Neoma's turn to hesitate after a huffing, irritated breath partially caused by his revelation and partially by the sounds of footsteps passing the empty flat where they had taken refuge long enough for her daughter to use the toilet. They had lost their place in line, but Neoma would not allow the child to suffer the indignity of soiled pants. Nor would she suffer the indignity of sour stares that would blame her for the girl's less-than-perfect appearance. They were Kemways. That would never do. With her Talker escorts scouting the walks outside and Nanny poking through the kitchen to find something to eat and drink, Neoma had dubbed this the best time to reach out to Tamner again.

Her efforts before had failed. Her efforts to climb through the Levs would be futile if she could not reach him. She had to do this now.

"That's why it has to be you. You've got more important things to do than pretend to arrest me. Ulynda's a child. Haythem's child. You understand how crucial it is to protect her. She knows your son. There's nowhere better…no one better…so long as she's in your care, I'll know she is safe."

"Where are you?"

"Lev 13." With so many stairs, so many turns and double-backs, Neoma had lost track of precisely where she was. But she counted lifts on the way up, thus she felt confident of her Lev location.

She thought, from his next pause, he would tell her no. Tell her he was too busy. Tell her it could not be done. She imagined he was contemplating ways to double-cross her and divert the bugorra to her location. But he was Ulynda's best chance of getting out of Hebenon, and at least, if Neoma was arrested, she would be taken out alive too.

Finally, she heard him groan. "Keep the ping on. Stay put if you can. Things are…it'll take some time to get to you…but I'll be there as soon as I can get free…"

"You'll get here now, Doctor…and you'll get her Outside. And you'll do one more thing for me."

Failing to hide the venom in her tone, she heard his hissed breath and cut off whatever retort he was about to make for the demands she was setting forth. "You'll keep her away from Aldrich."

"Mam…"

"Promise me, Doctor…or we'll take our chances here."

The pause was longer that time. "I'll do my best, Mam."

She did not believe him. The crackle through the ICD link was disrupted by the creaking bathroom door. Neoma dropped her arm to hide the communication. There were things Neoma needed to do if the name of Kemway was to continue to thrive and hold sway, things she could not do with a child dragging behind her like a weight in the river's sludge.

She sank onto a cushioned chair, comfortable enough to push a sigh out of her lungs, and as Nanny came into the room with a tray of what food this home offered, Ulynda entered from another with an armload of towels, and the flat door opened so that Cyrus could join them. Neoma huffed, took a towel to wrap around her shoulders for warmth, and grunted, "We'll rest here."

They could rub themselves dry and eat. Maybe there were blankets they could use to get warm. Ulynda could nap.

They were all excuses to hide Neoma's actual purpose.

Waiting for Doctor Tamner.

❧*❧

"What do you mean he's not available?"

Tappy avoided the punching end of Vanderwall's pointed finger by bending toward the table to reach for the passchip he had set on the other side when he entered the room. The images it contained were the same ones that had aired city-wide moments before Hebenon had fallen into this eerie, deafening silence. He did not know if his boss had seen the prods, had hoped to get the passchip to him before it aired, but the absence of usable lifts had made his descent through the Levs slower than expected.

Breathless and sweaty, he waited to straighten until Vanderwall's thick arm dropped to his side.

"Not just him," Tappy indicated grudgingly. "A lot of them, they're on their way Outside. There's talk that Hebenon's gonna fall, and there's the Nau's evac order…"

"They're not…"

"They're hungry and cold. They've got families. Probably best if we all…"

"Flats and vindis are empty. They can take what they want, what they need." He growled at the smaller man, snatched the passchip from his hand, and muttered, "Suppose you're off too?"

Tappy shrugged. "Haven't thought about it. Wife's got the kids on the way…but I figure there's things to do…and this isn't gonna last. Shouldn't give up our hold so easy. You, sir?"

Again, Vanderwall grunted. "You saw the prods?"

Though he did not verbally agree or argue, Tappy did answer with a nod. There had been mention earlier of evacuation checkpoints to coordinate an orderly exodus. With Uriah Frankel's face exposed to however many people had seen the brief flash of an image shown before the prods had gone offline, trying to go Out meant the possibility of arrest. He did not imagine the boss would take that risk.

"Heard talk about taking the river out to the sea…Now that it's dry," he offered to be helpful.

"And risk being swept out when it runs again?" Vanderwall snorted. "This ain't gonna last, like you said. We take advantage of this opportunity as long as we have it. Little Kemway's gonna have the same problem, so we can find him, and Mam, as they work their way up." He paused to slip the passchip into the currently inoperable P1 and asked, "Wulfe's boys? Bugorra?"

"Turning tail too…at least a lot of them from what we can see. Buggers got their hands full with the evac."

"Good. Good. We can use that."

Vanderwall's positive change of mood made Tappy's shoulders relax. "I can get the ones together who are still…if you want…?"

"Do it. Get them to the soaper…as many as you can…and tell them comms on." So long as the generators in the soaper had the power to emit the background signal that bypassed the Hub and its failing resources, Vanderwall could direct his people no matter where they were in the Levs. No matter how many he had on hand, he would make the most of them too, in addition to the city's growing vacancy.

Hebenon was going to hell, but the brako weren't going anywhere.

❧*❧

Leaving the Uppers for the stark darkness of the Levs, the absence of sound elevated to an ear-ringing eeriness, Tamner paused as he reached the bottom of the stairs as though stopped by a solid, immovable force. Four blue alglamps provided a glow leading away from the jerky, interminably slow lift, directing his way forward, and the battery lantern in his hand illuminated the path. It had taken a lot of pull to direct power to the lifts long enough to open the door, free fall a few stories, and then apply the brakes to lurch to a halt, but he had made it this far.

Once he made it to Neoma, going back up would take a long time.

The seldom-used staircase provided largely for the bugorra, the work crews, and for past occasions when the Founder had wanted a photo op in the Levs without going very far into the distasteful cold and damp, had not yet been discovered by the hordes of families seeking an escape route. His plan to get this far before being forced to take the stairs had been in his favor.

But he had not expected to find anyone here.

Perhaps it was the woman in white, seven acolytes with her, and the collection of herpa behind, that generated the force that stopped his feet from moving.

"Doctor Tamner."

The woman stepped toward him, extending her bone-thin hand with a friendly expression made harsh and serious by the straight-banged, fashionable cut of black hair framing her narrow face. It did not surprise him that she might know his name, his face, as his public profile continued to evolve thanks to the Nau and Captain Grainger. He did not know her, but he knew one thing.

Igraci

"Eido," she added in introduction.

He accepted the handshake with a nod. "Were you waiting for me?" There was no reason she, or anyone else should be, unless

Neoma had sent them, had known he would take this route. It was an idea as absurd as this whole situation was becoming.

"We've come up to offer assistance in the evacuation. We think we could be of service," replied one of the herpa, gesturing to the array of packs, sacks, and bundles they each wore and carried. "It isn't much, but we do have experience easing people's fears…"

Eido's head bobbed slightly. "I believe you know what we do."

"I do." Teach the old ways, the arts of growing things, building fires, the history of Outside, and how to survive in it, skills that most in Hebanthe Falls had long ago stopped caring about or paying attention to. While it was primarily book knowledge, intellectual rather than practical, it was better than the current systemic ignorance of basic survival skills.

People were going to need that education to survive Outside. Whatever the future held for Hebenon's population, the Igraci were likely to be an integral part of the transition.

Tamner glanced at his ICD. This was not something he could present to the Nau. There was no time for that, and they were occupied with more pressing matters. And as long as Neoma stayed put as he had asked, she and her daughter would be safe long enough for him to put this unexpected aid to good use. The needs of the entirety of the city's population were weighed against the needs of two.

Though he was suspicious about the Igraci's motives, the herpa, he believed, could be trusted. Their reputations made them so.

"Follow me. I'll get you through…and the bugorra can get you set up at the checkpoints."

Hebenon needed this intervention. Neoma would have to wait a little longer.

*

"Can't take the chance."

Otta smoothed her hair from her face, forcing a smile she knew he could read through. Colyx was helping the children collect their meager belongings, had provided them brightly colored school packs to carry them in, and was showing them how to pack them. Otta and Skelter's foray to provide enough to feed them all for another day or two had brought them home to her father's intervention, and though Skelter was skeptical of his initiative, he did appreciate the sentiment.

"I'm not one of them. No one knows I'm here." She aimed her barbed glower at her father and set the sack of nessies on the table, moving away from Skelter with a huff of annoyance.

"If Molly gets to 'em first, they will."

"He's not after me," she muttered.

"But he is after me."

"If he can get to Skelt through you," Colyx muttered without looking at the arguing pair, "you know the little fotz will do it. Probably already on his way Out…buying his way with your lives…"

"And risk arrest?" She did not believe Molly had enough fortitude to try that.

"He'd find a way." Molly, like Switz, could be a scheming, slippery mierdita when it was in his best interest. The possibility that he would find a way to blame Skelter for Kemway's death, now that his face had been revealed city-wide as a person of interest, weighed more and more on Skelter's thoughts after the stairway incident. He could not pin the murder on Otta, as she had an alibi in the children.

Skelter did not have the same luxury.

"Colyx can get all of you to…" Skelter began.

The bigger man frowned and shook his head no. "Maemi needs…"

"Vapors is closed," Skelter reminded him.

"Still brako out there…with the buggers occupied, they're thick," he protested, helping one child tighten her pack straps so as not to meet Skelter's gaze. "Promised her I'd be there. But you should go…"

"Let 'em take paso. Better than our lives." But a promise to Maemi was something Skelter would have kept, too. Vacating Hebenon could wait long enough for that.

Otta picked up folded clothes that an older boy was trying to stuff into the pack in a wadded ball. "If anyone should get Out, it's you. There's no business here…"

"Zara needs me. She doesn't have anyone else." Skelter sighed and said unapologetically, "He needs me here to…a little bit longer."

Scarecrow.

Bristling, Otta stomped through the arch into the kitchen with some of the food they had found and began to divide it onto disposable plates for the children. "Why?"

"Why?" Skelter followed her as far as the arch and leaned against it while Colyx, slightly stoop-shouldered, shuffled toward the children's room. He watched the older man go, years of experience in reading people telling him that something was off, was being hidden. Colyx knew something he was not sharing.

But this was not the time to corner or confront him.

"Why?" Otta repeated sourly.

"It's not that. It's not like…I told you; she doesn't have anyone." His excuse was not entirely accurate. He knew it. Otta knew it too. Zara had Maemi, Tox, and her dancers. She was one of the most resourceful people he knew.

But she was also his oldest and dearest friend. She would stay for as long as Rhyd needed her. Tox would too.

Skelter felt likewise compelled.

"Why does he need you? You're not like him…"

He stepped behind her and wrapped his arms around her waist so that his hands covered her pregnant belly. "Don't have to be like him to do the right thing. He helped us get out…I need to help get everyone else out, too. We're gonna get everyone safe, as many as we can…and he's gonna stop Vanderwall while we do. I can't do any of that if you and the kids…all the kids…are where Molly can get you. Venn's there…he'll see that you're settled right…"

"We need you too."

He kissed her cheek and pressed his to hers. She did not voice such emotion often, any more than she expressed jealousy. He appreciated her sentiment and wanted to be sure to reward it. "Know you do…and I need you. Nothin's gonna happen to me. I'll be fine. Not gonna be out there hunting or looking for fights like he does…just gonna make sure he's got everything he needs to do what needs doing. Soon as it's done, I'll be Out with you…or we'll have the lights back and you'll come home. Just…think about it, Otta."

Small faces peeped around the arch and he wrapped one arm around the closest child. "If not for me…for all of them. They shouldn't have to wait down here living like this. We got them out once…we need to do it again." When Otta grunted and pushed plates along the counter for the children to take, he kissed her cheek again. "Think about it. Don't need an answer now, but think about it."

The answer had to come soon. Getting out of the city was becoming increasingly difficult as more people joined the evacuation lines. Every moment of delay was one moment closer to Molly's potential betrayal. Molly would not consider the needs of the children. Skelter and Otta had to.

❧*❧

Jaron was on the sofa where he had left him, asleep this time when Rhyd dropped out of the vent and removed the hood and mask. The bottle of Zaolei rescued after the quake, surprisingly undamaged, lay on its side on the sofa table where it had been, left from the efforts to sterilize wounds and medical instruments used to restore Jaron to health. The bottle was nearly empty, a few swallows of amber remaining at the bottom, and he knew there were no other bottles left.

This drink, unless he could locate a bottle or two somewhere else, would probably have to hold him until the darkness lifted and goods from the Source began to flow again.

He did not consider how long that might take. How much he might suffer before that happened.

He wanted this drink before he went back into the streets. He could not shake the feeling that he was going to need it.

When his gloved hand closed around the neck of the bottle, another hand closed around his wrist. He froze, turned his head, and met Jaron's sleepy-eyed gaze.

His breath caught at the unexpected images the contact created, images of waking up in a bed with those eyes, that soft mouth, that face haloed in tousled black curls, staring at him from the adjoining pillow. That hand on his wrist, pulling his hand closer, coaxing him to touch the smooth, pale skin beneath the softly glowing speecher at the hollow of his throat.

Rhyd thanked the whole of creation that whatever thoughts might be going through Jaron's head were not directed to the speecher.

"You didn't gather your things," he stammered, pulling his arm free so he could open the bottle and empty it into his throat before his courage to remain in this room, with this man, failed him or prompted him to do something he was likely going to regret.

"Too much effort." The welcome digital buzz behind the voice made Rhyd's heart flutter with the relief of hearing it again. He knew those words were an excuse, that Jaron continued to stubbornly assert remaining below, but it was an excuse for lack of action that Rhyd could accept.

Jaron was convalescing. It had only been what…two…three days? Rhyd set the empty bottle on the table. "I'll get you some things."

"Not gonna need 'em…"

"Jaron…"

Jaron shook his head and sighed with a defeated expression of acceptance. There had been time to think about Rhyd's wishes, the things Rhyd had said. Time to make the wisest decision he could make. "Not gonna need them for that long. They'll get the power restored, and I'll come home, so long as you promise you'll be here."

As he spoke, he tried to push himself to sit, and then stand, wanting to be eye to eye as they talked. The blankets fell away, revealing the baggy trousers he wore…Rhyd's trousers…that he neither drew attention to nor tried to hide. The shirt Zara had brought him still lay on the table. When he wavered on his feet, Rhyd reflexively caught him, and Jaron's arms wrapped impulsively around him in return.

Rhyd could not help himself. The chaotic rush of emotion, relief, regret, fear…and something else he did not try to name, compelled him to turn to Jaron and find some measure of desperate solace in a kiss. He wished for the absence of gloves, for the feel of skin against skin. He wished for time, for opportunity, for something he had not wished for in a long time. The embrace, the kiss, were the closest he could get to a promise he could not speak, the closest he could get to the promise of a future he both longed for and dreaded.

They were unspoken promises that Jaron accepted and clutched to his heart as his fingers sought purchase in Rhyd's damp hair.

If the words were never spoken, the unsolicited kiss was enough.

There was a knock on the door.

Rhyd growled.

Maybe he could ignore it. Maybe he could stay with Jaron, shed Scarecrow's protective shell, give up the need to put Vanderwall down, and never leave this flat again.

But the knock came a second time, a code he recognized. Hebenon could not be ignored. Some things needed to be done if Jaron was to be safe.

Jaron, reluctantly, reached the same conclusion and released him when Rhyd drew away.

"Get dressed," Rhyd hissed, his gruffness masking his tumultuous emotions as he pulled the mask and hood back into place, thankful that the taste of Jaron's mouth lingered where it could be savored behind the security of anonymity. Only when he was hidden again, with Jaron trudging and shuffling about behind him to dress, did he go to the door.

The baggy black tee hung loose around his shoulders. The socks Zara had left fit well enough, and the work boots Rhyd kept by the door, which had seen many years of service in Hebenon's shafts, were an uncomfortable but serviceable fit. He did not have anything of his own here to wear. Rhyd's clothes would have to do.

Knowing Jaron wore those things gave Rhyd an unanticipated flash of giddy satisfaction.

On the other side of the door, Ginna and eight older Spinks, children who looked big enough, capable enough, to provide a degree of protection should Jaron need it, huddled beneath the glow of Rhyd's green exterior alglamp. Several cats loitered around Lash's door, despite his recent failure to feed them, watching the strangers with wary, unswerving eyes.

After scanning the streets and rooftops, searching for threats the Spinks might have unwittingly brought to his door, Scarecrow motioned them inside. As he closed it, he pulled the coat from the wall hook at the side of the door and tossed it onto the sofa where Jaron sat lacing up the boots.

"Where's the others?"

"Not ready…they'll come later."

Thankfully, they could not see his expression, judging that Zara's andi were reluctant to leave her behind, that they would need another, sterner talking-to. There was nothing he could do about it now.

Jaron had to go, with or without them.

"Safer if you go out here." Scarecrow gestured to the open panel as he removed a P1 from one of his many pockets. "You know what you need to do?"

Ginna nodded and smiled sheepishly at the bruised and battered-looking man on the sofa. "Get Mr. Rei Outside."

"And avoid the brako and bugorra."

"Avoid the brako and bugorra," one of the Spinks agreed. He looked at Jaron, who refused to lift his head, as though he hoped that if he did not speak and remained inconspicuous, the others would forget he was there.

The girl who had addressed him by name would not allow him that luxury.

"This'll get you up and out. Path's programmed in…and a couple of alternates if you need them. When you get close, look for Captain Grainger…" Within his hood, his gaze shifted to Jaron, who tilted his head at last to share an exchanged glance with the mirrored eyepieces. He nodded grimly.

Regardless of the length of the evacuation line, as soon as Oliver knew Jaron was there, he would do anything necessary to get Jaron out of Hebenon. There was no need to dredge up jealousies. That prior relationship was Jaron's best bet for safety.

"And you'll stay there with him."

"Outside?" squeaked another girl in the group, the tallest of the Spinks, but, from the tone of her voice, probably not the oldest.

"Until things are right, it's better to be there. Don't think the brako will be there, but I want you to keep him safe until I send for him."

The Spinks glanced at one another and then bobbed their heads. They were eager, if nervous, to see Outside, and even more eager to help Scarecrow. Only Ginna did not offer her agreement to the orders.

Scarecrow knew why.

She would come back for other Spinks. She would guide as many as she could to safety. She would come for the dancers, for Maemi, for her sister. For anyone else who needed help. It was a sacrifice he did not want her to make, but it was one Scarecrow understood.

Ginna hoisted herself into the shaft and helped three others up behind her. The other three would take up the rear, guarding Jaron's back, and so those three hesitated as Scarecrow aided the weak, reluctant man from the sofa and to the hatch.

Jaron was unsteady on his feet. His movements would be slow and uneven, but there was no other way.

Scarecrow left him leaning against the wall long enough to collect the medical supplies from the table into the sack they had been brought in, and gave it to one of the children in the shaft. As he prepared to help Jaron up, the dark-haired man put his hand on Scarecrow's chest and murmured, "Remember…you promised."

Jaron could not see a reaction, could not hear one, and he grimly understood that, against Vanderwall, such a promise might be one Rhyd could not keep. But he wanted to hear him say it, even if it was a lie. He was not willing to budge until he did.

"I'll remember," Scarecrow eventually replied, accepting that Jaron would not leave without some final word between them.

As he aided Jaron into the shaft, doing his best not to cause additional pain, Scarecrow knew another truth, too.

The last three Spinks followed, scooting back once inside so Jaron could reach for Scarecrow's hand. Without considering whether the gesture would make him appear weak or vulnerable, Scarecrow squeezed the offered hand and repeated, "I will remember."

He closed the grate and listened as Ginna led the others into the wider, taller corridor of the vent system.

He waited until the echoes of their passage were no longer heard.

Jaron was gone.

Scarecrow did not move for a very long time.

❧Chapter 38❧

Feena stopped midway up the stairs, watching the big man pass, his head down and covered by his cloak hood, his shoulders stooped as if broken by the weight of the darkness. She could have snapped at him for his disrespect as he pushed by, but the effort did not seem worth it. She put her hand on Tyrisi's arm to stay him and the dozen men with them as well, and together they waited for the stranger to reach the landing below and continue on his way.

The creak of his leg braces reminded her of someone she had encountered in the past. If not for the braces, she might have thought the stranger was Vanderwall.

If it was Vanderwall, using those braces as a disguise, she thought he would have acknowledged her, even if in a challenge.

The promenade at the top of the stairs was nearly empty. A single dimly lit vindi powered by a sputtering battery generator hosted a collection of five buggers huddled around it clutching steaming drinks. No water flowed in the fountain at the promenade's center, no citizens gathered to share company amidst the outdoor garden, and ahead of her, the open door of Primary Hall hosted no Talkers, no visitors coming or going beneath the frame of alglamps. The Echo beside it, its screen black, crackled with the audio-only prodcast which had begun much earlier. Kenneth and Soleia, reporting from one of the evacuation points, narrating the work of buggers, Talkers, herpa, Igraci, and others as they transitioned Hebenon's population from the darkness and into an unfamiliar Outside world.

Their discussion of when they, too, would take that final step beyond the fall city's shell, the potential pros and cons of that decision, did not deter Feena from her choice. She wondered as she climbed the Hall steps, if Kal had already made his.

The Senior stood at the podium, back to the door, staring with arms crossed at the stained-glass mosaic of Duncan Kemway, once illuminated to form a multi-colored halo around any individual standing in that spot to speak to the flock. Now it was as dark as everything else, a reminder as she approached that, whenever the power was restored, Hebanthe Falls would not be the same.

Without a Founder, the city could not go back to what it had been. Pragmatic, Feena was prepared for the inevitability of change.

The man who turned toward the sound of her footsteps, dour-faced and pensive, was less so.

"So…you're going." Feena carried only her handbag and the now unnecessary umbra, but the men with her carried the bundles and packs that announced his ally's intent.

"I prefer the light," she said with a shrug. "Where's Bene?"

Kal cocked his head to gesture beyond the Hall. He did not know where his aide was exactly. Bene had been given duties, acts of Faith and service Kal expected him to accomplish. For all he knew, however, Bene could have opted to evacuate the city too.

He changed the subject. "Aldrich?"

"I've got people looking for him…as I'm sure you do. If he's smart, he's already gone out."

Kal snorted. "If he's smart, he'd take the opportunity we offered."

"He still may…in time. This," she gestured toward the unlit high ceiling of the Hall, "is not the time."

"This is precisely the time."

Difference of opinion aside, Feena shrugged. "You should come."

"I've got people out there," he said with a second snort. "I need to be steadfast for them. Those staying, those suffering, need me." But there was no one here to help, and the quavering note in his tone, the shifting of his eyes away from her, spoke of a reality she expected to hear. The Cult of the Follower was rooted in fear, in the inaccessibility of Outside, the security that the Kemways and Hebanthe Falls provided to humanity. Since the Coup, since the opening of the Outside doors, since the abduction and death of Haythem Kemway, their relevance continued to erode until little else was left except fear.

As the Senior of the faith, Kal would cling to those ingrained beliefs until forced to confront the changes…or until they killed him.

"I brought you something."

From her bag, she produced a bottle of Wulfe's Head wine. He looked between her face and the bottle several times without taking it, his frown, the creases at the corners of his eyes, his general countenance shifting into an expression of discomfort. When he did not take it, she set it on the podium and dropped her hand.

He clutched the edges of the stand, his knuckles turning white. He knew what the offering meant.

She knew it too. He was afraid of being left alone…but he was more afraid of leaving. If she went out, there was a chance she would not return. He might never see her again.

Time would tell whether the Wulfe's Head label could survive.

"Leaving these four with you," she motioned some of the men with her to step forward. "I don't know what Vanderwall…what Neoma…but I'm sure he's not risking the bugorra."

"He'd be a fool to try." The only reason Feena could risk the checkpoints was that her hand in brako leadership had remained invisible. Outwardly, she was a respectable businesswoman. The gorra would not think twice about allowing her to pass.

Kal ignored the four men left as protectors while silently acknowledging that leaving them was her promise that she intended to pick up where she was leaving off as soon as the city had enough power to allow it.

"Save that for when I'm back," she offered with a smile, her confidence in her return bringing the first lightening to his countenance she had seen since entering the Hall. "We'll have a drink, laugh about this foolishness, and turn our focus to getting Aldrich onto the Founder's seat. We need a new plan."

"If you've got a better one," he muttered, "I want to hear it."

"I'll keep my eyes open for him. I promise you I'll have one as soon as I return. Stay safe, Kal. I'll see you soon."

Not soon enough, he thought bitterly as he listened to her retreat, refusing to offer a handshake or an embrace that would mark their parting with a finality both chose to deny. He would ride out this storm where he stood. He would be right here when it was over.

He would prove that the Voices of Faith were as loyal to Hebanthe Falls and the Founder as they had ever been. He would not abandon his beliefs now.

⮎*⮌

It felt as though they had been in the shaft system for hours. Though the battery in her ICD functioned, Ginna resisted checking the time and wasting power to light the screen in favor of conserving it for when they would need it most. The battery in the P1 was down by a quarter, the glow from the screen illuminating their way as she followed the path Scarecrow had marked. She had another battery but she did not want to waste it either.

She had no idea how long this trip would take.

Each shaft, each intersection, looked so much alike, despite being marked by symbols, letters, and numbers, that she wondered how Scarecrow or the shaft workers they were careful to avoid could find their way around.

Without the P1, she doubted she would be able to do so.

"I need to rest."

Jaron sank to the floor at the top of the incline they had just climbed, back against the wall, paying no attention to the moisture or grime at his back as he closed his eyes and tried to will the weakness out of his legs. His head hurt. His lungs hurt. His feet throbbed inside of Rhyd's work boots, and he longed for something to eat, something to drink. Suspecting he would need them before he reached fresh air, he had pocketed the bottle of pain meds Tamner left before Rhyd collected the rest of the medical supplies and handed them to one of the Spinks. As tempted as he was to use them, however, he did no more than clutch the bottle without taking it out of his pocket.

"Roger." Ginna removed a plastic water bottle from her pack, handed it to one of the Spinks, and pointed to a shaft opening they had passed at the bottom of the incline where the unmoving figure of a streeter sprawled, his foot caught between the open edge of the grate and the wall. "See if you can find some more water." The bottle had been full when they started, but Jaron had consumed most of it already. She had thought to discourage him from doing so, but she knew some medication made people thirsty…and if he was suffering dehydration from his period of captivity, she did not want to be responsible for more suffering that might either hinder them from reaching their destination or that might anger or disappoint Scarecrow.

"We'll rest here until you're back. But hurry."

The boy nodded, slid down the incline, picked his way over the streeter as though he had done so many times before, and squeezed through the partially open grate. The other Spinks squatted, knelt, or sat nearby, listening, watching for signs of other streeters or work crews as Ginna knelt beside Jaron with her hand on his arm.

"You okay?"

Irritated that he was at the mercy of the kindness and care of children, Jaron muttered, "Few minutes of rest…that's all I need."

"You'll have it 'til Roger's back," she promised.

"How far we got?" asked one of the Spinks.

Ginna studied the P1. She did not know how to read the map's details. How many Levs they had traveled, how much distance existed between points, was impossible for her to gauge. Their position was marked by a flashing blip on the screen, and the route immediately ahead was shaded red for them to follow. However, she did not know how to adjust the view to show the entire route. The best she could offer was a guess. "About halfway, I'd say."

Jaron side-eyed her wearily, his expression skeptical, but the Spinks accepted her claim without question.

It did not matter how far they had come. It was not far enough.

❧*❧

She knew the haunts they had shared as children, promenades and gymnasiums, deks and flops that were sometimes empty as streeters moved about the city in search of meals, Heb, or goods to ting. She knew the more prominent places frequented by secretive mercs where they exchanged information, jobs, and the ticks they acquired for goods that others in the guild had to trade. All those places were empty now as people flocked to stairwells to merge into the slow-moving line of those seeking a path Outside.

She was surprised the lines were moving this far down the Levs, as those above cut into the lines seeking an exodus. Buggers and medical workers had their hands full breaking up fights and tending to injuries as tempers flared. Herpa and Igraci wove among them, offering respite and trying to keep people calm and patient.

The redistribution of officers meant there were fewer patrolling the streets. Broken-doored flats and vindis sat open to the elements, looted by the unscrupulous, by the beaked brako she sometimes passed carrying armloads of goods, primarily the now too-scarce nessies they refused to share with those impatiently waiting in line.

She passed men standing watch at warehouses, some locked in combat with beaked assailants, not knowing if those guards were mercs, employees, or members of the unmasked segment of brako. Sometimes the masked brako won. Sometimes they did not. She felt she should arbitrate, but she was only one officer, recovering from a serious injury. She would never stand a chance in those fights.

Besides, she was on a mission.

She passed the masked figures who had fallen victim to Scarecrow's fists, some moaning, some silent, left where they had dropped, the fruits of their raids strewn about to be scavenged by others who passed. Scarecrow, it seemed, was busy doing the bugorra's jobs for them.

Thank the Creator for that.

Ilya checked her ICD again, pinging the tracker for Blayd's location, resending the plea that he should leave the city, too. If he read her message as sincere concern and took her advice, he would be stopped at the city's doors, and detained for questioning again. Or he would seek her out, in which case she would be the one to detain him. His ICD had gone silent not long after leaving the Uppers. So far, there was no trace of him in any of the places she thought he might be. So far, if he knew she was looking for him, if he suspected her motives, he was avoiding her call.

This was one task she could not lay at Scarecrow's feet. Blayd, she felt, was her responsibility. She shone her battery torch into the bowels of an empty vindi, seeking him in the shadows. On rooftops, in the hidden places, in the hopes that it was a duty she could fulfill.

❧*❧

Following a trail of unconscious men he presumed to be brako, bodies he had not left, Scarecrow tracked Tox to an empty street where two sets of men, masked and unmasked, fought over access, or to prevent access, to a string of locked warehouses. There were too many, more than a dozen that he could count, for Tox to confront, even if she took the side of the unmasked individuals who appeared to be the victims of the beaked men's assault. Four of the beaked brako were already down, felled by her fists or by the clubs and poppers the unmasked contingent wielded.

The odds, he judged, remained against her.

Wanting to extract her from the fray and offer a much safer means of assisting him, jumping into the fight was a prospect he could not pass up. Fueled by the exhilaration of his ongoing hunt, he chose not to resist the opportunity.

None of them wore Vanderwall's yellow armband. None of them moved like he did, fought like he did. To Scarecrow, that was irrelevant. If he could keep at least one man on each side alive, he might be able to discover where the elusive man was hiding.

Not in the soaper. Scarecrow had already been there. There had to be a secondary hideout, or possibly more than one. Someone had to know where that was.

He swung up from the half-Lev roof below the fight, a mole in their midst in a swiping move that knocked the nearest masked man off his feet. The trajectory of the man's fall caused his head to strike the walkway rail. The mask was knocked free; he did not move. Tox shoved the brako she grappled with into Scarecrow's path so that, as he leaped to his feet, he caught the fellow in the kidney with his glove fist. The blow propelled the brako sideways, into the range of an unmasked man's club, where he was struck across the ribs and laid out flat on the path.

A nearby black-screened Echo hummed the ongoing report from the city doors. The words were a murmured backdrop beneath the ringing of metal beneath boots, cries and shouts of the angry, the injured, the breaking of glass, and the endless thumps of bodies against the walls, rails, and stairs as they fell. Scarecrow did not count the bodies as they dropped or the number of blows he landed. Only when a word, a phrase, stood out to him from the prodcast's drone, only when the number of unmasked outmanned the masked, did he grab Tox by the arm and yank her out of the fight.

"Leave them to it," he hissed against her resistance. "Let them sort it out. Something I need you to do."

Tox growled but followed him onto the rooftop where he had been before joining the fight. Leaving the ringing of the brawl, they moved through the shadows into an alley, across an empty intersection, without speaking until Tox realized where they were heading.

Planting her feet in the between-vindi passage they had dropped into, she shook her head. "Long as you're doing this, I'm not going…" She was favoring her right leg, rubbing her hip, but her injuries, as far as Scarecrow could tell, were not life-threatening.

"I know." There was no point in arguing the inevitable. "But we need to get the dancers out before the buggers come knocking…and you're the only one I can trust to…"

"I thought you were going to…"

"Something's come up…and they're not going to convince Maemi or Zar without…"

"You know she's not going to…"

"She's got the equipment. She can lead. Once up there, she can hook into the Hub, into a primary power source, and communicate with me from there."

Battery power here was not going to last long enough. Any help Zara could give would last only as long as she had the means to communicate. He believed she would recognize the logic of the choice once it was presented to her. He should have thought of it sooner.

He also believed that Grainger was the best shot of keeping Zara plugged in and safe.

"Jaron's on his way up. He's gonna need…"

Tox huffed, muttered sounds he thought to be a slow, annoyance-relieving count, and then said, "I'll try…but whatever they do…I'm coming back for you. You're not going after him alone."

Despite that being precisely what he intended to do, Scarecrow nodded. Once she was up, he hoped she would choose to stay. Before she could return, he hoped the struggle to find Vanderwall and end him would be over.

❧*❧

"Eido. Here."

Tamner was more surprised that Lash knew the woman than he realized he should be. Expelled from the Uppers, punished by losing his tongue with the intent that he would keep the Founder's secrets, it would have been natural for a man like Edgar Quincy to seek out those in the market for the sort of information he held. Wondering how many of Hebenon's woes stretched back to that event, how much history influenced the tribulations he was trying to untangle, he escorted the woman and her collection of Igraci and herpa towards the man who summoned them.

The bugorra he saw were busy breaking up an argument between a cluster of people making demands of a bureaucrat with a T1 trying to process their evacuation. Two women had been pulled to the side, vaguely familiar twin faces that Tamner thought he had seen during the processing of the Core survivors. Without asking, he could not be sure. Grainger was not here to supervise.

There were three other doors. The captain could be at any of them.

He might be at his desk.

"Edgar…I didn't know you'd be here." Eido clasped his hands, bent towards him, and kissed both cheeks.

"Not much choice." He looked at Tamner without malice or accusation and shrugged. "Here to help?"

"If we can."

"We can use cooler heads, ones not wielding poppers or who want to solve conflicts with the ends of their thumpers."

"If you can get them up to speed, I've got somewhere I'm supposed to be…and I'm already late." It had taken too long to get through the congested corridors, to find a gorra in charge to direct him through the crowd to this particular door where the tracks of trade once ran…where he had expected the captain to be. Neoma might wait for him, but she would not wait indefinitely.

"We know what to do," said one of the herpa.

"I'll take it from here," Lash promised as someone nearby shouted and began to run.

One bugger ran after him. Another took a shot.

There was no blood as the fugitive fell, only a sparking plume of smoke as the circuits in his bald head burned. A cluster of people in line shouted in outrage while a frightened group of parah offering blankets and food to those coming Outside lurched in surprise and dropped what they carried.

The first andi to fall without so much as an examination or a trial.

From the protection of the doorway, Soleia reported the tragedy to anyone in Hebanthe Falls who was listening.

Tamner groaned, pinched the bridge of his nose, exchanged a glance with Lash and Eido, and muttered, "See what you can do to avoid more of that."

"We'll do our best," Eido promised.

❧*❧

The children huddled around Otta, wide-eyed in anxious wonder at the adventure they had been told they were undertaking, one not so different from the escape from the Core they had undertaken several weeks before, looked towards the rattling beaded curtain as Tox passed through it. Their crestfallen expressions suggested they had been expecting someone else, but with Otta already beside them, and Skelter and Zara and the dancers leaning on the bar, Tox was unsure of who they were expecting.

Judging by Ebenee's pout, she guessed they expected Scarecrow.

The prodcast's commotion, shouted demands to halt, the crack of a popper, and the accompanying screams ended with Soleia's mortified, "He's andi..."

The dancers looked at each other and shuddered.

"Here to take you all up," Tox announced, although how she could protect the trio, she did not know. She had stopped in her flat to pull on baggy workout clothes and a loose long coat over her body armor and regretted now the time she had taken to do so. If she had gotten here sooner, the dancers might not have heard about the death of one of their own.

It might, she decided as she locked eyes with Zara, be the incentive they needed to go with her. Or it would make them too afraid to leave the Levs.

"Scarecrow said…" started Hiana.

"He's been detained…asked me to help. Zar…if you can lead us through the shafts…"

The blonde shook her head. "I don't have enough comms to…"

"But you would if you can get to the Factories, if you can patch into the Hub and power grid there. You have the contacts…" She motioned to the Echo at Zara's elbow. "You can chart a way past most of the lines…and you're the only one who can get them past the checkpoints."

It was either that or leave Nigel, Hiana, and Ebenee in Vapors.

"All of us?" asked one of the children.

"Not another tunnel like…" squeaked another.

Otta pulled that second child closer and ruffled his hair. "No, not like that. No crawling."

At least there would be none that she was aware of.

Zara reached across the bar and covered Maemi's hand with hers. "You're coming with me. We go together; we come back together."

"Colyx isn't…" began Otta with a frown. Her father had last been seen saying he had something to do for Maemi. He had not been here when Otta and the children arrived, and Maemi denied having sent him anywhere. No one had seen him.

"You go," Skelter said, turning that same determined gaze from Otta to Maemi to Zara. "I'll find him; I'll get him out." He had no idea where to begin looking, whether Colyx had fallen or had someone he was determined to assist without his daughter knowing. Finding the big man gave him an excuse to stay behind.

The women understood that the offer was equal parts aiding Colyx and equal parts an excuse to do what he had intended to do anyhow.

Maemi looked at the hand covering hers and back at the empty bar shelves where once the bottles of her trade had been displayed. The mirror was lit only with the glow of the alglamps on the bar. There were no chattering voices, no sizzle of cooking from the kitchen, the clink of glasses, or the echoes of entertainment from the dance stage. Without power, there was nothing for her here. With everyone except Rhyd, all of those she loved, seeking refuge Outside, there was no reason to remain here except stubbornness and nostalgia.

Jonner had not come back. If there was any chance he was Outside, perhaps she could find him there.

"Let me get some things and meet you out front in fifteen."

"Fifteen," Tox agreed.

Stools pushed back from the bar counter. Otta, after sharing a kiss with Skelter and whispering words no one else heard, herded the children through the curtain Tox held open. As Maemi retreated through the kitchen to the door and stairs to her flat above Vapors, Zara exchanged one last embrace with Skelter.

"I'll see you soon," she promised. "Stay safe…keep him…"

Skelter embraced her too, pressing his nose into her hair, kissing her ear, and met Tox's gaze over Zara's shoulder. "Keep 'em safe."

Tox nodded grimly. "You know I will."

Going up and Out was the safest thing.

It was Skelter and those staying below who were the ones at risk.

"Wait here…I'll make sure it's clear."

Jaron gratefully sank to the floor one more time, something that felt like it happened more frequently the longer they walked. They had come as far as the map of the shafts would take them, to a grate that opened near the ceiling into a corridor bathed with flashing emergency lighting, the red color Jaron knew to be common in the Uppers. With the Spinks clustered around him, a shield from anyone below or behind, Ginna knew she had to go first, be the one to make contact with the gorra. Her sister's status might buy her clearance and, she hoped, influence Captain Grainger to take charge of her wards.

Scarecrow had said to get Jaron to the captain. He had not told her why or what to do next.

The clattering of the vent grate onto the floor when it slipped from her hands brought a man in a medic uniform from the left. Surprised to see her as she tumbled out in her effort to catch the grate, he reached her in time to help her to her feet.

"Miss? Are you alright?"

He did not seem suspicious of her being here, of her emerging from the shaft. Her clothes, no longer damp from the Levs but gray and grungy with shaft grime, stood her apart from those in the Uppers, but with all city residents required to pass through the white halls to evacuate, her presence might not be automatically suspect. Maybe, she thought as she took his hand, she and those with her were not the first to attempt to evacuate this way.

"Ginna Young," she murmured breathlessly, offering her most courteous, if worried and distressed, smile. "I'm looking for my sister…Lieutenant Ilya…"

"Young, yes…I know her." When Ginna blinked in surprise, he blushed and shrugged and said, "I know of her…from working…not like we're friends or…"

"An officer below told me she'd be here…or to find Captain Grainger…please…if you'll help us."

She picked up the grate, propped it against the wall, and knocked on the edge of the open shaft. One by one, small faces appeared, and the Spinks began to drop out. Jaron was the last, reluctantly, to emerge.

"He said to come this way or we'd never get through…to get Mr. Rei to the captain…"

Fortunately for Jaron, as he tried to maneuver out of the shaft, the medic was there to catch him when he fell.

"He's…expecting me…" Jaron rasped, arms clinging around the man's neck as he tried to force his legs to support his weight a little longer. The medic looked alarmed and confused at Jaron's condition, and as a credit to his profession, he chose not to question a man in obvious need of medical assistance.

"I just came from there. Come with me."

The Spink Roger supported Jaron on the left as the medic propped him up on the right. With the other Spinks following, blocking Ginna from view, and the medic fussing over Jaron's weak condition, he did not notice that Ginna remained behind.

By the time he looked back to question her, she was gone.

❧*❧

Maemi gazed around the room, barely illuminated in blue and green by the alglamps she was choosing to leave behind. The dance pole remained on its side, yet to be repaired. The shelves were empty, the kitchen dark, the chairs around each table pushed in, vacant. There were no glasses to clean, no customers to attend, no aromas of whiskey and curlers flooding the room with their fragrant perfume.

Tears gathered at the corners of her eyes until she blinked them away. It wasn't supposed to be like this. Creator help her, she did not intend to let things end this way.

She adjusted the pair of shoulder bags she carried and tightened her grip on the door latch. The sacks contained every possession of importance she owned, flotsam she was determined to keep out of the hands of looters whose echoes could be heard in the Levs around her. Other memories, of those she called friends, of family lost and living, of days of celebration and mourning, were embraced by Vapors' walls. Those were things she could not pack up and take with her. Vapors would have to safeguard them until she returned.

The memories would only otherwise persist in her head and heart.

For the first time since she had taken ownership of the bar, the hemplastic door was drawn shut and locked behind her so that the beaded curtain hung between it and the outside world. Looters could break through it, but she hoped the lock, her standing in the neighborhood, and the respect her clientele had always had for her rules, would be enough of a deterrent to keep those memories safe.

There was nothing of value inside now for anyone to take.

It was not a goodbye, she promised silently as she turned to follow Tox and Otta, the first time she had ever willingly walked away from her life.

It felt like leaving family behind.

*

This was not the same door where, in weeks past, Jaron had stood behind Rhyd to experience his first glimpse of the world beyond Hebanthe Falls. That door, where the commodity rails ushered hemp into the city and other goods out of it, was far to his right, where he could see people rather than product emerging near the eastern Factories. This door, and the other out of Factory West, had been sealed shut at the city's birth, closing people inside and the rest of the destroyed world out. This door was nearest to a once-empty plain now being filled with hastily erected canvas tents, corrugated lean-tos, and benches upon which the displaced insiders gathered in muted, uncomfortable, disheartened bands.

Jaron had beheld this beauty before. The dusky mountains in the west. The fading blue sky. The fields of hemp and grain swaying in the breeze while sheep, goats, and cattle grazed nearby. This time, however, the tributary beds were devoid of water, and a significant portion of parah and prossers scurried around a distant point where it appeared the water had been cut off.

He could not tell what they were doing. He assumed they were trying to unbind the water. His breath caught, and for a few moments, he held it as if in doing so he could will the waters to flow again so that Hebanthe Falls might live.

While their medic guide spoke to the pair of buggers who intercepted them at the door, pointing at them, sharing words he did not attempt to overhear, a pair of herpa and a young woman in Igraci white took down their names and offered small packets of food, cups of water, and blankets or canvas to ward off the coming chill of night. Parah guided evacuees towards the encampment, their speech stunted by their effort to communicate in an unfamiliar dialect, and Jaron sought the comfort of the familiar in anyone he knew.

Rhyd should be here.

Oliver was not. There was not a single face he recognized amongst those coming and going, those directing, those asking questions, until one high, gleeful voice punctuated the dwindling day.

"Mr. Jaron!"

The children pushed through the crowd, the girl Agnys and Tamner's son Cori, the last people Jaron expected to see or to have recognize him. Not far behind them, dragged along by the girl's tugging hand, another dark-haired man whose face expressed his efforts to hide his displeasure, but also hope, at seeing Jaron here.

"Agnys."

He did not know the girl. They had seen each other once across the distance between Marbordo's collection of homes and the city door. He suspected she knew of him through Rhyd, possibly through Venn, and through any other acquaintances the men shared. What he knew of her likewise came through those same channels, and through the rumors and stories he had heard about the parah girl who, in conjunction with Scarecrow, had changed the course of history. There was no reason he could think of that she should recognize him.

He recognized her only from the ICD images Rhyd had saved.

Maybe he had shared the same with her.

Venn, he knew too well, although in many ways, not well enough.

He felt Venn's critical, scrutinizing gaze rake over him as the man dropped the bound bundle of hemp cloth blankets where others were being distributed. Cori, likewise, dropped his smaller bundle and retrieved the one that Agnys had dropped before running to greet the curly-haired man. Jaron wrapped one weak arm around the girl embracing his waist. He did not want a confrontation. He wanted to sit, to rest, to eat and drink, and wait for Rhyd to come.

"Is he here?" The cluster of Spinks who emerged with him had already wandered away unattended towards people they could see in the distance, where food was cooking and a handful of musicians played in the hopes of helping the displaced feel more at ease. Streeter children, Jaron…but not the person Venn wanted to see.

The unsettled, disgruntled glance Jaron gave him was the only answer he received.

"You should have made him…"

"No one makes him do anything."

Agnys steered him toward the edge of the canvas-covered processing area and helped him sit on a bench when someone else vacated a space for the injured man. Jaron wanted to go further, be away from Venn, but he also did not want to leave the doorway in case Rhyd emerged through it. If he got too far away from Hebanthe Falls, he was sure he would never see Rhyd again. "You, more than anyone, should know that."

Venn grunted. "So, you left him to…"

"You want to go down and get him? You want to be the distraction that gets him…"

He did not say the last word in deference to the children, but both knew the answer to those questions. Venn had every opportunity to go to the home he and Rhyd had shared. He had resisted until he was no longer welcome. He would not go back now, into a city without ample power, into a city with multiple forms of new, thriving danger.

If Rhyd was doing what they both knew him to be doing, the distraction of either of them was the last thing he needed. Venn would never go back.

But Jaron wanted to.

"Come, Agnys…we should get back to…"

Sitting on the bench beside Jaron with her leg pressed to his, her feet swinging with nervous energy, Agnys shook her head. "I'm staying here. Maybe he'll…"

"He's not coming, Agnys," Venn muttered. "He made his choice."

She crossed her arms over her chest stubbornly and pouted. "He might. You don't know that. I'm staying."

Huffing, annoyed that another person appeared to have taken Jaron's side, though more accurately, Agnys had taken Rhyd's side, Venn muttered, "Suit yourself," and started back toward the village.

Cori nodded at Jaron, picking up his hand to inspect the bruises the way his father would have, and said, "Wait here; my father will take care of these. I'll bring you food and see if I can find him."

Jaron nodded too and looked into Agnys' wide, blue eyes. If anyone could prompt Rhyd to come out, it would be the child he had once risked his life to save. Agnys had not been enough to keep him out before, but maybe this time would be different.

❧Chapter 39❧

Service shaft 20-F1-B16AA.

That was what the message had said, a message from one of the last people he expected to hear from.

Not knowing the shaft designations, and with Hub access infrequent and unreliable, by the time Grainger cornered a heizer to learn where that particular shaft was located, he feared he would miss her. Fail her.

He did not lie to himself that he burned with more than a little hope that if Zara was evacuating, she was bringing Jaron with her.

The corridor was empty when he reached it, a splinter path into storage and maintenance Sheds out of the way of the unending lines of refugees cluttering the white halls of the Uppers. Those people had either looked at him wearily, warily, as he strode past, had shied away from his resolute demeanor, or else ignored him and his uniform as though he were but one more person there to inhibit their progress. He barely noted their faces, all variations on the same frustrated, frightened theme. Now he was alone, pacing back and forth in front of the service shaft grate. Waiting.

"Do you need something, Captain?"

"No…no." He waved off the spener without looking at her. This was an odd place for the bugorra captain to wait, to pace, but it was out of the way of the lines in the corridors. The possibility that he was waiting for one of the Shed bosses to give a status report was feasible enough that the woman who ducked past him into the nearby Shed merely nodded and let the captain be.

The door closed.

His fists and jaw clenched.

Moments later…footsteps. In the shaft.

Anxiously, he pried the grate free with his fingers, ignoring the pain as a sharp edge sliced across one of them, ignoring the strangling bile that rose into his throat and refused to be swallowed. Once it was free, he dropped it against the wall at the side of the opening and took the hand of the woman who was the first to emerge.

"Zara…"

He did not care if the word, the way he spoke it, was more intimate than intended. She was here, she was safe, she was one less person for him to worry about.

"Oliver." She turned her face away to mask the flush on her pale cheeks, a blush made more noticeable by the exertion she had spent to get here. She looked instead at the dark-skinned woman surrounded by the collection of children who emerged one by one, out of the shaft.

"I'm sorry we came like this…"

"No, don't be." Now that he saw her here, he was surprised that more people had not tried to utilize the shafts to avoid the caterpillar-crawl up the myriads of Lev stairs. Most, however, gave little thought to the shaft system unless their water, heat, filtration, or waste systems failed to work.

Many who might consider using that path would have no idea how to navigate that even darker, unfamiliar world.

By the P1 in her hand, of course, Zara would know how.

Another woman came next, the swiver from Vapors, a face he recognized from the times he had been there. And behind her, the dancers whose presence here put all of them in a precarious position.

"They can't…" he stammered, listening to the retreat of footsteps inside the shaft, someone he could not see. Not Jaron, he thought with a sigh and a cough as nervous bile broke free and burned into his belly.

Scarecrow?

"Oh, they're not going Outside, not yet," Zara countered, shifting her Echo bag on her shoulder. "They're coming with me. I need a port…power…if you could patch me into a Factory switch or…"

His head bobbed eagerly, though his gaze continued to flicker past her into the unlit shaft. Movement there had ceased, but a part of him continued to hope.

"Yes, of course." He did not ask why she needed those things. She had helped identify Vanderwall. She had helped save Jaron's life. She had helped generate the now-sabotaged array and more. She had also been unfailingly kind to him, despite the bugorra uniform, when few others would have been. She might still have more she intended to give their city if her skills as haikara were put to good use. It was why, he believed, she had chosen this shaft location. It put them near the door to one of the many interior Factory entrances. If she wanted, needed, access to Factory resources, he would see that she had it. He owed her that much.

Keeping the andi with her, out of sight of anyone suspicious enough to arrest them by avoiding the evacuation points, would protect the ageless dancers until some decision could be made on their behalf or he could find some other way to get them Outside unnoticed.

"Jaron?"

"Already out," she said with a noticeably stifled sound that made him regret his question as soon as it was spoken. "Or he should be."

Surprised, he wondered where or when Jaron had gotten past him. There were too many exits to monitor alone. Too many places for him to be, too much for him to do. And no one had been instructed to watch for Jaron Rei or told to notify the captain when he emerged.

He would have to seek out the younger man and see that he was well. The last time he had seen Jaron…however many hours ago that had been…he had not been well at all.

"The rest of you?"

"We're going out," Otta replied, stepping forward, shouldering the responsibility of breaking away from the Levs so that Maemi did not have to. The older woman's face was unreadable, but Otta could feel her reluctance and trepidation to move another step.

"Come with me." Into the Factory, where he would see that Zara had everything she needed, and then Outside. "You three…stay close to her." The workers in the Factory were too busy to ask questions about four strangers, but it was best if the andi took no chances.

The hand he had not realized was still clutching his squeezed. He looked at the shared link between them and up into Zara's eyes as she nodded and murmured, "Thank you, Oliver."

He nodded too and reluctantly let her go.

⤷*⤶

The retaining wall protecting the western outcropping had been shored into place, built high enough and sturdy enough that Jonner had assured Enoch, and Enoch had, in turn, assured the parah, that it should hold for many years so long as the weather maintained its normal ebb and flow and no further land movement occurred to undermine it. The river's overflow had destroyed crops and some homes at the northern end of Marbordo and had damaged others before the flow had been confined to the sixth tributary by a wall of stone, wood, hemp, and sacks of beach sand and earthen clay. Where seepage appeared, people continued to work to prevent further erosion. The work to trench through the collapse would begin once an evening meal had filled the bellies of the exhausted villagers and those from Hebenon they had recruited, and a night's rest revived overworked muscles.

Over the sea's horizon, dark clouds gathered, the coming of rain, the parah said, if the southerly racing clouds pressed nearer to land. Rain meant the need for more evacuation shelters, for more blankets and bedding, so some people shifted their labor from the river banks to the aid of the growing encampment of the displaced population.

It had grown clearer as the day passed that if those people remained outside, they would require re-education in addition to housing few had ever had to build, and food and clothes that most had never had to provide for themselves. They would need ongoing intervention to integrate into the already exhausted parah civilization.

Enoch did not know how they would accomplish any of those things, as many within the mass collection of prossers seemed to believe they were entitled to whatever the parah had. But he was determined to see that they did.

He tried to impress upon those he passed that, if they wanted to return to the city, the tributaries needed to flow. They needed to help. Not as many of them helped as he hoped, but the parah, thus far, had been remarkably accommodating. They had homes to protect, refugees or not. They shared what they had despite the evacuees' refusal to do more. They helped where they could, even as the number of migrants grew to a size the parah could never have imagined.

They should have been the ones afraid. Instead, it was amidst the swell of the homeless that paranoia and hostility grew, towards the parah, towards each other.

There was only one person who seemed able to mediate between them. And Tamner was not here.

A tiny glimmer in the mud, steel in the torchlight, something exposed by the oversplash of the river's push against the collapsed mud and stone, drew Enoch cautiously down the embankment. Holding the torch aloft in one hand, he pried the object free and with his thumb rubbed off as much mud from it as he could. A smudge of black, like candle soot, came off too, smearing across his hand like the substance people used to line their eyes.

It was just a fragment, small and flat, jagged and nondescript in function, curled at the edge as if forced apart from something larger. He sat in the mud, planted the end of the torch into the earth, and worked the dirt from it so that when he held it up to the torchlight, he was able to examine it more closely.

It was impossible to gauge what it was or what it had been.

An outburst along the border of the refugee camp, a skirmish of pushing and shoving that he could barely see, made Enoch look up. Others broke up the disagreement, pulling the combatants apart, although the participants continued to shout at each other as more bystanders filled the gap between them to prevent further violence.

Where the sky met the sea, the air crackled with tines of sizzling light. It was a distraction from the fight, as those from inside the city turned to marvel at a fearsome sight they had never seen. Enoch looked up too.

The bit of metal nicked his thumb.

He frowned, shoved his finger into his mouth, ignoring the dirt, and shifted his gaze to the continuing stream of people shuffling out of Hebanthe Falls.

The parah did not craft metal. They used it, tools and objects they had traded the city-dwellers for, items they relied on the Factories to repair when they broke or grew dull. Blades for cutting timber, carving wood, plowing earth, or the slaughter and preparation of animals. Whatever he cupped in his calloused palm, this was not that.

Something washed downriver from another settlement, perhaps? A fleck of something used in the building of the retaining wall? A relic of the world that had been, before Hebenon was constructed, perhaps left during the city's birth. Or was it, he thought with a sick feeling as he looked at the ground beneath his feet that had, for centuries, been covered with water, the remains of something more sinister?

He did not think he could ever know. He was not sure he wanted to. But with the future of Hebenon on the line, he wondered.

❧*❧

With the settling of night and the potential of a lightning storm charging the air, Jonner had intended to join those who returned to the heart of Marbordo for an evening meal but made a detour instead to the primary city door. Aware that Enoch remained alone at the construction site, he continued to glance over his shoulder as he walked, but could no longer see him. There had been questions from the start, about the collapse, about construction delays that were, Jonner assured everyone, to be expected if things were to be done correctly. Questions about the plume of smoke that few had noticed, or recognized as smoke rather than a dust cloud. Jonner did not believe that any evidence remained that would suggest sabotage or tie him to it, but he remained cautious throughout every hour they worked. He was especially attentive and vigilant after learning of the detainment of the Core survivors earlier.

Lash said there were concerns about an assassin among them. Jonner could not imagine who that might be, who would risk their new freedom to kill the Founder. He wanted to be sure he was not detained for that crime, that no one discovered the one he was guilty of.

Was it such a bad thing if it accomplished the goals he intended, the objective Hebenon needed? Was it wrong to force the extraction of humanity out of their prison in the falls?

"Jonner?"

The hand on his arm startled him and jerked him around, but the familiar voice prompted an embrace rather than an impulsive strike against someone who might seek to arrest him. The fine line between the right thing and the guilt yoked around his neck for the homes and lives lost prompted him to bury his face against the woman's hair after a partial nod at Otta and the saucer-eyed children with her.

The young ones had lived their entire lives in the Core. They had never dreamed of stepping into a world such as this.

Their wondrous, if fearful, expressions made him feel good about the choices he had made.

"You made it."

"No choice," Maemi said, accepting the embrace stiffly, her conflicting emotions pulling in too many directions for her to give way to any one of them. "Is this…real…?"

"Couldn't be more real," he assured her and those with her. As they carried the bundles the herpa, Igraci, and parah volunteers provided each person that came out, Jonner assumed they had just gotten free. There was so much he wanted to show them.

"Are you…is everything…?" Having feared him dead, she studied his face looking for any trace of injury. All she saw was evidence of a day spent working to save the village and set the river free.

"It's all good. Everything is good. Or almost everything." He could not imagine his life being any more perfect than it was, now that Maemi was here. "Follow me and I'll show you."

He had a tent. He had his own fire. So long as Maemi stayed at his side, he would share it with all of them.

Maemi nodded hesitantly, her gaze now turning to the flashes of light over the sea. The children flinched and cowered behind Otta, who scanned the faces she could see in the hopes that Skelter and Colyx would be there.

"It'll be okay," Otta murmured, meeting Jonner's gaze, expecting the same reassurance.

Jonner smiled and nodded. "It's all gonna be okay."

❧*❧

"Look like you're helping," Zara hissed to Nigel on her left and Ebenee on her right as Hiana finished wiring the Echos into the ports Grainger had given them access to. Factory workers rushing to create and assemble the parts needed to repair the solar array eyed the thin, androgynous blonde, a figure obviously out of place amongst the Factory staff, here at the captain's orders as she arranged the table to her satisfaction and set up each of the Echos she had brought.

Being here with Oliver's approval might buy them favor, but it might not be enough to avoid unwanted questions if the three people with her did not appear to have some part in whatever Zara was here to undertake.

Cables connected, Hiana sat down too at the rickety end of the bench that was barely long enough for the four of them. One by one, the screens flickered to life. Zara directed the data, Hub access, SCAM access to the few SCAMs around the areas where she expected Rhyd and Skelter to be, and tuned her earbud audio to monitor the bugorra communications. She had those with her listen to the chatter fed to Oliver throughout the Hub and transmitted over the prods, as well as reports coming from each of Hebenon's exits, seeking mention of arrests and violence at the city's doors. She wanted Rhyd to know everything that might affect the work he was undertaking.

She wanted validation that Jaron, Maemi, and everyone else were safe. She wanted to be sure that Vanderwall did not slip through. If he reared his head anywhere, Rhyd would know that too. With three other sets of eyes and ears to help her, Zara did not intend to miss anything.

☙*❧

She waited as long as she cared to. The flat was nice enough, clean and once comfortable, but without heat and water, after a shared meal of everything in the pantry and cool box worth consuming, Neoma refused to stay put. Against the Talkers' advice, now that they knew they were awaiting Doctor Tamner's arrival, Neoma bundled up her daughter and herded everyone into the empty street.

The last collection of footsteps of evacuees from this street had shuffled past with loud, grumbling voices over an hour before.

It seemed safe enough to risk continuing their upward journey with the intent of meeting the doctor somewhere along the way.

She muttered to herself as Ulynda trudged behind with her head down and pack clutched tightly against her chest. There was a host of reasons that might have delayed Tamner's arrival, a myriad of reasons why no one had come in his stead, but the reasons she dwelt on that seemed the most plausible, centered on a single, bitter theme.

Abandonment and betrayal.

No one cared about the survival and security of the Founder's family now that Haythem was dead.

No one was coming for them.

Even the buggers they passed, pulling and herding streeters and addicts out of alleys and flops and the mouths of this shaft, paid the women surrounded by the small collection of Talkers little attention.

Some of the streeters moved willingly, lured by the promise of food or Hebbies. Some fought back, resisting relocation, resisting being Taken as so many had been in the past. Their reluctance sometimes resulted in short-lived brawls that required all of the bugorra's attention. They had no time to heed anyone obeying the evacuation order on their own.

Still, Neoma continued to scowl as they skirted the edges of an intersection and the collection of people the bugorra had collected there. She did not raise her head or look at them as she passed but she firmly believed that someone should recognize them, that someone should care about Haythem's child if nothing more.

If she wanted to protect the only leverage she had, it was up to her to get Ulynda out of Hebenon while she and her escorts had light enough to see by.

Up another set of stairs. What Lev were they on now? Without asking, doubting the Talkers knew, Neoma scanned the path and the square they entered. The esplanade was dark, surrounded by unlit vindis, silent deks, a vacant herpa hall, and black-screened Echos that provided audio instruction for the immediate evacuation of Hebanthe Falls. Behind her, Ulynda tripped on the topmost step, one wet shoe catching on the lip as the other slid beneath her and pitched her against her mother's legs. Neoma turned with a hand raised, a growl on her lips and annoyance in her eyes as Nanny caught the child's shoulders to right her and pull her into an embrace to protect her.

"It's her!"

Peering from the doorway of the herpa hall where they had sought refuge from a flurry of bugorra boots marching the latest herd of streeters past, Molly yanked Switz back so they would not be seen by the Talkers coming up the stairs.

"Who?" grumbled Switz, his hand curled around the handle of the sharp cooking knife swiped from an abandoned vindi, his focus distracted by the shadow he had been watching before Molly's disruption. The shadow could have been anyone, or no one, but its stride, the swing of its arms, had set off alarms in Switz's head that prompted him to hide until it, and the bugorra footsteps, had passed.

He thought the shade had disappeared into a vindi to their left. He preferred to wait for it to re-emerge and continue on its way.

Molly chose differently.

Waiving one hand to attract the woman's attention, the only hope he thought he had of making it out of Hebenon, the only one who might protect him, protect them both, from those who intended to arrest them for the crime of being Core residents…if not for any actual crime, Molly cried, "Mam! It's me! It's Molly! I know the way up!" as he pulled his companion along behind him.

Switz tried to dig in his heels, but the slippery plating offered no purchase and he slid forward, yelping, "What the cazzing…?"

He knew that voice. It brought Blayd up from the vindi kiosk stool he had settled on and prompted him to leave the partially consumed bottle of alcohol on the sticky, unattended counter. The vindi had seemed an adequate place to wait out the ping of bugger boots on the grated walks above and below him, to catch his breath and plot another move in a secure location.

Ilya was looking for him. Likely other buggers too. Whatever she knew, or wanted to know, he had to avoid her for as long as he could in the hopes that Hebenon's chaos would override her interest in him. Given enough time, enough distance, he would be forgotten and she would go Out.

He had no intent to do likewise.

He would exist in this darkness for as long as he had to.

He was not afraid of the Talkers he noted to his left. The only Talker he cared about was Kal, and as far as he could determine, the Senior was not part of this group. He had no interest in the stranger pulling free of the smaller man who held him back. It was the unwitting man pulled into the street, who clutched the herpa hall door frame to avoid falling or being exposed…the last person who could betray Blayd to the buggers, to Ilya, who should be his only focus.

But another voice followed, one of frustrated annoyance snapping, "Why are you so clumsy?" that made Blayd's ears burn and his breath catch. That voice was enough to turn his attention from Switz, back to the Talkers as Molly's words burned in his ears…and then to the sound of boots on the descending stairs across from him…that made his heart pound and forced his attention away from everyone else.

Switz and Neoma be damned. Neither was worth being caught by Ilya and the bugorra.

Seven brako, their faces hidden behind long beaks, arms laden with sacks, boxes, and crates of loot collected along their way, stopped behind the one in front of them, a man with a yellow armband, big and bulky enough to command the attention of everyone in the square.

He knew Molly, though the little haikara addict meant nothing to him. The merc and the other man clutching the herpa hall doorframe were irrelevant, although he wondered if one of those two was one of the suspects the bugorra were looking for. Worth a potential bounty, but one that could not match the prize to his right.

The remaining two Kemways were worth everything else combined.

"Want her alive!" he barked with a gesture that prompted those behind him to drop what they carried and rush past down the stairs.

Scarecrow had followed Molly this far, not thinking the man worth the wrath of his fists but curious to see where they would lead. Both Molly and the man with him, who had aided in extracting the children from the Core, were wanted in connection to the Founder's murder, so it seemed time better spent to notify Lieutenant Young of their location and take advantage of a brief rest on this vindi rooftop as he waited for the bugorra to arrive. Removing the threat of Molly from Skelter's life was in his friend's best interest; finding the Founder's assassin was in Hebenon's.

The merc was of interest too, another link to the Founder he knew the bugorra sought. The Talkers were irrelevant, those they escorted unidentified before the approaching shadows of brako reached the top of the nearby stairs across from him.

The brako were the quarry he sought, the targets Scarecrow was most interested in. Particularly when the one in the lead, empty-handed and towering, voiced his command.

Scarecrow did not need the yellow armband to know who the big man was. And with that command and the woman's voice on his left, he did not need to see her face, or the child's behind her, to know who Vanderwall's target was.

There was no time for strategy. The need for vengeance, for justice, the need to protect the innocent, were the only things that mattered. Using the power pole at the edge of the vindi for leverage, Scarecrow spun around it, swung down, and dropped into the square directly in front of the merc's path.

Blayd rocked back, away from the unexpected movement in front of him, a fist thrust wildly at the perceived assailant as the brako charged. The blow missed its intended mark as Scarecrow rolled to his feet, the vigi focused on reaching the man on the stairs. His trajectory brought him into the path of the seven men barreling towards the Talkers and the women and children with them. With a roar of frustration made more frightening by the digitized speech unit, Scarecrow turned on the more immediate threat in time to catch one of the brako in the temple with his fist.

The man was thrown sideways and landed with a clatter on the grated ground.

Vanderwall remained at the base of the stairs.

His minions were enough to handle unarmed Talkers, two scrawny streeters, and one vigi. The merc, for the moment, did not appear to be a threat.

Molly, already across the promenade, threw himself at the Talkers in the hopes of taking shelter among them, but those Talkers in front, perceiving him to be a threat, pushed him back into the path of the oncoming brako. Blayd, with popper drawn, decided to enter the fray by barreling forward too. While the Talkers at the rear of the group pulled Neoma, Ulynda, and Nanny stumblingly behind them, blocking the brako's entrance to the stairs, Molly lost his footing and fell.

The remaining brako swerved past, ignoring him.

Believing that Blayd was more interested in the prestige of protecting Mam Kemway from the brako than he would be in the one little man with a knife in his hand, having nowhere to run that would not put him into harm's way except back into the herpa hall, Switz decided on the last course of action anyone would have expected. He scrambled forward, grabbed Molly's arm, and began to drag him to safety. Molly tried to push to his feet in that grasping hold, ducked to avoid Scarecrow's kick that knocked another brako out of the charge and stumbled into Switz's path.

Talkers screamed in outrage as the front-most brako plowed into their barricade, and a grappling struggle began. The man who had been kicked to the side before Scarecrow caught another by the collar of his coat was thrown against Blayd, and the merc, not expecting it, was tossed to fall between Switz and Molly.

Molly was torn from Switz's grasp. Realizing where he was in that roll, Blayd landed on his back with the popper aimed at Switz's head. Molly's scramble to right himself forced a split-second readjustment of the popper so that Switz, unbalanced by the loss of his dragging hold, lurched to the side and took the popper pellet in his shoulder.

It should have been enough to propel him off his feet, throw him against a nearby vindi cart looted of its goods and tipped on its side. Instead, he staggered, stunned and wide-eyed, long enough for Molly to wrap his arms around Blayd's legs in the hopes of preventing him from rising in pursuit. Blayd, in his fury, twisted his torso and took a second shot. The pellet that should have buried itself between Molly's eyes instead lodged inside the popper, causing it to jerk and twist in Blayd's hand. Blayd screamed, dropped the too-hot popper, and clutched his hand to his chest.

"Go!" Molly shouted. Assuming he would be lucky enough to extract himself from this unexpected melee alive because he had always lived a lucky life, Molly had no intention of remaining in it any longer than necessary. He expected Switz to do the same, particularly now that the kicked-aside brako was staggering to his feet to loom over the merc and his pair of assailants.

The brako, however, thinking the popper had been aimed at him, swiped low with the shock stick he carried, swinging with enough force to knock the useless popper away. With Blayd's attention on the brako and his injured hand, Molly let him go and used his arms and feet to crab hastily away…just as Switz charged.

The knife in his hand sank into the merc's neck.

Blayd, wild-eyed as he lurched to his feet to charge, bull-like, into the brako, crashed against Molly.

The buzzer came down with enough force to stun Molly, and he, too, landed heavily on the wet ground.

Switz, one bloody hand covering his bloodier shoulder, retreated into the herpa hall.

Always aware of Vanderwall on the periphery, Scarecrow was also aware that the Talkers were engaged in a losing fight with the brako, despite his effort to intervene. With Ulynda wailing in Nanny's arms as the woman pulled her towards the door of an open flat, four of the Talkers had already fallen victim to the assault. Scarecrow's efforts had felled three of the seven brako and sent a fourth crashing over the promenade rail, when the brako broke free of his skirmish with the merc and caught Scarecrow with charging arms around his waist, one of the remaining three sliced through the throat of the last Talker while the other reached for Neoma's arm.

She had no combat skills, no self-defense training, no weapons with which to defend herself. There had never been any need for those things in the Uppers, as the wife of Founder Kemway. What Neoma did have, however, was desperation, determination, and outrage, enough of each, now that she had no one to protect her, to fuel her madly flailing limbs armed with one heavy bag of personal belongings and another she had scooped up from the bottom of the stairs as she was forced to retreat and take a stance in front of the door where Ulynda was sheltered.

"How dare you!" she bellowed, one swinging bag catching the first grappling brako across the head.

He fell against the rail with cracking ribs and was pushed over it by the sudden arrival of another man, nondescript and unidentifiable, who pushed between her and the last, knife-wielding brako.

With a strong hold on the man clinging to his back and a snap forward, the attacker was hurled away. He bumped and clattered down the stairs to land behind his only surviving companion.

Nanny leaped from the doorway to pull Neoma back into it.

The brako with the blade took his chance.

The stranger, with a long piece of pipe in hand, shouted, "Go! Get him!" with a point behind Scarecrow as he swung and caught the knife-wielding brako across the shoulder. He fell to the side, the knife no longer in his grasp.

Scarecrow's gaze and his first step followed the stranger's gesture.

Vanderwall.

Two popper shots.

Neoma yelped.

Nanny screeched.

Scarecrow looked back to see the stranger stagger and slump against the wall of the flat, his hands tight around the last brako's wrist so that the popper dropped, clattered, and skittered away before bouncing over the edge of the rooftop below. With the women now unprotected, Vanderwall would have to wait. Scarecrow threw two bladed stars taken from the strap across his breast, trusting his aim without the guarantee that they would find their mark, before dashing across the promenade, expecting to be followed, to be ambushed, to be tackled.

The sounds behind him, sounds of Vanderwall's pain as the stars bit into flesh, eased Scarecrow's frustration at once more losing the quarry he wanted desperately to catch.

Two men fought on the ground at the bottom of the stairs, in front of the open door, their boots screeching against the grating as one fought to be free of the arm around his neck beneath the edge of the Crow mask he wore. Nanny's face was misshapen by the point-blank popper pellet that had shattered one cheekbone and made pulp out of one eye. Neoma, oblivious to the grime of the wet ground as she knelt, hunched forward, leaning over the other woman's body. The stranger, himself bloody and sporting several gashes across days-old bruises and burns, made one final jerking motion, snapping the neck of the man he clenched against his chest with one arm. The brako went slack.

"Did you…?"

Scarecrow did not reply as he squatted beside Neoma and put a hand on her back.

"Too bad…least these got what they deserved…" The stranger's sighing, disappointed breath rattled in his chest, but there were few visible fresh wounds Scarecrow could see. "Get them to…"

"Don't," Neoma hissed, jerking away from Scarecrow with a flinch of pain. "Get her to Tamner…he promised…"

"Momma…" From the dark of the flat behind Nanny's head, Ulynda's little voice squeaked in alarm. For all of her anger, fear, and hatred of the woman in front of her, Neoma was still her mother.

"I'll get you both to…"

"You need to go…there'll be more…" croaked the stranger.

"I'll stay with her," Neoma gestured to Nanny with a bloody hand her daughter could not see as she turned the older woman's face away from Ulynda. "I'll wait for the medics and join you later. You have to go, Ulynda…"

Hebenon rang with the clatter of the foretold boots. Scarecrow, assessing Neoma's hand, noting the blood that dripped from her side onto the grate in her hands and knees stance, nodded as he got to his feet and held his hand out to Ulynda.

"I'll stay," the stranger promised. "Just know…we're not…they are not…all bad by choice." Vanderwall had left him to his fate when he had fallen over a Lev rail; men he thought he could trust had done likewise. But they weren't all bad by choice…any more than he had been. He hoped this final act had been enough to prove that.

Brako.

Scarecrow wished he had time to speak with the man further, to learn the brako secrets that might lead him to Vanderwall. But there was no time.

"Go, Ulynda. He'll protect you. I'll be there as soon as I can."

Scarecrow paused to scoop up several nearby weapons and put them in the stranger's lap as Ulynda gingerly stepped over Nanny's outstretched arm, unable to see the woman's face and refusing to look at her mother's. When she hesitantly accepted the vigi's hand, Neoma hissed and glowered at him. "You will keep her safe," she demanded. "You owe him that much."

Again, Scarecrow nodded. He did not believe he owed Neoma, or the Founder, anything for all they had taken from him and the whole of Hebanthe Falls. But Ulynda was not to blame for anything. He would keep her safe, even if it temporarily deterred him from his primary mission.

"Come."

Ulynda paused, turned back, and slowly bent as if she would tearily kiss her mother's cheek. He could not tell if she was successful before Neoma turned her face away and snorted, "Go."

There was no farewell.

She would not give in to that particular expression of weakness. She would make sure Ulynda remembered her as the strong woman she had always portrayed herself to be.

Scarecrow hoisted the girl in one arm and stepped past the fallen brako and Talkers upon the stairs as she clung to his neck. Neoma waited until she could no longer hear them before moving, shifting off her knees to sit with her back against the wall of the flat. For a moment, she was silent beneath the dripping eave, exchanging glances with the stranger as the approaching footsteps drew closer. She did not look toward them as she closed her eyes with a groan, shutting out the dying darkness of the city that had betrayed her.

If she had ever done one good thing with her life, she hoped this was it. That this was enough to make a difference to whatever forces held fate in their hands.

Blood seeped through her clenched fingers as she pressed her hand against her side. The warmth of it was the last sensation she felt; the screech of the shift change whistle, the rumble of footsteps, the dripping of water, and the slowing thunder of her pulse in her ears were the last things Neoma heard.

❧Chapter 40❧

The woman's hand on his arm stopped him as he tried to squeeze past the winding queue of refugees clogging the corridor. The space between Delora Carville's grey eyes was pinched with worry as she and her husband shuffled their treasures between their feet and clutched the bags and satchels of clothes and other items that aided in slowing their forward progress toward the Factory door Grainger had just left. Open doors revealed Upper residents scrambling to collect mementos of their lives that they did not want to be pilfered during their absence instead of clothes and food, preferring to live without nessies and to believe that they would only be gone a short period in favor of protecting their treasures. Families argued about what to take, what to leave, and when they left, they locked their doors against the possibility of looters from the Levs.

None of the Lev evacuees were permitted in this section of the Uppers, being directed instead to the city exits. There was little reason to fear…but after the Coup, they feared nonetheless.

Grainger wondered how many were thinking about the previous evacuations into the Factories, how many were considering the fates of those past Founders had banished to the Outside. Had they shared the same fears? Had they entertained any hope of ever coming back?

He suspected, as his gaze swept over the pensive faces, that most considered no one except themselves and their families.

"You are coming with us, Captain?"

He smiled at Delora as soothingly as he could. "In time," he promised with a nod, glancing at his ICD, thankful for the interruption. He hoped it would be a message from his lieutenant, a reply indicating she had received his summons and was on her way up.

He could not shake the feeling that he would need her more here in this corridor than he needed her commanding the Levs. He needed better crowd control as the city slowly emptied.

They still needed to interrogate their captive before they lost the generator light to see him. They needed to interrogate him where he was before they could decide where it was wisest to move him to. Taking him, Borne, or the Talker Hall vandals Outside past the already anxious throng would cause a panic Grainger did not want to entertain.

With as many people as he had seen through his open office door, trudging down the corridor toward their designated exit, he could not imagine there were many people left in the Levs to evacuate.

"Is the Nau…?" he asked absently, sensing she was waiting for him to say more.

"Oh yes, most of us are already out, I believe," she assured him. "I don't think the Pissos have come yet…and Andre's in the Factory overseeing the printing…but you must come too. We'll need you."

"Doing my job," he reminded her. "Making sure everyone's out and the repairs get done."

It looked as if she would argue, but instead, she nodded and patted his arm. "Bless you, Captain. I don't think any of this…once we have the killer…when the water flows and the array's fixed…we will all come home, won't we?"

Her husband snorted before Grainger could reply and muttered, "Of course, we're coming home. Where else would we go? They wouldn't dare lock us out."

Grainger bit his tongue, thinking of how many times the Doctet had done just that to others, and instead said, "When it's safe, of course. Now…" he tapped his ICD, "if you'll excuse me."

"When it's safe," Delora agreed in a tremulous voice, letting him go as the line inched forward.

Her husband's grip on her elbow urged her on.

*

"You're not him."

Ginna and the Spinks with her, the smallest and youngest she had been able to round up in her last sweep of the lower Levs, had begun their ascent through the shafts, avoiding work crews who paid the children little mind as they focused on stabilizing the city systems for the eventual return of power. Her heart soared at the first glimpse of the figure descending one of the shaft ladders but when she realized that this was a woman, every one of the children stopped behind Ginna's outstretched arms.

"Maemi's safe," Tox said without speaking the obvious. "Otta and the children, too. I sent them out with Mr. Rei. You should go too."

Ginna narrowed her gaze and held her ground. "Who are you?"

The woman's attire looked similar to Scarecrow's, made, it appeared, of the same material. The cut of her mask was much the same, though not identical. She had heard rumors over the past several hours of another vigi, a woman, protecting evacuees and fighting with the brako, but until this moment, Ginna had thought the stories to be no more than mistaken sightings of Scarecrow.

It appeared the rumors were true.

Maybe in this desperate hour, Scarecrow was not protecting the citizens of the city alone.

The female vigi held up her palm, offering the same round toxin symbol throwing blade that Scarecrow used.

Maybe she had stolen it or found it at the scene of one of Scarecrow's fights, but Ginna did not think so.

"Have you seen him? Do you know where he is? Have you seen Vanderwall?"

"All we saw was a fight…Lev Six by Eastside deks," said one of the Spinks, eager to be helpful, more accepting of the unfamiliar vigi and her similarities to Scarecrow than Ginna was. "Then he left following a pair of streeters. We haven't seen him since."

"How long ago?"

The child shrugged. "Dunno. Been awhile…"

"Shift change," said another.

"There's no shift change," argued a third.

A fourth elbowed the third and hissed, "Still the whistle…"

Lev Six. Tox listened to the voice in her earpiece that indicated she had another four Levs to go to reach that position. There was no guarantee Scarecrow would be there, but it was a place to start. Her location was a detail Zara would pass on to Rhyd as well.

Both hoped Rhyd would accept the offer of working together.

"Thank you." She put the round blade in Ginna's hand and stepped back. "Go up and stay safe."

"If you see him, tell him I'll be back," Ginna said as she tucked the blade away. "Tell him we're here if he needs us."

Though she wanted to again compel Ginna to go Out and not come back until the city was safe, Tox kept those admonitions to herself. Ginna would not heed the warning any more than Tox was doing. Hebenon needed Scarecrow, and Scarecrow needed people like them.

It made a return to the dark bowels necessary if he, and the city, were to survive.

Hand still clutching his shoulder when the pain and the buzzing hum of a generator pulled him back to consciousness, Switz forced himself to sit up despite the dizziness. His injury caused him to lurch as his wrist met the manacled restraint that bound him to the frame of the medi cot he found himself on, and he swore beneath his breath. There were others in the room too, likewise restrained to their beds, men and women sporting an assortment of injuries, moaning in pain, confusion, and distress. This was not a clinic, looked more like a flop-turned-emergency-triage center. What he did know was that he was still in the Levs. The flicker of the lights, the rancid smell of old sweat and antiseptic, and the bitter taste of copper that lingered on his tongue suggested that this was a place he did not want to be.

Of those he could see nearest him, Molly was not one of them.

Nor did he see Blayd among the silent bodies of those whose gray pallor announced them as deceased. He did not remember what had happened beyond disjointed snippets of imagery…brako, Molly, and the Talkers…Scarecrow…and Blayd. He recalled the popper, the buzzer, the knife in his hand. He remembered the give of flesh beneath his striking, clenched fist. He was not certain of anything else, but he was reasonably certain Blayd was dead.

Maybe whoever had brought him here had left the merc's body to the elements. Maybe Molly was dead too.

He pulled at the restraint but could not break free. He growled as another woman was wheeled into the crowded room and was lifted onto an empty cot and likewise restrained. He watched in silence, determined not to attract attention, as a dead man was carried out.

If he was being held pending his arrest, he did not want attention.

He had gotten out of worse spots than this. He could get out of this one. But not, he decided as a pair of young medics came to his side and pulled up his loose sweater to examine and clean the wound on his shoulder, until he was convinced he would not bleed to death.

A plast, maybe a meal like those being offered to a few patients at the far end of the room, and then he would get free of this place.

He would find Molly and find out what the cazz had happened.

"Are you there?"

The static in his earpiece had crackled earlier, popped in and out of silence several times as Scarecrow took Ulynda through the shafts, the fastest way to travel without interruptions from the brako or anyone else. Whether stronger than he expected or traumatized beyond words, Ulynda remained quiet, close to his side without questioning his choice or directions. Once inside the shaft, she released his hand and refused to be touched or carried, choices he did not disobey except when it was necessary to aid her up a ladder, through a hatch, or into particularly narrow or unpleasant passages.

There was always hesitation. Sometimes she accepted the offer.

Most of the time, she did not. Now she waited behind him, their path illuminated by the open grate at the head of the shaft several yards ahead. This is where he had sent Zara, to the entrance shaft used by the Shed crews with the factory nearby.

If her gear worked, if she had power, if Grainger had helped rather than harmed her, Scarecrow expected to hear her voice in his ear.

He was more relieved than expected when she replied, "I'm here."

"Need Tamner…"

He heard Zara's breath hiss through her teeth in anxious fear. Beside him, with small fingers curled around his belt, he could feel Ulynda's quavering touch.

"I'm okay. Need him at the shaft where you came up. Someone needs his help. Tell him it's important. It's urgent."

"Don't know if I can reach him, but I'll try. You want me to…?"

"I can meet you there," said Hiana

"And I can go look for the doctor," Nigel offered.

Scarecrow could almost feel Zara's frown, almost see her shaking head. So far, the three were safe. "Give me fifteen…", she eventually said, the soft clacking of her keyboard supporting the request.

"Fifteen," Scarecrow agreed, looking over his shoulder at the dark passage they had crossed. There was a utility door there, a place where they could wait out of sight of anyone who might pass this way. Shift change was more than an hour away by his calculation. No one should come this way so they would be safe. Guiding Ulynda by her hold on his belt, he found the door and used his A-Pass to open a door still powered out of the necessity to keep as many systems as possible operating and repaired so they could run full force when electricity was restored.

"We'll be safe here."

He crouched after pulling the door closed, noting the mournful shake of her head as she knelt beside him, mimicking his gestures.

"Don't think I'll ever be…" she whispered.

"You're not your father or your mother. Doctor Tamner will come…he and Enoch will see that you're safe."

Her head continued to shake from side to side but she whispered, "He's here? My uncle?"

It seemed to soothe her to know that she was not completely alone, and so he nodded and replied, "He went Out." The only information he had was that Enoch had been on his way up. They had not spoken since the dwarf's decision to escape those who wanted to elevate him into a position he did not want, make him into something he wasn't.

Unless by some miracle Neoma made it out of the Levs alive, Enoch was the only kin Ulynda had. That knowledge appeared to satisfy her, and she wrapped her arms around herself to wait.

He would look into Neoma's fate when he journeyed back down. As he had with Agnys, he would stay with the girl until he was sure she was in good hands.

One delay after another, questions and summons from members of the Nau, overfilled stairwells, inoperable lifts, and a conversation with his son that had taken longer than expected, had prevented Tamner from reaching the promised rendezvous with Mam Kemway, but with the continuing emptying of the Levs, he clung to the hope that she and her daughter had chosen to come up without him, that they were safe, if cold and uncomfortable. The recent summons, a request from Grainger to intervene at one of the checkpoints where a fight had broken out between evacuees who each believed their needs were more important than the others, had been intercepted by another request, a more peculiar message summoning him to the Shed near one of the Factory entrances.

Assuming he would be met with an injury, and because it would take him to the evacuation point where Grainger had sent him, he turned into the corridor, noting the open shaft and closed Shed doors. No one was in the corridor.

He checked the message to verify his location, then knocked on one of the doors. When no one answered, he tried another. No one responded. A creak like an opening door echoed inside the shaft and Tamner gripped both sides of the entrance to peer inside. "Hello?"

There were rustling, skittering sounds joined by footsteps approaching out of the dark. Scarecrow came first, a sight that made this summons less surprising, but the girl who came behind him was entirely unexpected. Her hands were bruised and dirty, her face as well, and her clothes were spattered by what he recognized as dried blood. Her shifting, expressionless eyes made Tamner's heart sink.

He had done this, whatever it was, as surely as anyone else had. "Where's…?"

Scarecrow shook his head as he lightly prompted Ulynda forward. She obeyed but did not speak.

"Was asked to bring her to you…think Enoch should…"

Swallowing his guilt, Tamner murmured, "Yes…yes…of course." He offered Ulynda his shaky hand. She did not hesitate to take it. Another time, another place, another girl in these Uppers corridors. The sense of déjà vu made him shiver. Scarecrow had entrusted him with that child, too. It was as if everything was beginning again. Squeezing her hand reassuringly, helping her down from the lip of the shaft, he asked, "Are you going to…there's some people out there who'll want to know if you're…"

"Tell them I'm fine."

Tamner looked the vigi over. There were stains on his body armor but not likely his blood. If anything was bruised or broken, he could not see it. He noted no evidence of pain or trauma in Scarecrow's movement.

"Did Jaron…?"

"He's out. Can't say he's happy about it…"

Jaron's happiness, for the moment, mattered less to Rhyd than his safety did. "Tell him…tell them all…"

"I will. Be careful."

Instead of making that promise, Scarecrow muttered, "You'll know when it's done."

As he began to retreat, Ulynda tilted her chin up from her floor-level gaze and asked, "You will see if she's…?"

"I will look for her."

Ulynda nodded and stared again at the floor.

❧Chapter 41❧

"Perhaps I can help."

Shouts and curses and a woman's voice reached Tamner's ears before he made it to the front of the line of refugees with Ulynda's hand in his. The accents and choices of words and phrases identified the parah and the refugees, without his needing to see them, hot-headed, frightened men trying to bully and berate those they were indoctrinated to believe were monstrous, inferior things. No doubt, the doctor thought with a sigh, finding out that the parah were not so different from them, at least in appearance, increased the worries of those forced to confront a world they had been taught to fear.

The steady rain lightly falling from the clouds that had swept in off of the sea, bringing occasional flashes of lightning with it, was keeping most of the evacuees huddled under whatever shelter they could find, the newness of the forks of light and rumbling air heightening tensions even more.

The argument and the unfamiliar woman standing between the warring factions were welcome distractions from his guilty, dismal thoughts. Though he did not know what had happened or where Neoma was, he interpreted from Ulynda's traumatized silence and Scarecrow's stilted words that Mam Kemway would not join her daughter Outside. Maybe she had chosen not to.

Maybe she could not.

Whatever the case, he was certain things would be different if he had gotten to them sooner. If he had gone to her when she had asked.

He wondered if Ulynda believed he was to blame.

"Ulynda!"

It was a relief to find his son and Agnys near the door, along with Venn and Enoch who were doing their best to intervene in the dispute over the distribution of the dwindling food supplies. Whoever the woman was, tall and stately with a commanding presence, the rough men from Hebenon with her deferred to her in a way that suggested influence. Enoch refused to look at her as though he knew her and wished he did not, but she held herself aloof. When Tamner reached them, the woman looked at Ulynda as if she recognized her too, but she did not immediately speak. Jaron sat on a stool nearby, his experience as an Archivist lending itself to the documentation and registration of refugee residents; he seemed to find a degree of solace in the company of those who likewise knew Rhyd Ballard, even if it was obvious in the physical distance between them that Venn did not want the other dark-haired man there.

Many here hoped Ballard would come through this door and put their minds at ease.

How peculiar it was that they happened to be here now.

Ulynda's eyes lit up for the first time upon seeing the only friends she had, but it was seeing Enoch beyond them that brought a squeak from the back of her throat and prompted her to release Tamner's hand, rush forward, and throw her arms around the dwarf's neck.

She appeared not to notice any other details about an Outside world she had heard so much about and yet had never seen.

Enoch looked at Tamner, startled, seeking an explanation the doctor did not have.

"Scarecrow brought her up."

The stately stranger cocked her head and studied Tamner as if this was a morsel of news she could use. The men from Hebenon tensed.

"Is he…" began Venn, wrestling with the diminishing struggles of the parah he had pulled out of the fight. Two others dragged the grumbling refugees back to where four others were detained alongside men and women held in shackles and ropes in a line against Hebenon's shell. One parah sat on the ground, where Maemi wiped the blood from his nose, and another, sour-faced and frustrated, brushed off his clothes as though he had been knocked down and gotten up again.

"Where is…?" added Jaron, trying to stand but quickly aborting the attempt.

"Is he coming?" Agnys piped, her attempted embrace of the other girl taken in easy stride.

Ignoring the stranger's interest in his familiarity with Scarecrow and the familiarity of those around him, Tamner shrugged one shoulder and raked his opposite hand through his hair. "Wanted me to let you know he's okay, but…"

Jaron's shoulders sagged. "He's not coming." It was too soon, too much to ask for…but he had hoped.

Venn muttered something under his breath.

To Enoch, Tamner said, "Do you need…?"

"I'll see to her if Cori and Agnys will…?"

"We'll get you settled," Cori promised sympathetically, wrapping an arm around Ulynda's shoulders.

"If you need anything," the woman offered, looking at Enoch at last, "please let me know…"

Enoch snorted, tilted his head toward her politely, and muttered, "Feena," in appreciation of an offer he had no intention of accepting.

Tamner sniffed. Feena Wulfe.

He was surprised to see her here.

Ulynda nodded to Cori and leaned her head briefly upon Agnys' shoulder, but her drained expression did not change as she wiped her cheeks and refused to let Enoch go."

"I'm tired," she whispered. "It's been a long walk up…"

"It was. You can stay with me," Agnys said. She knew what it was to feel lost, to feel alone, to be in a strange place with strangers she could not trust. She knew that climb through the city, too. However Ulynda had come Up, it had taken a long time to reach the door. "We can show you everything later. Cori'll bring you something to eat and I'll give you a blanket."

"Thank you," murmured Enoch, steering Ulynda from the crowd towards Agnys' home at the heart of Marbordo. He glanced back at Tamner with an expression that promised he would seek answers later.

Tamner bobbed his head. Nearby, Jonner aided the seated parah to his feet with an unhidden look of discomfort that might have meant anything. At this moment, Tamner felt uncomfortable too.

Agnys looked back, but it was Jaron's gaze she met. She offered a sympathetic smile.

Jaron sighed and closed his eyes. It was so hard to hope when others around him were losing faith.

❧*❦

One more fight, another lone thug, possibly an unmasked brako prevented from taking everything a stooped pair of shuffling stragglers carried, and then, bruised, battered, and sore, Tox returned to her flat to exchange her body armor for a meager, unheated meal, a wash-down with a cold, damp rag, and then an unbroken sleep for as long as her body needed it. She had not run into Rhyd again on her way down through the city, but she had seen the evidence of his passing, unconscious figures left where they had fallen, for there was no one to move them or take them for treatment. Buggers rounding up streeters, knocking on doors to be sure the residents were out, were plentiful, but most were more focused on managing the evacuation than on confronting looters. They, too, left the brako where they had fallen.

The closer to home she got, the fewer active brako she saw.

She glanced at herself in the full-length mirror, her form illuminated and shadowed by the alglamp at her back. She did not need to see the outline of bruises to know they were there. She probed her ribs, her cheekbones, her arms and legs, seeking evidence of broken bones she could not identify from pain alone. Breaks she did not feel. If there were fractures, she would not be able to identify them until the bones snapped. She should take a few days to recover from the abuse she had pushed her body through.

But there was no time for that so long as Vanderwall was active and Rhyd continued to hunt him. The prods had not declared his capture, and Rhyd had not reported in, so she knew both men were still out there. Somewhere.

She winced as she turned. How did he keep doing this?

How was he not yet dead?

She swallowed a couple of pain pills, chased them with the dregs of her last bottle of juice from the cool box, and plopped into the recliner rather than her bed.

The bed would tempt her to stay too long. The recliner, despite her exhaustion, would prompt her to action sooner.

She would not be able to truly rest until this was over.

❧*❧

"How is she?"

His trudge across fields of muck where the river's overflow had washed away several homes and damaged others was a welcome respite, despite the grimness of destruction, from the onslaught of discontent, arguments, and ongoing efforts to maneuver cooperation between the disproportionately greater number of refugees and the parah whose world they were invading. Tamner had expected difficulties in the transition, fear and distrust building as more and more people emerged from the shell, but he had not planned to be the primary person responsible for making that transition as smooth as possible. Thank the Creator for Lash, for Venn, for Enoch, and the calmer heads of the Pisso brothers and Stace Sargins. Thank the Creator that Nunn and the more negative voices were neck-deep in the fabrication process of solar parts, and for Grainger keeping his bugorra inside to oversee the safety of those still evacuating instead of sending them Outside to impose militaristic might onto the too-tense situation.

Enoch's request to meet him at the river's edge, where the still-falling rain eroded more and more of the collapse away, was a welcome, if disturbing, distraction.

He had not seen the river bed close up before, had not seen the earthen collapse that had caused Hebanthe Falls so much turmoil.

"Sleeping. Cori and Agnys stayed with her."

"She say anything?"

Enoch shook his head. "What do you know?"

"He made it sound like Neoma's not coming…but I don't know anything more. She called me…I told her to stay put, to wait for me…should have gone when she…"

"If she didn't stay put, it was her fault. She should have been more careful." Though he knew less than Tamner did, he was confident that whatever had happened, Neoma had brought it upon herself.

"Maybe." Tamner shielded his eyes against the rain with one hand to watch the surging water push against the dam that created finger trickles over the crest and into its original bed.

Enoch shifted his attention, too. "Thankfully, most of it's found a new path to the sea," he grunted, pointing toward the water that rushed through the soft earth of former fields to meander towards the sea cliffs. "Not sure what this'll mean to Hebenon once we dig out the trenches…let it flow again…"

"Sounds dangerous."

"Jonner thinks if we do it right…" Enoch shrugged. "Rain's doing some of it for us. Harder it falls, you know. Wanted to show you this." He opened his palm to reveal the piece of charred, bent metal he had found. "I'm no expert…about metal, about what's upriver, about what may have been here before…when they built the city…but I don't think this is a relic.

Tamner took it from him and held it up as though to see it better by the light hiding behind the storm clouds and thrown by Enoch's torch. "You think this…someone did this deliberately?"

"Not someone from here. Parah wouldn't have the know-how. It would take tech, knowledge they don't have." There was no reliable record of who had been sent out before and after the doors to Outside were opened, Grainger had not kept a record of prossers and crossers. No one had thought it was necessary.

There were undoubtedly disgruntled men and women among them, before and after, but Tamner did not think that even the Igraci, for all of their belief in the destiny of man to move out of Hebanthe Falls, would callously harm fellow residents or cause distress to so many, but how well did he know their philosophies? Their intentions?

He would have to ask Eido.

There were other possibilities, other malcontents who could have done this, but the Igraci was a place to start asking questions. Even if the woman knew the truth, he did not expect her to tell him, and right now, the growing contingent of evacuating Players aiding at the checkpoints was sorely needed.

"Keep this to ourselves." There was an abduction, an assassination, and sabotage to contend with, on top of the logistics of relocating and managing so many people for as long as they needed to be here. There were andi and the survivors from the Core to process. There was lightning and thunder and rain and the pressing need for more food that needed to be addressed.

Another instance of sabotage, if that was what this had been, would spark more distrust and violence…and likely result in more blame thrown at the andi.

Enoch agreed. For now, they needed to keep any suspicions quiet.

Thunder crackled again. At the center of the mounded earth, mud and stone crumbled and tumbled a little more, and the fingers of water became a child-sized fist.

The men exchanged looks.

It might not be long now. If the rain continued or got heavier, the Five Falls might flow again before morning.

❧*❧

Reamon Folwell's handsome face, bathed with dripping sweat created by the increasingly stagnant air in the closed room, glowered at the pair of officers who finally opened the sealed doors and returned to the interrogation room where he had been held in the dark for more hours than he had been able to count. His calm, docile demeanor had grown harsh with annoyance as his solitary captivity stretched on, and before the door closed, he thumped one fist against the table and demanded, "What's going on out there? The air's getting…"

"No worse than where I found you," started Ilya, equally irritated to be dragged out of the Levs without finding a trace of Blayd. He had to still be there, or else was lingering in one of the many lines of people trying to evacuate.

She could find him. She needed more time.

But the captain's summons could not be ignored in this time of tribulation. Finding Blayd was important, but so was this interrogation.

The captain's side-eyed glance cut her off.

"What was your part in the Founder's kidnapping?" Grainger began, pulling out one of the chairs to sit casually across from Folwell. He motioned for Ilya to sit as well. For several moments, she did not move.

"That wasn't me! I didn't have any part in that."

"But you know who did? Senior Kal? We know they were Talkers…"

"Haven't been a Talker in years," Folwell retorted, trying to sit back but unable to do so without pulling tight against the cuffs that bound him to the table. "No idea what they're up to, or why, but it wouldn't surprise me."

The last came with a snort, prompting Ilya to sit down. "Why's that? He said you left the…?"

Folwell shook his head, pursed his lips, and refused to say more.

"How'd you support yourself after you left the Voices? Can't imagine it was easy to find work?" encouraged Grainger. "Says in the file you were an economist?"

"I know books, figures, checks and measures, inventory management."

"But not for the Founder or…"

"Always people looking for those skills."

"Vanderwall?"

Folwell looked away. Grainger glanced at Ilya.

"Must've been quite a grudge to give up your faith and side with the brako…

"Never gave up my faith. Founder's the life of Hebanthe Falls. Their blood's our blood."

"So why did you kidnap him?"

"Said I didn't…"

"But you did shoot him?"

"Hijo di puta took my wife!" His open hand slammed down with a fury that rocked the table. "I couldn't serve the Faith after that, but I never abandoned the tenets…"

It wasn't a confession, but it was closer than before. Grainger filled a cup of water from the pitcher he had brought in and pushed it toward their prisoner. "Wasn't always his orders," Grainger murmured, thinking back over the long list of Vanishing arrests he had made over his career, particularly during the twilight of Haythem's rule. "The Doctet could authorize…"

"He let it happen!"

"Why'd Senior Kal want to kidnap the Founder?"

"Ask him. Regain some influence, I'd say…nothing's like it was…not since Founder let Hebenon go to paso."

"Understandable. Knowing you were out of the direct umbra of his influence, you must have been one of the first he approached to pull it off. Must have been easy from outside, find some accomplices, borrow some robes, use your Voices access to the Uppers to…"

"If I'd had access up here, I'd have found my wife," he spat. "I don't know who kidnapped him or what they did with him…to him. From what I hear, he was dying anyway…"

"I admit he wasn't well," Grainger agreed.

"But after your wife was Taken," started Ilya, "you wanted him to pay for taking her…wanted him dead?"

"I want a founder who can do his cazzing job without hurting everyone. He should have been out of the way already. I want his brother where he should have been years ago. I want a Founder who thinks of us normal people and isn't afraid of change."

Grainger nodded for Ilya to continue with her questions.

"That would never happen so long as he was…"

"It wouldn't. Couldn't…not even with the Voices backing him."

"You needed the Founder out of the way to…"

"Yes! And I'd do it again!"

The room was silent, its stagnation complete as the admission sucked the last of the air out. Captain and lieutenant stared at the former Talker, and he stared back, his previous exasperation giving way to what looked to be relief.

Ilya asked one more question. "You acted alone?"

With nothing left to hide, Folwell muttered, "Opportunity was there; I wasn't going to waste it…only needed one shot. Wasn't expecting it…but there we were…"

Grainger rose with a menacing slowness and cool expression that would have made many seated across from him cower. "Then the second shot wasn't you."

"Didn't need it. My aim was good."

A hand gesture prompted Ilya to stand.

"You took my wife for less," Folwell spat at Grainger, this time with a different sort of anger, one with direct blame. "You were there. You can't leave me in here. I demand to be heard. I want you to know what you've done."

Deciding he would have to look back through old case files to determine if the name Folwell appeared in any of them, Grainger nodded. "You'll be heard; I assure you. It's not up to me to assign guilt or justification to your case. Founder Kemway is dead. You did that.

We have more important matters to contend with. You'll have your day, Mr. Folwell…just not today."

❧*❧

The lines of people spewing out of the city seemed as if they would never end, and it was at one of those doors, still on the stool where she had last seen him, that Agnys found Jaron. He no longer took notes or filed records, as the hour had long passed when he should have left the post for sleep, but he remained where he was, head drooping against his chest, his balance precarious as he perched on the precipice of sleep and waking. Other men and women did his job now, herpa and Igraci, but still, he waited there with a forlorn expression Agnys recognized very well.

Venn had worn it too, but Venn had no desire to return to the metal nest. Whatever he felt for Rhyd, the relationship was something he had given up on, something he had exchanged for a mix of longing and resentment that the girl did not understand.

If he wanted Rhyd in his life, why did he not go after him?

She did not ask. She already knew the cellist's inevitable answer.

Jaron was different.

"I brought tea," she murmured when she stopped next to him, a small hand on his arm before she spoke so that she did not startle him when extending the wooden cup of the same pungent, steaming liquid he had been offered before.

He accepted the cup with a wan smile. "Thank you." The algtea would stir his senses, wake him up, make him more alert. If Rhyd passed this way, he was determined he would not miss him.

He had meant to step into this world for the first time at Rhyd's side. Rhyd should be here too.

Jaron should not be here without him.

"Walk with me." Agnys wove her fingers through his empty ones, but Jaron shook his head.

"I can't…"

Lowering her voice so those around them would not hear, though no one paid attention to the increasingly familiar parah girl and the sleepy man with the speecher, Agnys whispered, "You want to be with him…you want to go back where he is." She did not give him a chance to reply before adding, "He's not gonna come…but if you walk with me, I can take you to him. Maybe we can change his mind."

Jaron stared at her with a fretful pout. Agnys stared back with the defiant determination of a child seeking her way. It was a similar sort of determination that he had noted often on Rhyd's face.

No wonder he and Agnys had bonded.

"He shouldn't be alone," she continued. "If you come, I'll take you."

He did not ask how she could manage such a thing. She was a child; he did not know if he should allow her to. Her family would be furious if something happened to her. Rhyd would be too. But desire overrode common sense; he nodded, the algtea still in his hand, and followed her through the drizzling night towards the primary trade door. He did not think they could get past the herpa, the Igraci, the bugorra working there, but if Agnys was not afraid, he chose not to be afraid either.

For Rhyd, Jaron was willing to risk anything.

⁊CHAPTER 42⁊

ome was empty. Home was cold. Home was the quietest it had been since the day Rhyd had returned to it after his shift after Venn had been ripped out of his life. That memory, those nightmares, felt distant and unreal as he peeled off Scarecrow's skin, hung it over the backs of chairs around the room, and stripped out of the sweat-soaked undergarments he had worn for too many hours.

Intellectually, he knew that horror had led him to this moment. Emotionally, he was exhausted, so far removed from that night, those events, that he wondered how and why he had started down this path. In many ways, it felt like he had been on this path his entire life.

Water barely dribbled from the faucet when he turned it on, lukewarm and carrying the slight odor of inadequately filtered chemicals. There was enough to dampen a dishcloth and rake it across his sticky skin in the hopes he would feel clean. Outside the window, the cats fought for dominance over bowls that had been empty for days. Their yowls and hisses formed the background ambiance that the falls normally filled. There was nothing else, not even the comforting hum of the filt systems. It was impossible not to listen for those sounds. It was impossible not to notice they were gone.

He frowned, hung the cloth over the lip of the sink, and trudged into the main room where he sank onto the sofa and wrapped his worn blankets around his torso and shoulders. He was used to emptiness; he was used to solitude…but he wanted neither. Not like this. What he wanted did not matter, however. The only thing that mattered was uprooting Vanderwall so that Jaron and all of Hebenon could be safe.

Ignoring the snarky voice in the back of his head that asked why this was his responsibility, whether he would be content to give up the mask when Vanderwall was put down…and someone else inevitably rose to fill that void, he reached for the packet of mixed nuts and a partial bottle of whiskey taken from one of the bars he had cleared of looting brako. It was not Zaolei, it was barely satisfying for his long-empty stomach, and he felt vaguely guilty for taking it without pay, but he rationalized his efforts to stop the destructive brako to be worth the half-empty bottle left by some now-vacated patron and the unopened bag of nuts one of the brako had dropped.

After, when the power was restored, when the tick readers worked and city life returned to normal, he would make financial restitution. For now, he was hungry and needed rest if he was to go back into the empty streets to continue the hunt for Vanderwall.

He would have to do it himself. The Spinks were being escorted Outside. The bugorra presence was thinning. Zara had gone Out and he suspected Skelter had too. He hoped Tox had done the same. Soon, there would be no one left.

No one except those he was determined to stop. Those who were determined to stop him.

He connected his sleep mask to one of the oxygen canisters left by Tamner and positioned it over his mouth and nose before settling into the familiar lumpy cushions. Once again, this was his bed of choice, the place he felt he should be until Jaron returned to him. The oxygen mask prevented the other man's scent from reaching his nostrils, but the remembrance of these blankets last being wrapped around Jaron's body lent itself to imagining those arms wrapped around Rhyd now. In that imaginary embrace, he closed his eyes and allowed too-long absent sleep to quickly drag him under.

❧*❦

Wisdom beginning to get the better of him, Jaron sternly whispered, "You shouldn't do this," as he ignored her shushing finger-to-her-lips gesture and shaking head. She dragged him with her other hand on a weaving path through the line of weary, fretful refugees stepping out of the city into the glow of pre-dawn. They appeared to be streeters now, fishermen and farmers and others from the city's lowest Levs, lending hope the population hemorrhage was nearing its end. With three other exits, three other lines that did not appear to be slowing either, however, that end still seemed a long way off.

The bowed heads, the dirty, weary faces, paid little attention to the pair pushing backward through them toward the as-yet-unseen end of the line. The bugorra, the Igraci, and the herpa aiding in the evacuation and resettling process were likewise too preoccupied to notice the pair. That inattention allowed Agnys to lead Jaron to a vented grate behind a stack of unpacked hemp stocks waiting for distribution and processing. She released his hand, pointed with the other, and began prying at the corners of the grate with her small fingers.

She had been here before. She was confident she could remember the path down. All she had to do was go down and down until there was no more down to go, and then she believed she would find Scarecrow. Or he would find her.

"Not safe for you," Jaron repeated as he pried the other side of the grate. It popped off easily, with little sound, and he propped it up against the crates, looking over his shoulder for anyone who might stop them.

"Do you know the way?"

"How hard can it be?" Down was down. Once he reached the bottom, he knew many places where Rhyd, Tox, and Skelter might be. Rhyd should not have to fight alone. Weak and unsteady as he felt, there were still things Jaron could do if Rhyd would allow it. Jaron would not wait Outside for a day he feared would never come.

Agnys did not answer or wait for him to stop her. She slithered into the tunnel, crept a few feet to one side, and then dropped through the first angled opening she reached.

Jaron swore, looked over his shoulder again to be sure they were not being followed, were not seen, and then hurried in after her. She would do this with or without him. He was going to do this with or without her. Now that she was inside, he might as well follow her lead. They might as well do this together.

With a masked bugger on his other side, the cuffed man Ilya led by a tight grip on his arm grimaced and blinked as she did when her rank finally allowed her to muscle to the front of the evacuation line and step into the first dawn she had ever felt tingle across her skin. She had resisted being sent Outside when she believed her duty should be inside, in the Levs, but she understood this duty too. Captain Grainger refused to trust this particular prisoner to anyone else's care…not after having lost Founder Kemway during his transfer.

After that failure, Ilya was determined not to fail again. Blayd or not, she would not lose this prisoner.

The brightening glow in the cloudy sky, something only witnessed through the captain's window, the crisp tang of salt in the air, the squishing muddy earth beneath her boots, made her reluctant to take another step. In the distance, the structures of the parah community glowed with early morning fires, and to her left, between her and the nearest dribbling tributary, the people of Hebenon huddled in a writhing, unhappy mass. For the first time since the evacuation had begun, she wondered if people were better off here.

At least here they could breathe. At least here they had sunlight.

But here they were just as cold, just as wet, as they had been in their dark, stagnant homes.

What had they done?

"Lieutenant."

Startled, she turned. She had not noticed Doctor Tamner when she passed the city's threshold. Another voice from the other side, from a small man she recognized from recent encounters and who she quickly realized had to be the missing Kemway so many were talking about, asked, "Doctor, have you seen Jaron?"

Reamon Folwell's arm tensed in her grasp as he, too, stared at Enoch, his attentive focus seeming to prove her suspicions. Enoch eyed the captive uncomfortably and sidestepped away from him.

Tamner shook his head. "Not since last night," he replied. There were so many people, scattered over such a large area, that knowing where anyone was at any given time had become impossible. The Hub provided limited messaging ability here. Outside was forcing the need to consider some other form of communication. It forced Tamner, the Nau, and the bugorra to stay as near to the city's walls as possible.

"You see him, let him know I'm looking for him."

"Ballard?" The note in Tamner's voice was more hopeful than he intended it to be.

Enoch shook his head and continued about his business. He had heard nothing from the vigi either.

Frowning, Tamner turned to Ilya. "Who's this?"

"Someone we need to keep an eye on." Who Folwell was and why he was in custody needed to be kept quiet until a decision was made about what to do with him. Death at the hands of an already uneasy mob was not the end the captain or Ilya wanted for Folwell.

"Don't exactly have a prison out here." He glanced at the andi and Core survivors lined up along the shell and then over her shoulder as if expecting Grainger to be behind her. "Bringing others too?"

"Not if we don't have to. Just this one…and maybe three more."

"Okay…follow me."

"Is Ginna…?" she began as she followed. There seemed to be dirty children everywhere, weaving in and out of the crowd, racing back and forth between the village, Hebenon's doors, and the refugee camp. They were so similarly dressed that Ilya could not tell which were Spinks, which were streeters, and which were parah.

She had never seen the parah close up. As a group of women passed with their arms loaded with blankets and food, it was the first time that Ilya realized how alike they were.

The Outside monsters of her childhood were a myth.

But she was not convinced, as she kept the stumbling Folwell from tripping, that Ginna could be safe among them.

"Here somewhere. She and her kids've been helping as runners…getting people what they need, taking messages." Noting the lieutenant's frown, he tried to smile as he waved to Lash, Jonner, and the crew heading off towards the damn through the misting rain. "Should be proud of her, lieutenant. She's making a place for herself. Can't ask much more than that."

Ilya grunted. She would feel more confident if she saw her sister for herself.

Better she was here, however, despite the discomforts, than inside where Ilya could no longer protect her.

Grainger had told Ilya to go Outside, to stay with their prisoner.

Vanderwall or not, so long as Folwell was in her care, Ilya was forced to do as ordered.

❧*☙

He could hear them outside, the raucous shouts of hoodlums looting the vindis around the promenade, warring brako factions hurling verbal barbs, punches, and anything they could pick up, their heavy boot steps now and then racing past the doors of the nearly vacant Talker Hall.

Vacant except for him, a lone man still at the podium, his hands clutching its edges, staring through the dim glow of his battery candle as though his sullen frown could ward off any who dared to trespass.

No one did. Maybe the brako respected the sanctity of the Voices of Faith.

Maybe the men Feena left to protect him, stationed outside the open doors, were a deterrent.

Maybe none of them knew he was here or cared enough to try to loot the Hall.

He tried to trace events back through his memory to determine the moment when everything had gone wrong. When the fall had started.

Many blamed the parah girl.

Considering the Founders' history of paranoia, though he could not pinpoint the precise moment the future had fallen away, Kal knew that one parah child was not to blame. No, the shift had begun long before Kal's rise to power. Long before his birth.

But he did not know when.

A flare, a flash, and the rise of oily smoke blossomed across the promenade, an upended vindi fryer finding enough of a spark, enough fuel when dashed to the side by the brako pushed into it, to spill and ignite around it. Without the spray of the Falls and the pervasive, permanent damp, there was little to prevent the spread. The warring brako, except for the individual who screamed and flailed as his coat began to burn, gave up their fight to put out the fire. Feena's men at the Hall raced to assist. Without a fire squad or bugorra officers, if they failed, there would be nothing to stop the fire.

Kal wondered if he should help.

He did not move, only stared at the glow that lent brightness to the promenade that had been absent for too many days.

Let it burn. Let it all burn.

He would not move until the world was made right, but he would be dammed if he would do any more than he had already done.

"Not many of them left it seems."

Having been jerked awake by another catfight outside and prevented from returning to it by the rumbling in his stomach that he could not appease with empty shelves, Rhyd returned to the streets to resume his hunt and find something to eat. Moving methodically from one known brako safe house to another, following the sounds of looting that had become the dwindling ambient sound of the lower Levs, he found handfuls of things he could eat, and every brako he found he put down...but he did not find the one he was looking for. Following the sounds and trail of bodies, he found the woman in near-identical attire leaning against an abandoned vindi stall, sipping from a bottle liberated from the contents knocked free and scattered across the walkway. She picked up another and handed it to him when he dropped from the roof to stand beside her, showing no surprise at his arrival. Unlike her, he did not lift the edges of his mask to consume the precious offering.

He heard no one nearby, saw no one, neither brako, vindi owner, bugger, or citizen, but he felt too exposed here in the open. The city might not have the power for normal lighting, but it did not mean he was safe from being seen.

"There's enough." He set the bottle on the upturned side of the vindi cart. In one of his pockets, it would eventually be broken.

"Zar say anything?"

"No." The lack of news only meant that Vanderwall was playing it smart, avoiding going Outside past people who could recognize him now that his face had been made public and continued to be randomly displayed across the Echos that voiced encouragement for evacuation to people who were no longer here or to the stragglers who remained, diehards who refused to leave or stayed to protect what was theirs. The brako were prevalent among them.

Despite the emptiness, finding one man in the Levs was still akin to seeking a fleck of gold in a mining pan full of rocks and silt.

Scarecrow did not know if he would find his quarry without the Spinks to assist him or the bugorra reports to alert him to brako activity, but he would continue to try.

"Should go out now."

Tox snorted. "You know we're not gonna so long as you're here."

Scarecrow frowned. He assumed by 'we' she meant herself and Skelter, although he had not seen the redhead in hours. To his knowledge, they would be the only two here. The evacuation lines were growing shorter, but not short enough. "What's he…?"

"Looking for Colyx. Zara's not reported him Out yet. I'm heading to the hostel to see if he's there."

"Haven't seen him; if I do, I'll send him your way, let you know." He tapped the ICD. "You find him, take him up, okay? No point in…"

"No point for you either."

She was cut off by the echo of shouting voices somewhere above and to the left of their position. He was already sprinting across the intersection before Tox could reply or readjust her mask.

He knew there was less and less point in remaining in the Levs, hunting ghosts he could not find, but so long as the brako continued to loot and harass the stubborn residents who remained, it gave him impetus and purpose enough to stay. If the brako lingered, it meant Vanderwall was still here. So long as Vanderwall breathed, Scarecrow would too.

Tox imagined he would not give up even when Vanderwall was out of the picture. There was no place for Scarecrow Outside. Scarecrow was who he was now…even more than he was Rhyd Ballard.

❧Hyperion's Bier❧

❧CHAPTER 43❧

Following the ping of the ICD, a nearly silent buzz that grew stronger as he approached the source, Skelter paused and frowned at the slow trickle of water that once again tried to push through the riverbed towards the sea. It was not enough to sustain the city nor the fish in the fisheries that appeared to be his destination, but it was water enough to inspire hope that the hydros would soon provide at least a fraction of the power Hebanthe Falls needed to survive. The fish in the fisheries would be dead and the gardens that fed the city would begin to struggle without water to sustain them. There would be a struggle when the falls flowed again, but Hebenon would survive.

They had survived worse: the end of the world, paranoid Founders, being hunted by Crows for the sport of it. They had survived Heb, they had survived the Coup, they survived the brako. They would survive this too.

But what in the name of the Founder was Colyx doing down here?

Having failed to find the big man in any of the places he expected him to be, it had been easy to convince Zara to tap into the man's ICD signal to feed it back to Skelter to follow through the city like breadcrumbs on a path. It was a tactic the Crows once used to hunt the dissidents the Founder wanted to be arrested, but it was only possible if the individual was known. Tracking ticks and passcards only worked if they were used at lifts or vindis or one's front door, but an ICD, so long as it was not deactivated, would accompany its owner everywhere. Using ICD tracking was a tactic Grainger, it seemed, was reluctant to employ.

Fortunately, the technology was embedded in the Hub's code.

For a long time, the signal he followed did not move. He expected to find that the man had fallen, that his damaged legs had given out, or that he had gotten into a brawl with the brako and been left wherever he had dropped. Dead or alive, Skelter would only know when he found him. If Colyx was injured or dead, there would be no way for Skelter to move him alone.

That was a problem he would sort out after he found him.

The signal began to move again on a slow, straight path toward the edge of the city where the silent hydros waited for the falls to roar through them. Not dead then, maybe not injured, but his location made no sense. He did not know what Colyx did during his hours away from Vapors, but working at the hydros was not the sort of business Skelter expected from him.

For all their time together in the Core, Skelter did not know Colyx well. He was not the sort of man to share secrets, even with his adopted daughter. Skelter had never been inclined to press for information he did not need. Maybe he had once been a hydro worker. Maybe a fisher. Learning those details now would not be a surprise.

What did come as a surprise, when Skelter struggled with his walking stick up the steep, ladder-like steps to the hydro platform where the signal was strongest, was the hemp satchel between the man's braced legs from which he was removing several fist-sized items. He worked by the light of day that filled the gap between the city and the cliff that was once filled with the river's torrent and the unnecessary light of a miner's lantern strapped around his head. When he looked at Skelter, the beam shone directly into the redhead's eyes and caused him to raise one hand to shield them.

Skelter did not need to know what manner of devices they were to know their purpose. What he did not know, and needed to know, was what Colyx was doing with them.

"What the cazz…?"

Colyx looked at him with an initial expression of guilty surprise that quickly gave way to a stoic, neutral look as he straightened with his hand on his cracking back. He used his other hand to adjust the head lantern so that its glare no longer shone in Skelter's eyes.

"Thought you were someone else," Colyx grunted, arranging the devices in the pack and snapping the flap closed again. The side was misshapen and uneven, as if some of the original contents were missing, a detail that prompted Skelter to scan as much of the platform as he could see. He could not see anything amiss.

"What are you doing? Why aren't you with…?"

"Was told to deliver these…waiting for a handoff. Then I'll…"

"Hand off to who? Those are bombs."

Colyx shrugged. 'Not my business."

"Didn't know you…did you build…were they used on the river?"

Again, Colyx shrugged and snorted. "Think I know how to rig a bomb? Not my business what they're used for…who made 'em. Doin' what I'm paid to…making sure Otta gets the life she deserves out there with you and the…"

"She's got nothing to do with this!" Skelter knocked the walking stick against the pack before Colyx pushed it out of his reach with one foot. "She'd never want you doing something like this. What are you planning?"

"Not planning," Colyx growled defensively.

"Then what…?"

The screech that cut Skelter off, a shout of insult and outrage that erupted from the hydro shed, was accompanied by the wildcat leap of a small man determined to take advantage of the opportunity fate and the Ace of Spades presented. Molly latched arms and legs around Skelter, knocking him to the ground while Colyx snatched the shoulder strap of the pack and pulled it away. The walking stick dropped from Skelter's hand and was kicked sideways as he fell.

"Pledges are meant to be kept!"

Flailing, the knife in Molly's hand sought purchase in Skelter's skin. The thickness of his raincoat, his velvet undercoat, and the defense of the body armor vest Tox had made, allowed only nicks and small cuts on his arms and hands as Skelter fought to extract himself from the leeching man's grappling hold. As he wiggled back, caught one of Molly's arms, and tried to turn him away, the blade slashed across Skelter's hand, the back of his wrist, and down one thigh before he could break free and retreat far enough to get to his feet.

Molly charged again, knocking him down a second time so that his forehead struck the metal handrail. A sharp protrusion created by the bent stanchion raked across his forehead. With blood trickling down his face, Skelter twisted to the side so that Molly's next charge brought him up short against the rail with a yelp of pain created both by the bar across his ribs and the sudden striking blow across his back.

The walking stick Colyx retrieved slid from his wet hands after the strike and was sent spinning beyond the rail to land at the muddy base of the nearest dry cliff.

Molly lurched around and charged at Colyx this time with a roar of outrage, the wisdom of attacking the much larger man offset by his fury. It allowed Skelter time to get up and throw himself in Molly's path, hoping to protect the handicapped man, but as that knife dug into his shoulder where the vest did not protect him, Colyx charged too, with a roaring battle cry that both men recognized. Skelter was flung aside with cracking force against the unlit lamppost. There was a brief look of wide-eyed horror as Colyx's great mass barreled into Molly with enough momentum to cause the bent rail stanchion to fracture. Both men were hurled over the precipice.

Bones cracked as solid flesh smashed into the rock and mud of the riverbed. Once the water's flow would have carried both of them into the now-sagging dredging nets where they would have drowned or been pummeled by other debris plummeting over the falls. Now they lay still and limp.

"Colyx!" Skelter pulled the knife free and dropped it, grabbed the satchel of explosives so that, whoever Colyx intended to give them to would not get them, and began the climb down.

He hoped he could pull Colyx out of the riverbed if he could reach him. Molly was nearly impossible to see beneath the weight of the body on top of him. Skelter paced the lower platform, judging its height, weighing his options. There were no ladders and no ropes, no stairs to take him down. It was an eight-foot, maybe ten-foot, drop into the riverbed. There was no way he would survive jumping that far. But if there was any chance that Colyx was alive, Skelter could not leave him there. Otta would never forgive him for not trying.

Giving up was not the sort of secret Skelter could keep from her.

Securing the satchel across his chest and shoulder, ignoring the pain and blood of various injuries, ignoring the gash in his thigh that slowed his steps, he sat at the lip of the river and made his choice. The bank was angled enough to wiggle and slide his way down into a swearing, disjointed heap at the bottom, now cut by sharp stones as well. He sat in that spot for several moments, staring up into the angular array of walkways and structures that made up Hebanthe Falls, marveling at a view of the city few had ever witnessed. Little fingers of daylight clawed past the cliffside into the city, making this side of Hebenon the only place to have light in the absence of electricity, making spider-lace art that pushed as far across the city as the prevailing darkness permitted. As his discomfort subsided to a bearable level, Skelter noticed something else too…the trickles of water that fell with the light and dribbled in such a way to reach his head and soak his hair where he lay on the drying earth.

If those trickles grew, if the falls flowed, they would drown.

The thought was enough to prompt him to roll and crawl to the prone men, ignoring the mud that stained the velvet and lace he wore. Blinking blood from his eyes, he reached to shake Colyx's shoulder but stopped short of touching him.

The two men had fallen and had struck the ground with enough speed and force that their broken skulls appeared to have merged into one misshapen mass.

Skelter turned his face and wretched, barely missing his hand.

"Paso…" he muttered.

The rivulets of water stroking past his knees seemed thicker.

"I'll take care of her, Col…I promise you that." He squeezed the man's deflated shoulder, used the man's body to struggle to his feet, and turned his back on them. There was nothing he could do for Colyx except make damn sure that no one ever knew about the contents of the satchel. No one would ever speculate what Colyx may have intended to do with them or why.

They would only know that he had given his life to save Skelter.

❧CHAPTER 44❧

There had been the briefest glimpse of a yellow armband amidst the band of combative brako Scarecrow had come across, a flag that thrust him into the fray with furious intent in the hopes that the end of his self-appointed mission was in sight. Men with beaked masks, men without, nearly two dozen in all, an army larger than any he had fought before, but the number was not the deterrent it should have been. It was the one with the masks he wanted, those swarming around the bulky brute who led them, so those were the targets he chose. He wove in and out of the fray, dodging blows, landing kicks and punches meant to clear a path toward the root of Hebenon's troubles. He was met with enough counterstrikes, however, pipes and thumpers, fists and feet, that the progress he hoped for failed to materialize, and by the time he made it to the place where Vanderwall had fought his own fight, the brako boss was no longer there.

Scarecrow hesitated to shoot a glance over his shoulder across the swath of bodies he had cut down as the remaining handful of brako continued to fight. Too late, he felt the strike, the blow against his spine, the twisting of his arm in its socket. Too late, he turned to meet the threat when the weaponless fist struck against the side of his head as he wrenched his arm away and threw a punch. Vanderwall. Doubling over in wincing pain, gasping for breath at the blow that caught him in the hollow beneath his ribcage, the beaked man gasped. His impotent blade was flung aside.

A popper shot whistled past Scarecrow's ear. Barely registering the click before the shot was taken, he arched out of the pellet's path and tumbled down the stairs.

Maybe the shot was meant for him.

Maybe it was meant for the one behind him who, as the pellet cut across his wrist and veered to catch the right edge of his beaked mask, was forced to let Scarecrow go. Cupping his bloody wrist, the brako boss staggered in the opposite direction, tripped, and fell through the vindi window that shattered on impact.

The unmasked men no longer engaged in combat swarmed forward to reach him. His beaked minions surged in to shield their fallen leader who was climbing to his feet inside the vindi. He had been shot. But it did not appear to be a fatal hit.

At the bottom of the stairs, one arm dangling awkwardly below his dislocated shoulder, a sharp pain running up and down his back, his knees throbbing from the falling impact, and his ears ringing from the popper shot and the fist that had struck him there, Scarecrow crawled to the nearest wall that could provide leverage and hoisted himself to his feet. Berating himself for his lack of caution, for the man's escape, determined to finish what he had started, he took a dizzy, blurry step towards the stairs, intending to climb them, intending to start again. But the crash and clatter of the ongoing fight continued within the vindi, shattered chairs and boxes thrown that splintered as they struck whatever obstacles were in their paths. The sounds shifted away as the barrier between adjoining vindis was punctured and the war moved away with guttural swearing and another crack of popper fire.

Scarecrow flinched, an intuitive response even though he knew the shot was too far away to hit him and was aimed in a non-threatening direction. His body's reflective reaction wrenched his shoulder and back, eliciting snarls and slurred curses. By the time the fight tumbled back into the street, three beaked men carried the fourth, hustling him away, protected at the rear by three others. Scarecrow remained where he was, clutching the rail, watching them go.

In peak condition, he could take them.

With the ringing in his ear distorting the sounds around him, each twist shooting fire along his spine, and his arm incapacitated, charging back into the fight now would be suicide.

He saw no yellow armband now, but he knew it had been there. And he believed, or chose to believe, that the popper shot had injured Vanderwall more than either of them had expected.

Those without masks would deal with their opponents, or Vanderwall would again elude them.

He hoped they failed. Vanderwall was his.

Without seeing the man fall with his own eyes, Scarecrow would never believe his threat to be thwarted.

Without Vanderwall…what purpose did Scarecrow have?

❧*❧

When they skittered like bugs in the darkness past the marker plate that Jaron assumed signified the passing from the Uppers into the Levs, he tried once more to convince Agnys to go back, to return to her village where her people must, by now, be looking for her. She looked at him with a wide-eyed expression as though suggesting no comprehension of his words before pulling ahead and turning down an inclining path that took her out of visual range. Unwilling to remain in the shafts alone, less confident of his direction than she appeared to be, he limped hurriedly after her. Only once had she led them into a dead-end corridor that required them to backtrack.

Always down.

Eventually, there would be no more down. If they reached Lev 1, Jaron could find his way to Rhyd's flat, to Vapors or Skelter's home, or even to his own home that he had not been to in longer than he could remember. Perhaps then Agnys would do the right thing and turn back.

He should have insisted that she go home, that she stay Outside. But he hadn't. They were too far into the bowels of the city to go back. The desire to find Rhyd would not let him.

Nor would it allow Agnys to retreat.

He continued to follow without argument.

❧*❧

"Take my hand."

Skelter accepted the offered aid after handing his walking stick and the satchel up onto the platform and, using both the gloved hand and the slippery, slime-covered dredge net, pulled himself out of the riverbed, breathing hard, heart pounding beneath his armored vest. His feet slipped and sloshed in the sliver of flowing water about the width of his hand. Both looked towards the cliff where the falls should be, and though they were silent, the streamlet held promise.

He collapsed at her feet and closed his eyes. It was fortunate she had reached him when she had. It was good that Zara had been able to direct her to Skelter's shifting location to draw him up before the river surged. If it did.

"You're bleeding."

"I'm fine." He stared again at the world of Hebenon stretching upwards, darker here than it had been upstream without the light of day to illuminate it. He had not been confident that his ICD message to Zara had gotten through the miasma of interfering electrical silence. He had expected Scarecrow to be the one to come to his aid.

He was not disappointed to see Tox.

Despite her digitized voice, this had to be Tox. He could not imagine it being anyone else.

She grunted and helped him to his feet, the sounds of men passing somewhere overhead being incentive enough to get the redhead off the street. He did not resist, paused only long enough to pick up the items he had dropped, but his steps as he juggled the pack and stick and tried to cling to the woman for aid were sluggish and weak. His weight rested heavily against her, his feet moved more by her dragging him than by their own volition. In no condition to climb multiple flights of stairs to reach somewhere familiar, Skelter accepted her steerage into

❧530❧

the nearest, foul-smelling waste processing facility and sank onto the desk stool when she maneuvered him to it.

The satchel was placed at his feet to reduce the risk of an accidental explosion. The walking stick lay across the desk, kept within reach in case any troublemakers burst in upon their refuge.

Nor did he resist when she wrestled off her mask and hood, pulled off her gloves, and peeled back his raincoat, the velvet suitcoat, the armored vest, and the gauzy white shirt beneath to examine the injury. He was satisfied she was who he had thought her to be. Her dark hair was disheveled and damp, her mouth set in a thin, stern line, but the harshness of her expression softened as she worked.

"I'm fine," he repeated, adjusting the eye patch with one hand and twisting his head to see the wound for himself. Bleeding still, aggravated by his stumbling haste to escape the dead, escape the river bed, he forced himself to remain quiet about what he had seen and instead asked, "How long've you…?" with a gesture at the body armor she wore.

Tox shrugged. "Long enough." Not long at all, but she did not want to discuss that. She rummaged in the desk looking for anything she could use; the search produced a partial bottle of some pale amber liquid that she set atop the desk as she continued her search.

"He know what you're doing?"

"Does now." Not finding anything useful except a pair of scissors, she used them to cut off the stained sleeve of his shirt. "Brako do this?"

"Molly. Not a problem now, though. Took care of it." He had not wanted the other man to die, had never been one to take a life if he could avoid it, but the details were ones he was not ready to share. Not until he talked to Otta first.

Next time the nets were dredged, if the river ran again, both bodies would be found. He was confident that by then, there would be few discoverable clues about how they had gotten there, who they were.

Tox nodded too, ignoring his wincing grumbles as the amber fluid with the pungent alcohol smell was poured over each of his wounds that were then dabbed clean with the cut-off sleeve before the first was tied around his shoulder to stop the bleeding.

"What's in the bag?"

Muttering under his breath, cupping his hand over his shoulder and squeezing to subdue the alcohol burn, he slid the pack towards her with his foot. "Evidence of my life's folly." She lifted the flap, peered inside, and looked back at him with an incredulous expression.

"Molly?"

As a kesfek, Tox knew explosives when she saw them. He did not need to tell her what she saw. "Don't think so, but maybe." He could not rule out the possibility that Molly had been Colyx's contact, but collusion between Colyx and the miserable little man who threatened his daughter and grandchild's security did not seem likely. "Found this by Hydro 1…where he jumped me. I think there's at least one missing…all stuff I provided…"

"To who?" When Skelter shrugged, Tox could not tell if he was being evasive. "What do you think…?"

"Dunno. Didn't get a chance to look around before Molly popped up. But this much paso…can't be good."

"This all of it?"

He knew there should be more. With all of the supplies he had sold, there had to be. "All I moved? Not by a long shot. Could be anywhere. If it's in use…if it was used to dam the river…if there's something else…I did this."

"You're not responsible for what people do with…"

"No? Think the bugorra will see it that way?" He snorted and crossed his arms, ignoring the pulling pain that shot down his bicep into his elbow. Once, he would have agreed with her. Once, he had given little thought to what goods he supplied to whom and what they used them for. So long as their uses did not bring the Crows to his door, so long as his name was kept out of any criminal investigations, he had been satisfied to keep doing what he did best.

Finding that his time in the Core and the impending prospect of fatherhood had birthed a spark of conscience was more bothersome than he expected.

"Should go out and find…"

"Don't even know where to look…or for who."

"Where you found it?"

He shook his head a little too vehemently in sync with his hasty, "Won't be anything there…'cept Molly…and I'd rather let the dead rest." He picked up the bottle and said, "Share a drink? Imagine whoever wants this is gonna come looking. Whatever they did with the rest…it isn't going anywhere. Maybe they can't do anything without this. Besides…" He ran his hand over the sleeve of her body armor and continued, "Imagine he still needs you out there."

Tox scowled but accepted the bottle and took one long swallow before handing it back. Explosives were a brako trick, though usually, they used something smaller, something to create smoke or blow down a door. Maybe if she found a few more brako, she could get some answers. There might be fewer of them now, but she did not think any of them, or anyone else, would be stupid enough to rig these in the already fragile city. She put the missing pieces of armor back on as he finished the bottle, and then nodded to him from the door.

"Stay here. Rest. I'll bring you some answers if I can find them," she promised.

"Just bring yourself in one piece…him too…and I'll be happy."

❧*❧

The grate ahead was open, the designation on the wall that should have announced their Lev unreadable as erosion had eaten away at the neon paint, and the unattended alglamp above it had lost its glow. The smell of the fisheries was strong, announcing their arrival at Lev 1 despite the absence of the river's roar. Jaron pushed past Agnys, his desire to reach his goal overriding the fear that recent memories of that smell brought in a surge to the forefront of his thought.

Agnys' hand upon his arm, strong enough to hold him back, forced him to stop. Voices and footsteps that he had not noticed forced him to suck in his breath and hold it as his heart began to hammer.

"Well now…"

Jaron's breath whistled out of his constricted throat in a squeaking sound of terror.

He knew that voice.

Agnys did not, but she understood the look, the sound, of fear. With the impulsive intent of making a difference, hoping to protect the man she had led to this place, she squeezed around his side as she released his arm, out of the shaft, and stood defiantly in front of him with her arms crossed over her chest. The man in front of her, his face hidden behind the mask of a Crow she had not seen in a long time, was the biggest she had ever seen.

No longer did she believe the mask was a monstrous thing. Behind it, however tall and broad he was, he was only a man. Men could hurt her, could hurt Jaron, but he and the five with him were only men. He looked injured.

"Got no business with you," she huffed indignantly. "Let us go."

The man chuckled, the sound acknowledging her childish insolence through the tilt of his head, the seeming focus of his eyes remaining on Jaron. "You don't…but I have business with you…don't I, Mr. Rei."

Jaron's lips parted. He blinked away the trickle of sweat that had beaded and dribbled into his eye. No sound came out of the speecher.

"To be fair, I know your business here." The girl, another Spink most likely, was inconsequential. She had likely been tasked of delivering this man to her idol, or out of the city to safety. Two morsels of bait, however, were better than one, a lure that could bring Scarecrow to him one more time.

He had almost had him before. He knew Scarecrow was injured, just as he was. But Vanderwall did not think himself injured enough not to be able to get the best of the troublesome vigi.

There were few bugorra now to interfere. Few Spinks or civilians. Few brako on either side of the party line to involve themselves in a fight that was his alone. The prestige he would garner by removing the vigi irritant was the prize he wanted. Every man who wore the badge of brako would respect him then. He could bring them together at last.

A Spink and the Archivist Jaron Rei were the perfect bait.

He flicked one hand, a gesture Agnys thought looked painful, and said, "I'll take you to him," as three of the five with him came forward. Two grabbed the unmoving, unresisting Jaron by his arms. The third snatched for the child but came up empty-handed when she scampered out of his reach. The trajectory of her intended escape, however, brought her too close to the mountainous man, and he caught her by the hair, causing her to yelp and thrash. He held her that way long enough for the other man to wrap his arms around her, pinning her arms to her sides, and hoisting her off her feet.

"Scarecrow will come for you soon enough," the big man said, shrugging off the previous aide of his escorts to struggle toward the edge of Hebanthe Falls.

"He'll never…" Agnys screeched, even while knowing that, when it came to protecting those he loved, Scarecrow would do anything…including risking his life.

The man in front of her, leading the way, chuckled again as her words confirmed what he already knew, a foreboding sound that made Jaron shiver as he was dragged without resistance at the back of the column.

"Oh, I think he will."

Vanderwall was counting on it.

❧*❧

For the first time in his life, the first time since discovering this place as a young adult, Vapors' door was closed and locked behind the beaded curtain, closing out the lingering damp air and shutting inside what little alglamp glow remained. It was the first time coming out of the bathroom vent and emerging into the common room that Vapors was utterly silent, devoid of music, laughter, and chatter, the sounds of dancing and the clink and clatter of glassware and plates as people enjoyed a release from the daily tedium of their life's cares. It was the first time the smells of alcohol, curlers, sweat, and perfume did not assail him as he struggled to remove his hood with his good hand.

Maemi was gone. Outside, he hoped, along with Zara and all the other faces he was accustomed to seeing here, people he had learned to care about. With the door closed and locked, no one would find him unless they noticed his movement in Vapors' only window.

It was better this way. No one would see Scarecrow unmasked. No one knew he was here.

On the end of the bar, at the place where he typically sat whenever he came to Vapors alone, a single bottle of Zaolei sat with a folded napkin beside it. He scanned the room again to assure himself he was alone before approaching the bar, laying his mask on his favorite well-worn stool, and opening the napkin with gloved fingers.

Only one word.

Rhyd.

The grip of his injured arm was not what it should be and created bolts of pain from his shoulder into his fingertips as he clutched the neck of the bottle, but it was strong enough to hold the bottle still while he unsealed it with his good hand. The whiskey's pressurized perfume was expelled into his face, a smell that awakened a thirst he had been forced to suppress since his home supply had been depleted. His hand shook as he brought the bottle to his parted lips, tipped it enough to permit the last of the fumes to roll across his tongue, and then followed that taste with the first sip from the virgin bottle. The nectar burned its way into his empty belly, but it was a familiar and welcome sensation that he focused on with closed eyes until it settled and disseminated throughout his body.

He wobbled a little on his feet, the exhaustion of his last untold hours of combat and lack of a decent meal warring with the whiskey's forceful lure, but the wobble caused his injured arm to bump against the bar, refreshing the pain, reminding him of his primary reason for seeking shelter here.

He took a packaged sandwich from his pocket, put it on the counter, and remained still until the pain subsided.

Vapors had been his nearest haven. He needed somewhere safe to reset his shoulder, someplace he would not be ambushed. There was no one to assist him, but this was a bodily enemy he had battled before.

The Zaolei would help dull the pain.

He shuffled towards the dancers' stage, bottle in hand, wondering if they, too, had gotten out safely. The usual sounds of wet soles on the floor, of the skitter and squeak of the grit and dropped bits of food were absent, the floor swept cleaner than he had ever seen it. The pole, sheared loose during the quake, lay across the platform, and the materials Nigel had used to attempt to repair it sat nearby.

When it came time for Vapors to reopen for business, this would need to be addressed.

Rhyd could help with that. There were instruments and fasteners in his tooler that would be useful in securing the pole to the floor and ceiling. For now, there were no dancers to use it.

If the andi ban went into effect, Zara's friends might never return.

Perhaps, after disposing of Vanderwall, he would focus on championing a future for the andi. That seemed a worthy cause.

Rhyd set the bottle on the platform within easy reach, lay his gloves beside it, and then stretched out gingerly on his back, favoring his shoulder as he went down. He lay there for several minutes, aware of the pain in his ribs, in his back, staring at himself in the mirror above with a frown. Paso, he looked old, he thought with a frown. What did Jaron see in him?

He considered reaching for the bottle, taking another drink before he began, but he did not want it badly enough to endure the pain of propping himself up to drink it. After the worst of it, it would be soon enough to enjoy the rest of the whiskey as the new pain bled away.

Slowly, as he forced his muscles to relax by focusing on the dancing specks of alglamp light that flickered on the mirrored ceiling, he stretched his dislocated arm out to the side and then up, gradually reaching over his head using his good hand to grasp it and pull against the damaged limb as the discomfort increased. He had to shift his body to rotate his forearm as if to scratch the back of his neck. Little by little, his hand slid further, toward the opposite shoulder, the muscles shifting, tendons and ligaments stretching, bone grating against bone.

His eyes teared. His teeth ground together as his jaws clenched. The muscles of his abdomen tightened around the whiskey in his belly, threatening to force the fluid up and out as the pain intensified. Then came the pop, the ball returning to the place it was meant to be, and the worst of the pain flashed and began its gradual fade into memory.

Facing the bar, facing the dwindling ache as he rolled his arm slowly back to his side, rolling it in its socket to test the success of his effort, his gaze traveled from his mask on the stool towards another stool, the place where he had sat the first time he had come here, the place where Venn had found him. Or where he had found Venn. Those details were distant and hazy, dulled by time and pain and the trauma left behind when Venn was ripped out of his life. He remembered that first sheepish smile, Tox's introduction, how he had noticed the softness of the cellist's hand in his in that first greeting handshake. Both of them had been little more than boys then, children of different Levs, backgrounds, and education. Rhyd had been struck from the first with the belief that he, a lowly bilger, could ever be enough for the creative force that was Venn Weir. He had thought even then that they could not last. He did not know what Venn had seen in him.

The years of happiness that came after, strained at times though they were by Venn's efforts to grow beyond himself, his station, had dulled that belief behind the veneer of contentment.

Then the Crows had come.

And Scarecrow had been born.

Nothing had been the same since that day.

Nothing would be the same now that his heart had chosen to begin again.

A banging tap, a fist against hemplastic glass, a startling sound that yanked him out of a period of slumber he had not intended to take. He jerked up, failing to notice the residual ache of abused muscles and the stronger one in his back and ribs, and listened to the sound. A shadow at the window, a flat hand pressed against it for a moment before curling to knock again.

"Scarecrow? Ya there?"

The youthfulness of the voice declared the speaker to be one of the Spinks. Someone could have followed him. Someone could have seen a shadow in the window and assumed it was him. He had encouraged Ginna to get them out, but the Spinks were too numerous to count, spread all over the Levs. This could be one of the children who chose to stay behind because they believed their idol needed them. It didn't matter. If the Spinks were looking for him, he presumed the summons was important.

He reached for his gloves, bypassing the bottle long enough to pull them on. One more drink before stashing the bottle behind the bar where he could find it when he returned, he pulled the hood and mask into place, reconnected the oxygen tubes and voice modulator, and then unlocked and opened Vapors' front door. The child was not in sight. Scowling behind the mask, rolling his shoulder again, and stretching his back to test his condition, he whistled.

Footsteps clattered around the end of Tox's kesfek vindi, a boy of about thirteen returning at a run with a look of panic. Spink whistles and chirps echoed around them, their messages filling the earlier silent void that had grown with the upward exodus of Hebenon's population.

"He's got 'em…got 'em both."

"Who?" Tox? Skelter? The Zaolei in his belly burned hotter.

"Vanderwall. He's got a girl…and Mr. Rei…down on Lev 1."

Fist balling at his side, swallowing the whiskey bile that tried to burst free, Scarecrow growled, "Take me there."

❧Chapter 45❧

The throbbing in his leg was more noticeable tonight as he stood at the office window watching spots of fire, alglamps, and battery light pop up across the landscape of a world not at all comparable to the one he had been raised to believe lay outside Hebanthe Falls. Fat raindrops spattered against the dome, a sound similar and yet different from the ever-constant dripping those in the Levs lived with every day. This sound felt jarring, as though each drop pricked the nerves of his skin with fire, and when the lightning came, the flash made him wince as its accompanying thunder roll shook the window.

There had been storms before. Many in the Uppers had experienced them. Tonight, it felt different.

The tiny moving specks on the ground were not recognizable as people and most, as the rain came harder, hurried to find shelter. Hebenon's refugees, those still being processed, had little shelter to find and were huddled together in tight masses to stay dry beneath sheets of hemp canvas. They looked like yellow-gray blobs against the storm-darkened green and brown of the Marbordo landscape. Soon, there would be a muddy riot on Tamner's hands, and his, when frightened people decided that returning to the security of Hebenon was their best option.

There was no electricity Outside either, despite the ongoing effort to provide it. What did it matter if they suffered cold and damp inside or out? At least inside, they had beds and the refuge of four walls.

Jaron was out in that storm. Ilya had reported that to him when she had checked in to report that their assassin prisoner was secure. Maybe he would be willing to aid Tamner in keeping the peace. Ilya, the Nau, and the dwarf Kemway heir would undoubtedly do likewise, just as the herpa and Igraci were doing.

Grainger should be there too…but not yet. The city was not empty. Bugorra remained within, rounding up stragglers. He had to stay as long as he directed them to. Replacement parts for the array had been printed. When the rain ceased and daylight came, installation would start. He had to stay the course.

Lightning flashed again. Lights bobbed at the edges of Marbordo's fields, where the bank collapse had occurred. No doubt, the rain was having an effect there and along the flood barrier built to protect the village. Maybe he should be helping. But what did he know about dams and flooding?

Another excuse.

They were all excuses.

Pushing down the anxiety, he gripped the windowsill with a determined nod and a long, reluctant sigh.

∾*∾

He had been here before, watching the soaper, knowing it was a brako stronghold. Only once had he found evidence of Vanderwall's presence, but he had been unable to take action then. Periodically raided by law enforcement as it was, from the days of the Crows on through the reign of the bugorra, Vanderwall would have been a fool to make this his primary haven.

Now, Lev 1 was nearly empty. The bugorra were elsewhere, seeing to the exiting refugees. Many of the brako who remained in Hebenon were likewise scattered, taking advantage of that emptiness on the boss' behalf. From his perch in the rafters, having crept silently in from the Lev 2 shafts, crawling on silent feet along the beams and pipes that supported the vats, the stacks, and the upper rooms, Scarecrow could see three of the six men surrounding their bait in the empty corner nearest the soaper's entry. Two more stood at the door with poppers in hand, peering into the street outside in the direction of the fisheries, hothouses, and food processing businesses on his left and then toward the southern shell of the city on his right, as if expecting their quarry to be so bold, or foolish, as to enter from the street.

His Spink guide was there in the shadows, along with a collection of eight other teens, silent and unseen, where Scarecrow had left them. He suspected they had scavenged the poppers, thumpers, and stingers from brako who lay incapacitated around the Levs, but he had not taken the time to ask. They were armed, they were big enough, old enough, to fight if they chose. But he hoped they would not have to.

His calculating gaze swept over the brako again as he listened to the tense, muted chatter of the four before focusing on the lures that had brought him here.

The brako were unaware of him there, but they expected him.

Jaron. Agnys.

He blinked the stinging, nervous sweat out of his eyes.

Neither was bound. There was no need for it when the pair could be easily overpowered by the men guarding them. Jaron's bruised hands were clasped in his lap, his wandering gaze steadfastly avoiding the man at the desk across the room. Agnys leaned forward on her chair, feet swinging, hands gripping the edge of the seat as she watched one brako at a time as if looking for a detail, a weakness, she could use against them.

It should not surprise him that Jaron was here. The dark-haired man had more heart than sense, in Rhyd's opinion, led by intuition and impulse and an expressed love that was going to be his downfall. He should not be here, Rhyd thought with a frown as nervous fingers found purchase on a loose bolt and began to twist it loose from the beam at his feet. Jaron was weak in his recovery, swollen-eyed and weary. Coming back into Hebenon was a foolish risk. Yet if he was strong enough to make his way to Lev 1, perhaps he was strong enough to fight for his freedom when the moment came to act.

Agnys, on the other hand, was a child. A resourceful, stubborn child, but a child all the same. Whether she had learned her alert wariness, curiosity, and scrutiny from him or if it had always been an innate part of who she was, the things that had brought her into the city to begin with, she was no match for the four who served as a wall to cut her off from the man who had dragged them here. Vanderwall would not know who she was, what she meant to Scarecrow, but she was with Jaron, and that made her valuable. Why she had risked coming here, on her own volition or at prompting from Jaron, were unknown, unanswerable questions. Perhaps it came down to fate.

All of this had begun with this one parah child.

Perhaps her presence was an omen. Perhaps, once Vanderwall was no longer a threat, Scarecrow would finally know peace.

Poking at the flickering screen of the only functioning Echo in the room, powered by a generator whose spluttering growl suggested it was nearly out of fuel, the big, bald man lifted his gaze now and then to look toward the door, toward his prisoners, and then back down, the tension of his shoulders and his absent pecking suggesting the distraction of waiting was inevitable.

If he had been shot, Scarecrow could not see the damage.

None of them wore masks. None had the advantage of Crow tech to hear, to see, to sense.

One well-aimed bladed disc would be all it would take. Between the eyes. Across the throat, into the back of his neck at the base of his skull. Vanderwall would go down, and that would be the end of it.

It had to be a kill shot. Reluctance to kill aside, it was the only way.

But making Vanderwall his primary target would leave Jaron and Agnys at the mercy of those guarding them.

Scarecrow could not take that risk. He had to distract them first, separate the guards from their captives, and then strike Vanderwall.

With the freed bolt between his fingers, Scarecrow slid further along the beam, pushing his outrage and fears into a focused ball in his belly, judging the ideal place from which to make his move. Once satisfied with his position, he spun the bolt so that it landed on Jaron's lap and froze, hidden in the darkness, waiting.

Startled, Jaron jumped and looked into the unlit shadows of the upper reaches of the soaper. The bolt clattered to the floor. The sound and his movement made the guarding brako turn their attention to him. One shoved him back into the chair, the gesture rough enough to knock Agnys' chair to the side and tip her out of it. Another scooped up the bolt with a sneer.

"Think this'll protect you?"

The other looked into the rafters to see what Jaron was staring at.

Curious, Vanderwall stood up, slowed by injuries recently sustained.

There was a whistle. From the street, the Spinks interpreted the voices from the long-silent soaper as the signal they needed. Someone gave a whooping yell and they let loose a spray of popper fire aimed at the pair at the door. One of the two ducked back, firing in return while the other dropped to his knees, also returning fire at the dirty streeters daring to assail them.

Two stars from Scarecrow's hands sliced the air. One bit across the side of the head of the man with his hands on Jaron. He lurched back, cupping the place where his ear had been, blood spraying between his fingers. The second star sank into the back of the neck of the man who had scooped up the bolt when Jaron's thrashing kick flung him back into the third. Agnys rolled to the side as both men fell, eluding flailing hands that tried to close around her ankles. As the two brako worked to disentangle themselves, and the Spinks, their popper rounds now spent, lured the still upright guard into the street, Scarecrow took the opportunity that presented itself.

He dropped. He rolled. The pain in his back and ribs jarred at the abuse as he came up into a shielding crouch between Jaron, Agnys, and Vanderwall.

"Go!"

He released his remaining two stars as he crabbed backward, urging the pair out the door. One star cut across Vanderwall's cheek, drawing a line of blood; the other was deflected by a sweeping arm as though it were nothing more than a fly as he charged. Scarecrow's dodging sideways blow, a fist into the face of the uninjured brako who had picked himself up from the floor, meant that Vanderwall tripped and fell face-first to the floor before he reached them. Agnys screamed. Jaron snagged her arm and yanked her toward the door. The henchman fell, blood gushing from his nose and mouth. Vanderwall, having used both arms to break his fall, roared in pain and rolled away from Scarecrow to regain his footing. Scarecrow spun, kicked him with one foot, and then landed in a shielding posture in the doorway after Jaron and Agnys stumbled over the fallen man there and hurried into the street.

The Spinks came out of hiding to surround them, a wall to protect them as they herded them away.

Vanderwall charged with another roar, pushed Scarecrow so that he flew over the dead brako on the steps, and then crushed him against the walkway rail with a bellowing cry.

*

"Out!" bellowed Enoch, stretching his hand to aide one of the workers standing upon the collapsed earthen dam, while Jonner, Lash, Tamner, and others reached for anyone they could as the black clouds opened and unleashed a blinding torrent from the sky and the mud of the land collapse began to give way.

His reach came up short.

Tamner, however, caught the flailing hand, and the man reaching for Jonner caught Enoch's wrist instead.

Feet scrambled for purchase in the soft earth. People pulled, screamed, and tumbled back onto the sloping riverbank. Others did their best to yank them to safety.

The mud and rock gave way.

The water pent up behind the dam cut through the narrow troughs and burst free, surging again in the deep beds of the five tributaries toward the cliffs that had once fed life to Hebanthe Falls. The unfortunate were swept along with it.

❧*❧

The teenage Spink, who had been Scarecrow's guide, threw his spent popper with enough force and accuracy that it struck Vanderwall in the temple. The bigger man snarled and reflexively turned toward the new attack. The boy was far enough away on a nearby rooftop that Vanderwall could not reach him, but the act and Vanderwall's distraction were enough to allow Scarecrow to slip out of the bigger man's pinning hold and roll away in the direction of the city's shell. Ribs aching, gasping for breath that would allow him to shift his focus away from pain, he looped his arm around the rail so that, when Vanderwall came at him again, he used the leverage to kick the man in the chest.

Scarecrow heard the sound, the impending gurgling roar, the furious whining of the inactive hydros…as Vanderwall caught his leg and twisted. The river's sudden surge beneath them and the violent shudder that ran through Hebenon from bottom to top, enough to throw Vanderwall to his knees, forced him to release his hold on Scarecrow. Scarecrow used the momentum of release to brace himself against the grated floor and slam his fist into the brako boss' face.

❧*❧

"What the fotz is…?" Skelter shouted, staggering to his feet, and tripping towards the door of their shelter when his walking stick dropped out of his hand. Tox caught him in both arms, and they fell together, her body taking the brunt of the impact as they landed.

❧*❧

In the flash of lightning, he saw the river gush up over its dam. He could not hear the screams, could not see the sudden dash of panic that erupted between Hebanthe Falls, Marbordo, and the angry river.

Grainger could only watch in horror as the falls surged to life once more…and the city quaked in violent response.

❧*❦

It came without warning. It happened without prelude. One by one, as the hydros tried to spin to life between the Falls' assaulting force, there came an explosion, an eruption of fire and smoke that clogged the Levs and filled the air with steam and soot and flame. Ancient stanchions sheared and warped and pulled away from the earth anchors that had kept the Levs upright for the centuries in which Hebanthe Falls had stood. Other stabilizing points bent and buckled as the collapsing weight from above sank beneath gravity's attack. Another explosion.

The ground beneath Scarecrow's feet tilted toward the river, towards the edge of the city where he had once led an assault on the Core. His hold on the rail prevented him from sliding. Vanderwall caught his other, recently dislocated arm, as his heavier weight dragged him down the slope.

The digitally distorted scream of pain echoed the cries of people further up the Levs and in the Uppers who now pushed and shoved in their desperation to make it out of their city alive.

As the Spinks pulled Agnys and Jaron into the nearest, still-stable structure, the pair screamed in unison, "Rhyd!"

❧*❦

The roof collapsed, pinning them to the floor. Skelter's head bounced with the force of it, his skull cracking against Tox's. He made a sound, something abrupt and sickening that made her scream his name. As the floor tilted and water rushed up around their legs, the river's roar was the only response she heard.

❧*❧

He did not hear the rush of the falls. He did not hear the resurgence of the river. He felt only the abrupt shuddering of the city, heard the rattle and shimmy of the stained-glass windows that decorated the walls of Talker Hall Prime…in the moments preceding an explosion that threw that same glass and the molding that encased them across the width of the building. Shards slashed at him with their fractured teeth as he was thrown against the nearest wall, where he was buried by the unexpected collapse of rubble from above.

Feena's men might still be at the door, but Kal could not see them, could not hear them. There was smoke, embers from the fallen incense pots he imagined, but the thing he was most acutely aware of was another explosion…falling…falling…and then nothing.

❧*❧

Thrown off his feet, backward across the office as the room tilted sharply to the south, Grainger rolled and came to rest only when he hit the wall. Sliding chairs, objects from the desk, the Echo, were thrown with him, and though his arms protected his face, the rest of his body endured impact after impact.

Through the window that had once displayed Marbordo's fields, the river tributaries, and the distant mountains, he now saw only the inky rolling clouds and the streaks of light through the splatter pattern of rain against the glass.

What a fitting place, fitting way, he mused grimly, to die.

❧*❧

"Get them out!"

❧549❧

Ilya did not recognize the woman beside her as anything more than Igraci as they, along with the herpa and bugorra, yanked at the reaching hands to pull people out of the congested doorway. Smoke and flame mixed with the ozone smell of rain and lightning as explosion after explosion rocked the city and caused the Upper dome to list dangerously to one side, the lip of the city digging into the rocky earth so that the passages into the Factories twisted and warped. Fate and future mattered little in the face of fear, and the stability of the Factories through which other refugees fled was not considered.

Any people still caught in the halls of the Uppers, any stranded on the walks of the Levs were in danger.

❧*❧

"Rhyd, is it?" Vanderwall chortled, blood bubbling from his lips as Scarecrow kicked him again to dislodge the man's hold on his dislocated arm. "Think she's had enough of us both…" Blood stained the big man's side, the place where the popper shot had lodged in his gut, giving Scarecrow an idea.

"Then I think it's time for you to go."

Another kick, this time low enough that the toe of his boot slammed into Vanderwall's bloody side, came at the moment when the walks of Lev 1 shifted again, allowing the river's spray to splash into their faces. Vanderwall's shout of pain and his fall when he let go of Scarecrow's arm ended with his feet braced against the distorted portion of the buckled soaper wall. Rhyd swung from the rail to kick again, but his attempt missed. The brute's arm wrapped around both of Scarecrow's legs, and with a yank, he tried to bring Scarecrow down with him.

Scarecrow turned as he dropped, and his hold on the rail broke. His fingers found purchase in the grated walkway; it was enough to break his fall, but the force of Vanderwall's weight, when the man's feet slipped, popped his shoulder out of the socket again.

"Rhyd!" Jaron tried to charge towards him as another explosion, delayed from the rest, on the south side of the city, tore a hole in the rock, and pulled a supporting pylon free. Agnys' hand around his wrist and the pulling hands of the Spinks, however, held him back.

The support beneath Vanderwall's feet gave out, throwing him away from the walkway rails or anything else that he might have found his footing on, leaving him nothing to cling to except Scarecrow's legs. With the first look of terror Scarecrow had ever seen on the other man's face, he pulled as if to climb up the vigi's body to safety. His weight continued to stretch and tear the ligaments in Scarecrow's injured arm, and though he tried to get a better grasp of the grate with his other hand to shake Vanderwall free, the deepening rush of the river that now pulled against the brako's feet made the effort futile.

For a moment, his body stilled, his effort to fight the current, to fight Vanderwall softened by a kernel of knowledge that he had always suspected would be. From the day Venn had been Taken, to the day Jaron was rescued, until this moment, Rhyd had known there would only be one way he would ever be able to stop this fight.

Head twisting to the side, he looked through the smoke and river's mist to the younger man's grief-stricken face. So soft. So gentle. So beautiful in the hope it had given him for a future he had never believed he would have. He listened to the water's crash and tumble, listened to the distant falls' roar, and the dying, struggling whine of the damaged hydros, to the crackle of distant fire and the sobs that Jaron needed no speecher to express.

Jaron did not need to see the whiskey-brown eyes behind the mask to read them. He did not need to see Rhyd's face to understand the inevitable.

Rhyd did not need to say it.

His actions alone would express the love he bore as he made a decision that would keep Jaron, Hebenon, and those he loved, safe.

He jerked and twisted until he could press the ICD button.

"Zara?"

"I'm here."

Her voice brought with it a swirl of memories that filled his eyes with tears and produced a moment of regret. He hesitated as the emotion passed, unable to take his eyes from Jaron's face as Vanderwall continued his climbing effort and the pulling pain in his shoulder grew more acute. One hard swallow past the lump in his throat and a long intake of breath.

"Take care of Jaron."

"Rhyd?"

He let go of the grate.

Scarecrow and Vanderwall fell together, had breath stolen by the impact with the icy tumbling rapids, and were swept through the river's teeth toward the distant sea with Jaron's cry of "Rhyd!" sweeping along behind them.

❧Chapter 46❧

Dawn brought the cessation of rain and a full assessment of the damage done to the city in the falls. Smoke continued to rise in a few places but the warped collapse had enabled the rain to penetrate places in the Levs where Outside had never penetrated in more years than the current population had lived there. Though bugorra and Igraci continued to sift people out through the Factory doors into the rain-washed open air, wafting cries lifted from further down in the twisted bowels. Stricken faces peered from the height of the falls, seeking guidance, seeking answers, while others combed through the host of evacuees looking for those they had not yet found.

Oliver Grainger, Tamner quickly realized, was one of the missing.

"Gonna take a long time to get people out of there," Enoch muttered at the doctor's side, clutching Ulynda's hand as the girl stared, numb and wide-eyed, into the abyss with the rest of them. Neoma would be listed among the missing even though both of them understood that Mam had likely been dead before the city's collapse.

That did not mean that Ulynda did not both hope and dread that her mother would somehow make it out of the city.

"We can't abandon them," started Jonner from Ulynda's other side, his tone awash with something Enoch interpreted as guilt.

"No one said we're abandoning them." Tamner glanced at the woman who joined them, her face lined with grime and exhaustion as she chugged from the water flask she carried and dragged her other arm across her eyes and forehead. Lieutenant Young had been helping pull people out of the city most of the night, despite the rain. It was about time she took a break.

Before he could ask her opinion, Lash said, "We got bilgers, skolpers, more…we can get in there if we're careful. They'll be used to the climbs; they'll know the back ways to get around."

"Shafts'll be collapsed too, but maybe…" Enoch looked towards the Core survivors and the handful of andi who had been weeded out of the evacuees. "They could get around in the Core, they can get around down there too…so can the andi. And any of us who'll volunteer…I've been there…I can do it…"

Tamner shook his head. "Need you up here. The people need…"

"I'm not…"

"Nau needs leadership…and the injured are gonna need triage management. If you can handle that," Tamner looked from Ilya to the ongoing processing at the Factory doors, "and you two can coordinate extraction and excavation…" he looked between Lash and Jonner, one a victim of the Core, the other a victim of the Levs, "get all shaft workers, athletes, emergency crews…any buggers the Lieutenant can spare…we get as many out as we can. I'll see we have the manpower and resources to take care of them if we've got it and bring some medical staff together. In the meantime, someone has to interface with the Nau, keep them calm, keep things running…and like it or not, there's no one they're more likely to cooperate with than a Kemway."

Enoch scowled. Ulynda squeezed his hand and murmured, "Make that two Kemways," in a strained, small voice.

Enoch wanted to protest. He wanted to argue his way out of this responsibility. But in this time of crisis, everyone had to do their part. This, unfortunately, was his. "Until the last person's out of there," he muttered with a sigh. "Not a minute longer."

That last person, he imagined, was going to be Ballard. There was no trace of the man Outside. Somewhere down there, hunting still, the vigi would be difficult to extract until there was proof that Vanderwall was dead.

His hope for Skelter and Tox was equally thin.

"Good enough," Tamner agreed.

❧*❧

The warmth of sunlight on her face, a peculiar but pleasant sensation she had never felt before, announced the end of the shifting city walks and the sliding of the world from its' centuries-long axis and prompted Tox to open her eyes to witness the world the new day had given them. The removal of her mask, of placing the breathing filter over Skelter's face, was a hazy memory, but the rise and fall of his chest where his weight rested on her proved that her effort to protect him was worth it. The collapse of city structures had diverted the river away from their legs, preventing prolonged immersion in the frigid water, but the damp was still too cold to be healthy. She was protected by her body armor for a while longer, but Skelter was not. She had to get him out of their demolished shelter and into the welcome sunlight. She had to get him secured so she could assess the night's damage.

She had to pursue the cry lingering in the air's memory that filled her with a chill that had nothing to do with the rain or the river.

She pushed against the collapsed roof sheathing. It barely budged. When she pushed again, she heard a youthful voice call, "Hold on…we'll help."

Rubble shifted. Wet debris spattered down on them, prompting her to turn her face while she continued to push against the material above and tried to protect Skelter's head from further damage. He moaned a few times as the weight moved and changed, but it wasn't until they were exposed to the glare of dawn and a host of reaching hands that she could maneuver Skelter and herself free of the trap.

Tox did not notice the state of Hebenon. She barely recognized the flow of the city's lifeblood through the bed below them. At the back of the collection of young, dirty faces, street kids and Spinks she assumed, who had worked together to get her and Skelter free, was the mournful face of the man she had not wanted to believe she would see.

The origin of the night's distraught plea.

Her lips quivered as she sat and relinquished Skelter's care to the Spinks and the familiar parah girl with them. "Is he…what…?"

Bruised and bloody, wet and covered with bilge that dribbled into the river from a nearby broken shaft pipe, Jaron shook his head and pointed in the direction of the sea.

When he closed his eyes, Tox did likewise. What ifs and whys pushed to be asked, but she forced herself to swallow the wash of hopelessness and square her shoulders.

The river was brutal, but Ballard had endured worse.

So long as she could hope, Rhyd might be alive.

❧*❧

"Sir? Sir, can you hear me?"

Grainger did not think he had blacked out, although the only remembrance he had after the world tipped and crashed was the rainclouds and lightning through the window. It was daylight now, the ponderous black billows had given way to brilliant blue that he could see as the Echo that partially obstructed his view was dragged away by a bulky, dark-skinned fellow and the skinny one called Lash behind him. He did not remember the Echo being there.

The gap in his memory made him scowl.

A gaggle of others was likewise sifting through the room's debris, harnessed men and women maneuvering a canvas stretcher between them that Grainger brushed off as he wiggled into an awkward sitting position. His knees throbbed, and his left leg from hip to foot began to tingle with pins and needles as circulation rushed into it. That feeling made him wince too, but again, he pushed away the hands that tried to grab and steady him.

"What happened?" he growled, using the gruff tone of annoyance to push distance between himself and any perceived helplessness.

Lash shrugged as he maneuvered back to allow the captain room to stand. "Don't know yet…the dam burst, so the river ran in. There were explosions…could have been the strain on the hydros. Won't

❧556❧

know until we get teams down that far. Right now, we're working on getting everyone out, pulling engineers together to…"

"I need to get…"

"Doctor Tamner's gonna have a good look at you first, and your lieutenant out there's gonna want a word…" started Jonner.

"A few others, too," Lash interrupted.

Jonner nodded. "Need to get you up to speed." When Grainger's balance wobbled on the uneven floor, Jonner caught his wrist and helped him up. Their gazes met. "You get the clear, then we can use all the help we can get."

Grainger grunted. The room swayed as his head spun, and he used that mutual wrist grapple to remain upright when his vision began to darken around the edges. But the moment passed without any need for coddling, and he grunted again and nodded. Starting with Tamner and Ilya would be best. Hebenon might not be strong but he needed to be sure his people were. And he needed to be strong for them in return.

From the room he was in, he could tell very little. From the Outside, he would be able to assess the extent of the damage. He could avoid going Out no longer.

"Get me out then…I want to see what we've got."

❧*❧

In the recesses of recent memory, there were snippets of disjointed imagery that Kal could not connect as the fabric sling that supported him swayed and turned as the pulley rig drew him up and up between misshapen walkways, collapsed and tilted flats and vindis, toward an overwhelming brightness. Loud voices, shouted commands, and curses. When he was free of the weight that had covered his body like a blanket, the totality of his abused body's pain rushed through him until the malleable threads of consciousness were absorbed and left him again in darkness.

He remembered being lifted, carried up an incline, and then moved between popping sparks of sputtering neon. Acrid electrical smoke…but he remembered no fires. There was nothing else until the jostling fabric sling began to draw him up.

The afterlife awaited in the light.

It was what the Cult of the Founder taught.

Maybe he was dead.

Death would explain so much.

The rising paused periodically as hands maneuvered the ropes and pulleys to keep the cargo clear of impediments and dangers. He was not aware of the why or how, only increasingly aware of each delay until the final swinging motion brought him into the hands of a multitude of others, hands that unfastened straps and buckles and the hook of the hoist that was sent back into the bowels with an empty canvas attached, intended to extract the next unfortunate soul. Someone gingerly cupped the back of his head, lifted and tilted it, and bid him to drink by pressing a flask to his lips.

He expected it to be wine.

It was only water.

Forcing his swollen eyes to open in his bruise-mottled face, he saw her first…Feena…and though his split, blood-caked lips parted to speak her name, no sound came out. Beyond her, he saw others too, Aldrich…Ulynda…the Kemway heirs who no longer needed his support. No sign of Neoma. He saw trees…fields of hemp crop…and the mountain rim beyond that. He beheld the blue sky of Outside…and the golden sun.

His body trembled. His hands flexed in terror, in outrage at being brought here against his will, in wonder, and finally in surrender as indoctrination clashed headlong into reality. Who was he now if the Cult of the Founder was dead?

There was no going back.

His old life, everything he knew, was over.

Kal closed his eyes…and wept.

⮞*⮜

From the pantry of the still-level, undamaged flat in which they had taken refuge, Jaron passed the tin of sweet wafers to the Spinks, listening to Skelter swear as he tightened the makeshift bindings around his ribs to ease their ache, while Tox rummaged through a back room for clean clothes any of them could use. Without the periodic wail of the shift whistle, the ICDs no longer offering contact or function, there was no way to measure how long they had climbed. Slowed by mangled walks, sheared stairs, and collapsed rooftops, floors, and walls, they had spent as much time finding a safe route as they had spent climbing, with only the rays of sunlight that poked through the collapse here and there to suggest the passage of time.

Three days it had been, judging by Jaron's calculation. They could hear voices above, workers aiding in extracting the trapped and the injured, cries of the hurt and dying, calls for help. Those who could do so were likewise climbing upwards, but it was going to take a week or more for the crews to reach the bottommost Levs. If anyone was trapped there, they would be lucky to be alive by the time rescue came.

There were other flats and vindis, like this one, that had not suffered significant damage from the shaking, the explosions and fire, the collapse. Perhaps Hebanthe Falls could be rebuilt, in part at least. But why, Jaron mused as he met Tox's gaze when she emerged with an armload of clothing, would anyone want to come back here?

Hebenon was no longer stable, no longer safe.

And Scarecrow, he thought morosely, was gone.

The woman pulled a pair of baggy pants and a long-sleeved, knee-length sweater over her body armor, hiding the evidence that no one else knew anything about. The Spinks understood she was not Scarecrow. They had seen their idol fall. But they agreed that the gradually nearing voices from above did not need to know either truth. They agreed to protect her secret, even from others in their group.

She nodded as she helped Skelter into another sweater to replace the blood-soaked clothes he continued to wear since being trapped, as the Spinks sorted through the pile looking for items they too could use.

They had similarly raided other flats as they climbed, and by now, they each had suitably warm, sturdy shoes and clothes to protect them from all but the most jagged twists of grate, wall, and stanchion.

Only Agnys declined, her sullen face pressed to the window at every stop, always looking behind. She did not need to voice her thoughts or feelings for Jaron and Tox to know them.

If they had not been there, if they had not been a distraction, Rhyd might be alive. Unlike Jaron, however, Agnys watched behind them with hope.

Sooner or later, she believed he would be there. Sooner or later, he would reach them. He would come back for her.

He always had before.

Again, Jaron nodded, closing the cupboard after tucking the bottle of Zaolei into his pouch and securing it from falling out, protecting it from breakage. It was the only bottle he had seen since the start of their climb.

He had wanted to return there.

There was no time. They had to get Skelter and Agnys out of the city. And as Tox had said, Rhyd was not going to be there.

Jaron tried to cling to that hope regardless.

With Tox leading the way, testing the mettle of the path to move them along the safest route, and the Spinks who had survived the encounter with Vanderwall, bringing up the rear, offered hands pulling and pushing each other along when the support was needed, they began again. Beams of light that replaced all but the brightest alglamp glows shifted from one side of the city to the other, marking the passing of another day, and brought them to the source of the nearest, loudest voices they had been following. Like edged blades, streaks of light crisscrossed an expansive open area, a collapsed rooftop that Jaron believed had once covered the sport's arena complex. There were many gathered here, some huddled together for comfort, others moaning in pain and traumatized terror, some in silence, while men and women in herpa and Igraci robes walked among them, offering food, blankets, and hope until it was their turn to be hoisted Outside on flat pallets that made journey after journey to take people out.

Tox barely made it over the lip of her climb when she heard a shout from the middle of the throng, her name a relieved cry from a familiar voice she was grateful to hear. Rather than race to greet him, she turned to help Skelter over the incline and onto the flat ground. By the time he lay still, panting, staring at the tangle of Hebenon above him, Tox turned and welcomed her cousin's embrace.

"Thank the fates," Venn swore, face buried in the woman's hair, not heeding the movement beside them as Agnys scrambled out on her own and threw her arms around his waist. Surprised, he looked at her, past her, to see the man climbing after her and the group of Spinks who came behind. His lips trembled at the details the collection of individuals revealed, the realization that there was one face he expected to see among them but did not.

Jaron's foot slipped. Instinctively, without thought of jealousy, anger, or bitterness, Venn caught one of Jaron's wrists while Tox caught the other. Their gazes met, but they did not speak as they pulled Jaron to safety and then lent a hand to the Spinks.

Questions would come later. With Agnys sobbing softly against his side, Venn understood well enough.

For now, no words needed to be said.

The end of the fight had come for Rhyd…as Venn had feared it would.

¦Chapter 47¦

Oliver Grainger sank onto the wood plank bench and wiped his dusty forearm across his sweaty face, less out of exhaustion, less to shield his eyes from the midday sun, then it was an attempt to block Zara Peru from sight when she passed with an Echo in hand as she discussed with Lash, Caminda Vaughn, and Lydon Folaw how to establish and maintain a communication and power grid for the array of clay brick and wood structures perpetually under construction in the distance that would house the refugee host and begin to replace the businesses that had been lost.

They had not spoken since the collapse of Hebanthe Falls.

He did not expect they would speak again, despite the occasional glances exchanged across safe distances as their duties pulled them in separate directions. There was no reason they should.

Their past, such as it was, was behind them. Here Outside, with an assembly of musicians gathered under Venn Weir's leadership playing some spry, upbeat number on a haphazardly erected stage near one of the Factory entrances, on instruments that had been scavenged from the collapsed city, destiny forced humanity to begin again, to build a new life, find a new purpose. Grainger had found his. It appeared that Zara and her ever-present entourage of a dozen andi had found theirs as well.

The Nau and the Marbordo Council, merged into a single governing entity to serve the population surge, were due to meet in the evening after the Pisso brothers emerged from Hebenon. There was still debris to clear, materials to scavenge, to salvage, but those duties continued to halt every evening as Tamner, Enoch, Ulynda, and the Marbordo chief, jointly made leaders as the long-separated populations learned to merge into one people, brought them together to sort through each day's trials.

Those trials were many. Bridges were being built to cross the river so that the homeless could stretch out there rather than infringe upon the crop fields that had expanded to feed everyone. Efforts were being made to establish fisheries along the river and the ocean shore. The Factories churned day and night, fed by the expanded solar arrays. One of the city's many hydros had been dismantled to be rebuilt elsewhere in the hopes that it, too, would provide the power the people of Hebanthe Falls were accustomed to. It, like many other things, was a difficult hurdle for a single person to manage, but the council, with the aid of two surviving Kemways and Tamner, was coming together.

The doctor, once a man of relatively little significance under Haythem Kemway's rule, was proving up to the task. Enoch and Ulynda might be the figureheads of the newly emerging state, their voices listened to when they had opinions to share, but Rafe Tamner was its leader. There was no Founder. Those days were gone. Tamner, though currently without a title, was the de facto voice everyone gravitated toward for answers. He was a man of science as Duncan Kemway had been.

To Grainger, the transition felt fitting. The people needed a voice of science to build a new world, a clearheaded, charismatic man to guide them through this transition. What came next, a new dynasty of leaders or something else, remained to be determined.

Grainger wanted no part of it. He was grateful to have given up the ill-suited role and the problems that came with it in exchange for the ongoing responsibility of everyday peacekeeping.

The city crews under the man Jonner's leadership cleared debris, collected anything useable, rescued animals, and continued to extract the dead and barely living. Others worked to stabilize portions of Hebenon that might one day be usable again, while the majority focused on building lives Outside. Whether inside or out, the need for the bugorra remained. Hebenon's death toll had been high, and as clashes between Insiders and Outsiders continued, Grainger and his force had their hands full, breaking up brawls and intervening in feuds, wherever the Nau thought they were needed.

The brako appeared to have gone to ground, but there were other troubles to manage. Many people, displaced from jobs that no longer existed, joined his ranks to manage the chaos.

The changes suited Grainger well enough.

Near the doors of the Factory where carts of hemp went in as other goods came out, the lieutenant's sister, the woman Otta, and a host of others had created a haven in which to collect the children orphaned by the collapse. Streeters and Spinks and those left without families needed care and attention. While some, especially the older ones with survival experience, put their hands to use inside, the rest were being cared for, taught, and integrated into Marbordo's existing society.

From what he witnessed day by day, Granger thought the children were having an easier time adapting to the changes than the adults.

The familiar redhead, a friend of Zara's only recognized by face, and the woman Tox who had once been a victim of the Founder's sadism, had integrated with the herpa, the Igraci, and members of the directionless Talkers to manage trade, to teach, to negotiate, and fill the needs of those who had so little.

Those who had once sold food, drink, and clothing were maneuvered into positions of growing, cooking, and sewing to keep the masses fed and clothed. It meant the management of supply, distribution, and production.

Thank the stars for men like Stace and the Pissos and those once shadowy organizations and individuals that already had a network spread throughout the refugee sprawl.

Senior Kal, most frequently confined to a chair as he continued to struggle against the injuries sustained in the collapse, was not part of the efforts. Grainger saw him most often staring toward the mountains, silent, withdrawn, as though imagining what lay beyond them. Though he refused to speak to the captain when they passed one another,

Grainger imagined that, if the Senior ever got back on his feet, he would join the trickle of those who had bled off in all directions in search of the wonders this new world had to offer.

Or he would linger in sullen, displaced silence in Feena Wulfe's company as the Wulfe's Head Label worked toward prominence once more.

Grainger did not care so long as Kal stayed out of his way. The kidnapping had never been solved, but the matter had been set aside now. What did it matter here on the Outside? The captain decided to let the past go. The Senior and his Voices of Faith had caused enough problems. For now, the Cult of the Founder was dead.

So too, it was assumed, was Reamon Folwell. In the aftermath of Hebenon's fall, the man had slipped custody to disappear into the masses, into the world. Witnesses claimed to have seen a man fleeing the tent where he was held, racing toward the river only to fall into the released surge and get swept over the cliffs. Numerous bodies, those who had been thrown into the water when the city twisted, those Outside caught unaware and unable to escape the bursting dam, were still being dredged from the nets.

Maybe he was one of those.

As mutilated and bloated as most of them were, it would likely be impossible to identify them. Lieutenant Young, berating herself for losing the Founder's assassin, another failure she blamed upon herself, accepted the responsibility of keeping peace inside the city and, in the moments she could spare, focused on the identification of the dead.

She would find Folwell. She would find Blayd. If either were alive, she would see that both men suffered for the damage they had done. She would find Neoma Kemway for her daughter's peace of mind and so that the people of Hebenon could put that piece of their communal history to rest.

She would find them all.

Just as she found Vanderwall.

Tangled in the jagged rocks beyond Hebenon's crumpled southern shell, the brute's body had been spotted bobbing furiously on the river's renewed current. Using ropes and chains that dug into the corpse's water-softened flesh, the body was pulled out and taken to the nearest secure location for identification.

He wore the yellow band of his station. And Ilya never forgot a face. Marred as it was from bruising and bloating, she knew him.

Vanderwall was dead.

Grainger saw it too. He was at peace.

Wherever Ballard was, the one face Grainger looked unceasingly for in the sea of displaced faces, the one man he hoped to find so that he could see Jaron smile again…even if that smile was never meant for him…Grainger hoped Scarecrow was at peace as well.

The haunted sorrow in Jaron's eyes and the cold knot in Grainger's belly every time he saw it begged for a different sort of peace for the man who had fought so hard for Hebanthe Falls.

Grainger never asked Jaron what happened on that last night.

He never spoke to Jaron at all.

He did not have to.

Scarecrow had become the bier on which Hyperion was born each day since the city's collapse. Grainger knew the sparrow had fallen…and only the gods, if there were any out there…knew his fate.

There was no body.

Though out of sight, however, Scarecrow's legend continued in the stories told by those gathered around dinner fires and those still crawling through the shafts and streets of Hebanthe Falls looking for survivors, looking for the dead. Some claimed to see him on rooftops, in the shafts, in the shadows. Many believed Scarecrow lived within Hebenon still.

Jaron and others continued to hope and believe.

But Rhyd Ballard was not seen again.

Only the gods knew the truth.

❧EPILOGUE❧

She stooped at the water's edge where the day's calm sea washed over her bare toes and splashed up around her ankles, to retrieve the item wedged between the rocks in the pool the tide had left. Tiny crabs skittered away from the scratched and dented surface as the hem of her hemp tunic dress dragged in the dusk-kissed surf.

She held her breath. She could not believe her eyes and had to rub her hand over the scratched surface. She had never thought she would see this again.

With eager excitement, she scanned up and down the beach, towards the mouth of the river where the Five Falls flow met the retreating surf and back towards the clattering construction of long platforms that stretched into the waves to provide mooring for the growing collection of fishing boats built and sent forth in the hopes of feeding more people than she had ever thought could exist.

Only discarded shells, stones, and shreds of uprooted kelp dotted the sand. Only seabirds haunted the empty beach. The one she hoped to see was not there.

No one was.

Beyond the river's mouth, perhaps, where the black sand stretched for many days' travel, an area largely ignored and unexplored by the people of Marbordo in the days when they had been able to provide everything they needed where they were. Perhaps there, in those distant places, there were other havens, caves for refuge, or other villages. Perhaps he had been found by one of them, cared for or killed as a frightening outsider. Perhaps he was out there, injured and alone. Perhaps he needed her as she had once needed him.

Perhaps Tox and Venn and Enoch and all of the naysayers were wrong. Perhaps Jaron was right.

With an excited squeal, she turned and raced up the beach with her treasure held tight in her hands.

Of course, Jaron was right. Agnys had the mask and cowl to prove it.

She missed his smile, his scowl, his pensive face. She was not the only one. Perhaps Vanderwall, the river, the sea, and Hebenon's darkest era had not defeated Rhyd Ballard after all. Hebanthe Falls might no longer stand as it once had, but its people needed their hero.

Jaron needed him, too. They all did.

Perhaps there was hope. Perhaps the rumors that he lingered inside the shadows of the metal nest were true.

Perhaps Scarecrow was alive.

THE END

❧GLOSSARY❦

algtea: algae tea

andi: androids; artificial humans made most often for the sex trade and as dancers. Sometimes used to perform other undesirable duties.

bilger: those who work on dehumidifying systems

bozhe moy: my god

brako: thugs

bugger: nickname for new law enforcement due to the new breathing apparatus having a bug-like appearance. Also called bugorra or gorras

bugorra (bughat): nickname for new law enforcement due to the new breathing apparatus having a bug-like appearance. Also called buggers or gorras.

buzzers: tasers used to stun victims.

cazzo: fuck/dick(Italian)

cazzing: fucking

Crows: police/military force, someone not to be trusted; a snitch

crosser: those who have moved outside of the city; also, those who work outside but live inside

crucksake: combination of Christ and fuck's sake, one of the more common swear terms.

deks: holodek suites used for recreation/vacations, since there is nowhere else for those in the city to go.

Doctet: Hebanthe Fall's Council of 10 that used to run the city in conjunction with the Founder

eblan: dumbass (Russian)

Echosys (also XCO/ekso/echo): computer; Current model is the 237 as they are frequently redesigned and built over 5 to 10 years. There are four basic models:

w (home view screens)

d (public view screens)

p1 (personal Echos)

t2 (portable tablet echos)

All are linked to the city's Hub at the time of manufacture. They are customizable and can be, illegally, removed from the Hub network.

filt: breathing filtration system

fotz: bitch (German)

gorra: nickname for new law enforcement due to the new breathing apparatus having a bug-like appearance. Also called bugorra or buggers

haikara: cybercriminal, hacktivist, hacker (Punjabi)

Hebenon: 1) name of the drug produced by official sources, intended as population control for use by the Crows but long ago made available to the public after its addictive properties became known; 2) The nickname Hebanthe Falls gained after the rise of the drug in the streets. The word Hebenon was taken from the Shakespeare play Hamlet due to the similarities in side effects experienced by its users.

Heb: the injected form of the drug Hebenon.

Hebbies: the drug Hebenon in pill form

heizer (also denki): those who work on heating systems

herpa: (from Japanese for helper) pastors, men of religious faiths outside of the Church of the Founder.

hijo de puta: son of a whore (son of a bitch)

Hub: the central broadcasting & computer system in the city.

ICD Images: still images captured with an ICD by passersby.

ICD: Interpersonal Communication Device

Igraci: The Players, (Bosnian in origin) group determined to move mankind out of Hebanthe Falls now that the city is open.

injectors: air guns that fire needles laced with Hebenon

kaheao: one who dabbles in many trades; has their fingers in many pies

kesfek: a tinker, a repairman, one who repairs things

komeada: jackass (Japanese)

Levs: refers to any of the lower 20 city levels. Houses most businesses and most of the population of the city.

malakes: from the Greek, plural of malaka(s); literally masturbators but as slang used as a curse word similar to asshole or idiot.

Marbordo: Seaside/Seacliff; what the parah call their village

mierdita: little shit

moli: Molotov cocktail explosive.

Nau: The Nine, the group that replaced the Doctet; potentials are selected by the whole of the city, but posts appointed by Grainger. Some were members of the original Doctet, most were not (because they were locked in the factories for so long and some died) No longer a lifetime or hereditary appointment but set for a term of five years. Can repeat service at Grainger's discretion. 1) material production; 2) distribution; 3) news/programming; 4) SCAMs and computer systems; 5) medical sciences, research, and care; 6) technical systems (including life support systems); 7) food production & distribution; 8) outside/inside relations (also monitors religious activities); 9) construction, city maintenance, and upkeep (including life support systems)

parah: a corruption of the word pariah, used for those 'humans' who are living outside of the Hebanthe Falls in a world polluted by mankind's failings.

parah (2): refers to those born on the outside, although now sometimes used to refer to those who have moved outside as well.

payaso: clown/fool (Spanish)

poppers: air guns, firing small synthetic pellets.

poq Gai: "Go die in the street", a general-purpose swearword (Chinese)

posa: shit

prodcast: broadcast productions aired through the Echosys, ranging from news, to sports, to entertainment and educational subjects.

prosser: those who have moved from the outside into the city; also, those who work inside but live outside.

qinai: dear (Chinese)

SCAMs: security cams used for monitoring public behavior. There are no SCAMs on the Uppers.

schweinhund: pig dog (German)

Shed: facility out of which shaft crews work.

soaper: where Hebbies are made by the brako on Lev 1

Source: the center of all material goods and food distribution.

speaks: speakers

speecher: digital implant units, typically in three parts, that allow mute individuals the ability to speak. One unit is located over the larynx, the other two at the temples, allowing electrical thought impulses to be converted into computerized speech.

spener: those who work on plumbing

streeter: those living on the streets

swiver: someone who owns a food/beverage serving establishment or who serves food or drink; a bartender, waiter, waitress

Talkers: priests of the Voices of Faith established religion.

thumper: police stick used for beating prisoners to subdue them.

ticks: currency points used for the acquisition of food and supplies and services. Distributed by the Doctet on a predetermined scale.

tinger: someone who takes things, thief, vagrant living off of others

tinging: begging

Vapors: Maemi's club/bar

verpiss dich: piss off/fuck off (German)

vigi: vigilante

vindi/vind: venders, shops

Voices of Faith: the 'religion' supported by the Founder and Doctet which supports the Kemways' divine right to run Hebanthe Falls; they produce prodcasts angled toward religious faith, community cohesiveness, and Kemway support.

XCO/ekso/echo: computer; current model is the 237 as they are frequently redesigned and built over 5 to 10 years
  w (home view screens)
  d (public view screens)
  p1 (personal Echos)
  t2 (portable tablet echos)

Zaolei: algae whiskey

About the Author

With fantasy and sci-fi as her passions, Tamara has written multiple novels to date, including the five books of the Kestrel Harper Saga, two installments of The Blood Wild Chronicles, and the stand-alone novel Suspicion's Gate. Cozenage is the third book in The Scarecrow Trials series.

When not indulging in her love of words, Tamara relaxes in the company of her pack of Papillons, her horde of cats, and an ever-growing collection of films.

Learn more about Tamara's work at www.agdhani.com

9 781737 186984